Swan Song

Kelleigh Greenberg-Jephcott

✳ WINDMILL BOOKS

'Told as different "Variations", one of this impressive novel's delicious achievements is the collective voice used as a Greek chorus to convey the wealthy women united against "the androgynous sprite".'
Sunday Times

'This **sparkling** debut divines the deep and true feeling beneath the wicked cocktail party chatter of the twentieth century's most powerfully glamorous women ... **Fabulous.**'
Damian Barr

'**Incredible ... Funny, sharp and moving,** this wonderful book marks the debut of a **major talent.**'
Kate Williams, author of *Rival Queens*

'Sharp, racy, beautifully written, it's **an utter corker.**'
Fiona Melrose, author of *Johannesburg*

1 3 5 7 9 10 8 6 4 2

Windmill Books
20 Vauxhall Bridge Road
London SW1V 2SA

Windmill Books is part of the Penguin Random House group
of companies whose addresses can be found
at global.penguinrandomhouse.com

Penguin
Random House
UK

First published by Hutchinson in 2018
First published in paperback by Windmill Books in 2019

www.penguin.co.uk

A CIP catalogue record for this book is available
from the British Library.

ISBN 9781786090188

Typeset in 9.84/13.4 pt Century Expanded LT Std
by Integra Software Services Pvt. Ltd, Pondicherry

Printed and bound in Great Britain by Clays Ltd, Elcograf S.p.A.

*For my parents, Les & Marty, who have
enabled my love of words,
without which this would not exist;*

*and for Dominic,
who has given voice to every syllable,
ten times over.*

*Ironically, words fail when it comes
to my gratitude.*

We tell ourselves stories in order to live. The princess is caged in the consulate. The man with the candy will lead the children into the sea. The naked woman on the ledge outside the window on the sixteenth floor is a victim of accidie, or the naked woman is an exhibitionist, and it would be "interesting" to know which. We tell ourselves that it makes some difference whether the naked woman is about to commit a mortal sin or is about to register a political protest or is about to be, the Aristophanic view, snatched back to the human condition by the fireman in priest's clothing just visible in the window behind her, the one smiling at the telephoto lens. We look for the sermon in the suicide, for the social or moral lesson in the murder of five. We interpret what we see, select the most workable of the multiple choices. We live entirely, especially if we are writers, by the imposition of a narrative line upon disparate images, by the "ideas" with which we have learned to freeze the shifting phantasmagoria which is our actual experience.

Or at least we do for a while.

Joan Didion
The White Album

ONE

1974

THEME

FOR THE FIRST TIME IN HIS LIFE, the words refuse to come.

He lies in bed, propped on a pile of chintz pillows, their suffocating tangle of tea roses faintly reminiscent of a Southern grande dame's parlor.

We've each mused, at one time or another, that somewhere beneath his gnarled-gnome exterior lurks a genteel New Orleans matron, mortified by her host-form's crassness.

He stares vacantly at the page before him, thoughts elsewhere. On delivery dates he hasn't met, on advances already spent. On the Fabergé paperweight he's just nabbed at auction, how it changes hue when the light shines through it just so, citrine tones conjuring Babe's miniature vegetables, darling little carrots that only grow so big.

On the eight hundred pages of lies he has or hasn't told, depending on who you ask. Depending on what he's said and to whom.

For all his boasts to the contrary, the paper—curled around the barrel of the Smith Corona balanced on his protuberant stomach—is barren. A stack of sunny legal pads proves equally unfruitful, his spider-like scrawl more scribbled through than not.

He reaches for an ashtray full of half-smoked cigarettes and grabs his pack of Trues—a brand he's sworn to each of us had been named after him. He trembles as he lights one, causing the flame to quiver before he sucks the nicotine into his lungs. He runs a hand through his tissue-fine hair, a gesture of old, when a mop of thick corn-silk fringe swept across his forehead. The fringe, like so much else, is long gone, with only a habitual gesture to remind us of a tow-haired boy we once adored. A boy pampered and indulged well into middle age, courtesy of his unquestioned genius.

In madras pajamas and ratty pink cardigan, the aging wunderkind seems less the literary lion, less still the social barracuda of public perception. Alone in the darkened room, stripped of bravura, he looks like what he is—'just a pissant rug rat from Monroeville, Alabama, shit-scared as ever.' (His phrase, not ours.)

The Tiny Terror is in many ways still the terrified toddler who sobbed when his Mama left him locked in fleabag motels while she stole out with her lovers. Lillie Mae, who traded her small-town, small-time name for the more exotic 'Nina,' a further removal from the role she never wanted: Mother to the odd Lilliputian boy with the snow-hair, toad-face, and girlish voice, the child whose very oddness repulsed her.

HE'D SAT, HE'S TOLD US, on the 'Big-Bed,' chubby fingers sticky with sugar from the bag of beignets that had been bought to bribe his silence. He watched her dressing as he chewed, wide eyes peering from his cherub face. She was barely more than a girl herself, and were it not for his gnawing at the scrap of fried dough, one might mistake him for her baby doll, propped against the pillows—rather than her great mistake. A live baby, who she never asked for, from whom she just needed a few hours' escape to try to salvage her *wreck-of-a-life*.

She'd told him this in dulcet tones, almost a lullaby, which he couldn't help but think of as good, given her smile as she cradled him close.

She was beauty and light. His whole tiny universe.

He'd studied her as she sat at the vanity in a sheer black slip, taming a honeyed pin-curl into place. He watched as she unscrewed a tube of lipstick—red like the tin fire engine a man called Daddy once gave him. She smacked a pout at her reflection. Across the room he mimicked the same, spreading sticky sugar between invisible lips. She grinned at him, and he giggled.

He pulled another beignet from his bag as she slithered into a silky dress, the green-gray hue of Spanish moss. She'd told him that was the name of the stuff that hung from the trees there, those spider arms blowing in the breeze that used to scare him, the rustle of which he had come to think of as home.

She moved to a hotplate in the corner. His eyes followed, transfixed by the colored lights that shone through the window onto her face, flashing Red-Green-Blue, Red-Green-Blue—like a Christmas tree. A trumpet-wail from the open window battled a jangling pianola from another room. She'd shaken her hips to the ragtime of the latter, as she stirred a saucepan of milk, pouring a healthy splash from the glass bottle of 'Mama-juice' she always kept on her nightstand. He loved to look at that bottle, its amber liquid sparkling in the lamplight, even when there was precious little left inside.

She had poured a cocktail of warm milk and Mama-juice into a tin cup and presented it to him. She stroked his hair, telling him what a fine boy he was as he sipped, the fire trickling down his throat. He nuzzled against her, inhaling her perfume. It reminded him of the scent of jasmine in the lobby they walked through each day, sneaking past the fat man behind the desk who, like a broken gramophone record, asked in an angry voice when she intended to pay. She'd made it a game—run, *run!* she told him—and his chubby little legs raced to keep up with hers.

Here in the Big-Bed, she stroked the white straw that topped his head, the warmth of her thigh the last thing he remembered before sinking into deepest sleep.

When he woke the room was dark. He reached for her, but she was gone.

He sat up, groggy, feeling like syrup had been poured through his brain. The colors of the Christmas neon still flashed in through the window. He could still faintly hear the player-piano, drowned by the blare of a brass band.

He slid off the Big-Bed, feet dangling, falling with a thud to the floor. He teetered toward the door, reaching upward for the cold brass knob. He turned it—one way, then the other. Wouldn't budge. He put his cheek against the crack and cried out, 'Mama . . . ?'

No answer.

He called again, 'Mama—?! *Mama!!*'

Only music and shrieks of pleasure from below.

Terrified, he howled—desperate that someone might hear him. He worried that she'd gone away for good and forgotten to take him. He pounded tiny fists against the door, screams muffled by ragtime and laughter and grown-up things he didn't understand. He slumped to a heap on the floorboards, sobbing till he just couldn't sob anymore.

He'd cried himself asleep by the time she returned. She scooped him up, dumping him in a threadbare armchair. He stirred—and through exhausted half-slumber he could just make out the man she led into the room. A man in a smart white suit, sharing a sloppy gulp of Mama-juice as their mouths collided, just before they fell into the Big-Bed, crushing his bag of beignets, stuffed between the pillows.

Of course, sometimes the details change . . .

The color of her dress. Beignets or cake, ragtime or blues. Who the man might be. Whether the Mama-juice was clear or amber. Whether she'd instructed the motel staff to ignore his screams. He's always left behind, locked inside. Alone. Abandoned. Terrified.

That's the important part, as the tale is told and retold—

Alone. Abandoned. Terrified.

The details, frankly, are interchangeable.

WE'VE ALL HEARD HIS STORIES, a hundred times over.

These were Truman's playing cards. How could they fail but rouse our sympathy? How could we not reciprocate with our own

4

tragic tales, each believing ourselves to have privilege over one another . . . ? Each believing ourselves to be his Favorite.

We loved him, after all. We welcomed him into our homes—our multiple homes—into our pools and yachts and planes. Accepted him into our celebrated families—Paleys. Guinnesses. Guests and Keiths. Agnellis and Bouviers. All vigor and tans, fresh-cut flowers and pure-bred pups. With our money and our manners, we picked up his tabs and lifted his stature. We festooned him with cachet.

We were the wives he'd never know. The mothers he wished he'd had. We loved him as we loved our own broods—more so, perhaps. No one would dare leave Truman behind with the nanny. His childlike zeal and raunchy wit proved too heady a cocktail. He'd even seduced the husbands. Those alpha males who launched networks and empires, who found themselves confiding in our androgynous sprite in ways they couldn't confide in us.

He seduced us all with words—and Truman knows full well the power of his words. They're both armor and weapon, the one thing he's sure of. They alone have never failed him, their lyricism hinting at the beauty trapped within his stunted body, not to mention his conflicted soul.

But now the muses have gone silent. For the first time since he set up a spartan desk in his childhood bedroom, armed with a composition book and a thimble of whiskey, the muses refuse to speak. Blind to the elusive gossamer threads, from which he once wove such intricate verbal webs. Deaf to the delicate balance of tones he used to strike so effortlessly. Stripped of that singular gift to find just the right word to make a phrase reverberate.

While the right words elude him, the *wrong* ones are another matter. Waffle and bile increasingly spew from his thinning lips— half-baked thoughts, easy insults. He can hardly stop himself. And *loooord-eeee*, the boasts!

'Honey, I was *born* to write this book. I'm the *only* one who could write it. Let's face it, no one else has the guts to say what

I'm prepared to say. I've seen spoiled monsters first-hand and, baby, they ain't pretty. *Trust* me, this story is the one true thing I know.'

We've heard him preach this gospel, to anyone who'll listen. Columnists. Chat-show hosts. Friends, strangers. Enemies, sycophants—come one, come all. He's been writing it for ages. Told everyone he was doing it. He's taunted with bits and pieces, read snippets to some of us, quoted lines to others, and hashed and rehashed the plot. For years Truman's warned we just might find ourselves making an appearance. He's tailored hand-carved coffins for each of us.

'It's called *Answered Prayers*. And if all goes well, it'll answer mine.'

There's been a lot of buzz, *alotta* talk. But it's becoming cheap dime-store talk. Shit on a shingle, masquerading as pâté on Tiffany silver—'It's positively epic, the thing I've been crafting. Everyone I've ever met. Everything I've *seen*. I'm constructing this book like a gun. There's the handle, the trigger, the barrel, and, finally, the bullet. And when it's fired it's gonna come out with a speed and power you've never seen—*WHAM!!*'

Yet now the words elude him, like snowflakes on a balmy day, evaporating before he can grasp them. Without his precious words, he is nothing. Panicked.

And when Truman panics . . .

He props himself upright, steals a glance at the clock. Nine thirty. It's five o'clock somewhere. He removes the typewriter from his distended gut and drags his otherwise shrunken carcass from the bed, treading carefully over the landmines of his thoughts.

BARE FEET WADE THROUGH A THICK SHAG CARPET, woolen strands threading between his toes. He proceeds through an open-plan living room, glass walls revealing a brittle desert landscape beyond. He's donned swimming trunks and a terrycloth robe, which hangs loosely around his minuscule frame. Oversized sunglasses hook over tortoise specs. The thinning hair is hidden beneath a panama hat and apart from the middle-aged paunch, he could pass as a ten-year-old boy, drowning in adult clothing.

He slides a transparent door open, squinting against the glare.

Lying catatonic on the patio is an English bulldog, Maggie, slobber dribbling from her protruding tongue. Truman steps over her, making a beeline for a wet bar. He pauses at the mini-fridge, torn between options. Shouts back to the slumbering lump— 'What'll it be, Mag-pie . . . ? A Bloody-Blood or my *Orange Drink* . . . ?'

The rolls of canine flesh fail to respond beyond a steady, listless panting.

'That's what *I* thought . . . OJ it is.' He reaches for a carton of concentrate. Removes a hundred-proof bottle of Stoli from the freezer. He fills half a highball with the vodka, adding the tiniest smidgeon of juice. Demurely sips—then tops up the hooch for good measure.

'*Na zdorovye,*' he quips in thick Russian dialect, toasting lazy ole Mags as he shuffles past. Heading for a lounger, Truman collects an apricot princess phone, rigged with an exceptionally long wire, linking him to the house as if by coiled umbilical cord. He reclines in the sun, Orange Drink in hand. He takes a swig, pulling a black book from the pocket of his voluminous robe. He finds the desired number. Dials. And in that adolescent-girl whine we've all come to recognize in a single syllable, he commands the receiver.

'Hello, precious. Mr. Don Erickson, *s'il vous plaît,*' then, surprised by the receptionist's apparent ignorance, 'Why, honey, it's Mr. Truman Streckfus Persons Capote, if you didn't know.'

He balances the phone on his shoulder, and like a contortionist he twists around, shimmying out of the bathrobe and retrieving his drink with surprising dexterity.

From the other line, anxious, 'Mr. Capote?'

'Donny. Greetings and salutations.'

'And to you, Mr. Capote.'

'I'm not your daddy, for Chrissakes! Call me Truman.'

'Mr.— Truman. I want to thank you for returning our call. We're very excited, and may I stress *very* excited, at the prospect of publishing your stories—'

'*Chapters,*' Truman corrects. 'The first *chapters* of my magnum opus. *Looooong*-awaited chapters. Fifteen years in the making. Think of this as a little sneak peek . . . A few chapters to keep 'em guessing.'

'Yes. Chapters. I just want to express, on behalf of the *Esquire* staff—'

'Let's cut to the juicy bit, shall we? The *New Yorker*'s offered me twenty thousand. Care to sweeten the pot . . . ?'

The line goes silent. Truman frowns, dabbing the pooling sweat collecting in the reservoir between his chest and belly. His 'man-tits,' he'd been amused to inform us while sunbathing on board the *Agneta*, sailing cobalt waters off the Amalfi Coast, slathering the 'most divine' shea butter on his beloved Babe's porcelain skin.

We had all, of course, told him what a silly creature he was, that he was far too prepubescent to have tits of any sort.

'Donnn-eeee . . . ? Cat got your tongue?' Truman ventures, pressing the charm offensive, somewhere between a purr and a growl.

From the other end, palpable disappointment.

'We were prepared to go to sixteen. I'm sorry, Truman. We'd do anything to keep our hat in the ring. We know how big this will—'

'*Aaaac*-tually, I don't think you do.'

'We do! We're simply a smaller operation than—'

'Sugar, you have no *idea* how big this book is gonna be.'

Truman rises, dragging the mile-long phone cord past Maggie, who lifts her head as it grazes her lumpy back. At the wet bar he mixes himself another Orange Drink, the once icy vodka bottle weeping in the heat.

'We *know*. We knew with *Breakfast*, didn't we? We just don't have the resources to go any higher. Try as we might, we can't outbid the *New Yorker*.'

Truman pours himself an extra capful of Stoli, tosses back the shot.

'Give me one good reason why I should go with *Esquire* for four grand less. You've got sixty seconds, Donny-Boy. Convince me.'

A sharp intake of breath, then— 'Who would you like your readership to be?'

Truman pauses. '*Well* . . . I don't want 'em kicking the bucket midway through. I *suppooose* I'd like a younger readership. One that doesn't give a flying hoot about The Rules.'

'Okay. Demographically, do you know what the occupation of the greatest percentage of *New Yorker* subscribers is?'

'No.'

'Dentists.'

'Dentists—?'

'Yes—*dentists*. Purchased as what's known in the trade as Lobby Lit. There's your audience. Sad fucks with toothaches waiting for a root canal.'

Truman chews an ice cube, ingesting this, drumming his claws against the highball.

'You know I'll have certain *demands* . . .'

'Anything.'

'I want cover approval.'

'You got it.'

'And you cannot change a *word* of text. I mean it! Not a *syllable*!'

'All right . . .'

'I'm flying to the Yucatán to see Lee—do you know Lee Radziwill? She's *utterly* divine. *Far* more stunning than her sister . . . I mean, I *love* Jackie, don't get me wrong. She was one smart cookie back in the day—surprisingly well read—but she can be so *severe*, don't you think? The whole weepy-widow routine . . . No man would touch that with a ten-foot pole! And face it, she *can* look a bit like a drag queen in pearls from certain angles. Of course Ari . . . Well. *He's* no looker. He did sleep with Lee first . . . but that's another story. Anyhooooo. Seeing Lee in Mexico, then on to

9

Key West, where I've found the most deliciously trashy seaside motel. I only have one copy of my book. Only one in the whole wide world. You'll have to come down and pick up the manuscript. Personally.'

'Done.'

Truman dumps the last of the ice cubes into his glass.

'*Weeee-uull* . . . okay then, hon. *Esquire* it is. And on that note, I'm gonna do a jig and pour myself one last little something to celebrate . . .'

A splash more Orange, splash(es) more hundred-proof. Truman teeters with drink and phone toward the swimming pool. Maggie, half-eye on alert, rolls resentfully clear of his path.

On the line the mood shifts to one of triumph.

'Wow. Truman, that really is terrific!'

'I'm delighted, Don. Simply over the *moon*.'

He sets the phone base at the pool's edge, dipping his toe in the chlorine bath.

'But Donny . . . be forewarned.' Truman pauses, wading waist-deep into warm water, relishing the moment. 'I'm about to detonate a bomb.'

'You always do. I'm sure this will prove no exception.'

'Ohhh, but it *will*. They ain't seen nothin' yet . . .'

'Well. I can assure you— You won't regret this.'

'Nooooo,' Truman ponders, 'I don't think I will. But *you* might.' Satisfied, he places the handset back in its cradle.

Faintly . . .

You don't think you'll regret it, Truman?

Truman polishes off his OJ, sets his glass beside the phone.

Part of you isn't worried about what we'll say when we find out . . . ?

His brow furrows. Ours is not the Calliope voice he's been longing to hear.

Turning to his morning exercise, Truman dog-paddles the length of the pool, keeping both head and hat above water. At the deep end he grasps the diving board, stretching his arms, feet dangling into the depths below. He makes a U-turn and paddles back to the shallow end.

You know, there's only one thing that cannot be forgiven . . .

Betrayal, in black and white.

'Stop it,' Truman says aloud, to no one in particular. Maggie raises her head at the sound of a phrase she recognizes. He laughs. 'Not you, Mags.'

Bitchery and butchery, in Century Expanded type. Are you sure you won't regret . . . ?

Holding his breath, he ducks his head beneath the water. It's serene. Peaceful. But in the glugging, amniotic solitude, a voice, Our voice, persists . . .

As a rule, people are far more hurt by what they read than what they hear.

Truman allows his weight to sink, leaving his panama hat bobbing gently on the glassy surface.

A WEEK LATER, A LIMOUSINE PULLS UP in front of Capote's modest desert retreat. A chauffeur collects his luggage: a pair of worn Vuitton suitcases, découpaged with labels.

'My bags have been positively everywhere,' Truman often boasts. 'They've traveled *twice* as much as me. It's not my fault . . . They have their own little legs that run on ahead!'

As he carefully locks the deadbolt—we've been told there have been break-ins in his absences—the chauffeur returns for the final item of luggage. A thick, rectangular parcel, meticulously wrapped in brown butcher paper, tied with kitchen twine. As he reaches for the parcel, Truman lunges in his path.

'Nooooo thank you, Mr. Hauptmann. This baby's not leaving Daddy Tru-bergh's *sight*!' The chauffeur, a heavyset Mediterranean, backs away. Truman laughs heartily.

'Gracious! I'm like a little ole junkyard dog! Bless your cotton socks. To whom do I have the pleasure . . . ?'

'I'm Vincent, sir.'

'Vi-*chen*-teee . . .' Truman rolls the name around on his tongue. 'Well, you simply must tell me *all* about yourself . . .'

IN THE BACK OF THE LIMOUSINE, Truman sits with parcel in place of honor on the seat beside him. He taps the partition. Flashes a grin in the rearview mirror.

'Say, Vicente . . . ? You wouldn't mind if I popped this delicious bottle of bubbly, would you? I can't think of anything more *rude* than to drink while you're driving. But would you mind *terribly* . . . ?'

'No, sir. Help yourself.'

'It's medicinal, you know. I just have to wash down the *teensiest* of pills, and they're always *so* much nicer with my old friend Dominic P.—' Truman reaches greedily for the chilled bottle of Dom Perignon, giggling when the cork pops, like a child with a Christmas cracker. He removes a Quaalude from an enamel Victorian snuffbox in his pocket. Slides a turquoise pill into his mouth, then a jade one, together fanning into the colors of a peacock's tail.

'Vicente what?'

'Angelotti.'

'Angelotti. *Quel* divine! You're *Italian*, I presume.'

'Yes, sir.'

'Well, isn't that just the most *exotic* thing to be. And where did you say you were from?'

'My family came from Sicily, but I grew up in Hoboken.'

'What an extraordinary coincidence! My friend Francis comes from Hoboken. He's a singer . . . Perhaps you know him?' Truman's accordion-grin expands. Celebrity never ceases to thrill him as a topic. 'Francis . . . ? Francis *Sinatra* . . . ?' He watches the driver's eyes widen. 'You know, he wanted to buy the film rights to my book. Now as much as I love Francis dearly, he's *notoriously* stingy, and my Big Mama—that's my *very* close friend Slim—she was acting as my agent at the time, and she said to hold out for a million.'

12

'Sinatra,' the driver stammers. 'You know *Frank* Sinatra?'

'Vinny, I know everybody. So Slim, she was married to Howard Hawks before she left him for Leland Hayward, who left *her* for that slut Pam Churchill—as in Winston, Pam having bagged his son Randolph (. . . and just about anything else with a pulse!) Anyhow, I had met Howard through Bogart, who met his darling wife Betty through Slim, who *literally* discovered her—not that that misogynist rat Hawks gave credit where credit was due, and—'

'You knew Bogie too . . . ?'

'*Knew* him? He called me Caposey. I beat him at arm-wrestling. Three times. I won two hundred bucks off him, which in those days was alotta dough. But when I body-slammed Bogie— he dared me!—and took him out of commission for three days, Big John Huston was not too happy with Li'l Ole Caposey, let me tell you! Where was I—? Oh yes. Back to Slim . . .'

BY THE TIME THE CAR PULLS UP to the Sputnik facade of LAX in two hours' time, Truman has told Vincent the life histories and bed-hopping of almost everyone in our circle.

The chauffeur has listened, incredulous, not sure whether this pint-sized raconteur is a teller of truths or crazy as a coconut. Truman, having exhausted himself with a potent cocktail of gossip, dolls, and champagne, slumps in his seat, mid-catnap.

Vincent collects his luggage from the trunk and sets it by the curb. He opens the back door and gently shakes his snoring passenger. Truman wills himself awake, peacock-plume-eyed, empty champagne bottle in his lap. He squints toward the open door, where the chauffeur stands with the sun at his back, features obscured, surrounded by a halo of light.

'Mr. *Angel*-otti . . . have we reached the City of Your Kind?'

'Welcome to Los Angeles, Mr. Capote.'

'Give me your arm, dear angel boy, and help me to fly.'

The chauffeur hoists Truman to his feet—no easy task, his featherweight form leaden with fatigue. As porters arrive to drag suitcases inside, Truman removes his watch. A flashy Cartier affair. He presses it into Vincent's palm, who stares at the offering, flabbergasted.

'For you, Vicente.'

'But sir—I couldn't possibly—'

'Don't offend me, Angel. Bogie had one, Francis has one, I've got a dozen.'

Vincent's protests cease as Truman rolls back the sleeve of his uniform, tenderly fastening the watch strap around his wrist. He pats the chauffeur's arm. '*Bellissimo.*'

He lowers his insect shades and follows the porters into the terminal.

IT'S NOT UNTIL HE DRIFTS PAST the rush of travelers, languidly swimming against the stream of hustle and bustle, following his bags—which indeed have their own legs today (we've always insisted there's generally a sliver of truth in what Truman says . . .)

Not until he's sauntered up to the Aeroméxico counter without a care in the world, been checked in, ticket printed by a doe-eyed señorita in the smartest pillbox hat ('Just like Jackie used to wear,' we knew he'd tell her, 'until that terrible day, the Pepto-Bismol pink pillbox, splattered with Jack's blood . . .')

Not until he's slurred a final '*Adios, amiga,*' pausing to contemplate that the masculine version of that farewell had been—as he'd tearfully informed us—Perry Smith's final words before he'd watched him hang, the killer having limped forward, kissed his cheek and whispered, '*Amigo* . . .' into Truman's ear. He'd felt the breath coming from Perry's warm lips in the icy warehouse, noticed his exhaled puffs, coming faster as he mounted the scaffold steps, where a delicate black mask was tied over his eyes. Visible breath—same as the lawmen and journalists watching. A last exhalation of vapor gave the illusion of hovering when the floor dropped out from under him and the breath was no more. Too late did Truman realize that he'd never be able to jettison those images, of Perry and Dick's fragile necks snapping, or of the shotgun blasts for which they paid—four shots that snuffed out the Clutter clan, upstanding folks by all accounts, in a single blood-soaked night. He couldn't escape the feeling that theirs was his own funeral, and that the boy with the fringe had died with them in that freezing warehouse, leaving a shell of a man in his place.

Not until he's allowed himself a groggy moment of self-pity for all that he has lost, for the price that he has paid for his art . . .

Not until *then* does Truman remember . . .

He looks around, horrified, groping for the thick brown parcel, deciding it *must* have been tossed into his luggage. Bags are retrieved, flung open, guts rifled, and every conceivable item tossed from their cavities. Tablets covered in Truman's fussy scrawl. The weighty Smith Corona, concealed in its leather sheath. Paisley swimming trunks. Black silk pajamas. Scarves of unacceptable lengths. T-shirts. Corduroys. Furs— —

Furs? In the Yucatán? We've always said he couldn't pack. How many times has one or another of us neatly packed his bags for far-flung jaunts, removing wildly inappropriate items he's always managed to sneak back in last minute . . . ? While he, the pampered son, sits curled at the foot of our beds, part pasha, part Pekinese, observing our efforts, rhapsodizing, 'But darling, that's *amazing*,' delighted by our labor on his behalf.

At the feet of the startled señoritas of Aeroméxico, Truman tosses his hallowed treasures, searching in vain for the only item that matters.

'Oh-my-god-oh-my-god *oh my GAWD*,' he wails, a peacock screech, which in itself is not unlike a woman's scream. (Were he operating at full capacity he would have appreciated this detail, having more than once pointed out in the Central Park Zoo that the New York City Police have often been called to investigate a shrieking 'genus *Pavo*' on this very basis.)

'I can't believe . . . Fifteen years of my life—*fifteen YEARS!*'

15

The Misses Aeroméxico exchange uncomfortable glances.

'I can't—I'll *never* be able to duplicate . . . !'

He reaches the bottom of the final case and sits back on his haunches, his portable world scattered pitifully around him. (So pitiful we could *almost* feel sorry for him . . .) He sees his last minuscule chance receding into nothingness, which is even more frightening than the Nothing he's been grappling with. He realizes that this may well signal the end of the line. He doesn't have the strength to start again.

But Hemingway did, when it happened to him, we'd assure him—

'I hate that pompous old fart,' he'd say, per script. 'Homophobic faux-macho cunt. Bore, bore, *BORE*.' Those of us who'd known Papa would argue otherwise and Truman, claws extended, would inevitably snap, 'Well, he was practically a *child* back then—Mr. Shotgun-for-Breakfast could hardly do much *now*!'

The elfin body rounds in defeat. His bony shoulders begin to shake, with them the spine, as ordered and defined as a string of freshwater pearls.

A concerned señor, the counter manager, appears and kindly offers to phone the 'young man's' hotel. Truman shakes his head in his skeletal hands, knowing full well that all is lost.

The voices, *Our* voice—soloists, overlapping now—

You should have known, Truman, that it was beneath you.

Flinging fine-boned skeletons from our walk-in closets . . .

Airing our thousand-count, bloodstained linens for all to see!

Leaving us reeling that our trust could be so utterly betrayed by our closest confidant . . .

'*Noooooo!*' Truman wails. Señor Aeroméxico withdraws, mistaking the protest for him.

We can just hear the headlines—'Capote kills in cold blood. Ladies who lunch—eviscerated in Manhattan's most fashionable eatery by their best friend?!'

16

'I didn't mean to . . . I didn't *mean*—'

Our best friend . . .

Aeroméxico has summoned the porters.

'Where did he come from?' asks the befuddled manager.

'He was dropped off, sir. In a big black limousine.'

You—with whom we sipped Cristal and spilled our souls! Shared juicy gossip over bubbling pots of Soufflé Furstenberg, egg yolks oozing into milky custard as we dished the latest dirt. We confided, in tipsy tête-à-têtes, our most guarded, martini-soaked secrets, while you listened with the attention our husbands failed to provide.

You ungrateful little dwarf! Low-level social climber—

'You've always made that mistake about me! I was an artist! Always an artist!'

Señor Manager is on the phone now, ringing car companies, calling for reinforcements. A well-heeled queue has formed at the counter. Most ignore the display, unwilling to acknowledge such theatrics in a public place, and one as glamorous as the *airport.*

A child waiting in line, clutching her mother's hand, stares at Truman with fixed, frightened eyes. He looks to her, making a tearful appeal—'Who did they think they *had* . . . ? What did they think I *was* . . . ?!!'

'Mama . . .' The girl retreats behind her mother's skirt.

Then, another voice, across the room . . .

'Mr. Capote . . . ?'

The voice of an angel, floating toward him.

Truman looks to see the flash of a golden wing—an appendage wrapped in Cartier.

Just like that, Saint Vincent Angelotti is standing over him, offering the sacred object . . . Eight hundred pages, wrapped in brown paper, carefully tied with string, which might as well be the Christ Child wrapped in swaddling clothes.

'I'm sorry, sir. I came as soon as I realized. You left this on the backseat.'

Truman Capote reaches out, recovering his destiny, clutching it to his concave chest.

'Ohhhhhhh, *grazie*, Angel! *Grazie!*'

And suddenly he knows, definitively—regardless of the outcome—sometimes the wrong words are better than no words at all.

TWO

1975

VARIATION NO. 1

LADY SLIM KEITH—formerly Mrs. Leland Hayward, formerly Mrs. Howard Hawks, formerly scrawny Nancy Gross of Salinas, California—is startled when the phone rings just before eight. She's reading the morning papers in bed, her routine of late. It's what divorcées do, she's told herself—even reluctant divorcées, when forced to create new rituals. She's always been an early bird, up with the sun, relishing the lazy hours before the rest of the world has risen to join her. Yet the unexpected ring alarms.

No one calls until ten. It just isn't done.

Her mind races . . . The asylum? Has Billy pulled another prison break? If so, should she contact Leland, or should she wait . . . ? He and horrid *whore*-ed Pam have neglected Billy awfully. She herself has tried to intervene, but then, as we've reminded her, it isn't her responsibility; he isn't her son any longer, if a stepson ever was.

When the phone goes quiet, she feels the relief of reprieve. Probably just some rat in London who hasn't had the decency to check the time.

Then—a fresh round of ringing punctures the stillness.

It *must* be Billy. Or Bridget? The Hayward brood gone haywire. It wouldn't be the first time, and Slim doubts it will be the last. She feels a sharp stab of anxiety, the same she felt when the phone went at sunrise years ago, with grim news about Papa. Ernest had not been well. 'I'm sick of it all, Miss Slimsky,' he'd said when she last left Havana, and he'd meant it. They'd been dove shooting one last time, she later confirmed, with the very gun he'd used to— —

Christ. Not Billy too . . .

Bracing herself for the worst, Slim reaches for the receiver. Before she can answer, Babe's voice, strained—higher than its usual smooth, silvery perfection.

'Have you read it?'

Thank God—just Babe.

With a wash of relief, Slim reaches for the papers. '*Times* or *Post*?'

She'd already flipped through Suzy and Charlotte's gossip columns, scanned picayune slings and arrows hours before. The usual birdbrain socialites jostling for see-and-be-seen preeminence. Par for the course.

No Paleys. No Haywards. Nothing to warrant an 8 a.m. alarm.

'Truman's piece in *Esquire*,' says Babe, in an un-Babe-like rush. 'Have you read it . . . ?'

'*Esquire* . . . ? No.'

'Well, get it right away. Read it and call me back.' Click. Click? From the Queen of Manners? *Decidedly* un-Babe-like . . . What could possibly—?

Slim rings for her maid, hands her some change from the vanity drawer, and sends her scampering down to the corner newsstand.

AN HOUR LATER, SLIM SITS at her kitchen table nursing a bottle of Scotch, the pages of *Esquire* spread open before her, confronting her fictional doppelgänger.

Lady Slim Keith, meet Lady Ina Coolbirth . . .

Both carefree, Californian broads, thrice divorced. Both damn good-looking, yet one of the boys. Sultry gals-next-door, whose laid-back cool makes trousers and suede jackets and slip-on flats alluring. Both poster girls for the man's-man's ideal woman. A woman who drinks deep and lives large, who fishes, rides, and shoots big game. Who'll spin a helluva yarn once the cocktails start flowing . . . Trouble is, the booze and the spiel tend to flow together.

And there they all are. Our precious, protected secrets. Shared in hushed voices among members of our set, bandied like tennis balls at our most exclusive clubs. Courtside, poolside small talk. Harmless enough. But guarded with hawklike vigilance from anyone *outside*.

We're all there. The whole goddamn cast. Some of us appearing under our real names—Babe and Betsey, Jackie and Lee—others under thinly veiled pseudonyms. All at our signature tables at La Côte Basque, unknowingly weathering the barbed insults of the fictional Lady Ina . . . *clearly* Slim, dishing the foulest dirt with a gigolo queen named 'Jonesy' . . . obviously Truman.

But it's not 'Jonesy' from whose lips the slander drips . . . It's *hers*.

Slim feels a cold chill run through her body . . . the arctic chill of panic.

Oh, Truheart. You little motherfucker. What have you done?!

That's before she reads the worst of it . . . When she gets to the bloodstained sheets, she fumbles for the phone. Babe answers on the first ring.

'Well?'

'I feel like I just got punched in the gut.'

'Yes, but what did you *think* . . . ?'

'Pure garbage. Bitchy, catty trash,' Slim says unequivocally. She tries to sound dismissive, but they both know this is bigger than that.

It's a declaration of war.

'That story . . .' Babe pauses. 'Do you think that it's true?'

Slim holds her breath, knowing *exactly* which one Babe means . . .

The Sheets.

Slim can't bear to tell her. With her cancer . . . with the treatments. We *all* know about Bill's women. But with Babe looking

21

death in the eye, to *mention* them seems exceptionally cruel. 'Truman's a fantasist. I've always told you that.' *Cannot tell her . . . Can't . . .*

'But there's always some truth in what he says,' Babe persists. 'Clearly "Ann Hopkins" is Ann Woodward. The pretend intruder, the dead husband . . .'

'Okay, so that bit's true. My God, to dredge that up . . .'

'What was he *thinking*?'

'Christ. I hope Ann's okay . . .'

SLIM DOESN'T YET KNOW, but Ann is *not* okay. Someone smuggled her an advanced copy of Truman's article days ago. Needless to say, poor Ann Woodward was horrified by the prospect of having her long-buried demons revisited, sickened by the thought of being dragged through the mud, branded 'BIGAMIST' and 'MURDERESS' in blazing scarlet letters, all over again.

She'd always admitted to shooting her husband, mistaking him for a prowler. She'd certainly set up the idea, The Prowler being the Woodwards' sole topic of conversation at the dinner they'd attended for the Duchess of Windsor the very night in question—Ann in particular having *banged on* about it (Truman's sardonic pun). They'd been worried about the break-ins in their Oyster Bay hamlet. Had taken to sleeping with shotguns by the bed. What they failed to mention were the separate bedrooms, so broken was the marriage, hanging at that point by a thumbnail. Ann had heard an intruder and shot without looking. But there was something fishy in the position of her husband's naked body when police responded to her frantic call.

Truman relished the salaciousness of it all, and had a new detail to share each time he told the tale around an enraptured luncheon table, as if he peeked into the Oyster Bay police files on a regular basis.

'She *says* she'd grabbed her musket—*à la* Annie-Get-Your-Gun—and unloaded that bespoke baby into blackest pitch. *Bang! Bang!*' Truman enthused. 'Then she flipped the light switch on, and *who* should she find—*quelle surprise*—but her dear, departed Billy, positively riddled with buckshot. Only *this* unlucky buck was lying limp in the hallway, stretched between their boudoirs. The sheriff arrived to find li'l Miss Oakley poised atop the body—a position she so often occupied in life,' (he loved to add with a smirk.) 'She sobbed those great big crocodile tears, still sporting her blighted nighty, splattered with blood like a crimson Jackson Pollock.

"I did it! I killed him! It was dark—I couldn't see!" At a measly twenty-foot distance?! Ha! Well, the cops didn't need but two brain cells to rub together to suss out in a jiff that *that* didn't add up. The hall was a fine story—mighty fine. I give Annie an 'A' for effort. Excluding one small point: that *wasn't* where he was killed . . .'

When we'd asked Tru how he could be so sure, he retorted, with forensic zeal, tidbits that had been withheld from the press. 'Honey, the police found the corpse inside a glassed-in shower. *Naked* for Chrissakes! The water was still running and the door was shattered with bullets. Now *you* tell *me* . . . ? How did he die . . . ?'

He'd then slurp a spoonful of soup, or drain a martini, satisfied.

The scandal had faded, to Tru's dismay, with Ann's acquittal, her mother-in-law Elsie having refused to press charges. She was a vestige of the Gilded Age of Astors and Vanderbilts, when one didn't taint the family name with shame, even if it meant setting a murderess free. Elsie Woodward believed one should only see one's name in print twice—once at one's birth and once at one's death (not even marriage currying favor, its lifespan being so fleeting.)

For Truman, however, the more ink the better. For him a good story never died, and he's waited with the patience of Job to resurrect *this* gem. Truman's a great one for grudges and for almost two decades, Ann's been at the top of his hit-list.

'Look at Capote, that horrid little faggot,' he'd told us Ann had sniped at a party in St. Moritz in the early Fifties. Other times he'd said he'd bumped into her on the packed El Morocco dance floor, stepped on her clodhopper toes in a frenzied, tipsy jitterbug.

'Watch it, *Fag* . . .' she'd hissed.

'Watch *yourself*, Bang-Bang,' he said he'd fired back.

Whichever version, however vicious or not, she'd gotten her comeuppance, on the knifepoint of his pen. She's the main attraction in his *Esquire* sideshow, the production simply dripping in Truman's malice. She's billed as 'Ann Hopkins', a flame-haired widow in a black Mainbocher suit and veil, sitting with a Gibson-swilling priest, who consoles her over the death of a husband called 'David'.

'Ann was a two-bit Showgirl—Call girl, more like,' Lady Ina tells Jonesy in Truman's tale, sinking a spoon into her Soufflé Furstenberg. 'Desperate to grind her way out of the chorus, Ann found a *patron* in David Hopkins Senior before moving on to Junior, who married her for her ... talents. But when David found out that his Daddy'd beaten him to the punch, the marriage went south quick ...

'David wanted out, without the hefty price tag, so he hired a crack P.I. to see who else's bones were hiding in Ann's closets. And before you could blink, he had photographic proof of Ann mounting each member of the Piping Rock Polo Club (one-by-one-by-one, then the whole team, *tous ensemble* . . .) Enough to warrant an arrest, not to mention a divorce! But in a twisted turn of fate, clever Private Dick decided to poke around Ann's old homestead—

'He interviewed her toothless relatives, who had never known her in the highfalutin' role of Mrs. David Hopkins—' Lady Ina relishes this bit in particular— 'But as Angeline Lucille Crumb, tomboy brat of a taxi-rank Madame, operating from the men's room of the movie palace of her shit-kicker midwest town. Little 'Angie' got hitched fast to get outta Mama's house—child bride to one Joe-Bob Barnes, a hillbilly leatherneck, promptly shipped to Okinawa. But no sooner had Joe-Bob's convoy set sail, Angie fled the scene, turning up in Manhattan, repackaged as 'Ann Eden'. Years hence, Clever Dick dredged up those ancient marriage scraps and unearthed said Joe-Bob Barnes, and got him to testify that he'd married one Angeline Crumb, never divorced her, and that the last time he checked she was still his Missus. Billy threw down, having learned Ann's dirty secret, which rendered *their* marriage null and void. He threatened to leave her shamed; he would've taken the children. She'd worked too hard to fall back down to the bottom of the heap. That must've been what did it . . . Backed into a corner, bigamy exposed: her first rung on a mile-long ladder out of the inbred gutter. What was left for Ann but to shoot him? *La matadora*, she was dubbed by the press—the woman who kills. A fate beyond her control, poor dear, determined by an accident of birth; a lethal cocktail of trash and ambition, a gold-digging, shameless whore of a — —'

'But I never *met* Truman Capote, and he never met me!' Ann had insisted when she was told about the article. Whatever the truth, after reading Tru's sordid *Esquire* tale, Ann marked the date of its release in her pocket diary. She had retreated to her Fifth Avenue prison and drawn the curtains, her maid Miss Reever would later tell our maids. She'd asked Reever to hold her hand and pray with her.

That night, in a blue-flowering nightgown, Ann fished a note-pad from the bedside table, 'DON'T FORGET . . .' printed in typeface as its heading. She scrawled 'Ann Woodward' beneath, and placed it by her beige Bakelite telephone. Instead of the mask of cold cream she usually slept in, Ann, still the showgirl of her youth, painted her face, applying pancake base, rosy cheeks, and gobs of green mascara, as if going on stage for a final, grotesque curtain call.

Then, grappling with the ghosts of her messy, guilt-racked past, Ann Woodward went to bed, took a fatal dose of Seconal and never woke up. (The same drug that killed Lillie-Mae-Nina-Capote, we'll later remind one another, gobsmacked by the irony.)

Punished for an insult spat eighteen years earlier, Ann is Truman's first victim.

A PAUSE FROM THE OTHER END OF THE LINE. Babe's slightly labored breathing. Forty years of L&Ms, finally taking their toll. When she speaks again, it's careful . . .

'That story . . . The Sheets. Who do you think it is . . . ?'

'Who knows. Could be anybody,' quips Slim, a little too quickly.

Another pause, soft wheezing, then, 'I can't figure out who the woman is, but I think I know who the *man* might be . . .'

Slim downs her drink . . . Here we go.

Babe pauses, then, cautiously, 'Slim . . . do you think it could be Bill?'

Slim, with feigned certainty, 'It's fiction, Babe. Half-baked fiction at that. Don't waste a minute more on it.' Changing the subject, 'Where are we lunching? Quo Vadis?'

'But he's Jewish, "Sidney Dillon" . . .'

'So is half of Manhattan.'

On the line Babe calms her breath. 'It can't be. Truman wouldn't do that . . . Not to *me*. Not to us.' The thought seems to mollify her.

At the St. Pierre, Slim pours another Scotch. She wishes she could agree.

He'll pay, that sick little fuck. He'll pay for selling our secrets like some cheap back-alley pimp. For putting *his* bile in *her* mouth.

'Like I've said—Truman's out for Truman.'

'But you *love* Truman.'

'I love him. But I've never trusted him.'

Oh, but Slim *had*. She hadn't meant to, but Truman had a way of getting you talking. Getting you drinking and getting you gabbing. Slim racks her brain to separate fact from fiction. Had she told Truman the rumor of Bill's attempt to bed the Governor's Wife while Babe was out of town, only to have the lady in question menstruate vats of blood onto the Paleys' marital sheets? When Babe had called and announced her early return, Bill, in a darkly slapstick turn, had stripped the bed in a panic and thrown the linens in the bath. The idea of the great Bill Paley, CBS mogul, at tub's-edge on all fours scrubbing bodily fluid from fine Egyptian cotton like an old Russian washerwoman had seemed amusing at the time, as long as it was kept from Babe. More amusing still was Bill's alarm—after depleting multiple bars of Guerlain's *Fleurs des Alpes* guest–soaps—that the bedding might fail to dry in time. The lauded laundryman had stuffed the sheets into the oven, baking their restored pallor to a vanilla linen crisp.

Surely it was *Tru* who had told that tale to *Slim*—or had it been the other way around? *Oh God* . . . 'Lady Ina' feels a pang of remorse for not remembering.

They had shared so much, the pair of them, having told each other tale after tale with competitive zeal, it all seemed to bleed together.

And Jesus, had they talked. They'd talked through hundreds of lunches over twenty years. Over cognac chicken hash in the Oak Bar at the Plaza. Over the Colony's lobster Thermidor and boeuf à la mode. Past the cast-iron lawn jockeys in their jewel-toned silks on the way into 21. Across smoggy tables at the Stork Club. At dinner parties, over quivering aspic. At galas, shunning banquet fare. In loungers, sipping gimlets, on poolside terraces and shipboard poop decks. They'd talked in taxis stuck in traffic. On Vespas whizzing through Madrid. At thirty thousand feet on board transatlantic flights, smoking at the bar to pass the time. On freezing trains through barren Russian landscapes, clinging to each other for warmth.

It was after those surreal days in Moscow—after a vodka-drenched rail journey to Leningrad, sinking shot after shot, wrapped in multiple coats to stave off the ferocious cold, singing folk songs they'd been taught by the locals Truman had befriended, toasting '*Na zdorovye*' with each toss-back of succor, enjoying the feeling of crystal-clear Mama-juice as it trickled like lava down their throats—that Truman suddenly cocked his head and stared at Slim.

'You never confide in me, Big Mama,' he'd mused, a twinge of hurt in his voice.

'Truheart, *please*. We talk all the time! I tell you *everything*.'

'Yes . . . But you never *confide* in me. About *you*.'

Slim had smiled, 'No, I don't, darling, you're right.'

'Why don't you confide in me?' he pressed, Stoli stripping defenses like paint thinner.

'Well, Truman,' Slim slurred, 'it's very simple. I don't trust you.'

Papa had always told her, 'Miss Slimsky, you have a first-rate, bona fide bullshit detector,' and Slim had detected early on that Truman was a master of the art. She'd in short order spotted what most of us denied: If Truman could run around blabbing to each of us about the others—'*in the strictest confidence, sugar*!'—it was pretty damn certain he was liable to be blabbing to everyone else about us, in an endless round-robin of chat.

We were his creations, whether rendered by mouth or pen, the Miss Golightlys no less real than the Mrs. Paleys or Guinnesses or Keiths—the Mrs. Keiths and Guinnesses and Paleys no more. The details of our lives supplied base metal for his tales, which through some strange alchemy he turned to shimmering, narrative gold, spanning themes and genres. We'd see shades of ourselves in his work; nothing you could pinpoint—we wouldn't stand for that. It was our *essence* that peopled his text. We floated in and out in different guises . . . Babe drifted through his tarnished fairy tales. Gloria's covert past stalked his thrillers. Marella's foreign cadence metered his librettos. Lee's longstifled envy simmered beneath his rivalries. The bridles and florals of C.Z.'s sporting life pervaded his pastorals. Slim spawned heroines in stark western gothics: Steinbeck-tinged seediness meets little girl lost.

'Big Mama had a brother who looked *exactly* like me. Same tow hair, same cherubic face. The spitting, *spitting* image. Edward was his name (after their Daddy—a big fish who owned half the sardine canneries in Cannery Row—) but folks only ever called Ed Junior "Buddy"—the very name my old cousin Sook called me as a boy . . . *Buddy.*'

We had each, on more than one occasion, listened as Truman spun the trauma of Slim's childhood into mythos, as he had for each of us in turn. 'He was mummified, you know—actually *mum-*

mified, like those sad souls in Pompeii. Poor little Buddy. Saddest thing. That tiny boy, in an old man's nightshirt, one he would never grow into. Flames lapping him up like a thousand serpents' tongues. Slim tried to save him—her name was Nancy then, and Nancy was a very brave girl and she adored her baby brother. They shared a secret language, just like Slim and *I* do.' Here he'd pause, wistful, sometimes removing his glasses for effect.

'I've always felt *quite* close to Slim—eerily so. From the moment we first met, in Mrs. Vreeland's living room, a room so *red* you could hear the walls sizzle. Well, I plopped down beside Slim on that crimson-patterned sofa, and I said to her, "Honey, I just *know* we've met before—another lifetime ago." I *recognized* her, see . . . ? It was like finding a missing scrap of my own mislaid self. We're old souls, Slim and me—we've been around the block a few times. Why, for all we know, I could be Buddy reincarnate!' (Most of us thought this last bit was asinine, and told him so—but we *nearly* saw his point about the rest.)

Whether Slim was born an old soul or was forced to become one remains uncertain, but grief had robbed her of a childhood, her youth incinerated alongside Buddy, when she was still little Nancy in Salinas. She'd been reborn as *we* know her in Death Valley, where she was sent to cure her spotted lung, a scrawny kid of seventeen. An ironic place to start a life, but start one she did, when Bill Powell plucked her from a motel in Mojave and christened her 'Slim Princess,' the 'Slim' sticking long after the 'Princess' had been dropped.

Even now, decades later, Slim has told us she *still* wakes in an icy sweat, having felt in her nightmares the blast of heat from the open grate. She comes to, rolling in bed, trying desperately to smother the flames that had licked the edge of Buddy's nightshirt; flames that traveled as if through wild brush through the cotton fibers.

When the surviving Grosses later stood at the cemetery watching his body being entombed in the mausoleum her father had bitterly purchased, Nancy had noticed that there were only plaques enough for four of their five. On an unseasonably cold day for the California valley, Nancy wondered which of them her father had blamed for Buddy's death and denied a place in the family plot, in some sick game of permanent musical chairs. She decided in short order that *that* was the last place in the world she wanted to end up, and quietly vowed to bequeath her spot to whomever had been slighted.

The men she had chosen from that day on were, each in his own way, the father she'd been denied. Her string of husbands, revolving door of lovers—there was something of the patriarch in each. 'Big Mama's on the hunt for a Big Daddy, because her real one was so absent,' Truman noted. 'He only cared for Buddy, and when *he* went away, so did Mr. Gross. You never get over being left like that . . .' This was the cue to replace his glasses, with a practiced shift in tone. 'I *know* this, you see, because *I* had absent parents too.'

They'd been chasing them since. A head-shrinker's field day, the pair of them. Filthy ole Freud's wet dream—Slim searching for Daddy, and Truman for Mommy, he desperate to recast Nina with a swanlike being, one who would love him with unwavering devotion. He had us now, en masse. And Slim realized, in Russia more than ever, just how desperately Truman needed the love that Nina had denied him.

IT WAS AFTER AN EVEN LONGER JOURNEY to Copenhagen, after they'd checked into the Hotel d'Angleterre and basked in the rediscovered luxury of creature comforts, that Slim saw Truman shed his armor. And it was in that moment that she understood him. Or thought that she did . . .

They'd had an idyllic day out, devoured an absurdly indulgent lunch of pickled herring and schnapps, followed by a heaving platter of *smørrebrød*—though they concurred that anything would have seemed indulgent after weeks of freezing borscht. Even what Truman pointed out were, let's face it, little more than open-faced sandwiches with fancy Danish names.

On their way back to the hotel, Slim stopped to photograph a group of local children tossing coins into a fountain. When she turned around, Truman was gone. Slim popped her head into a row of shops, checking them one by one. No Tru. She continued on to the hotel when he suddenly appeared at her side once more. He slipped a wrapped box into her coat pocket.

'For you, Big Mama. That's because I want you to have things as pretty as you are.'

Slim opened the box to find an exquisite antique ring: brilliant canary gemstones, linked in a delicate band. Truman had disappeared into a shop as she walked, and managed to find a gift more suited to her tastes than her husbands and lovers combined. He could, when he chose to, be the most thoughtful creature alive. He *knew* us, Truman. This was one of the myriad reasons we loved him. And Slim, despite her cynicism, was not immune.

EACH EVENING ON THEIR TRAVELS they had shared a nightcap, and Truman had walked Slim to her room, kissed her goodnight, and retired to his own. Their last evening in Denmark they repeated the ritual, only this time Truman stopped at her door.

'I'm gonna come tuck my Big Mama in, that's how much I love her,' Truman insisted in an oddly hushed voice.

Slim unlocked the door and Truman followed her into the suite. He sat on the edge of the bed, watching as she undressed, studying her long body with wide eyes. She walked naked to the bathroom, as she would in front of a child. Easy, devoid of self-consciousness. She returned wearing a thin silk robe.

'You just do what you usually do, then I'll put you to bed,' he almost crooned.

Slim settled in at the vanity, proceeding step by step through her nightly beauty ritual. Truman watched with rapt attention as she removed her makeup, as if witnessing the dance of the seven veils as Slim shed each cosmetic layer with tantalizing promise, until her bare flesh was revealed. He studied her face in its natural state, the earliest traces of sunburst lines forming around her eyes.

'Beautiful,' he exhaled. The sunburst rays spread as she smiled at him in the mirror, as Lillie Mae once had while he chewed sugared beignets, another lifetime ago.

He watched, enraptured, as she slathered a layer of cream onto her skin. She loosened her hair around her shoulders—a seasoned blonde, darker than it once had been, the color of winter wheat. With soft boar bristles she brushed each side, exactly fifty strokes.

Finally Slim rose, walked to the bed, and removed her robe. And like a tender lover, childlike father, or both combined, Truman lifted the covers for her. She slipped inside, and he gently tucked the soft blankets around her.

'I'm doing this, Big Mama, because I love you. I love you very much.' His eyes met hers, welling with sincerity.

'I love you too, Truman.'

'No, you don't,' he frowned, turning from her.

'Of course I do,' she insisted, reaching her arm out to touch his rounded back.

'*No*—you *DON'T!*' He jerked away.

Slim sat up, startled. She turned him to face her, his visage flushed the color of rotting cherries. Teeth clenched, tears streaming down his hot, puffy cheeks.

'Truman, whatever's wrong?'

'*No* one loves me.'

'That's not true. *I* do. And Babe. And Jack—'

'You *don't*. None of you. Well—*maybe* Jack . . .' he allowed. 'Because Jack sees me for exactly who I am.'

Slim reached for his arm and he snapped. A feral animal, caught in a cage. Protecting the one thing he had: knowledge.

'You don't think I *know*? You don't think I know what I look like? What I sound like? You don't think I see people cringe when they meet me? Or wince when I speak?' He rubbed his eyes. 'I'm a freak. I'm a monstrous little freak and everybody thinks it.'

Slim started to protest, but he cut her short.

'Oh sure, people get used to me. People can adjust. But every time they see or hear me, it starts all over, the *adjustment*—to get past the freak show to all that's trapped inside. Be honest, Big Mama. Don't pretend you don't know what I mean.'

Slim sat quietly. As much as she hated to admit it, she *did* know what he meant. She'd watched it happen, again and again— we all had—watched a room forced to acclimatize to his mannerisms. She'd felt it herself—not once, but the tiniest bit every time she saw him, before she slipped into his delicious Trumanisms once more.

She *did* know, and he knew that she understood.

He hung his weighty head, hiccuping silent, choking sobs. 'I'm unlovable. No one could ever love me the way I want to be loved.'

With a surge of warmth, Slim wrapped her arms around him and held on tight, trying to smother the flames of Truman's misery as she'd once attempted to smother the flames lapping at Buddy's nightshirt.

TO BE FAIR, TRUMAN HAD WARNED HER about his *Esquire* bombshell weeks ago at the Russian Tea Room, where they like to wax nostalgic over their Moscow venture. They laugh at the notion of the stark Soviet haunts they'd braved bearing any resemblance to the jade jewel-box dining room, gold-leaf phoenix reliefs swooping down on chattering Manhattanites. Slim looked doubly radiant in that space, bathed in the warm light reflected off its twenty-three-carat ceiling, light that even gave Truman an oddly flattering, if slightly jaundiced, glow.

'You're in it, Big Mama,' he'd smiled as they snuggled close in a circular banquette, sipping blood-red pickled-beet borscht and a round of Black Russians, chased by a round of White. 'Hold on to your hat . . . !' Slim had not thought about it since. She'd expected a cameo—not the leading goddamn role!

Well. He won't charm his way out of *this* mess, the snake.

Slim has a sudden flash of the pair of taxidermy cobras in Truman's United Nations Plaza apartment. They'd found them together in an antique shop in Madrid, thought they were kooky and fun. Scaly bodies stuffed upright, raised at the point of attack; mouths agape, sharp little fangs poised to sink into unsuspecting flesh. He'd laughed and laughed like Br'er Rabbit in his briar patch when each of us jumped at the lifelike reptiles, encountering them for the first time.

Oh, it's war all right.

Slim hears the click of Babe's Ronson on the line, and imagines her bringing the next in a string of L&Ms to her lips, nails buffed to perfection.

We can each picture Babe, fingering a stray lock of hair as she tends to when she's nervous—the bit tinged with premature silver, usually hidden in her neat bouffant.

'Slim. Tell me honestly. As my friend. If you know, tell me . . . Is it Bill?'

Slim takes care her answer comes neither too quickly, nor too slow:

'It isn't Bill.'

She downs her third Scotch and tells her first lie of the morning. It's not yet 10 a.m.

THREE

1932–?

VARIATION No. 2

THE BOY IS EIGHT, MAYBE NINE, WE'RE TOLD.

It's a sweltering day in Monroeville, the kind of day when lizards sizzle on the pavement, the kind that sears the tender pads of doggies' paws.

He reclines on the porch planks, listless, watching an ice cube melt atop the griddle of his chest, translucent dribble rolling between his bony ribs.

It's the kind of day when the heat seeps into your brain and sets it on fire. When you just have to stir something up or go out of your pent-up, heat-stroked skull.

He wills himself from the shade and his toy limbs follow, buttoning his shirt, trotting next door to Nelle's house. He knocks on the frame of the mosquito-proof screen, waiting for his friend.

Mr. Lee answers in his hybrid-cotton suit, a loose weave that, in theory, would allow breeze to blow through, should the breeze ever choose to cooperate.

'Well hey there, Truman,' he says in his molasses baritone. A lawyer's voice, trained to appeal to twelve good men and true—to the whole dang town, to be honest. He's the classiest act the boy has met, a beacon of what he thinks of as 'justice' when it's preached by folks who wouldn't know it if it smacked them in the kisser. Teachers and preachers, each dumber than a bucket of hair.

'Hiya, Mr. Lee. Might Nellie be available to play?' He bows with formality, a midget suitor, pushing the fringe from his sweat-soaked forehead.

'Nelle honey—Truman!' Mr. Lee calls, setting his scuffed brief-case by the door. He reaches for a hair comb and straw hat, turning to the kitchen mirror as the boy moves to the porch swing, the lat-ter wondering what it might feel like to wait there for a sweetheart.

He swings back and forth, his feet dangling, enjoying the creak of the metal chains, calling to mind the uneven croaks of bullfrogs at the swimming hole. Through an open window he can hear a voice inside the house, buzzing like a gadfly, presumably on the telephone, hardly pausing to land on one topic before irritatingly buzzing 'round to the next.

'. . . And I just told her to pack her things and get! But would she listen? With a man like that, poking every stuffing from here to Mobile, and all before the wedding cake was in the icebox? Well, who could *blame* Itty for running off with Scrub Mangram? But all the way to N'awlins—? She *did* though—Esther Reaben *saw* them check in! I swear it on a stack of Bibles! At the Pontchar-train Hotel on St. Charles. I *tell* you, Esther *saw* them at the Bayou Bar, clear as crystal! Well, Itty best watch out or she'll end up like this one next *door*—knocked up without two pennies to rub together, before she's old enough to order a cocktail. Dumping her brat with that bunch of spinsters . . . Mark my words—that boy'll turn out just like his con man Daddy, if you can call *him* a man, or call *that* a boy—'

'Nelllllllll—eeeeeeeee,' the boy screeches in his highest, most affected wail.

He wants the voice on the phone to know. He's *heard* her.

He's *listening*. Always listening . . .

'Listening and lurking,' he's heard her say about him, that busybody. Old Mrs. Busybody Lee! How could someone as decent as Mr. Lee have chosen such a witch? How could that biddy have spawned his precious Nelle, speak of the devil—

The coltish form that bolts onto the porch is as far a cry from sweetheart as the boy is from beau. The masculine to his femi-nine, with her bowl-cut bob, rolled blue jeans, and Keds that she can run in. She's his one true friend and he hers.

She joins him on the swing, each appreciating the harmony of creaking back and forth together, swinging higher and higher . . .

Then, from an upstairs window, the fly-buzz amps to a buzz-saw wail—'Nelle . . . ? Don't you *dare* leave this house with that little nancy!'

Mr. Lee flashes a wary grin on his way out. 'Y'all best be off before you get caught!' He stops the swing and gives the colt-girl a quick nuzzle before hurrying to trade the wrath of the missus for the sanctity of his office.

Nelle and the boy exchange a glance and leap from the swing in unison, running from the porch with the speed of a hurricane. Not a minute too soon, as the figure—absurdly plump for an insect—is in the doorway, her buzzing having escalated to the baying of a hound dog.

'Nelle Harper *Lee*! You come back here this *minute*! You've got a ballet lesson at two thirty!'

But they're off, making their getaway into the fields. Onto dirt roads outside town. Into treehouses and under porches, listening to unsuspecting voices they will both later repeat to one another, still later rehash in their prose. Sometimes the boy has Nelle take dictation, weaving tidbits into stories as he orates. Sometimes he types, on an old Remington with keys that stick, that he found in his cousins' attic.

As he furiously types that very night—the open window scant comfort in the sticky stillness—he relishes his revenge on Old Mrs. Busybody.

She'll get hers. He'll teach her to talk that way about — —

THE BOY IS NINE OR TEN, HE TELLS US—*certainly* no older. It's a sweltering day in Monroeville. Lizards sizzle on the pavement. Dogs scorch the pads of their paws.

He and Nelle wander along the train tracks, balancing on the rails, wondering how long it would take for the conductor to spot a body, were one tied to the tracks, and whether or not the brakes could stop in time to avoid hitting it. In an old abandoned depot at the fork in the road, they spy two derelicts. Local men, 'once nice family types,' the preachers caution, 'until they got hooked on the hooch.'

One looks to be asleep, a Stetson over his face—or maybe he's a body, dragged in off the tracks. The other, a shirtless figure, Skin and Bones, swigs from a bottle of Wild Turkey as he gives the reclining feller an earful, who, if he wasn't dead already, might *wish* that he was after all that talk.

The boy puts a finger to his lips, signaling Nelle to follow him around the back of the ramshackle structure. They lie in the tall grass, so hot it laps like flames at their sockless ankles. Eavesdropping ...

'Goddamn preachers'll tell you otherwise, but there ain't nothin' wrong with Faffy Bixter's roadside cathouse, sure as I live and breathe,' Skin and Bones assures his passed-out friend. 'Them's just honest gals, makin' an honest wage . . .' He takes another gulp, swilling the liquor through the gaps in his teeth. 'I'd haul these ole bones right on over there this minute, if I hadn't done lost the only quarter I had on the chicken fights ... I coulda just fried that no-good losing cockerel in a pan and gobbled him up myself—*still* madder than a wet hen!' He downs another mouthful of Turkey, directing a resentful gobble at the label.

The boy and Nelle suppress giggles as they listen to Skin and Bones' bourbon-drenched diatribe, when— —

THE BOY IS TEN, BUT ONLY JUST. He knows this because he just had a birthday the week before.

He was given as presents an eggshell herringbone suit (mailed in a box from his Mama), a slingshot (from Nelle), and a typewriter ribbon (from Mr. Lee). He had wanted a dog, and his Daddy had promised him . . . He'll bring one the next time he comes to visit.

Because it's September, just one day shy of the start of October, the boy is certain that the trees are losing their leaves.

He plays hooky twice a week these days, about as often as he can get away with without being sent to a home for wayward boys. He gets himself a stack of books from the library, waits until the grown-up Faulks have left for work, when it's only him and Cousin Sook left in the big drafty house. Sweet Sook—somewhere between sixteen and sixty, who people think as slow and odd as the boy himself. She brings him cups of hot chocolate as he lies in bed, propped up by pillows, escaping the dull gray town, reading his way through the great stories of the world, sharing his tiny room with the likes of Huck Finn and Oliver Twist, boys who have nobody, like himself, who live large, in primary colors splattered onto vast canvases.

Sook also brings the boy the morning paper, he being the only soul in the house full of aging cousins who has a lick of interest. He reads the obituaries out loud to her. She likes to hear about the people who have gone, and all the folks who'll carry on without them.

As Sook settles into her rocking chair and the boy flips through the newspaper, his eyes flick across the children's Sunshine Page. He usually skips this—it's kids' stuff after all. But his focus is drawn by a photo of a beagle puppy, the word CONTEST printed above. Folding the page carefully to the section in question, the boy reads aloud to Sook's gentle rocking, the old chair squeaking on her down-tilts. She smiles and nods, mending a pair of long johns, the Sunshine Page pleasing her every bit as much as the Obits. It's the boy's high, melodic voice that she loves.

'*The* Mobile Press Register *seeks short stories by children under the age of twelve. Any subject. Five hundred words. First prize, publication and . . . a* beagle PUPPY!'

He's just finished reading À *la Recherche du Temps Perdu*— at *ten*, he later loves to boast—and strangely enough, it felt . . . familiar. He's read it's what's called a *roman-à-clef*, which to him just seems to be a fancy French word for spreading rumors. He figures he could try his hand, Southern gothic style. While there isn't much in Monroeville, there *is* gossip. It peppers every porch chat from here to Mobile. And who better than the town muck-rakers to mine for narrative gold—serving up Mrs. Lee's and Skin and Bones' scuttlebutt as fiction, just like old Marcel had done? He's already written up Mrs. Lee's slew of lies. It'll serve her right for talking out of school.

Within the afternoon the boy has carefully typed a copy of what he now calls 'Mrs. Busybody' on clean white paper, has sealed it in a brown Manila envelope and hand-delivered it to Miss Bee McGhee at the post office.

'It's very important that this not get lost in the shuffle,' he's gravely instructed her, paying an extra nickel for first class.

Each afternoon the boy runs home to check the mailbox. Day after day, he loyally reads the Sunshine Page and fishes through bills and envelopes in the mail, searching for his name. When an official-looking letter arrives, he holds it in his pocket for a day and a half before he can bring himself to tear it open.

Mr. Truman Streckfus Persons, we are pleased to inform you . . .

Pleased?! The boy can hardly contain his joy. He's never won a cotton-picking thing, has never been told by anyone but Sook that he's good at anything (she having told him he was excellent at flying homemade kites). He cartwheels across the lawn to Nelle's house, shouting his triumph loud enough for Mrs. Lee to hear him.

His joy will be short-lived. As he tells it, his story was to be published in three installments in the *Mobile Press Register*, under his very own name, which the newspaper men call his *byline*.

The boy and Nelle wait on the Sunday for the paper to be tossed over the crumbling fence at the Faulk house. The minute it lands, thrown unceremoniously by a sluggish kid on a red bike pedaling *far* too slow for their taste, the pair races up to the boy's room to enjoy his tale, printed there in black and white for all the world to see.

He feels for the first time a rush of something like power.

That same moment, Mr. and Mrs. Lee are sitting down to plates of bacon, grits, and eggs, reading their own Sunday *Register*. Mr. Lee sees it first (the Lees' cook, Val, will later report), and begins to laugh in his hearty, good-natured way.

'Well, I'll be damned. Little Truman's gone and got himself published.' He folds his newspaper to the Sunshine Page, clears his throat and starts to read out loud:

'"Mrs. Busybody"—by Truman Streckfus Persons. Mrs. Busybody buzzed like a gadfly on the telephone, hardly pausing to land on one topic before irritatingly buzzing around to the next . . . "Well, Itty best watch out . . ." her fly-buzz amped to a buzz-saw wail, ". . . or she'll end up like this one next door—knocked up without two pennies to rub together, before she's old enough to order a cocktail!"'*

Mrs. Lee has, by the third sentence, at least had sense enough to recognize herself, and marches right on over to the Faulk house to tell the boy's spinster cousins what she thinks of him. She rings up the newspaper editor personally, demanding the next two installments under no circumstances be published. She has all her lady friends write letters threatening to cancel their subscriptions.

The boy writes his own letters in reply, about the beauty of art and the evils of censorship, but he never sees his byline in the *Mobile Press Register* again—not, that is, until he has long emerged from the chrysalis of self-conscious prepubescence and made his mark on the world.

Still ten, the boy also writes the *Mobile Press Register* about the dog that they had promised, but fails to get a reply. He calls them from the telephone in Mr. Lee's office in town, which he and Nelle had snuck into for that very purpose. He's told that his inquiry will be 'looked into.' He even saves his pocket change and skips school to take a Greyhound bus to Mobile, where he marches directly to the *Press Register*'s office, approaching a reception desk he can only just peer over. The receptionist with the horn-rimmed specs pretends not to know what he's talking about.

He's won their contest, fair and square, but he never sees the beagle that they promised. Or the one his Daddy had. Wouldn't get one until he was all grown up and moved away, to the city where no one cares what you— —

THE BOY IS EIGHT, BUT HE *REMEMBERS* BEING NINE. It's still fall, but closer to Halloween. He vividly recalls planning his costume: Fu Manchu, a long robe with a thin, dangling mustache.

He often brags about digging a hole from Monroeville to China, has even enlisted the labor of local bruisers to dig up his cousin Jenny's vegetable patch, promising payments of oriental treasure when they reach the other end.

This time he recalls concealing the identity of his subject, writing about Mrs. Lee, but putting her words in the mouth of Skin and Bones, the derelict from the railroad tracks:

'. . . *And I just told her ta pack her things and get!*' the boy has the fictional Skin and Bones rant to his hooched-up companion, passed out beside him in the abandoned train depot. He has recast the object of gossip as Skin and Bones' wayward wife, run off with a traveling salesman, '. . . *poking every stuffing from here to Mobile, before the weddin' cake was in the icebox . . . runnin' all the way to N'awlins, without two pennies to rub together . . . knocked up before she's old enough to order a whiskey . . .*'

Skin-and-Bones-on-Paper takes a guzzle of Wild Turkey for emphasis. The boy feels clever coming up with the amalgamation, a disguise that would surely prove crafty enough to elude any grown-up who might suspect his source and put the kibosh on his efforts.

He even allows himself to plot a sequel, in which Mrs. Lee shocks the ladies of Monroeville at the beauty parlor, spouting Skin and Bones' diatribe about cock fights and gambling and houses of ill repute, making a case for their various virtues. The thought of offending Mrs. Lee twice over—both by giving her words to a washed-up tramp *and* by forcing the tramp's whore-loving words into her pious mouth—pleases the boy enormously.

Within the afternoon he has carefully typed a copy of the first tale—what he now calls '*Mr.* Busybody'—on clean white paper, sealed it in a brown Manila envelope, and hand-delivered it to Miss Bee McGhee at the post office, insisting in his gravest squeal that she take special care, paying an extra nickel for first class.

The prize offered by the *Mobile Press Register* is a Shetland pony, something the boy wants badly. He thinks he remembers his Daddy promising to bring him one someday.

He recalls winning first prize, the first installment coming out under his very own byline. But Cousin Jenny comes home early from the dry-goods shop and hears the boy reading his piece to Sook and Nelle in the kitchen of the old drafty house, and recognizes Mrs. Lee's gossip. She calls the newspaper editor personally and tells him not to print installments two and three, and even makes the boy write a letter of apology for the lies that he has spread. He hopes against hope that he still might get the pony, and gallop into the sunset, or at least ride far away to the city where boys with talent might speak their minds without causing a fuss.

The pony never — —

THE BOY IS TWELVE. He's not sure if the sun is scorching or if the leaves are falling, but he senses that he's older. This time he's added a pejorative 'Old' to the 'Busybody,' but later forgets whether it was 'Old Mr.' or 'Old Mrs.,' and vacillates between the two.

In this version the first installment published under his byline in the *Mobile Press Register*, as the winner of the Sunshine Club prize.

The second installment is ready to go to press the next week, but is yanked in the ninth inning when the *Mobile Press Register* switchboard lights up with calls like a fireworks display.

The more the boy tells the tale, the madder folks seem to get, until you'd think there'd been an absolute riot in Monroeville over a tiny little story in the children's Sunshine Page.

The prize is 'a beagle dog *and* a Shetland pony'—sometimes with a bicycle thrown in for good measure. Not that Cousin Jenny will let him ride a bike, claiming his constitution too fragile. Since neither dog nor pony materializes, the boy develops a conspiracy theory and begins to write to other winners of children's contests across the country, asking if they had been given their prizes, and enlists Nelle to do the same. After fifty letters, their tongues numbed with the cardboard taste of licking stamps, neither is able to find a single case of dog or bike or pony being forked over.

THE BOY IS A MAN when he first tells us various versions.

It was the dead of winter—he's told Babe—when the skeletal trees rattled against the icy wind. That he'd shivered in a threadbare hand-me-down jacket—even though the average December temperature in Alabama flatlines at fifty degrees Fahrenheit.

He's told Lee, C.Z. and Marella it was spring, when the new azaleas had started to bloom atop the previous season's growth, in that brief lifespan we all know they have, just between Easter and May Day.

With Slim and Gloria it's back to that sweltering summer of old. The sizzling lizards. The scorched beagle paws—which he would tenderly have bandaged, had he been given one.

The summer scene he gives to Gloria because he thinks it might appeal to her hot Latin temperament, to Slim because he couldn't bear to pitch her any scene but sunny.

Both of the latter are too savvy to believe a word of it. But Gloria, being a hustler herself, appreciates the detail of the

44

feverish heat, whereas Slim just logs it as another reason not to trust him.

Nelle alone—never one of us, being armed with too much knowledge and too little beauty—knows the truth. And for that very reason he has kept her separate from our flock, for fear that she'd trumpet a definitive gospel.

FOUR

1975/1955

VARIATION No. 3

NATURALLY WE PRETEND THAT WE KNOW NOTHING of The Sheets, apart from what we've read.

When it becomes the prime topic of conversation around our tables at Vadis or Cirque—or even the eponymous La Côte Basque—we feign suitable horror.

We pretend not only—as Slim had—that we don't know that Sidney Dillon is Bill Paley, or the Governor's Wife Marie Harriman, but that the tale itself is new to us.

We don our most convincing expressions of offense, looking particularly appalled by details we make a concerted effort not to appear to anticipate. In the end we will offer that the whole thing sounds absurd—so slapstick it must be fiction. Isn't its author vile to have invented such a thing? However did he think of such graphic smut, the sick little fuck?

As we play our role in the drama, issue our lines with what we hope reads as naturalness—calibrating our timbre of concern, of shock, with just the right amount of vitriol—we feel *her* gaze lingering on us across the table as we move on to other topics. When we confer with one another in a series of phone calls afterward, most of us will feel nearly certain that we pulled it off.

Of *course* we'd heard the ludicrous story about The Sheets. Not only that, but we likely knew more about the Paley marriage than Babe herself, the details of which had kept us enthralled over *years'* worth of lunch trysts. The intelligence came courtesy of the one who served as a first-hand witness: the favored son who settled in at the foot of their beds each evening trading con-

46

fidences with wife and husband in turn, who might as well have snuggled in with each of them, so enmeshed was he. And by son we don't mean Tony Mortimer, Babe's from her first marriage, or Billy Paley, their shared one—both left behind at Kiluna with a retinue of nannies in early days, uninvited in later ones. We mean the *chosen* son, without whom we'd not seen the Paleys travel in over two decades—be the destination Jamaica or Venice, or Lyford Cay; Paris or London or Timbuktu. He was neatly packed and bundled from tarmac to tailwind, from restaurant to residence. As indispensable and as cozy as a favorite pair of slippers; as reliable and loyal (so we thought. . .) as the most devoted of pets. Confessor, confidant, consigliere, ever since that fateful day when he'd won Babe Paley's broken heart in the sky.

WHEN DAVID HAD ASKED OVER THE *pots de crème* if he and Jennifer might bring Truman along, of course they'd accepted. It was hardly a question. One simply couldn't say no.

'Please do,' Babe said, with trademark dazzling smile.

'It would be our pleasure,' Bill assured, scraping the sides of his ramekin, licking the last globules of chocolate from his spoon.

Our pleasure, thought Babe, with a silent laugh, knowing full well that the pains would be hers. What was one more body to Bill? Especially a prominent one.

Bill loved high-profile guests—the higher the better. What could be a bigger coup than a former head of state?

Two days and counting to Round Hill. And now a change in protocol.

Babe began to revise her mental inventory of minute details.

Would creamed chicken hash on toast be too casual? Would Harry Truman drink a Jamaican Mule? Did Harry Truman drink at all . . . ?

For Babe the addition meant nothing more than another meticulous checklist. Another set of carefully orchestrated arrangements to delegate. She planned their Caribbean trips like a general going into battle. She allowed for every contingency. Considered every comfort. She arranged indulgences from New York's gourmet vendors: cured salmon; rare truffles caked in earth; black cherries soaked in port; five varieties of heirloom tomatoes—six if she could find them; French wine—Pouilly-Fumé, packed on ice and stowed aboard the CBS plane.

A consummate hostess, Babe could throw a black-tie affair in mid-air if push came to shove, but then Babe could throw an incomparable gathering on the moon. It was her profession: keeping Bill happy.

The expected luxuries the Round Hill staff would handle. Unpacking luggage, whisking clothes off to be ironed and neatly folded in guests' dressers before they realized they were missing. The Paley households were known for their pampering, thanks to Babe's uncanny knack for anticipating guests' needs before they knew them themselves. Her near-obsessive attention to detail long ago cemented the Paleys as entertainers nonpareil.

She took care to fill each guest suite with fruit and flowers, wrapped soaps and bath oils, tailoring each aesthetic choice to that room's particular inhabitant. She hand-selected books for every guest; she ensured that three newspapers for each member of the household were neatly stacked outside their door with a pot of fresh-roasted coffee every morning.

First class all the way, those Paleys. Just as Bill liked it.

Of course anyone who knows the Cushings (and really who could escape them?) knows that Babe learned the tools of the trade from a shockingly early age. She had been raised to cultivate perfection, in a family where overachievement was an understatement. Who else's beloved father was a groundbreaking neurosurgeon and Harvard professor, whose leisure time casually produced a Nobel-winning biography? Who else had two permanent rivals in the form of near-identical older sisters? And what a trio of stunners they were, raised by a shrewdly ambitious mother who, like a modern mutation of a dowager empress, bred her girls to marry royalty. It was indeed thrones and dynasties Gogsie Cushing had in mind for her fine-boned daughters . . . But the courts she looked to conquer were those ruled by the scions of American industry. Vanderbilts. Astors. Whitneys and Roosevelts.

'Marry up' was the message drummed into their perfectly coiffed heads from their earliest consciousness. And like domestic courtesans they learned to please. From childhood the tools of the trade were imparted. How to prepare an impeccable luncheon: a classic lobster Thermidor with vegetables in miniature, or a cheese soufflé that rose just so. How to lay a flawless table with settings for every occasion, from an informal supper to a debutante ball. To stage a room with just the right mix of New Elegance and Old World shabbiness—preferably French—so that the scent of Old Wealth permeated, its musty chic confirming its inhabitants' pedigree. To dress one's lithe frame with effortless grace, wearing the most fashionable attire without letting *it* wear *you*. There were lessons in comportment, deportment, and etiquette. How to speak, to sit, to smoke . . . to please.

Neatness was the key to dressing well. A girl could stretch the same black dress over ten occasions and fool her critics with a subtle change in accessory. Grooming was everything. Visit the hairdresser at least twice a week. Attend to one's manicure diligently. Never go to bed without a thick coat of youth-preserving cold cream. And never, absolutely *never* be seen without your Face on.

From the age of fifteen, Babe Paley, formerly Mortimer, née Cushing was not once glimpsed without lips and cheeks subtly painted, without her eyelashes carefully applied, enhancing incomparable features—even if it meant applying one's Face in the hushed half-light of the vanity mirror, then slipping back into bed beside a snoring partner. Or waking at dawn before the first of a heaving house of guests had had the gall to rise.

Houseguest, lover . . . even one's own husband should never be subjected to anything other than the radiant perfection of a Fabulous Cushing Sister.

To her credit, Gogs' ambitious plotting had paid off in spades. Three daughters, two marriages apiece. Betsey: a Roosevelt and an Astor. Minnie: a Whitney and a Fosburgh. Gogsie couldn't have been more pleased. But for Barbara . . . her Babe . . . the sky was the limit. She held the biggest and most glimmering hopes for her youngest daughter, the beauty among beauties, the sylphlike creature with her father's height and her chiseled, delicate features—Babe, with her aristocratic air and unpretentious charm. She who possessed the involuntary power to turn each pair of eyes in every room into which she chanced to float. That she was kind and bright was but a bonus. Surely Babe would fulfill Gogsie's final ambition: to marry titled royalty. Of course, her mother worried that Babe's stint as an editor at *Vogue* risked branding her an Office Girl, but it did give her access to the sartorial offerings showered upon her by couturiers who encouraged her emerging status as a tastemaker. While the looming label of 'careerist' failed to win her approval, Gogsie was the first to appreciate the rewards that a high profile might yield for her glamorous daughter.

She was vaguely disappointed when Babe chose to marry oil heir Stanley Grafton Mortimer, Junior. He was rich enough, good family. Gogs chalked it up to a decent starter marriage. Two children in six years—a boy and a girl; then the marriage fell apart (the War . . . Stan drank), and Gogsie resumed her vigil. Imagine her shock when Babe, the prize thoroughbred in her stable of splendid offspring, then chose to marry *beneath her*.

Babe ignored the comments. The rumors. The polite inquiries, dressed up as interest: 'And what *club* does Bill belong to . . . ? Ah . . . too busy at the network . . . ? Dear me—what an absolute go-getter!' She ignored Waspy whispers as they breezed past tables at the Colony . . . 'He's *Jewish*, you know . . .' Even worse, the patronizing 'How . . . *exotic*!'

Instead, she eschewed Old Money snobbery and embraced Bill's new breed of power. Where New Wealth was born of ingenuity. Where an ambitious boy could turn profits from his immigrant family's cigar concern into a radio network acquisition, and end up a titan in the fledgling field of broadcasting.

She fell hard for Bill Paley's dynamism. His zeal was infectious. He wanted so desperately to belong to those grand old families, he became a tenacious apprentice; a mongrel sniffing and digging around pedigree pooches who'd had all the life inbred out of them. Babe found his avidness endearing. His passion for beauty, moving. She knew she was his most coveted acquisition. She'd become the object of perfection he fixed his greedy eye on. All that outsider Bill Paley—who'd been kept from the right schools, the right clubs—had ever desired in life. It was as flattering as it was unnerving. She had thought that once he had her, he would feel that he had arrived. She would feel safe in the love of a man for whom she held the keys to the rarefied kingdom. He would bask in the knowledge that his wife was the finest portrait of elegance, studied and admired by all, but his alone to keep.

She would make herself perfect for him. His acquired masterpiece. They'd conquer empires, with his power and her grace. Together. The Paleys. The Perfect Couple.

That was before she realized that Bill wasn't shopping for one masterpiece . . .

He wanted a collection.

'WE NEED OYSTERS!' BILL DECLARED to the Selznicks, cutting his eyes to Babe.

She stifled a sigh with a drag from her L&M.

It was now January in Manhattan and Babe knew that Bill's casual comment meant a reordering of her day. The next morning she had planned to go to Kenneth's. She needed her hair colored and her nails buffed. So much for that. She would instead be trudging through slush to the fishmonger in Chinatown, in order not to disappoint.

She tapped her ash, adjusting the long, gold cigarette holder she was never seen without. Bill adored shellfish—oysters especially—with an unnatural passion. His mother had kept a strict kosher kitchen. Perhaps that in part explained his insatiable appetite, his rebellious enthusiasm for all things gastronomical (crustaceans and pork products in particular). In one day, Bill Paley could quite literally consume up to eight meals. That he managed to keep a slim, athletic figure without lifting anything heavier than a fork was an affront to dieters everywhere.

'Kumamotos,' Bill enthused. 'Ice cold. The flavor is unsurpassed. The Japanese began importing them just after the war. They're the firmest, sweetest things you'll ever put in your mouth! We discovered them in LA, come to think. At Dave Chasen's. Speaking of which . . .' He leaned in toward his dinner companions, excitement mounting—

'. . . Have you tasted their chili?' Bill practically licked his lips.

'Heaven,' cooed Jennifer languorously. 'I'd give my left *arm* for a spoonful now.'

After the five-course meal they'd just polished off—shrimp in aspic, crab salad, corn bisque, baby rack of lamb, and the pots of chocolate custard—Babe doubted Jennifer Jones wanted anything other than to fall happily into a deep, comatose sleep.

But Bill . . . sweet Bill. His passion for food—consuming or discussing—knew no bounds.

'I think we can do better than that! Baby, darling, what do you say? Could Dave send some chili over on ice to Round Hill?' he asked, purloining Babe's untouched *pot de crème*, helping himself.

She reached for the miniature gold-framed notepad beside her plate, paired with a miniature gold pencil, kept close by at all times for jotting detailed notes on the eccentric errands she would be expected to run to keep the incomparable Paley legend alive and well. She wondered, if she managed all in record time, if she might still make a quick stop at the salon . . .

When she mentally clocked back into the conversation, mercifully Bill had dropped the topic of Chasen's menu before further strokes of inspiration occurred.

'Truman really is something,' David was rhapsodizing. 'An utterly original person.'

Babe allowed herself a moment, picturing the staid portraits of a bland liberal Democrat, lacking the charisma of FDR. Poor Harry Truman looked about as 'original' as a lipless, lifeless banker.

Babe shifted her eyes to Jennifer, who was saying, '. . . he's charming, Babe. Enchanting. You'll simply *adore* him.'

Babe smiled, mask of neutrality in place. But the divine Mrs. Paley had mentally moved on to her lists, pondering what kinds of fruit, books, and flowers a former President would like, and how to get chili from California to Jamaica in less than two days' time.

THEY COULDN'T HAVE APPEARED MORE DAZZLING, Mr. and Mrs. William S. Paley, as they boarded the CBS jet that freezing January morning. He in his Savile Row suit. She in a slim navy sheath and coat, Hermès *Harnais* scarf shielding her coif from the elements.

They smiled their thousand-watt smiles, greeting the pilot and staff. Bill offered Babe his arm, gallantly assisting her up the rolling passenger stairs. An unnecessary gesture, but how thoughtful. What care he took. How delighted she seemed.

Who ever could have guessed that the Paleys had fallen out?

On board Babe settled into her seat, flipping absently through *Women's Wear Daily* while Bill served up the silent treatment. He seldom lost his temper; he simply froze her out, leaving her to stew until she earned his favor back. She would rather weather anyone's rage than Bill's *disappointment*. It simply tore her apart.

'What would you like?' Bill, with polite indifference.

'Pouilly, please,' Babe answered, not looking up from her magazine.

Mr. Paley summoned the air hostess, while Mrs. Paley focused on 'The New Silhouette.'

AS IT TURNED OUT, BABE HAD FAILED.

Failure was unacceptable, and she was, beneath her guise of serenity, in a foul mood.

She'd managed the chili, but fallen short with the Kumamotos. Dave Chasen assured her that no one could get them. Apparently California oyster farmers had banned the Japanese supply when they discovered they could cultivate Kumamotos themselves. But Chasen swore the domestic variety wasn't the same. He recommended the European flats, Belons from Brittany. He promised they had a lovely seaweed-and-sharp-mineral taste. A meaty texture . . . almost a crunch to them.

She had gone on a three-shop hunt for Bill's favorite barbecue sauce, making her late for Kenneth. There was time for a set, but not a coloring. At forty, Babe's chestnut hair had started to reveal its first silver streaks and she agonized over what to do about it. She had planned to cover the traces of gray this last appointment, but after the oysters and the chili and the sauce . . .

Babe sat beneath the domed dryer, having her nails rounded and painted in a glossy oxblood lacquer, carefully maintained twice weekly—for with enough wear and tear, they, like anything, might chip and fray and eventually be broken.

WHEN BILL HAD LEARNED THAT THE KUMAMOTOS were off, he clenched his teeth and made a sandwich. He sawed at a loaf of rye, methodically layering cold cuts, disappointment palpable.

'Chasen said you just can't get them, darling. No one can,' Babe had explained.

Silence. He removed a jar of pickles from the icebox.

'It's on account of the oyster farmers . . .' She trailed off. Trying again: 'Chasen said the European flats are divine. Seaweed and mineral undertones—briny.'

'I don't like briny.'

Babe had sunk into a chair at the kitchen table. She rubbed her temple, sensing a migraine coming on. Bill sliced his sandwich in half. He ate it standing at the counter, his back to her.

'Darling, I did try,' Babe offered, defeated.

'I suppose the Selznicks won't know what a Kumamoto tastes like until they're back in California.' Then, evenly, 'It would have been nice if we could have kept our promises.'

THE SELZNICKS' CAR PULLED UP ALONGSIDE the plane just after set departure time. Without looking up, Babe could feel Bill glancing at his watch, hardly attempting to conceal his annoyance. He *hated* leaving late.

'Throws the whole schedule off,' he'd simmer.

Babe tensed, knowing that Bill Paley waited for no one. Not even a former President. And where *was* their illustrious guest? Not with David and Jennifer, she noted, glancing out the window.

As David removed luggage from the trunk, he was joined by an odd little man—the chauffeur, perhaps?—struggling to lift a suitcase twice the size of his body. His efforts were hindered by the most extraordinarily long scarf, flapping in the icy wind, tangling them in its wooly, stripy length. What a strange driver, thought Babe as she rose from her seat, preparing to meet-and-greet.

They boarded the plane, all kisses and smiles, the jovial Selznicks and the odd little man trailing behind them like an eager terrier.

He beamed at Babe, and it was as if the sun exploded. When he opened his mouth, it was the voice of a twelve-year-old girl that squealed with delight.

'Well, aren't you just the most stunning creature who ever was born? I'm *beside* myself.' He looked to Bill, whose brows had set in a permanent furrow at the bizarre, unexplained presence. The Terrier thrust his human paw forward, shaking Bill's hand with an unexpected grip. Strong. Confident. Like a macho lead in a Bogart film. At complete odds with the rest of his persona. 'Mr. Paley—may I call you Bill? Bill, you are just the luckiest man in the whole wide world! She really *is* exquisite. A Goddess—with a capital G! I must say, I've never met such a gorgeous couple in all my life!' To the Selznicks—'Not that you're chopped liver, angels!' Jennifer and David laughed. Bill stared, mouth agape.

The Terrier nudged past him and took Babe's arm, confidentially. As if they were longtime friends, sharing a vital confidence.

'Now, Mrs. P—I'll call you Babyling. Jenny says you're just the hostess-with-the-mostess. What do you say we get ourselves a little splash of something and have the nicest of chats . . . ?'

Babe couldn't help the smile that overcame her. He bombarded you with his warmth, this little man, this pup. It was disarming. It was magnetic. He was unlike anyone she knew.

Within no time they were huddled together in a corner of the plane, giggling, sipping champagne; oblivious to the others.

Bill ordered a round of drinks for David and Jennifer, and another Scotch for himself. He checked his watch again. Finally, to David, tersely, 'How long should we wait?'

'Hmmm?'

'Will he be here soon?'

'Will *who* be here soon?'

'*Harry Truman*, for Christsakes!'

David grinned at Jennifer, who broke into peals of laughter.

'Bill . . . *that's* Truman!'

Bewildered, Bill craned his head to study the Terrier, gossiping with his wife.

'I thought you said that Harry Truman—?!'

'We said *Truman*. As in *Capote*. We thought you knew!'

Bill frowned. 'Who the hell is Truman Capote . . . ?'

BY THIS POINT, ACROSS THE PLANE, BABE AND TRUMAN were busy falling madly, platonically in love.

At that very moment he was saying to her, 'We must go on a trip together, darling—just the two of us. I know! Let's run off to Tangier! There's the most *fabulous* little hotel I know . . .'

By the time they touched down in Jamaica, Truman and Babe had covered thirty years of history in four hours time. Family trees (hers illustrious, his illiterate). Educations, or lack thereof (she hardly had one, apart from etiquette; he flunked high school, apart from English). Preferences in art and music and books (Renoir, Bach, Proust). High above the Atlantic they developed a kind of shorthand, bordering on telepathy. It was as if they had known one another all their lives. This was more than Truman's stock charm routine. This was a merging of souls.

'You know, Babyling,' he had told her on the plane, leaning in, 'I'm going to tell you something I've *never* told anyone. Not another living soul. I know that we just met, but I feel as though I can trust you . . . Am I right? Can I trust you, darling?'

'Of *course*.'

He leaned in closer and whispered in her ear—

'My Mama died this last year.'

'How awful for you. I'm *so* sorry . . .'

Then he lowered his voice, almost a whisper. 'Yes . . . But she didn't die of cancer, or in an accident like I tell people when they ask. My Mama killed herself with a bottle of Seconal, chased with a bottle of Scotch.'

'Oh, Truman!' Babe's expression darkened. 'How *unbearable*.'

'And do you know the worst of it, Babyling?'

'What?'

He paused, cautious. 'Can I really, *really* trust you?'

'*Yes*,' she said, never meaning anything more. 'Yes, of *course*, you can trust me.'

'I loved her so much, you see, but I know she didn't love me. That's why she kept leaving me. She told me she had an abortion once because she said she couldn't bear to have another child like me. She thought I was grotesque.' The tears began to well in his eyes. 'I thought if I could be enough, she would love me. If I could only write enough—succeed enough. I thought if I could achieve enough, she'd have to change her mind. But in the end, I *wasn't* enough. She choked down that bottle of pills and it was like driving down that long dirt road for good. Just like she'd done a hundred times when I was just a boy in Monroeville. She left me time and again . . . With my spinster cousins. Or locked away in motel rooms. No matter how I adored her, she could never love me the way I wanted to be loved.'

He wiped the tears away quickly with the back of his hand, beaming at her grave expression, brows furrowed with compassion.

'My gawd, but you're beautiful. I think you're the most beautiful creature I've ever seen. And I can tell you're beautiful on the *inside* too—and that's what really counts.'

Babe had listened to his confession, wanting to scoop him in her arms and love him in a way his Mama had failed to. She watched him drain his drink (they'd moved on to dry martinis) and chew his olive, lost in an ocean of thoughts.

She felt a sudden impulse to share a truth with him in return.

'Can *I* trust *you*?' she asked out of nowhere, surprised to hear the words leave her mouth.

Babe *never* let her guard down. Not with private concerns. Mother Gogsie had trained her girls to be stoic. One didn't complain, one got on. One couldn't reveal one's pain to male conquests, for that would spoil the 'mystery.' One didn't show one's cards to female friends, for no matter how close (sisters included), they were one's competition. But Gogs certainly hadn't anticipated this lovely elfin thing—whatever he was. She'd given no warning for such a person, who fell between the cracks of categorization. Neither male conquest nor female friend, this little soul seemed a safe haven. For the first time in her life, Babe felt that she could share—if only a tiny piece of the puzzle. The elf-boy leaned in close, almost bursting with empathy.

'Yes, Babyling—you can trust me with anything. I'll never breathe a syllable, I *swear*.' (Something he would tell each of us in turn, but this was perhaps his most convincing of performances, for we genuinely feel that he meant it.) 'Cross my heart and hope to die.' That childhood gesture of old, which he'd so often shared with Nelle.

She glanced across the plane to Bill, yammering on at David, about some topic or another, as Jennifer pretended to flip through

Women's Wear, stealing jealous glances. Babe leaned in close to Truman's ear, whispering her own confession.

'I don't think my husband loves me.'

'That *can't* be true!' he took care to whisper back. 'Just *look* at you—you're perfection! How could anyone fail to appreciate such loveliness?'

Babe, more confident now, for having voiced it the first time—

'I know Bill doesn't love me.'

'That *must* be wrong . . .'

'I'm *useful* to him. I suit his image. He can appreciate me from afar—a thing on the mantel. But he doesn't love me. Like you said . . . not how I *want* to be loved.'

The imp took this in, and she felt certain he understood.

'Oh, Babyling. I know *exactly* how that feels. My poor darling.'

It was then that he reached out his tiny hand and touched her for the first time. He allowed himself to ever so gently sweep his fingers past the outline of her chiseled jaw.

As his flesh brushed hers, Babe had a flash of memory of standing in an empty ballroom years before, in the darkness. She'd gone back to fetch a stole or a clutch or a missing earring, after the guests had departed. She had heard a ghostly tinkling in the dimly lit chandelier above. She looked up to see a moth, caught in the crystal cage of the Baccarat droplets. Its gray tissue-wings battering the glass. Babe held her breath, looking upwards into the glare, hearing the soft rattle—the futility of its effort. She hated to see anything trapped, especially something so fragile. Her heart leapt when the moth dove beneath the lower tier of crystals and flew across the ballroom, liberated. Then, selecting its next random landing spot, the moth flew toward her, grazing her cheek, then neck.

She stood very still as it landed on her shoulder. A moment passed and it fluttered even lower, settling just inside the décolletage of her evening gown.

Babe held her breath, not daring to move as the moth beat its delicate wings against her heart—or breast—she couldn't remember which.

Something at once erotic and chaste.

Something she'd not felt since . . .

Until Truman's trembling fingers traced the line of her jaw.

She looked into his eyes and felt certain that he felt it too—a sensation that had no name beyond communion. They recognized something in each other, the lonely little boy from Alabama and the disappointed tycoon's wife. It was as if each had recovered a missing bit of themselves.

AS THEY DISEMBARKED in the sticky island heat, walking down the tarmac in the hibiscus-scented breeze, Truman slipped his arm through Babe's and whispered in her ear—

'Now you're my friend. A friend is someone you don't have to finish your sentences with.'

FIVE

1933/1966

VARIATION NO. 4

MR. TRUMAN STRECKFUS PERSONS

REQUESTS THE PLEASURE OF YOUR COMPANY

AT A HALLOWE'EN GOODBYE PARTY,

FRIDAY OCTOBER 28, 1933

7 O'CLOCK (IN THE EVENING!)

THE FAULK BACKYARD

COSTUMES A MUST—ELSE YOU'LL BE TURNED AWAY!!!

THE BOY IS *BESIDE* HIMSELF, perched at the farmhouse table in the drafty kitchen, typing up his first invitation on the Remington with keys that stick, having carefully threaded a new ribbon for the occasion.

'Just *beside* myself,' he rhapsodizes to Nelle, Sook, and just about anyone who'll listen. 'Absolutely pleased as punch!'

He's gonna give little ole Monroeville a night they won't soon forget. Long after he's moved to the city, his legend will loom, bigger than a tit through a telescope.

Yessir, after what *he* has in mind, they'll remember him when he's gone. He's made a special trip to the five and dime and bought a brand-new three-cent composition book: black confettied with white flecks, its pattern reminding him of granite slabs in the stoneyard.

In it he has, for the better part of two weeks, carefully recorded the name of every child in town. He's weighed with great consideration his feelings for each, and either placed a star by their name or drawn a line through it.

He's both judge and jury. He can choose benevolence—hadn't he crossed Summer Clewett off last week when she'd refused to let him skip rope, yet reinstated her when she shared the oyster po' boy from her lunch pail the very next day? In equal measure he could retaliate, having struck Chipper Daniels clean off when he'd mocked the boy's speaking voice in class.

The boy carries his composition book everywhere. To the playground. To the swimming hole, where he sits a distance from the ruckus, way up the mossy bank, shielding his precious pages from wayward splashes. It's his constant companion, the black-and-white book.

The kids watch with curiosity as he scribbles his secrets on the ruled sheets inside. He's not like the rest of them, in his sailor swimming trunks and smart linen jacket, sent in a box from his Mama. But they've learned that he's something of a magician—'a pocket Merlin,' Nelle calls him—never failing to come up with something to pass the time on days that seem slower than watching cream rise on last year's buttermilk. Whether it's building a sideshow from scratch in his cousin Jenny's shed, convincingly playing General Tom Thumb, World's Smallest Man, or sticking horsehair on Nelle's chin with spirit gum, transforming her into The Bearded Lady, or even convincing a couple of colored farmhands, Lucian Cole and John White, to play Siamese twins, their separate forms hidden behind a suit-draped hat rack—the boy can call in favors, he being friendly with *everyone* in town, black, white, or red all over.

The kids know he can be a spitfire too, and have learned to keep their distance when he's on the warpath. The boy enjoys the panic that flashes across their dull little faces when they see him cross a line through a name on his list, keeping the page in question close to his chest.

Kids worry that *they've* been the one he's crossed off, and bring him Snickers bars and chewing gum and fireflies caught in jars as offerings.

'Why thank you, sugar,' he gushes, scrawling notes in his ledger. 'Maybe I just *might* have to invite you to my shindig after all . . .'

Grown-ups say he's out of control. Gotten too big for his britches, they insist, ever since his crazy Mama's summoned him up to New York City.

'She's gone and married herself a *Yankee*, lordee mercy!'

'And of the *Latino* persuasion . . .'

Such is the chat that dominates Mrs. Lee's under-read book club. The Monroeville doyennes in their Sunday best loll on the porch, fanning themselves with their folded *Forum* magazines, pages dog-eared to Mr. Faulkner's 'A Rose for Emily.' From the bits they've skimmed, they like his heroine in her big drafty house, whose fiancé '*disappears*' one day.' She reminds them of at least a dozen shrews in town they know. That bunch of spinsters next door, especially.

'I'll bet a hundred dollars and my firstborn that ole Cousin Jenny's got a corpse rotting up in that dump too,' Mrs. Lee clucks wickedly, and they all cackle like a coop of satisfied hens.

The boy no longer cares what they say. He's already sprouted wings and flown high above their tawdry company.

'You know, I'm the first out of Monroeville to cross the Mason–Dixon Line,' he boasts to the kids down by the river dock. The first except his Mama, that is, who has returned for him as promised, with a brand-new life and a brand-new name. She's Cuban now—having traded the hillbilly 'Faulk' and Southern 'Persons' for the more exotic 'Capote.' The boy is about to become Cuban too, he brags. He promises he'll bring back crates of fancy cigars when he next comes to visit, that being the only thing Cuban that he's sure of.

Folks don't believe him. This sounds like another of the boy's tall tales, but then they say the poor little bastard seems so overjoyed, they can't help but be happy for him. He knows this because Nelle, moving in and out of shadows, perhaps her greatest talent, has heard them.

He's waited for this moment. Waited since he first watched his Mama drive away in a Silver Bullet convertible, backing out of the driveway of the Faulk cousins' house—barreling down the long dirt road, tires leaving clouds of red smoke billowing in their wake. The boy had run down the road after her, his screams drowned by the roar of the engine. He'd begged her to take him with her, promising he'd be *so* good, she'd hardly even notice him. He had sprinted like a little ole greyhound after that car, until his legs buckled beneath him and he crumpled to the ground, unable to run anymore. An abandoned racer pup, muscles smarting from the effort. (For added impact he makes sure that we all know that racing dogs who run too slow are either shot in the head or left in fields to starve, their purpose all used up.)

He's told us he'd cried himself to sleep the first time she'd driven away. The second time, he'd stolen a bottle of her perfume—Shalimar—and drunk the whole thing dry like a bottle of Mama-juice, part of him hoping to ingest her beauty and keep her inside him, part of him hoping to overdose on her rancid poison, relishing the thought of the tears she would shed when his little body was all laid out at Johnson's Funeral Parlor, pint-sized legs barely stretching halfway down, covered in hundreds of glorious calla— —

BUT THAT'S BEHIND HIM NOW. He has been *summoned*. All the way to New York City.

He'd been there before, mind you.

'I was *taken* there,' he frequently reminds us, 'on my own special merit.' He'd been taken there by the team of seersuckered researchers from the Mobile Works and Progress Administration, who had brought their box of IQ tests to the little ole country school.

He had scored so high, the men had furrowed their brows and made him take the test again. Yet again, the boy scored a perfect 215. Never had a child in the US scored as high on an IQ test, he's assured us. The men were so damn stunned they drove him all the way to New York City, where they only confirmed what the boy already knew—that he was a bona fide genius, so proclaimed by science.

And now he has been sent for, by *her*. He'll become Cuban like she has, perhaps change his name to *Juan* . . . Dye his white fringe black and begin his new life as a genius in the city where exotic boys with talent might speak their minds without causing a fuss.

But first, he wants to make sure Monroeville never forgets him. That's what's given him his idea . . . to throw a party like the hick little town has never seen before and likely'll never see again. A party to bask in his genius and good fortune. Sometimes he just wants to hug himself in a joyous chokehold, he *so* can't believe his luck. This is better than a *pack* of beagle dogs and a *herd* of Shetland ponies (which he now feels confident he's won for his stories in spades).

In a bold gesture, he's insisted on a nighttime gathering, even though most children under the age of ten have never been out much past sundown. He's decided on the weekend of Halloween to add a splash of drama. He adores a masquerade. Why, you could be practically anybody hiding behind all that——

MR. TRUMAN CAPOTE

REQUESTS THE PLEASURE OF

YOUR COMPANY

AT A BLACK AND WHITE DANCE

ON MONDAY, THE TWENTY-EIGHTH OF NOVEMBER,

NINETEEN HUNDRED AND SIXTY-SIX

TEN O'CLOCK

GRAND BALLROOM, THE PLAZA

R.S.V.P. MISS ELIZABETH DAVIS
485 PARK AVENUE

DRESS:

GENTLEMEN: BLACK TIE, MASK

LADIES: BLACK OR WHITE DRESS, MASK

TRUMAN IS BESIDE HIMSELF when he collects the box of embossed invitations from Tiffany's. Just *beside* himself, staring at the text, fresh from the printers, his enthusiasm dampened.

'Sugar,' he informs the manager of the stationery department in a clipped tone, not nearly so friendly as he'd been moments before, 'an 'E' seems to have gone missing from Miss Davies' name, and someone at four-*eight*-five will be *très* surprised to receive acceptance cards from five *hundred* of my close personal friends, while my publisher Mr. Cerf at four-*six*-five listens to the crickets chirping.'

The Tiffany salesman dons glasses, examining the card. At first glance it's exactly what his client ordered. An elegant, white embossed card, classic Emily Post, with Truman's playful touch of a sunrise border, gold and orange pinstripes framing the perimeter. Yet turning to the RSVP line, the secretary's name is indeed misspelled and the street address off by a number.

'I mean *honestly*, for all the free press I've given you, *you* should be giving *me* breakfast—and a set of Tiffany silver to boot!' Before Mr. Manager can grovel in earnest, Truman has snatched the stationers' box and left in a huff, taking comfort that he'll later milk the blunder for a discount. Truth be told, he's already planned to alter the invites by hand.

He's been struck with the sudden inspiration for his *pièce de résistance* . . . a Guest of Honor. Of course those of us who *know* him know this is merely a prop. Let's be honest: Truman's throwing a party for Truman.

Nevertheless, he's written our names down and weighed us each as candidates. Babe is the obvious choice; if this is Tru's version of a wedding, she's the closest thing he has to a bride. He knows, however, that *that* would be expected, and he's aiming for anything but. He considers Slim, alas away in London with Husband Number Three. Gloria, who we all know would lord it over Babe. Lee would shift the focus to the Kennedys, thoroughly unacceptable. C.Z., too twinset tweedy for what he has in mind. Marella, too *European* for a venue so steeped in American lore.

Truman has naturally selected the Plaza as the setting for his drama. It has, since his early days as a copyboy at the *New Yorker*, served as his haven, as he tucked into the Oak Bar on his lunch breaks, inhaling the signature cognac chicken hash—an upscale version of Sook's down-home cooking. He'd peered into the hushed opulence of the Grand Ballroom after those stolen lunches, before rushing back to the office, where his tardiness was being clocked with some regularity by exasperated superiors. He'd seen dancers in those shadows, visions swaying to the big bands in his mind, when he was little more than a loud-mouthed nobody. He'd always known that *this* was his Shangri-La. 'It's the last great ballroom left in Manhattan,' he's insisted ever since. With its lingering glamour and old-school mystique, the Plaza remains a glimmering symbol of Truman's most cherished, Gatsbyesque ambitions.

In the end, we all fail to qualify for the role of honoree. Of course we know the *real* reasons none of us is chosen. First, we are a 'We.' Truman knows women, and is savvy enough to foresee that plucking one from his chorus would be bound to offend the rest. More important—none of us *needs* a fairy tale. Our over-feted grace would deny Tru the credit that he craves, would strip him of the art of creation. He's planning his party with a focus normally reserved for his fiction. His real-life heroine will be no less vital to his legacy than his fictional Holly Golightly. Truman realizes, as any skilled dramatist would, that what he needs is the fantasy of transformation. An Ugly Duckling, ripe for metamorphosis.

And Truman has *just* the ugly duck in mind . . .

'Kay, sugar, it's Tru-baby,' he drawls, sitting at the desk in the vermillion study of his new United Nations Plaza apartment—a heady address by any account, bought with his hard-earned dough. His address book lies open to the G's, where he's drawn a star beside *GRAHAM, Kay*.

'Truman!' Kay brightens on the other end of the line.

With a blue fountain pen Truman carefully corrects the street number on the first in a stack of invitations, phone receiver shoved between his chin and shoulder.

'I've missed my precious Kay-Kay!'

'I've missed my Tru-babe.'

'Look, honey. We hafta have a chat. I've decided you're depressed, and I'm gonna cheer you up. I'm gonna throw you a little party to shake you out of it.'

In her *Washington Post* office, buried under a deadline, Kay seems more befuddled than pleased. 'But I'm not depressed.'

'Yes you are, sugar. You're depressed and need cheering up and I'm gonna be the one to do it. You see, I've got this vision . . . a *bal masqué*. A *sea* of black and white, with *you* as the belle of the ball.'

Kay, in her sensible suit, with her sensible haircut, snorts at the absurdity.

We know Kay, of course, some of us better than others.

Babe had introduced Tru to her a year ago and with Truman, as ever, the wooing process commenced. She's unusually dowdy for Tru's bag of chips, but she has kind eyes and razor smarts, things that he admires. As publisher of the *Washington Post*, Kay's an impressive addition to Truman's flock, even if her feathers aren't quite as smooth.

He'd brought her along as his 'own special date' for last August's *Agneta* cruise around the Greek and Turkish islands. The trip seemed cursed from the outset, Marella and Gianni having both come down with food poisoning—a batch of rotten oysters. They insisted, however, that Kay and Tru take the yacht as planned.

Truman had instantly taken to Kay, loving—as he does—a tragedy.

They were both, after all, shucking off death. He had just watched Dick Hickock and Perry Smith hanged in Kansas, the killers having requested that 'Friend Truman' be present at their executions. While we sensed Truman's grief, noticed that his lunchtime martini count had all but tripled as months rolled by, we all felt *wretched* for Kay . . . Philip Graham, her husband and publisher at the *Post*—*ghastly* man, manic depressive—checked himself into a D.C. nut-bin, then convinced the doctors to spring him for a weekend. Back in their Virginia farmhouse Phil had kissed Kay goodnight, left the room, and proceeded to blow his head off with a twenty-eight-gauge Winchester repeater. Kay had bottled her pain and assumed the mantle of publisher with dignified grace in the wake of the unmentionable.

Truman had restored for Kay the gift of pleasure on their yachting venture, where they sunbathed while cutting across the Aegean into Turkish waters. They sipped chilled retsina and ate fresh-caught fish, fried up and served with a mezze of salty cheese and sweet, ripe melon. All the while, Tru read to Kay from the galleys of *In Cold Blood*. In his final scene, Detective Dewey encounters the best friend of the murdered Clutter daughter in the cemetery, visiting their graves. She's home from college. Blossoming. She recalls how she and Nancy had hoped to go away to school together, had planned to be roommates at Kansas State. Parting ways, the lawman watches the girl walk away, thinking her all the things that Nancy might have become, had her lovely head been filled with thoughts of books and boys, rather than the lead from Perry's shotgun. Then Detective Dewey turns and wanders home for his dinner, imagining that he hears the voices of the silenced Clutters in the gentle breeze, rustling through the wheat.

Closing the book with the dramatist's flair, Tru looked to his audience, expectant.

'Truman, that's extraordinary. Absolutely extraordinary,' said Kay, wiping tears from her eyes.

Tru had hesitated, then leaned in close. 'Can I tell you a secret, Kay-Kay . . . ? Deep down, I think I know . . . I've finally written my masterpiece. And it scares the living shit out of me.'

'But why in the *world*—?'

'What's left?' he'd asked, forlorn. 'I'm scared to death I won't be able to do anything *nearly* as good again, and that this is the beginning of the end.'

Kay says she had dismissed this as preposterous, yet somewhere in the pit of his gut, Truman knew that he was right.

At night they smoked a hashish pipe furnished by islanders in turbans and collapsed woozy on the cushion-strewn deck, giggling in earnest for the first time since death had kissed them both. They lay cradling one another, staring into a star-littered sky.

AT THE TOP OF THE INVITATION CARD, Truman neatly writes: 'In honor of Mrs. Katharine Graham' in blue ink, shifting the phone receiver to his other shoulder as he slides it into an envelope.

'I'm sealing your invite as we speak—it's too late to say no.'

'Truman, I'm *not* depressed. I don't need—'

'Now Kay-Kay, I won't hear another word. You're having a ball and that's final.'

He hangs up, cutting the call unceremoniously short before his honoree has time to object. Satisfied, he turns focus and fountain pen to the next invitation, ready to insist four hundred and ninety-nine more times in his neat script that his dance has *nothing* to do with *In Cold Blood*, or feting his own Arrival. For those of us who *know* him, he isn't fooling anyone.

As we say, Truman's throwing a party for himself.

YESSIR, HE'S GONNA GIVE LITTLE OLE MANHATTAN a night it won't soon forget.

He's made a special trip to Woolworth's and bought a brand-new ten-cent composition book, the kind he uses for his work, black-and-white confetti-flecked, its pattern calling to mind the marble floor in the Paleys' foyer. He's written a single word—'DANCE'—on the cover, and has, for the better part of three months, carefully recorded the name of everyone he knows. Writers. Film stars. Politicians. Intellectuals. He's weighed with consideration his feelings for each, and either starred their name or drawn a line through it. He's relished assembling the perfect cast, like playing God at an Elysian cocktail party.

He's been benevolent—hadn't he listened sympathetically to an acquaintance who called to say his wife refused to leave her bed, so devastated was she not to have been included? There was something in the husband's sad dignity that moved Truman. Something about the wife's desperation that reminded him of Lillie-Mae-Nina-Capote. He had bandaged their wounded pride, spinning the omission into a mistake. 'Why honey, did your invite not arrive? Mercy me. It must have gotten lost in the mail. I'll have my secretary send another straight away. I would simply *looooove* to have you at my party.'

In equal measure he's used his list to settle old scores, having added Ann 'Bang-Bang' Woodward's name for the sole pleasure of striking her off for calling him 'a horrid little faggot' at El Morocco years ago. Just a graze now . . . he's saving his big guns for a later date.

He's carried his notebook everywhere. To the Colony. La Côte Basque. To 21, where he eschews his usual prime table for a booth in the corner, holding hushed meetings, shielding his precious pages from curious eyes. He brings it like a prized pet to our various swimming pools through those humid summer months.

'Lee, should we have Jackie, or is she playing 'Widow' all November . . . ?' We all know he can be a little bastard and have learned to keep our distance when he's on a jag. We can see him toying with us, a tomcat with a garbage pail of mice. Enjoying the panic that flickers across our carefully made-up faces when he cuts another name from his list. Being the inner, *inner* circle, we doubt we have to worry that we'll actually be axed, but you never *really* know with Truman.

The acquaintances, outsiders to our set, are practically tripping over themselves to get in his good graces. They send him Mont Blanc pens and theater tickets and five-figure checks as offerings. 'Why thank you, sugar,' he says with a smile. 'But my party's just for *cloooose* personal friends . . . and I don't waste time on folks I don't admire.'

Now a man of means, the boy can no longer be bribed.

THE PAPERS SAY IT'S OUT OF CONTROL. New York's been struck with Black-and-White fever, ever since Truman mailed his invites. 'In one day I made five hundred friends and five *thousand* enemies!' he relishes telling the press. Truman's roster of 'personal friends' reads like a new aristocracy—Sinatra, Mailer, Warhol, Bacall. CAPOTE'S COURT—AN INTERNATIONAL LIST FOR THE GUILLOTINE! Such is the fodder that dominates the headlines, comprised of six daily papers, plus *Vogue*, *Bazaar*, and *Esquire*. Even the *New Yorker*, who once fired the effete copyboy with the big ideas, now wants in on the act.

He's waited for this moment, waited since he first arrived in the wheat-fed Kansas wasteland, patiently befriending detectives and killers alike, he having a rare gift for walking delicate tightropes of loyalties. He's invited his *very* close Kansas friends to his dance—the ones who are still alive, that is—immortalized after six long years as characters in his masterpiece. And now they have been summoned, all the way to New York City.

'I was taken to the Plaza for the very first time,' he'll remind them when they've checked into the big hotel and tucked into lunch in the Oak Bar, 'not by Nina, not by my Daddy—but by the men in suits with their IQ tests.' A lifetime ago, when kids lined up for Chinese boxes and apple-bobbing in the Faulks' Monroeville yard, orchestrated by a midget outcast, hiding behind a Fu Manchu mustache.

The boy-turned-man has waited *ages* to celebrate his wild success. To show every moron teacher, every dimwit bully, everyone who ever doubted him just how wrong they were.

He's metamorphosed into Truman Capote, Great American Writer. And he got there on his own special merit. It only confirms what we already knew, the thing he's said over and over to anyone who'll listen: that he's a bona fide genius, as long proclaimed by science.

L OOKING BACK, MARELLA HAD SEEN THE STORM BREWING.
That's why she'd stopped speaking to him months before.
European Swan Numero Uno—as Truman long ago christened
her—is fortunate that Manhattan is not her natural habitat. She
visits, of course, but what better excuse than being isolated on a
yacht in the middle of an ocean to escape the lunch requests Truman continues to bombard us with. Invitations that, post-*Esquire*,
largely go unanswered.

It happened on board the *Agneta* in the last days of August, as
they sunbathed on the polished deck, sipping iced prosecco and
nibbling plates of antipasti.

'Uno, you simply must read my latest chapter.' He had
brought a stack of pages from his cabin. She'd been excited,
Marella. Long before she'd met Truman she had read his work
and thought him a genius. She was his fan before she was his
friend, having devoured translations of *Breakfast* . . . and
Other Voices . . . before he'd infiltrated her sphere. As he'd
done with each of us, he'd read her excerpts of *In Cold Blood*
before its release, and she'd listened, moved by the beauty of
his prose.

'*Bellissimo*, Truman. *Sei* Michelangelo,' she'd said, believing
him a modern master of his craft. Reading a sliver of his long-
awaited *Answered Prayers* would be a thrill for any of us, but
Marella took the charge as seriously as a Medici glimpsing the
Pietà in progress. She started the chapter, which was set neither
in the gothic South of his childhood, nor the barren plains of Kansas, but amid the cramped tables at La Côte Basque. After the

first ten pages, Marella began to question her abilities as a reader. English was not her first language. Perhaps she'd misunderstood . . . ? Someone called 'Lady Ina' seemed to be spitting insults at everyone in sight, at people that we knew. Marella had to wonder, was she missing something . . . ? It sounded like one of Truman's catty gossip sessions. Worse, in fact. (We've all noticed that Truman is generally on slightly better behavior around Marella. Call it the Princess Factor.)

Reclining on her stomach on a lounger, the graceful slope of her exposed back absorbing the midday heat, Marella had struggled through the text like a remedial schoolgirl, straining to grasp the nuances of a foreign tongue. Even so . . . surely this wasn't literature?

She turned to the author, who sat gnawing at a ribbon of Prosciutto, flipping through a paperback potboiler.

'Truman, *stai scherzando?*'

'What's that, Uno?'

She joined him at the table. 'Is this a jest? Where is your novel?'

His thin grin spread as he popped an olive into his mouth. 'You're looking at it.'

Marella frowned. 'Well, perhaps my English isn't good enough . . .'

'Oh yes, of course, sugar . . . It's *molto* colloquial. Here.' He wiped his greasy fingers on the tablecloth, extending an eager palm. 'Let me read it to you.'

He snatched the pages from Marella's lap. Then impulsively tossed them aside.

'Actually, I don't need that. It's all up here in my brain-box,' this, tapping his head. And with that he cleared his throat, and in the high, melodic voice the princess had come to love, almost as much as his old cousin Sook in Monroeville had, Truman began:

'*Bill*— oops! I mean *Dill* . . .' he gave Marella a conspicuous wink, '. . . couldn't come. Despite the gusto in the sack for which he was renowned (for what he lacked in technique he made up for in ambition . . .) he couldn't get a cock-hold. It felt as if he was drowning in a slick, soupy void. There was nothing about the Governor's wife that could be vaguely described as "tight", except perhaps the purse of her lips as she endured his efforts with a mix of disdain and ennui. If only he could rouse that dull, cadaverous form . . . He withdrew his flaccid snake from its hole, moving down the bed towards her snatch. That roused her, alright, though not in the manner he'd hoped. 'STOP!!' she commanded, tugging his hair like a pair of flimsy reins.

'You sure you don't want a nice licking?' Dill offered, solicitous, like a Good Humor ice cream man, throwing in a cone. 'CHRIST, no!' she snapped. He hoisted himself back up and said, 'Well then perhaps you'd care to suck me off and we'll just call it quits . . . ?"

By the time the stewards arrived with lunch, Truman had moved on to the moment in his narrative when the Governor's Wife rose to dress, leaving as a parting favour, he gleefully reported, a blood spot the size of Sumatra amidst the smooth, blue ocean of sheets.

'Ohhhhhh how perfect is that . . .' Truman enthused as cloche lids were lifted to reveal steaming plates of Spaghetti Puttanesca. '*Whore's* Pasta!'

Marella had long lost her appetite.

'Isn't it a scream . . . ?' he laughed, digging into the pungent tomato sauce. 'You see Dill only *wants* that blue blood bean-flicker to prove that he can have her. Because they'd kept the Yids out of their fundraisers and their country clubs . . . Ironic, given that he's just about the only atheist Jew in Manhattan!'

She had watched him, Marella told us, repulsed, when he'd asked her between greedy mouthfuls, 'So Uno . . . What do you think of my ditty . . . ?'

'I think it's vile, Truman. *Pettegolezzo.*'

That had straightened his spine. The Great Author bristled at the unfamiliar sting of criticism. Marella said it was as if something snapped, and the lapdog bared his Rottweiler teeth—that

75

he'd turned in an instant from toy-pup to butchers' dog, bred to pull meat to the market.

'Well you wouldn't really know, would you? You can't even speak the fucking language.'

'I've read what you've written before, and this is beneath you.'

'What the hell do you know. You're just a paid-for princess. Principessa *Puttana*,' he laughed. 'I'm gonna do to America what Proust did to France. It's utterly brilliant— it's bold and it's brave. *You* wouldn't know brilliance if it hit you in the *faccia*.'

Marella felt dizzy. She looked to her plate to avoid his grimace.

Why had she never noticed his teeth before, how the gums receded, how the canines tapered to sharp little points? She placed her napkin over her untouched Puttanesca, covering the pool of tomato sauce, Kalamata eyeballs staring up at her. Truman's manuscript pages fluttered in the breeze beneath her butter knife.

'What don't you like about it?' he demanded. 'Be *specific*.'

She'd reached for a page, reading slowly in her thick Italian accent, 'Why would a nouveau riche, narcissistic, sizably-packaged Jew go for a cardigan-ed, corduroyed giantess who wears spiked golf-shoes and reeks of tuberose and tal—talcum powder?'

'Talllll— taaaall— *tallllcum* powder . . .' Truman mocked her accent.

Marella pressed on, ignoring him. 'Particularly given that his wife was Cleo Dillon, the most sublime specimen of female perfection the world has ever known?'

She lowered the page and looked at Truman pointedly. 'What do you think *Babe* will have to say . . . ?'

Truman met her gaze, then looked away, leaving the question hovering in the air.

'This is gossip. It's nasty, vicious talk. Truman . . . *please* don't do this.'

For a moment his eyes glazed, then began to water. A salty sea breeze made him blink, its breath chilling the single tear that escaped down his cheek.

'Babe's not Babe when I'm writing.' He'd rubbed his eyes roughly, reaching for the bottle of prosecco. 'She'll understand.'

Marella had leant across the table and grasped his arm, trying to make him *see*.

'Truman . . . I don't think that she will.'

He ingested this before freeing himself and depleting his glass. 'Yeah, well, what do you know. *Non capisci un cazzo*—you're thick as a fucking plank.'

Truman rose, collecting his manuscript, tucking it carefully under his beach towel.

He looked to Gianni, swimming in the waters around the anchored yacht, skin brown as a butternut. The bronzed skin of privilege.

'*Miele*, Gianni's so rich he buys a new boat each time his old one gets wet!' Truman, in better spirits, loved to tease.

Heir to the vast Fiat fortune, Gianni had lost no time, it seemed, test-driving hundreds of the flashy bastards, chauffeuring around half the female population of Europe before he was forced to settle down and marry. Scion of an Italian industrialist father and American heiress mother—the latter of whom Marella seemed a slightly faded carbon copy—Gianni had complied. But not without resistance.

He preferred more oomph in his inamoratas, the famed Pam Churchill having tooted his horn with Satchmo-gusto for the better part of a decade. Her enthusiasm legendary, she'd worked her way through the brass sections of the fraternities of worldly men, and while each appreciated her performance, nobody married Pam Churchill. Never one to be deterred, Pam had set her sights on Gianni; had converted to the Catholic faith, enrolled in a crash course at Berlitz and taught herself Italian. (None of us could accuse her of being anything short of a go-getter.)

'For fucksakes, she even learned to roll his *nonna*'s meatballs!' Truman had exclaimed.

That was until Gianni's *famiglia* threatened to fling themselves off some picturesque Piedmont bridge if he considered such a scheme. When he'd driven his new '53 Fiat Otto Vu smack into a lorry (after a red-hot fight with Pam, it must be said, having been caught by her in flagrante with another of his playthings), he was finally slowed by broken bones, confined to bed rest. His sisters had ensured that Pam was barred from visitation, while Marella was driven past her, waiting at the hospital gates. The domineering *sorelle* closed ranks, having determined the princess-next-door be given preeminence, as if arranging a marriage of Borgian proportions.

'You can see why, can't you? Marella even *looks* pricey. If she and Babe were in the window at Tiffany's,' Truman often analyzed, 'Babe may be more elegant, but Marella would be more *expensive*.'

Indeed, with her aquiline profile, neck that went on for days, and pedigree to match, Princess Marella Caracciolo di Castagneto proved a more appropriate matrimonial option than the fast women who'd warmed the seats of Gianni's even faster cars.

It must be noted that Truman never had cared for speed. The lethargy of his Southern childhood still lingered in his blood, flowing as slow through his veins as tar through a gully. He'd never be as quick as the playboy with his streamlined strokes, cutting through the ocean below, nor as slick . . . except when it came to words. That's where Tru's quickness triple-lapped others, his verbal velocity outpacing Gianni's breaststrokes and racecars and speedboats combined. As ever, Truman took comfort in his words, which never failed to restore his wounded pride.

Armor and weapon . . .

As he turned to retreat to his cabin, Truman allowed himself a parting jab. He leaned in close and whispered in Marella's ear—

'By the way . . . the Governor's Wife? *Gianni* fucked her too.'

And brushing her earlobe with his prosecco-chilled lips, Truman was gone.

WE OF COURSE NOTICED THAT SOMETHING had altered between them.

Marella, who once so cherished Truman, who had preferred his company to all others, he being her own special travel companion ('*Dar*-ling, Marella and I are the only ones ever to sail the length of the Amalfi Coast not once, not twice, but *thrice* . . . !') has gone as quiet as the Sphinx on the topic of her *piccolo Vero*.

Stranger still, she now seems genuinely frightened of him.

But what went wrong? we'll ask when we see her, fishing for details like determined *pescatori*. *Did something ghastly happen?*

'Did he get sloshed and act an ass?' asks Lee, polishing off her own lunchtime Scotch, in a private chat with Marella. (Lee's third round, we're quick to note, from our adjacent tables.)

Marella shakes her head, and holds her terror close.

The most that she will say is, 'He told me something harmful— about someone I love—specifically to hurt me. Something . . . unforgivable.'

But what? What is it that he said?!

Surely Gianni's flagrant *dolce vita* conquests would have ceased to shock by this point, even were Marella in denial.

What could possibly be *that* bad . . . ?

'I dare not say,' Marella holds firm, for fear that Truman's sordid words might contain an ounce of truth, or at least that in repeating them, she might will them into being.

AT LEAST SHE'D SET THE SCENE.

It was in an antiques shop in Genoa, she tells those of us who prod. It was an autumn day, off-season, a day dense with split-pea fog. The first bone-rattling day of the season. It had just started to rain.

Marella and Truman had ducked into the shop, coats held high above their heads to block the icy droplets. It was one of the finest *antiquaires* in Europe, owned by a little old man with a limp. A cavernous place—thick with dust, packed with rarest booty.

79

They'd wandered through the space, glorious pieces polished and stacked high on every side, the lure of past lives lingering in their fibers.

Like a boy in a toyshop, Truman squealed when he spotted an elaborate red-lacquer sideboard, peeking through a pair of rococo wing chairs.

'Uno—just look at that candy-apple treat! Wouldn't she look divine in my parlor, under that stuffy ole Fosburgh? Lord knows it could use a splash of color!'

Marella confirmed the sideboard would indeed look sublime beneath Jimmy's portrait of Tru, Babe's brother-in-law having painted him in that ephemeral state between Boy Wonder and *Enfant Terrible*, looking uncharacteristically sober.

Truman had summoned the proprietor, 'who shuffled with the vigor of a three-toed sloth,' according to his prospective buyer, who with rapture began the haggling process.

Those of us who'd heard this had rolled our eyes and laughed, each with our own canon of Truman bargain-hunting tales. The Victoriana sofa, its stuffing poking through in cotton tufts, which he and Babe had bought for a song—and which she'd lovingly helped him re-cover in a delicious sherbet brocade. The chinoiserie he'd found with Lee, when they stalked jumble sales in rural France, to launch her fledgling decor biz. Slim's taxidermy cobras, wrapped and shipped from Spain, all the way to Truman's doorstep.

He had the ruthlessness of an ancient pawnbroker, with the gift of bluff and slick-jaw when it came to dropping a price.

In the combination tongue of pidgin and pantomime, Tru had asked the old man of the sideboard: 'How much?'

The sloth took his own sweet time pulling out a pair of bottle-thick specs, so clouded they themselves seemed a Chippendale relic. In an unintelligible dialect, the old man named a price that, whatever it had been, was unacceptable to Tru, on principle alone.

'*Grazie*, Signore Sloth! But that sounds *molto* high!'

The old man had grunted, shrugged, and stood his greedy ground.

'Uno, don't you think our friend is being *raw*-ther stingy?' Truman dropped to his hands and knees, inspecting the cabinet for flaws. 'The travesty is, he doesn't appreciate the beauty of this gem, as you or I might do. He's just trying to make a quick *dollaro*.'

'*Sì, sì . . . dollaros . . .*' The old man squinted through his glasses.

'*Sì, sì . . .*' Truman mocked his accent, as he had done with Marella's. 'You know, *miele . . .*' Tru continued, still looking at the sideboard, tossing out figures to the seller, his offerings plummeting in value, to the wrinkled prune's dismay, '. . . he's just like a European male—the most vile of all the species.'

Marella watched as Truman almost leaped with glee upon discovering the tiniest flaw in the centuries-old varnish—the thing that connoisseurs would find the most romantic, the proof of life and history. He motioned to the proprietor, pointing at the blemish.

'What about this *here*?' he demanded, American hands on hips.

Then, returning to Marella, a deliberate aside—'I mean, the European male—as a tribe, if you will—the *pay-dirt* species in particular—let's be honest: They are cunts. Cunts, the whole damn lot!'

Signore Sloth creaked to a bend, examining the surface through his glazier-fitted lenses, as Truman continued in a language Marella felt relieved the old man didn't understand.

'They either fail to realize the worth in what they have, or they overvalue something tawdry.' Tru tapped his nail impatiently on the sideboard's glossy top—

'*Più economico*,' he demanded. Then bluntly, in English—'Cheaper.'

The signore relented, Marella thought—if only to be rid of the brash little tightwad. As they followed him back to the front of the shop to pay, Truman had mused, removing a wad of bills from his pocket—'The only species worse is the European *feeee*-male, who allows herself to be bought and sold, like flesh-whipped ass in a livestock show.'

Was that it? Was that what he said, to make you disown him? we press, when we've coaxed this from Marella.

Again she shakes her head—'It was worse. Something vicious, that's all I can say. Something . . . *letale.* I saw a killer in those eyes . . . That like his *amico* Perry Smith, Truman could slice any of our throats and not lose a moment's sleep.'

Back on board the Agneta, she'd ignored him for three days; had spent the remainder of the journey hiding in her cabin. Finally, in the moments before they reached their final port, as with relief she watched the safety of land draw closer by the minute, she sat down beside him on the prow.

'Why did you tell me . . . ?' She'd asked him, unable to resist. He stared at her, blankly. 'Why did you say what you did . . . ?'

'I thought that you should know,' he said, simply. 'Everyone knew, *except* for you . . .' then, with a vestige of the old tenderness, he reached out to stroke her alabaster cheek—

'I love you, and I thought that you needed to know.'

Marella, having said this much, goes silent yet again, the look of a hunted fawn hanging around her eyes. Try as we might, we cannot persuade her to unburden her fears, to trust us with whatever threat or insult Truman had leveled against her amid the antiquaire's treasures.

All we know for certain is that Marella now shudders at the mention of his name.

MARELLA'S NOT THE ONLY ONE ALLOWED a glimpse into the mire in which Truman is about to sink.

Lee is granted access next.

Lee, his protégé, his paramour.

Lee, who hides behind a veneer of indifference—beneath Cassini suits and tawny locks, and a wicked nature to rival Tru's. Lee, who, kissed by the aura of halcyon Camelot, was propelled to fame by relation rather than merit.

Lee, who harbors a rage in her darkest soul—perhaps only matched by Truman's—incited by her envy for a sister who stole her place in history, leaving little Lee with nothing but the shallow sandboxes of society in which to play.

Lee confides in very few—and *certainly* not in us. Nearly a decade younger than Truman and lacking our assurance, Lee keeps to herself. Her sister was her confidante, until she stole too much for Lee to bear. That's why Truman is so prized.

He has his own ax to grind, mind you, having first been close with Jackie—when Jack was, according to Tru, 'Nothin' but a knife-sharp senator, with his Daddy's bootlegger eye on the White House prize.'

He'd been proud of his bond with Jackie; hooking the First Lady was quite the coup indeed, and Truman loved to let folks know just how close they were. When Jackie's infant son Patrick died, it's said Tru wrote her a missive so thoughtful, she'd saved it ever since.

'Jackie trusts me,' he'd run his mouth to the press. 'She tells me everything. Absolutely everything.' We wondered at the time if Jackie ever broached the topic of Truman's 'dear friend' Marilyn, who—after cementing herself in public minds as the Other Woman with a breathy, doped-up 'Happy Birthday, Mister Prezzzident'— must have cried on Truman's shoulder too. ('Why, Norma Jean, did those Kennedy boys fail to love you?' we can almost hear him ooze.)

'Jackie knew what Jack was up to—as I say, she is no dummy. But Jackie's not the kind of girl you simply knock one off in. Jackie is a thoroughbred, meant for show and breeding.'

It was then that Truman learned—or failed to learn—the lesson that might have saved him.

Cardinal rule *numerus unus*— never, *ever* talk out of school.

The transgression in this case was fairly tame—really nothing more than admitting their shared bond. But the moment he began to run his mouth in public, Jackie's calls to Truman ceased; his calls to Pennsylvania Avenue went tellingly unanswered. Perhaps sensing danger long before the pack, Jackie pulled away, withdrawing her courtly favor with the same bemused indifference with which she had bestowed it.

When in several years' time Tru was introduced to Lee, we wondered if his fervor was colored by her sister's slight.

Their first lunch date, a four-hour tryst at La Grenouille, in short order turned into a Jackie-bashing fest of epic proportions. Lee let rip the years of stifled fury—it all came tumbling out.

It was *she* who was the brilliant one, she assured him.

Lee who had the flair for style, the elegance, the taste. *Lee's* was the love of books, the artist's soul. It was *Lee* who had the knack for decorating a room; *Lee* had been the visualist, with her paints and pens, when they were girls, not Jackie and her horses! It made her blood boil watching Jackie lead TV crews through the White House, bragging in her dishrag voice about her renovations, as if French rococo revival was something she'd invented!

It was *Lee* the writer; *Lee* the actress; *Lee* the femme fatale, who men adored in more than just a distant way. It was *Lee* who was the genius, who should have had the spotlight—not be doomed to a life in the chill of Jackie's shadow, forever linked to a lesser being.

Yet oddly, in her vitriol, Truman found a kindred soul.

HE STEPS OFF THE AEROMÉXICO PLANE in the Yucatán with renewed conviction.

Now that he has lost—and found—his precious pages, he's sure that it's happened for a reason. He's been high on relief ever since, doped to the gills with gratitude to the unseen forces that be. This transcendental state proves a greater opiate than the uppers, downers, or in-betweeners he totes in his black doctor's bag.

His driver tells him, en route to the remote resort, that 'Yucatán' is taken from a Mayan name for language. A retreat in the land of language is something he sees as an omen.

Not only that—the landscape of the region speaks to Truman's soul. Its shallow, rocky earth giving rise to stunted trees, as diminutive and resilient as he sees himself as being. He likes its rust and ocher hues, its slow tequila sunsets. It's like Palm Springs, without the pain. Without days of empty pages, of loneliness . . . of terror. 'Hope's End,' his Jack had called the Californian desert, and it was there that Truman's hope had finally hit rock bottom.

Yet here, lying on a private beach in the Mayan Riviera, with lovely Lee beside him in matching insect shades, listening to the surf lapping gently in-and-out, with its steady, liquid breath—he is happy. Giddy, even. Because he's sure (or so he thinks . . .) that the thing that he's been doubting will trouble him no longer.

To publish or not to publish, that has been the question. Now at least he knows he has no choice. He's been relieved of the burden; fate has chosen for him.

As he and Lee sun themselves before clear-cut turquoise waters, sipping frothy piña coladas from coconut shells, Truman calls to his companion: 'Princess-Dear' (his name for Lee), 'would you like to hear a tidbit of my chapters . . . ?'

Not bothering to stir, Lee lazily purrs, 'Mmmmmmmm.'

'I'll take that as a yes.' He clears his throat, then begins to orate:

'La Côte Basque, that unrivaled temple of French cuisine, is a dining establishment in Midtown Manhattan, situated on East Fifty-fifth, directly opposite the St. Regis Hotel. It opened its doors in 1940, helmed by the venerable Henri Soulé, the Leonardo of the luncheon, famous for launching Le Pavilion at 57th and Park, frequented for their famed Beluga Caviar and Louis Roederer rosé champagne trysts. M. Soulé's demise would occur in the gentlemen's washroom of Basque (a stroke it was thought, for the great restaurateur was portly to say the least . . .) only to be found by the clean-up crew, the very next morn— —'

'Wait,' Lee interrupts, turning her head just enough to allow full view of the adjacent lounger. 'You're not reading . . . You're just talking.'

'Sugar—I have ninety-six percent total recall. That's a scientific *fact*.' Truman points to his enormous head. 'It's all here—the whole thing! All eight-hundred pages, seared in my noggin. Where was I . . . ? Oooooooo *wait!* I have the most maaaarvelous idea! I'll pitch you some characters and you guess who they are!'

Lee allows the flicker of a smile to play at the corners of her lips, the closest to excitement one might hope to wrench from her. 'I'm game.'

'Goody! What fun!' Truman pauses, dizzy with options.

'Okay, ready? Tell me who *this* is: Wifey *numéro deux* of a late-night chat-show buffoon, "Jane Baxter" is needy. Christ—she's even been fired by her *therapists* for chewing their ears off, leaving 'em a pack of maimed medicinal Van Gogh. And "Bobby Baxter"—he's a modernist Marquis de Sade, hiding in a three-piece polyester suit! The way *he* gets around town, poor Janie's been given a nasty case of the pox, with a robust round of clap-clap-clap—and *NOT* as in *applause* . . .'

'Joanne and Johnny Carson!' Lee snickers. 'Truman, that *is* talking out of school.'

'Let's do another! . . . Former New York Governor's wife—thankfully deceased. Positively porcine, with tree-trunk legs, who I reckon wore serge skivvies and looked like she could club you with her driving iron—'

'Marie Harriman? Couldn't be anyone else.'

'Correct again! How 'bout: The Duchess's tabs run as high as her hairline, covered by her coterie of courtiers—loaded broads who Her Graceless can always rely on to shell out the cash . . .'

'Easy—Wallis Simpson.'

'Notorious cheapskate! I wonder if she's ever picked up a check?'

'*You're* one to talk . . .'

Sucking through the straw so quickly he's hit with a stab of brain-freeze, Truman grasps his forehead. He turns onto his side, facing Lee directly, a gleam in his eye.

'Perhaps *this* one'll hit closer to home. Lady Ina Coolbirth—that's Slim, by the way—reports: . . . BLANK and her sister BLANK enter La Côte Basque. You can see those girls have caught a few big fish in their time. Most people I know can't stand either one of them—' He checks in with Lee, who listens, expressionless. '—Generally fellow females, which I can understand—as they have contempt for other women, and never have a kind word to say about any women but themselves, the Bouviers.' Lee eyes him as he pauses, sheepishly slurping the last of his colada from its shell.

'Fair enough,' she allows, ever one for honesty.

'But boy, they work magic with the menfolk! Like a pair of sorceresses, they weave their spells on the fellas, as if by some strange voodoo they might put their hex on rich suitors and render themselves indispensable.'

At this, Lee raises an eyebrow.

Truman shrugs, moving on to what he really wants to share, his own true soul, a love letter, from the mouth of Lady Ina: '. . . If *I* swung that way, I'd be head over heels for Lee. She's perfectly formed, like a lovely Grecian bronze . . . a gleaming, gold-brown girl, her whisper-warm voice ever-slightly vibrating . . .'

At this, Lee's lips part in a genuine smile.

Truman, via Lady Ina, continues: '. . . Jackie—not in the same league. She can take a helluva photo, sure, but in the *flesh*, she hurts the eye. Those features, so . . . *severe*. Like a drag queen masquerading as Mrs. Kennedy.' Truman breaks character, an aside to Lee, 'You *do* know she's their number one pick? I met a sensational Queen at The Anvil who goes by "Jackie Uh-Oh" . . .'

Lee's smile widens to a grin. She can't help but love when Truman takes potshots at Jackie. At least *someone* can. Someone who, praise fucking Jesus, doesn't see her as the vaunted widow, nor the grave madonna, but the conniving bitch who stole their Daddy's love from her—and Ari too, long ago, along with a million other thefts.

Truman returns her grin, conspiratorially.

'Weeulll darling, what do you think of what I wrote about *you* . . . ?'

Lee sits up to sip her drink, tossing her gold-brown hair with indifference.

'Frankly, I could care less.' (A lie, we suspect—though she'll later tell Marella that she meant it.)

'Anyhoo. That's the gist of the chapter. Of course I have some *fabulous* bits you haven't yet heard: about Cole Porter—remember the time he shook his exposed member at a Portuguese wine steward? And *naturally* Ann Woodward ... who could resist *that*? And Bill, of course.'

'Bill ... ?'

'Bill Paley.'

'*Paley* ... ? What about him ... ?'

Tru's countenance blackens with something like revenge. 'He needs to learn. He needs to appreciate what he has ...' (Unspoken: we know that he means Babe.)

Lee reaches for a magazine, fans herself languidly, veneer of neutrality in place.

'Truman, I could give a flying fuck what you say about us ... but haven't you considered what you stand to lose ... ?'

'I know what I stand to *gain*.'

'Have you thought about how mad they'll be? And what they'll do to hurt you?'

'Oh, honey—it's art. It's beautiful ... it's Proust! I haven't used their names.'

'You have for some. And the rest seem pretty clear.'

'Nah . . . They're too dumb. They won't even recognize themselves.'

Lee places a wide-brimmed sun hat over her face, and through its checkerboard weave she rasps, 'We'll see. If they *do* recognize themselves, they ain't gonna be too happy.'

BENEATH THE SHADE OF A CANOPY of Royal Palms on an estate in West Palm Beach, Gloria and C.Z. sit in matching wicker armchairs, remnants of lunch and a pitcher of iced tea between them.

They're a study in extremes.

Gloria with her raven hair, C.Z.'s palest platinum. The brunette in a black shift dress; the blonde, the same in ivory. The former, rich olive complexion. The latter iridescent, almost nacreous. The lava-hot Latina listens as the ice-cool Bostonian reports the extent of the damage, flipping through a copy of *Esquire*.

'My *ghaaaaaad*,' C.Z. intones in her Brahmin-stretched vowels. 'He writes this "Lady Ina" as a desperate, aging lush . . . On a transatlantic flight where her husband gives her the boot, and there she is, trapped beside the heartless bahstard for six more hours fullah *hell*.'

'*Dios mío!*' Gloria's eyes widen.

'Wait! It gets worse . . .' C.Z. skips down a few lines, absorbing the material.

'What does he say?' her companion leans forward, impatient.

'Oh it's simply *ahhhhhhwful* . . . .'

'Go on!'

'I cahn't.'

'You *must!*'

'Ahhlright . . . The author *implies* that Coolbirth's pahst her prime—at *forty* no less—thrice-divorced, facing the gallows of *Extra*-Womanhood . . .'

Gloria furrows a brow, as if it's a concept she's not had need to learn the meaning of. 'What do you mean by this, '*Extra*' . . . ?'

'Oh dahling, you know. The Spare. The one for whom the hosts feel obliged to import a 'suitable' Extra Man at dinnahs, in order to keep her company. Hosts that care about such bullshit . . . It's why *I* ahlways favor a nice communal buffet.'

'Why can't this "Coolbirth" simply find another husband?'

'They're thin on the ground, the Keepahs.'

'Could she not borrow someone else's . . . ?'

'We cahn't all be *you*, dahling.'

Reading a few more lines C.Z. reports—'My ghad . . . It ends with her simpering into her soufflé . . .' She lowers the magazine, sips her tea, rendering her verdict. 'Ahhhwful . . . but effective.'

Gloria laughs, shaking her head. '*Él tiene cojones, Diablito* . . .'

'What's that, dahling?'

'He has balls, our Truman.'

'*Thahht* he does.'

'But why this gossip—when he could write anything?

C.Z. shrugs. 'Writers write. One cahn't be surprised if they write what they know.'

'Poor Bebé. And Slim!'

'Yes, but *really*. What were they thinking?'

Gloria frowns. 'What do you mean?'

'We all knew what he was. They should have been talking to their shrinks, not a writer. What did they *think* he would do? Of *course* he was going to use all that mahterial, sooner or later.' C.Z. reaches for the pitcher, refilling their glasses. 'It's why I've never told him anything interesting enough to *mattah*.'

'Hmmm.' Gloria falls silent, suggesting that she perhaps had not been so wise.

'He doesn't say for certain if it's them,' C.Z. allows.

'Who else could this 'Coolbirth' be? We both know that 'Dill' is Bill . . .'

'Truman told me that story *years* ago—most of the others too.'

The palms rustle above them, accompanied by a low rumble of thunder.

'*Bueno*.' Gloria, with a deep breath. 'I'm prepared,'

'For whaht, dahling?'

'Skip ahead to what it says about *us*.'

C.Z. flips forward through the article, while Gloria waits with what she hopes might read as wariness—but what we'll later come to realize is, in fact, something more closely linked to *appetite* . . .

Reaching the end, C.Z. looks up, tossing the magazine on the table.

'Nothing.'

'What do you *mean*, nothing . . . ?!"

'Nada. Zilch. It seems we've escaped the shit-storm.'

Gloria grabs the magazine, scanning its column inches.

'How can that be . . . ?'

'We should thank our lucky *staaahrs* for small favours.'

Unconvinced, Gloria flips backwards through the pages herself.

Beads of rain begin to fall, at first in isolated droplets, then a gentle patter, ricocheting off the table. C.Z. rises to open a standing umbrella above them, as an autumn shower commences.

'**F**RANKLY, *FUCK PALEY*,' Babe practically spits, enjoying the fricatives of the consonants on her lips as she chases them with a long drag of her cigarette.

The swearing is new, something she relishes like a rebellious adolescent.

We've noticed it on bedside visits in these last molasses months, where we sip Manhattans as Babe chain-smokes her beloved L&Ms, musing they could hardly hurt her now, their damage already done.

Babe has changed these last few weeks. She is depleted, yet strangely full.

For those of us who know her, she's more herself than ever.

The cancer has robbed her of lingering vanities, stealing her lustrous hair, her gamine strength. Yet for all that it takes, it gives her something she's long denied herself.

A voice. Not her mellifluous voice, not the well-mannered one.

It's an uncensored Babe who's emerging.

She has come to find that death is far from an amiable house-guest. There's no seating arrangement that will encourage buoyant small talk. No place setting that will please, no delicacy that will satiate its ravenous appetite. And like the most night-marish of guests, it refuses to leave. It has even had the audacity to move into her bedroom, sits at the foot of her down-covered mattress.

It watches her in fitful, pain-racked sleep, greets her when she wakes each morning, ravaged. She has no privacy, even within the fabric-draped walls of her master suite—the fabric with Moroccan vines that she'd selected despite warnings that it might feel claustrophobic. These days she has ample time to study its intricate, serpentine lines. She finds their complexity comforting.

The few times a day she ventures downstairs to join the world of the living, her unwanted visitor's decaying perfume lingers in the hallways. Like any good hostess, she's tried to turn a blind eye to its impudence. She's developed a disquieting sense of calm when it comes to the presence that follows her. She even addresses it, speaking out loud to the 'Other,' only to find that she's talking to herself.

Babe talks a great deal more than she used to. The new alien voice bubbling from her elongated throat started with small tantrums. About a meal brought on a silver tray, food she cannot fathom an appetite for. About a male nurse with clammy hands who stabs at her withered arm in a vain attempt to find a vein, too thick to appreciate the irony, she tells him. Once she starts using her voice—the honest one, gravelly, no longer eager to please—she finds that she likes the sound of it. She realizes that it's an entity quite apart from her. She reserves a special round of daily vitriol for Truman, who she continues to loathe from a distance, who she hates all the more, knowing he's the one person who could have cheered her.

But the bulk of her rage is reserved for the man that robbed her of her beloved Truheart.

'Well, isn't it true? If Paley hadn't had his dick up anything that passed in a skirt, would Truman have bothered to write that shit in the first place?'

She calls him 'Paley' now, or 'the Old Bastard'—never 'Bill.' Not anymore. He has lost the privilege of intimacies, as much as the author himself.

'As if it made a goddamn iota of difference if Old Bastard Paley had aspic or mousse. Skippy or Jif. Over-easy or sunny side up.'

At the word 'sunny' she turns her laser gaze to Slim, who nearly always is described as such. Golden. Sun-kissed. *Breezy . . .*

'Babe, that's unfair. You did *want* to please him,' Slim ventures, sitting at her bedside, sipping her manhattan, taking her turn in the revolving-door of one or other of us paying daily visits. Babe stares at her with a peculiar expression, as if she has just recast her closest female friend as villainess. Hadn't Slim insisted, along with Bill, that she never, ever speak to Truman again?

IT WAS AT QUO VADIS, SIX MONTHS AFTER THE RIFT. We all remember slightly different versions of the encounter. Some of us recall Babe and Slim sitting at a prime table, in full view.

One knows exactly where one ranks in Manhattan's social pecking order by where they're seated. The more comfortable booths that line the perimeters of Vadis or Basque or Cirque, the ones that offer a modicum of privacy, are disastrous. If you're seated in a cozy, out-of-the-way banquette, you know that you're a nobody.

The Jackies and Lees of the world, the Babes and Slims of our set, are placed at the hellishly uncomfortable tables in the center of the restaurant. The closer to the door the better. Never mind the glacial chill that sweeps in each time the doorman swings the portal open to herald a new arrival. Ditto the hard, upright chairs, like something from a Puritan grade school. These are the prime tables, where one can be seen—by incoming patrons, or lurking paparazzi, or, better still, by one another. But we digress.

We'd made a pact not to speak to him. Ever, *ever* again. He was out. *Persona non grata*. Of course Slim and Babe—the most violated of us all by the *Esquire* chapter—were the most staunchly resolved. But there's more coming, he's always warned. Who knows when it could be our turn. And so we rally in a public display of solidarity.

Privately, we've each played our hands a bit differently.

Lee sees him, Lee's status exempting her from the need to follow the herd. As a slain President's sister-in-law and royalty through marriage, Lee can march to whatever drum she likes. She's continued on with little Tru, though her enthusiasm is waning.

C.Z. has stood by him, but then Truman has never hinted at her cool vanilla Hitchcock persona in his work. Gloria's schadenfreude at Babe and Slim's humiliation has been tempered by a growing anxiety that she herself is next. She hasn't cut Tru exactly, but her invitations to Gemini have ceased; Loel has forbidden them. As much as he misses Truman's company, his is a staunch world of protect-one's-own handshakes and greased palms, exchanged between titans. Bill is too close a friend (or too vital a business ally) to risk Truman's presence.

Marella was forced to sit beside him at a dinner at Lee's, dining *à trois*—naughty of Lee, really. It was her attempt to broach a reconciliation, at Truman's hangdog begging, no doubt. The three had a perfectly civilized meal, perched on Fez pouffes in Lee's Moorish pied-à-terre, picking at tagines of stewed prune and lamb. When dinner was over, Truman had insisted on escorting Marella home. She silently cursed Lee as she allowed the poisoned gnome to help her into her fox-hair coat, to take her arm with forced intimacy, walking her out of Lee's town house, into the whirling snow.

Truman had snuggled up against her in a taxi, she'd told us, resting his chin on her furry shoulder. 'Why haven't we seen each other, *miele*? Little Tru has missed his Numero Uno.'

'I couldn't bear to tell him that I'd seen something black and rotten in his soul that last day in Genoa. Instead I simply said, "Oh Truman, you live here, I live in Europe. It does make things difficult."' He'd taken her hand and patted it.

When the taxi had rolled to a stop in front of her hotel, Truman gallantly climbed out and walked her to the door. He'd presented his ruddy cheek, she said, its horizontal spread looking more reptilian than she'd remembered. In that moment Marella felt every inch the Italian princess in a twisted fairy tale, kissing the toad with the reverberating croak, in a scene Central Casting couldn't have orchestrated better. Truman's wide eyes searched hers for a sign—of rejection, of redemption. Marella had smiled, perfectly civil, perfectly polite. She couldn't tell if his voice trembled when he asked it, or if that's a detail she's imagined after the fact, when he turned to leave her.

'You'll call me, Uno? For lunch?'

'Yes, Truman. I'll call you.'

Marella said she had known as she quickened her pace into the sanctuary of the Ritz lobby that she would never call Truman again.

SOME OF US REMEMBER THAT AFTERNOON at Quo Vadis with Babe sitting at a prime table by the door, waiting for her lunch date to arrive.

Others recall Babe and Slim well into their meal when it happened. Still another camp recalls Truman arriving first, stalking the bar.

Lee remembers Tru holding court in a prime spot, Babe being forced to walk past his table to reach her lunch companion.

Majority rules, so the legend has, for the most part, gone the Slim-and-Babe route: Truman proceeding directly to the bar, ordering a double martini. After a few fortifying slurps, he'd breezed—this part is certain—up to Babe and Slim's table, seemingly without a care in the world. Slim refused to look up from her *Langue du Boeuf*, stabbing violently at the tongue on the plate. Babe sipped her Pouilly-Fumé, allowing her doe eyes to flick upward, unable to resist a quick glance. Truman had beamed his chandelier-smile at her as if nothing were wrong.

'Hello, Babyling,' he chirped.

Startled into habit, Babe's manners responded for her. 'Hello, Truman.'

Babe felt a sharp pain as Slim gave her a good kick under the table. She quickly cast her eyes back to her quiche, flaking at the outer crust daintily with her fork, managing one more peek . . . His demeanor was jaunty, but there was something in his eyes that spoke the truth. Those eyes, hidden behind the glasses . . . the eyes of a very small boy who still desperately hoped to be asked to play.

Her gaze met his, and for a moment they were locked.

Please, she could almost hear him say. *Please forgive me.*

Babe felt a pang in her heart, as acute as Slim's kick. How she wished that all of this would end. How she would have loved to have Truman pull up a chair and go back to the way things were. Their forgettable lunch would suddenly be sprinkled with his magic-dust. They'd be wrapped in the cocoon of conversation, doubled with laughter at his witticisms.

She had so much to tell him. About Kate joining a religious sect. About Billy's drug bust. Amanda's divorce. Disappointments all. (She always feared she was a shit mother.) Most of all, about Bill's renewed fervor . . .

Ever since her diagnosis, the strangest thing had happened. Bill Paley, philanderer extraordinaire, had fallen in love with his wife. It was as if the threat of losing her had opened the flood-gates of denied affection. He had been forced to recognize what he'd always had.

He'd tried to seduce her again, attempted daily to make love, something that had ceased years ago, after Billy's birth, at Bill's insistence. He had not wanted her perfection marred by carnality. There were other women for that.

Babe had been devastated when Bill had moved down the hall, ceasing to share their bed. One night she had crept down the dark-ened corridor to his suite. She dropped her robe and stood naked before him. Shivering. Vulnerable. Bill had looked on, as one might study a statue in a gallery and find it aesthetically pleasing. But when she took his hand and tried to move it between her legs, brushing the tangle of hair at her lips, Bill pulled away. He'd stroked her cheek and retreated to his study, flipping through the weekly network ratings, nibbling a leftover sandwich.

Babe had quietly retrieved her robe, returned to the maze of Moroccan vines in her own suite, and cried into a throw pillow needlepointed with jade-plumed lovebirds.

He had loved her once. Then he had stopped, once he had branded her Mrs. Bill Paley. Then, without warning, he loved her again. And Babe resented the hell out of him.

As Babe sat beside Slim in Quo Vadis with Truman's eyes begging her forgiveness, she longed to tell him everything.

He was the one person who would understand—if you wait long enough for something that never comes, you eventually cease to want it.

Babe broke Truman's gaze and looked back to her plate.

He shifted his focus to Slim with cheery resilience.

'Hello, Big Mama . . . Guess what? I've decided to forgive you.'

Slim, unamused, polished off her Scotch, looking beyond Truman as if he were invisible.

'Well, mercy me—seems I'm in need of a top-up. Back in a jiff.' He managed to sound upbeat as he trotted back toward the bar, smiling at each of us as he passed.

As Babe watched Truman's seemingly buoyant retreat, she wanted to run to him, to unburden her fractured heart, which may as well have been removed along with her blackened lung. But Bill—and Slim—had denied her.

EIGHT

1970/1962

MARELLA

DRAMMA GIOCOSO

A s a tribe, we migrate frequently and rapidly—largely because we can.

While we can recall with vague nostalgia the pleasures of a summer crossing on one of the great Cunard liners, departing from New York, arriving in Europe in a week's time, the 'getting there' having secretly pleased us as much as our stated destinations, that was before. Before the skies cracked opened and revealed their potential. Before the speed of metal wings granted us the luxury of restlessness. Before the urgency took hold, compelling us to make up for the years that we'd lost to the war. Before adrenaline infected our body clocks, tempted by thoughts of rarefied air and starry eyes and exotic booze in bars in far Bombay. Motion had corrupted us with wanderlust.

Who now would dream of wasting a week, even a day, stuck on board a tortoise of a cruiser if one might just as easily jet off to Paris for an afternoon's shopping spree—or on to Venice for a meal? With one's intimates possessing the ability to transport one at the drop of a passport, why ever—we asked ourselves, when the option first presented itself—would we limit our mobility?

Babe and Bill were such dears—they offered to drop me off in Rome on their way to Sardinia. They have the most adorably intimate plane—have you flown with them?

Darling, do you mind if we reschedule lunch on Thursday?
I'm hitching a ride to Acapulco with Gloria and Loel—just a few
days in the sun. I'm in desperate need of a tan.

What began as a novelty has become a way of life. We've transmuted, through a dizzying combination of technology and means, into a migrant set. Nomads. Globe-trotters. Internationalists. Ours is the pulse of motion, propelled by a frenetic desire to keep up with our peers; desperate to stay a healthy length ahead of our rivals. We thus spend our days in a state of flux, conveniently rootless.

Our circle has expanded from a cadre of friends to an army of *acquaintances*. How else might one ensure hospitality in every port?

We know in our bones where the next migration will be— where we might find the rest of the flock. The most fashionable months for each locale, though we avoid a place with cultivated disdain the moment it becomes too popular.

We travel for weddings—though curiously not funerals, which might slow our pace with grim thoughts of mortality. For hunts, races and sporting must-sees. For auctions, exhibits, and launches of fashion. We fly to the slopes of St. Moritz when the snow is good, and to the beaches of St. Tropez when the sun is at its peak. We cross continents for premieres in every metropolis—particularly rewarding if we beat one another to the punch.

Even the most tone-deaf among us consider the Salzburg Festival required attendance, especially with Herbert von Karajan conducting, we being friendly with his third wife, Eliette, the toast of French fashion for a time. And even the most strident opera-hater would sell a lung to hear Maria Callas sing anywhere—though we couldn't help but snicker when Gianni Agnelli described Callas singing *Medea* as 'two hours of pure torture.'

We like that about Gianni—he hasn't the time for dishonesty. In fact, Gianni might well be the cultural icon of our set, epitomizing the velocity of the age. Gianni has been known to wake in

Turin, put in an hour at his Fiat office, fly to Rome for lunch, then to the snow-capped Alps—where his helicopter drops him at mountain's peak, he having no patience for ski lifts, ending the day in the South of France, where he's more than once been known to leap from the aircraft, landing in his swimming pool below. He seldom will finish a book or a film, and cannot bear to linger over dinner. He likes his conversation short, sweet and to the point (and—we've heard from several *reliable* sources—the same might apply to his lovemaking).

If anyone, in contrast, offers a glimpse of a more graceful age it is, ironically, Marella. While nine years his junior, she feels an ancient soul with her steady, regal calm.

It's on one balmy summer evening in Salzburg that we find ourselves settling into our seats, contemplating such thoughts. As expected (given our presence), Karajan is conducting—and thank God he's spared us the shrieking Valkyries. (We'd told Eliette quite plainly that another round of *Götterdämmerung* and we might be 'otherwise occupied' slitting our throats on opening night.) Perhaps as a gesture of appeasement, he has revived last season's standby: *Don Giovanni*. It's his third revival in eight years of this particular staging, so, in the spirit of *been-there-done-that*, we turn our attention to the surrounding scene, allowing the opera to function as a pleasant background track to the dramas in our midst. We nudge our seat-mates, coughing ever so delicately, nodding toward recent divorcés, test-driving new models; to their former wives mere rows apart, arms linked through those of eager young escorts. We spot the usual spattering of starlets, alongside their directorial counterparts. The expected ratio of aristocrats and members of the smart set, all fresh off their various planes, yawning and napping in their boxes.

Scanning the crowd, how can our eyes but linger when they reach Marella?

Perched in a loge just above the stage, she gives the impression of some exotic avian creature. Not the swan of Truman's appellation—something more angular. A heron perhaps, slender neck extended from a high Pucci collar, skimming her cropped chestnut curls. There is indeed something birdlike in the way she cocks her head, poised atop that elongated throat, her aquiline nose a sort of fine-boned beak.

Seated beside her, Gianni, in his Battistoni suit, cut to perfection. His signature touches of loosened tie around a Brooks Brothers shirt, collar unbuttoned with the calculated insouciance of a rebel schoolboy. Ankle crossed over knee, hiking boots peeking from the leg of his fine wool trousers. Foot jiggling. Restlessness apparent. The epitome of Felliniesque visions of the beautiful life. Of restive playboys in slick suits, wading romantically into fountains, speeding in fast cars past jostling paparazzi, of Negroni-fueled nightclubs and ruins and reckless passions.

It's this last bit from which we draw the parallel, somewhere midway through the first act. It's there right in front of us—had it been one of Truman's cobras it might have bitten us. Mozart, it seems, was prophetic indeed! How closely does the rake singing his famed Champagne Aria on the stage before us resemble the Rake of the Riviera, Gianni's sobriquet in those wild days of post-war hedonism? Even the name is uncanny, Gianni's birth name being Giovanni, after his grandfather, the great Fiat chairman. Not that anyone calls our Gianni anything other than *L'Avvocato*, an affectionate nod to the law degree he'd discarded without a day of practice. Was he not an incorrigible seducer? To put it more crassly, were his fucks not famous . . . ? There were too many to catalog, their numbers rivaling those detailed in Mozart.

And of course! Good God—of *course*. We only *just* spot it . . .

Donna Elvira! The stoic, steadfast wife who suffers Giovanni's betrayals. Did Marella see it too? How could she not? From that dawning Act One realization, we each watch Donna Marella and Don Gianni like salacious hawks. Ten minutes into the second act—not long after Giovanni's crooning '*Deh, vieni alla finestra*,' accompanied (tellingly, it will later be whispered alongside the rumors . . .) by a lone mandolin—we note Gianni glancing at his Rolex, fastened, as is his habit, on the outside of his cuff, having famously proclaimed in the press that he is too busy to pull back his sleeve to check the time.

He watches the serenade, shifting in his seat.

We're a bit startled, we *must* say, when Gianni suddenly rises from his chair, mid-aria. We watch with fascination as he leans in close to Marella, whispering in her ear. She gives the faintest nod, not taking her eyes from the action on stage as he turns and slips out of the box. We strain to see if his exit has left an impact, but her features remain impassive, as if chiseled from fine Italian marble. An ever-stoic madonna.

It is only during Donna Elvira's final, conflicted aria, '*Mi tradì quell'alma ingrata*,' that we *think* we notice her heron's neck lengthen a fraction with what we can only assume is wistfulness. Some of us could swear we saw a tear roll down her cheek.

MARELLA WAS DETERMINED—after Truman said what he did in the *Antiquariato di Sloth* several months back—never to trust a soul with what had transpired between them.

She vowed she would never, *ever* repeat his odious words, not even to herself.

Frankly she ceased to care if what he said was true or false—only that he'd said it, and from that point on he ceased to exist for her.

She remembered that fateful day in fragments. The dampness of their coats. The hiss from the hotplate upon which the Signore Sloth had boiled a kettle. The fading leather of rows of antique volumes, upon whose fragile spines Truman had run his fingertips in passing, en route to pay for his cabinet. She'd watched him pause and stare longingly at the centuries-old tomes, with a purity of gaze she seldom saw him bestow upon the animate. While his initial appreciation seemed more for the assortment of works, his eyes seemed to light on a particular volume. A smile crept across his face—one that conveyed the mischief she'd once found irresistible, something that now made her queasy. He plucked it from the shelf, leaving a hole in the collection. He trotted to the counter to confront the proprietor once more, while Marella managed to slip out of the shop before the haggling process recommenced.

THEY HAD TAKEN A TAXI BACK TO THE PORT, where he sat snickering, turning the wrapped package around in his hands. It was as they neared the mooring that he handed it to her.

'For you, Uno. *Un regalo.*'

Marella regarded the offering warily. She managed a terse smile as she shook her head.

'*Grazie*, Truman, *ma no, grazie.*'

'*Whhaaaaat?* Thanks but no thanks?' His jaw dropped with mock offense. 'You're rejecting my prezzie, *miele*?'

'*Sì*, Truman. No thank you.'

'But Uno, you simply *must* take it. I picked it out for you *specially.*' He dropped the package into her lap, ignoring her reluctance. 'It's not like I can give it to anyone *else.* I's likes to be specific in my choices, and this really does suit you to a T. Go on ... Open it.'

His eyes were so earnest, she began to wonder if this was, in fact, a peace offering. An apology for his unfathomable disloyalty. Without speaking, she unwrapped the paper to find a small volume of cracked ivory leather, pages brittle with age.

Embossed in flaking gold: DON JUAN.

'It's *Byron, miele.* Of course you wouldn't be able to understand five syllables, it not being written in *I-talian* ... But I think *Gianni* might be just the man to summarize the plot.'

As Marella ran her fingers over the lettering, she noted the faintest traces of gold residue on her skin, along with a layer of dust.

'Of course I *wanted* to get you Ovid's *Heroides.* It's about wronged heroines, told in a series of epistolary poems to the menfolk who betrayed them. Do you know what "epistolary" means? Doubtful. It means *letters.* The letters of those poor wives whose husbands abandon them. Penelope to Ulysses, Medea to Jason.

103

Perhaps *L'Avvocato* might shed some light on this as well?' There it was again. That smug grimace.

'He came back, Ulysses. To Penelope. His *wife*.' Marella met Truman's gaze, her regal chin jutting as defiantly as his own.

He shrugged, a casualness to his malice. 'Sometimes theys do, sometimes theys don't. Face it, for the very rich, marriage is like travel these days . . . One stays as long as one's interest holds, then he—or she—but let's be honest, it's usually the *he*—moves on to the next port.' Then, pointed—'Sometimes one never knows how close one's come to loss.'

They sat in silence the rest of the drive. The moment the taxi pulled up to the quay, Marella was out the door and halfway up the gangplank, before her companion had bent to collect his faded treasures.

BACK ON BOARD THE *AGNETA*, Marella locked herself in her cabin, where she intended to stay in self-imposed exile for the rest of the journey. She prowled the master stateroom, which Gianni did not share, preferring to sleep in a guest berth so that he might come and go as he pleased. It was a luxurious cell to be sure, with its Carrara marble fireplace and priceless modern art, Rothkos and Bacons filling the space. Still, Marella resented her dubious guest having the run of the ship while she stewed below.

How dare the little beast! He with his ugliness and lies! And all because . . . what? She had the temerity to criticize his work? To have served as the sibyl predicting his demise, should he fail to heed her oracle? She could see the fate that awaited him should Babe ever read the filth he'd spouted on deck. It was then that it first began to dawn on her, that while she loved Truman-the-Artist and still felt a reverence for his gift, she found she no longer cared for Truman-the-Person. And for confusing one with the other she found herself ashamed. Perhaps because she had told him so much. About her marriage. About Gianni. About that wretched Churchill woman. About Mrs. John Fitzgerald Kennedy, about whom she still had suspicions. She had told Truman these tales, along with hundreds of others. She'd always shared with her *Piccolo Vero* her inner, innermost fears.

Marella paced the stateroom, recalling an occasion seven years before, which now felt chillingly similar. A reprise of an earlier chorus. A variation on a theme, played out time and again, with its operatic blend of farce and tragedy.

IT WAS AUGUST 1962, and Lee and Stas had taken a villa in Ravello.

Lee had gone to great pains—agonizing over every minute detail, she confessed to Marella—to host her sister Jackie, the latter desperate to escape the madness of Washington at the height of the Kennedy presidency. This was to be Mrs. Kennedy's Italian adventure, beginning with Lee in Rome, moving on to the Amalfi Coast. It was a lively party, the Radziwills having asked mutual friends to join. Photographer Benno Graziani and his wife Nicole, and lawyer Sandro D'Urso and his stockbroker son Mario were included in the guest list, so how could the Agnellis refuse? They were at the end of an Amalfi cruise as it was. It was a natural choice to point the *Agneta*'s sepia masts toward the tiny fishing port.

It proved an enchanted setting. Even Gianni slowed long enough to observe the scent emanating from the lemon trees on the rocks and the verbena wafting on the breeze, commenting on the flora of the region—something Marella had scarcely heard him mention in all the years she'd known him. Each morning the little party began the descent—three hundred steps to be exact—to the beach across the bay, under the watchful eye of the Kennedy Secret Service detail. How awkward that poor young Agent Hill looked, a pistol tucked into his bathing trunks, stark white legs extending like toothpicks; limbs that had scarcely seen the light of day.

Marella couldn't imagine how Jackie endured the burden of the entourage. She had admired her quiet grace when they'd met through the Roosevelts several years before, recognizing in the politician's wife something of her own public persona. When the Kennedys had hosted a White House state dinner for the Agnellis and Radziwills the previous fall, Marella had been impressed by the First Lady's attention to detail.

Signora Agnelli had worn black and diamonds, though she barely noticed Jack Kennedy's eyes fixating on her lengthy neck, her attention otherwise occupied with Gianni, the latter clearly mesmerized by Jackie.

Of course Marella had learned over the years to closely observe in such cases, but to keep her powder dry—for nothing was more abhorrent to Gianni than 'a scene.' He had been raised to keep emotion at bay. It was partly a matter of temperament, partly a self-imposed discipline, one she suspected he developed after losing both parents by the age of fourteen to accidents of speed—father flying his plane into a cliff, mother's lovely neck snapped in an auto crash, racing along the winding roads above the Riviera. For Gianni, expression of feeling—worse still, lack of control—was not just a sign of weakness; it was the worst of all transgressions.

It was *inelegant.*

She was under no illusion that her husband was faithful, but she did consider him loyal. His quickly discarded tarts may have their brief moments spinning in the warmth of his gaze, but it was *she* to whom he was devoted.

She knew of his conquests long before she married him—had read the tabloids that chronicled his exploits. His sisters had warned her, when Marella was but a schoolgirl, long before the flirtation began. After she was introduced to *L'Avvocato* at a party in Rome, the *sorelle* Agnelli had demanded—

'Did he pay you attention?'

'Not much,' she had conceded. 'In fact, none at all.'

'Run, then! Fast as you can! *Veloce!*'

Marella had smiled, eyes clouded with the dreamy infatuation of an eighteen-year-old girl. 'But he's magnificent, is he not?'

The *sorelle* laughed with affection and launched into a catalog of his conquests—'*Ascolta*, Marella. You are not the first and you won't be the last! Each town, each district, each country testifies to his affairs with women. In Italy, by the hundreds; in England, Spain and France—on the Riviera a thousand at least, we should think! In winter he likes fat ones, in summer thin ones. Tall or short. Young or old. It doesn't matter if she's rich or poor, ugly or beautiful; if she wears a skirt, you can guess what he does!'

They were exaggerating for effect . . . though not by much. And they would, when the time came, encourage Marella to marry their beloved *fratello*.

Marella had tried to heed their warning. She moved to Paris for a stint in art school, then to New York, where she was scouted to model for *Vogue*, her lissome frame providing an ideal manne-quin on which to drape the latest styles. It proved an endeavor that bored her above all others, until she was encouraged by the great Erwin Blumenfeld to step *behind* the camera.

He gave her a twin lens Rolleiflex and she submerged herself in surrealist imagery akin to his own. He trained his eager appren-tice in techniques of double exposures; of combination printing and solarization. Dismantling beauty and putting it back together— one's subject rendered all the more lovely in the end for having once been not so.

She scanned the papers for news of Gianni—most of it gossip. Of carousal at the playboy's Villa Leopolda on the Côte d'Azur, with film stars and aristos and wild nocturnal romps. In her sepa-rate world, Marella was satisfied waiting in a darkroom for images to emerge in those pungent chemical baths.

It was only when the Agnelli clan summoned Marella to their *Avvocato*'s bedside that the romance finally flourished, his nearly amputated leg preventing his flight. Though she willed it to be otherwise, Marella was under few illusions when he asked for her hand. Gianni still had his *ways*. She had always secretly worried that he had loved the scheming Pam Churchill rather than her at the time of their union, and that she had only won the matrimonial prize because his *sorelle* had forced a proposal. Or perhaps because she was already carrying in her womb Gianni's future heir.

The day of their nuptials was cursed with rain, which she refused to accept as an omen. She emerged from the chapel in Balenciaga lace, her arm threaded through Gianni's. He was dapper in a slim-cut morning coat, fragrant gardenia in his lapel. Yet the photos—taken by Robert Doisneau, whom *Vogue* had commissioned to capture the occasion—could not conceal the awkward presence of not one but *two* walking canes, upon which the handsome groom leaned throughout the service. He had been determined to wean himself off the crutches he had been dependent upon since his accident, the one that had occurred while fleeing his lover Pam Churchill. The gold-tipped canes were at least a gesture of sartorial eccentricity, but Marella saw them as nothing more than grotesque appendages—reminders of Pam on what was supposed to be *her* special day. It was as if her rival was there, a specter haunting the proceedings.

That first night, on a terrace perfumed with ripe blood oranges, Marella gathered the courage to ask her new husband the question that had weighed heavily on her since their formal courtship had commenced.

'*Amore mio* . . . you *are* in love with me, aren't you?' Her heart thrummed like a hummingbird's as she awaited his answer.

Gianni replied with his hearty, good-natured laugh. '*In* love? . . . *Angelo*, isn't that for valets and chambermaids?'

He had kissed her on the forehead like a younger sister, but not once had he told her—before, then, or ever—that he was in love with her.

She learned, over time, to intuit his conquests. She could sense when he was rushing off for a rendezvous and developed techniques to make her presence felt, filling his flat in Rome with enough signs of her presence to dampen his libido. A bed delivered to his bachelor pad, sheets monogrammed with their combined initials. Room service awaiting his arrival in a hotel suite, the meal carefully chosen to evoke familial memories. A well-timed phone call to mutual friends she suspected of aiding and abetting—providing open houses and plates of spaghetti for

Gianni's *maggiorate*, the curvy girls that were the Italian male ideal.

Still, Marella wasn't troubled. She had come to see his infidelities as a form of expression—his desire to possess a beautiful woman no different from his desire for a sculpture or painting. Affairs of aesthetics, rather than emotion. Even the most glamorous of these, the Cinecittà sirens—Anita Ekberg and her ilk—on the whole made their entrances and exits without consequence. She took solace in the fact that she was the one he had chosen. She was Donna Marella Agnelli. Gianni's *wife*. They were a pair—in time hardly anyone could mention *L'Avvocato* without mentioning Marella in the same breath. They were fused as one, in the eyes of their families, in the eyes of God.

It had taken one incident to shake this assumption to its foundation.

She was six months pregnant with their second child when it occurred to her that Gianni, for all his eccentric devotion, was, without question, a singular being. It would take another decade for Marella, sharing a languid lunch with Truman amid the bustle of the Piazza Navona, to attempt to articulate this concept.

'You know, Vero,' she observed, twisting a strand of linguine contemplatively around her fork, 'Gianni has never said "we." Only "I."'

'In what sense, *miele*?'

'He has never once said "we ski" or "we sail" . . . Just "I." Singular. Never plural.' She paused, lowering her fork. 'We ski or sail together, but when he speaks of right or left . . . or right or wrong, it's quite clearly *his* right that he means. Does that make sense?'

Truman's expression brightened with recognition. 'Of *course* it does! It's all a matter of point of view. Gianni is without question a first-person narrator, singular.'

Marella placed a hand on his arm, grateful that someone understood. It was why Truman was so vital to her.

As she'd go on to tell her *Piccolo Vero*, it was during her pregnancy that she began to suspect that something was amiss. Gianni's were not the telltale signs of the average philandering spouse, whose absences and skittishness might provide critical clues. With Gianni it was the opposite. He did what he never did . . . he *slowed*.

It was a lethargy she'd not seen in him. Even when bedridden with his injured leg he had possessed his signature agitation. Now he took his time. Sat in one place for hours, wearing a satisfied expression. Finished a meal and waited for others, rather than expecting them to match his pace. He seemed to emanate the dreamlike quality she knew too well, for recognizing it as that which had consumed her when she'd first fallen in love with him.

It didn't take long for Marella to identify the object of Gianni's suspected affections. A few phone calls to mutual friends, asking who he had been seen with at the nightspots around Via Veneto, the center of *Il Boom*, the Roman social whirl. It was in scouring the musings of the tabloid rags—*Momento-sera*, to be precise—that Marella found her evidence. There, captured by a paparazzo—leaning in to whisper in one another's ears at a thimble-sized table—was Gianni and a stunning female. This woman was no actress who could be tossed casually aside. She was no nomadic trust–fund brat who would be off to Monte Carlo on the next departing flight. This was a woman that she knew. A woman with a name—but not just *any* name. One as titled and lauded as Marella's own. Princess Laudomia Hercolani. 'Domietta' to friends, 'Dom' to her intimates. The photo revealed an aristocratic profile. Ashen hair marbled with honeycomb. Cigarette drooping from unnaturally long fingers, Princess Dom was a rival of mythic proportions. Visconti's scenic designer, inspiration for Ian Fleming's feminine ideal. Intense, headstrong, with a restlessness to match Gianni's own, the Princess Hercolani was more than Marella's equal. She was a genuine threat.

L'AVVOCATO TO WED HERCOLANI, the tabloid caption read. Marella felt the bluntness of it puncture her heart. To wed? But he was *already* wed! Perhaps it was her expectant state, but Marella raced to collect a coat, kiss little Edoardo, whom she left in the care of his *bambinaia*, and commandeered one of the fleet of Fiats at her disposal, speeding from Turin to Rome. As she drove, the thoughts played like a rondo in her mind, a recurring theme of envy and rage . . . *Are these the tricks he's used to betray me? Is this the reward for my loyalty and love? Must stop him, before he escapes—makes off . . . Must stop* . . . she thought again and again, stoking the embers of her fury.

IT WAS IN THE THIRD NIGHTCLUB that she found them. Unfamiliar with the hot spots of Via Veneto, she allowed the wolfpack of photographers to serve as her guide.

Windblown hair hidden beneath a silk kerchief, mackintosh concealing her protruding belly, she slipped into the establishment unnoticed. When she found them at a table surrounded by a cadre of Gianni's *amici*, she wasted no time in her approach.

'Giovanni?' she cried, disbelief in the discovery. As if being proven right was not what she'd expected.

'Marella, darling.' She watched Gianni remove his hand from Domietta's as he rose. Broad smile. Arms extended to embrace her, as if nothing was amiss.

'You monster. You criminal . . .'

'Come, my darling, calm yourself—'

'Pack of lies!' Marella looked to her rival, who was assessing her, lighting a cigarette with cool detachment.

'Charming insults,' she thought she heard Domietta say to Gianni's *amici*. 'She knows him well.' She exhaled an even stream of smoke, as if bored by the display.

'*Angelo*,' Gianni tried again, 'let me speak . . .'

Marella shook her head, the sting of tears in her eyes. 'What can you say, after such betrayal? You succeeded in seducing me. You wormed your way into my heart with your promises and your lies . . . I fell in love and you made me your wife. I bore you a child and now, with another on the way, you *abandon* me? Leaving me alone, with my regrets and tears? Is this my punishment for having loved you too much?' Her voice rose from melodic to shrill. Chatter at nearby tables lowered to a hush, all eager to listen in.

Gianni maintained an icy calm. 'I had reason to be in Rome.'

'What was that, if not your deceit? Thank God I found you here. At least now I *know* . . .'

'But my darling, Domietta is a *friend*.'

'She's clearly more than that!'

'You're making a scene.' His tone was even, though his eyes spoke volumes. 'Come and join us if you wish—or if you feel unwell, I'll have Mario drive you home.' He nodded toward a young man in his cadre with thick, black brows, which furrowed sympathetically at Marella.

'Is this all you have to say, after what you've done?'

'My dear woman, can't you see that I want to enjoy myself?'

'Enjoy yourself?! I know how you "enjoy" yourself!'

Onlookers had started to snicker.

Gianni, coolly, 'You're becoming a nuisance. I've done nothing. If you don't believe what I say, ask these gentlemen here.' He nodded toward his entourage, expressions ranging from bemusement to chagrin.

Domietta tucked a honeycomb strand behind one ear. Marella met her gaze.

'Don't believe this faithless heart! He's betrayed me. He'll betray you too.'

Gianni emitted an easy laugh. 'My poor wife is tired, my friends. It is her condition—it makes her . . . emotional. Women in her state are allowed to act crazy.'

Marella pulled her mac protectively around the evidence of her 'condition.'

'Betrayer,' she hissed. '*Betrayer!*'

Gianni took her arm and led her aside. '*Angelo*. People will *talk*. Be careful or you'll end up an object of gossip.'

Marella laughed bitterly. 'Don't place your hopes there. I've lost my sense of modesty! Your guilt can be known by all of Rome for all I care.'

And with a last look at the rival princess, who had the audacity to regard her with a vague expression of pity, Marella turned and left the club, bracing herself for the explosion of light that would inevitably issue from the paparazzi's waiting flashbulbs.

MARELLA KNEW SHE'D BEHAVED POORLY, had disappointed Gianni, but she didn't care. He was *hers* and she'd fight for him. An *armistizio* had been called as they limped through the familial Christmas rituals, strife simmering beneath the placid surface until, on New Year's Eve, she picked up the phone at midnight to catch Gianni on the line with Domietta Hercolani. A great scene was thrown on Marella's part, which Gianni refused to engage in. He sat quietly, enduring the tears and the wails, the stuff of Roman tragedy. His sole contribution to the encounter was a single word: 'Undignified.'

She had sought the counsel, in the ensuing days, of the *sorelle* Agnelli. She unburdened her soul to each in turn to find they had more or less the same reaction.

'*Cara*,' said one, 'in this life, sometimes it happens that a square is not a circle.'

'Whatever do you mean?' Marella asked, confused.

'Just that you should not try to fit a square peg into a round hole.'

Another: '*L'Avvocato* . . . he is devoted, not faithful.'

By the time she sat down with Suni, the eldest, on the terrace of her stately Argentine home, Marella had packed and unpacked her things time and again. She tearfully explained the *situazione* and gave voice to her great fear—'He's going to marry this woman.'

With a blunt clarity that mirrored Gianni's own, Suni took her hands.

'*Ascoltami*. He is not going to marry her. Not now, not ever. You are his wife. He will never leave you. Why ruin everything over something so trivial?'

Marella listened, and in doing so learned to bottle her fear. It was simply a matter of discipline. She packed her things one last time and returned to Turin with an odd sense of calm, assured that while Gianni might come and go, he would always return to her.

THUS IN THAT AUGUST OF '62, Marella was satisfied to spend time in the presence of the Bouvier sisters, both of whom had married well themselves. She knew and trusted Lee, and while Jackie, with her wispy voice and uncertain pauses, was more of an enigma, she was pleasant company, the glow of Kennedy Camelot emanating from her.

There were, of course, complications, which seemed incongruous with the sleepy island paradise. The omnipresent Secret Service, watching from speedboats bobbing close at hand. The prying eyes of the paparazzi with their telescopic lenses. But if one could ignore such intrusions and simply *live*—for that's what Jackie seemed to desire most—they were glorious days.

They floated in gem-kissed waters in the afternoon heat. They cut sea urchins from the rocks beneath the surface, cracking them open, slurping buttery innards from their shells. They explored emerald grottos, where the Romans had worshiped water nymphs centuries before—which Sandro insisted were still haunted by the spirits of doomed sailors and sea witches and long-dead gods. After a lunch of spaghetti with fresh-caught squid, they wandered into the town below, stopping to shop for sarongs in the local trading posts, 'WELCOME JACQUELINE!' signs fluttering from their storefronts. These excursions, while enjoyable, created a feeding frenzy among the photographers, who pursued their small party as they strolled through the village. A stop for *aperitivo* at a cafe in the Piazza Duomo had the power to incite a near riot as the mob scrambled for their shots.

'Eh, Jackie! *Sorriso*, Jackie!' They'd bare nicotine-stained grins to encourage a smile. '*Di "formaggio*," Jackie!' Marella saw the terror in those wide-set eyes as Jackie managed a weak half-smile, turning to ensure that Agent Hill was within arm's length. Behind her compliance, the panic of a fox facing down the hounds.

Having returned shaken but unscathed, the Radziwill party disappeared for leisurely baths or naps or to read on the terrace, reconvening well after ten for dinner overlooking the lights of the bay, serenaded by the fishermen's songs from boats anchored offshore. Sometimes they slept until noon, having not gone to bed until well past three. Then the leisurely routine began again, with coffee and ripe fruit served alongside the international papers, the delivery of which the Radziwills had prearranged. By the sixth day of their stay, the pages were plastered with paparazzi photos of Mrs. Kennedy and her entourage walking through the village—which was to be expected. And yet, a curious vanishing act had occurred. In the photos, Mrs. Kennedy's entourage was nowhere to be seen . . . apart, that is, from *L'Avvocato*.

GIANNI AND JACKIE'S ROMANTIC GETAWAY, the headlines read. **KENNEDY FIAT MERGER.**

A dozen such variations, translated into multiple languages; the photographs pictured a relaxed Jackie, in white capris and pastel V-necks, kerchiefs tied over chestnut hair. Strolling with Gianni—*alone*. Laughing—looking every inch the sun-kissed holiday couple.

Marella studied the images: Jackie gazing longingly at Gianni. Gianni pouring Jackie's drink. Gianni helping Jackie onto a speedboat, hand resting on the small of her back. One particularly tantalizing image captured Jackie holding a bottle of suntan oil, Gianni gripping her slender wrist. His head resting on her arm, premature patches of white at his temples, stark against his otherwise inky waves, brushing her bare skin.

In the background: a woman, reclining. Sunglasses shielding a myriad of secrets. Perhaps observing the intimacy of the couple in the foreground. Perhaps oblivious. Marella looked closely and thought that the woman might be her, but the figure was out of focus.

When Jackie emerged from her cabin, sundress over her bathing suit, sleep crusted in the corners of her eyes, Lee passed her a stack of newspapers. 'You'd better call Jack.'

Jackie took them, flipping through the pages, incredulous. 'But—' she began in her downy voice, halting before she resumed. 'But—how did they *manage* this?' The papers were circulated around the table, received with intense scrutiny and grave expressions.

Only Gianni seemed amused, chuckling at the headlines. Pleased with his fictional conquest. 'They have a good idea. Kennedy and Agnelli—it is an excellent merger, no?' adding, 'Businesswise, perhaps I should speak with Jack and we'll consider the matter.'

Marella barely heard him, preoccupied with the blurred image behind the wrist photo.

'They've cropped the rest of us out to sell their story,' said Benno Graziani, an expert in such things. 'Oldest trick in the book. *You* know that, Jackie.'

She nodded numbly. The two had become close as photojournalists for a Washington paper—the *Times Herald*—Marella seemed to recall, before Benno moved on to *Paris Match* and Jackie to no career at all.

Of course Marella herself knew all about the power of manipulating an image from her work at *Vogue* with Blumenfeld. Her *head* knew that this was craft. But her gut . . .

'We were all *together*—the entire *time*!' distress creeping into Jackie's tone. 'I just don't see how they achieved it.'

'Angles,' said Benno, looking over her shoulder.

Lee joined them. 'Look—there's the edge of my shirt!' There was, in one version of Jackie's stroll through the piazza with Gianni, a lemon-rind sliver of Lee's striped tunic. 'And Marella—there's your shadow.'

Next to Gianni there was a shade of a figure, cut from the image beyond a nebulous reflection, as if its owner had conveniently stepped just outside the frame.

'Did it make the *Times*?' Jackie asked.

Stas rifled through the papers. 'Yep.' Checking the next in the stack, '*Post* as well.'

Jackie sank into her chair, deflated. 'Perhaps we shouldn't go into town.'

'*Senza senso!*' Gianni scoffed. 'Rosa!' he called to the local woman Lee had employed as their cook, who had arrived to clear their plates. 'My dear woman, bring us champagne!'

Lee laughed. 'Champagne? For breakfast?'

Marella smiled. It was another Agnelli eccentricity. When his father had died and the adolescent Agnelli brood were left to their own devices by a mother as untamed as they, champagne and pineapple juice became their daily breakfast. The ritual was only questioned when they were discovered lounging around half dressed by the pool at the family's Cap-Martin villa by their grandmother. Gianni answered Lee's inquiry as Marella knew he would—with the words the young Agnellis had used in reply to their *nonna* when challenged—'Why not? It's good.'

Marella loved how well she knew him. She could predict what he would say before the words left his lips. He was her one great love—her *only* love. She was a bit of a sage when it came to Gianni. There was something she sensed in him at that very moment, something intensely alive. Stirring . . . awakening that old doubt in Marella which she thought she had banished for good. The feeling she'd tamed years earlier, with the exit of Domietta Hercolani. For the first time since, she felt the firm pedestal on which she balanced quake, reminding her of its impermanence.

Gianni whisked the bottle from Rosa when she reappeared, popping the cork with a flourish. 'We *won't* let these vultures spoil our pleasure!' he decreed, making his way around the table, filling glasses. 'Let's sail to Capri! And Positano—and everywhere in between! We'll drink wine till our heads spin—and mingle with *la bella gente* in the piazzas! We'll follow them to the nightclubs and let loose. We'll do the rumba and the cha-cha and the twist! Let's dance and sing and flirt with everything in sight!'

He pecked Jackie's cheek, then Lee's, then Benno's. By this point laughter reigned, the mood shifting from gloom to ebullience. Marella beamed, familiar with such transformations. He was a magus, *L'Avvocato*. In a very different way, he was much like Truman. Brimming with boyish mischief. Infecting those around him with the thrill of the possible.

Gianni raised his glass—'To *la bella vita!*'

The others followed suit. '*La bella vita!*'

He tossed back his glass and—laughing with exuberance in the spirit of excess—hurled it against the ancient stones, where it shattered into a thousand glorious pieces.

THE *AGNETA*, HER CLARET-COLORED SAILS rippling in the wind, was Gianni's kingdom. Here he indisputably was *il re*, and his credo was one of excess. He greeted his guests with embraces—Radziwills, Grazianis, D'Ursos, and lone Kennedy, Jacqueline (Caroline having remained ensconced at the Villa Episcopo with Secret Service detail, doubling as nannies).

'We call it Negroni.' Gianni presented a glass to Jackie, as if bestowing nectar of the gods. Vivid crimson liquid, ice and slivers of orange, passed on silver trays.

'What's in it?' she asked, bringing the glass to her lips.

'Campari—from Milan—vermouth di Torino from Piedmont at the foot of the Alps . . . and *uno spruzzo di* gin.' The grin suggested more than 'a splash' had been employed. 'It is more than a drink, Negroni; it is a way of life.'

His passengers imbibed the bitters and botanicals, which clung to them like a gentle opiate, rendering them drowsy. The Grazianis lounged—Nicole resting her pale head on Benno's ribcage; reconfigured, Benno using her orbed buttocks as a cushion. Sandro and Mario played chess for hours on end. Jackie read—or fell asleep with a book on her chest, the open page moist with suntan oil and perspiration.

Marella was far from certain, but did she not see Gianni appraise Jackie's athletic form as she sunbathed in her modest maillot (the President having forbidden the potential scandal of a bikini)? Was it her imagination, but lying in loungers beside one another, did their fingers brush on *purpose*, or by chance, as they changed positions? She summarily dismissed such thoughts, remembering too well a time in her past . . .

And yet, was it an accident that they seemed to forever be seated or walking close to one another? Yes, photographers could employ tricks to fuel their fictive narratives, but they could not create the proximity in the first place. A photograph could be manipulated, yet it could equally capture hidden truths.

Lee sketched, until she tired of it, or found herself distracted, as she was when—late on their second afternoon—a solitary speedboat was spotted, approaching in the distance. Jackie was roused from half-slumber, for fear it might be a pack of paparazzi having discovered their whereabouts. Marella thought it more likely to be one of the flotilla of Secret Service crafts bobbing just out of eyeshot, arranged by Agent Hill to keep a discreet distance. The motor's wasp-buzz increased in volume, though the vessel seemed inhabited not by insect, nor water beast, but by avian, perched on the prow. Enormous black wings flapping in the breeze—a black crow, at odds with water so green and a sky so blue they seemed to meet and evanesce in the most exquisitely blinding of suns. Drawing closer, the crow took the shape of a figure in priestly robes, clinging to the back of a motor launch traveling at speed.

'That must be for me,' Lee brightened. '*Stas!*' Her husband was roused from a nap in the shade and both Radziwills moved toward the stern, where they waved at the approaching figure.

Marella, sunbathing beside Jackie, watched the curious display. Turning in her lounger, Jackie relaxed once more, as she explained— 'It's an emissary from the Vatican.'

'From the *Vatican* . . . ?' Marella frowned.

'Yes. Lee and I went to see the Pope when we were in Rome. Officially it was me alone, but in fact it was both of us.' Then, with a thrill of imparting a secret, Jackie's voice grew more breathless than its breathy norm. 'Lee wants an annulment, you see.'

'From Stas?'

'Goodness no!' Jackie giggled. 'From her first husband—Michael Canfield. English. Publishing heir.' Then with disdain, 'A starter marriage. To get out from under our mother's thumb—or to beat me to the punch. Who knows. Anyhow, she wants to marry Stas—'

'I thought they were already . . .'

'In civil terms, yes. But they're desperate to be married properly. To erase that first messy business. One shouldn't say, but I do think our . . . situation. Jack being Catholic, the first Catholic *President* . . . Well, it *is* pulling some fairly delicate strings, but what can one do? Lee is family.'

Marella watched from a distance as the priest clambered from the speedboat onto the *Agneta* deck with the unsteadiness of a drunkard dismounting a rowboat. She had of course heard of such arrangements. In Italy, where divorce was illegal, annulments were the only means of ridding oneself of one spouse to make way for another. She found it alarming, the casualness with which they were approached, and the frequency. She knew at least a dozen wives who had been summarily disposed of in such a manner so that their husbands might marry again. She couldn't help but think of the Coupés coming off the assembly line at the Fiat factory in Lingotto—new autos customers were eager to trade their former models in for. How tenuous this century was; change was the ethos of the age. How different was Marella's thinking, for hers was a mindset that embraced something all the more for having been time-tested. A piece of antiquity, a Renaissance painting. A marriage . . .

It is what had terrified her about Gianni's flirtation with Domietta Hercolani. Now, watching Lee broker the details of her own arrangement with the Vatican envoy in her bikini from a lounge chair, Marella found it pushing the boundaries of absurdity.

Gianni appeared in a towel, drink in hand. Ever the gracious host, he delivered a Negroni to the perspiring priest. Then, removing the towel without a shred of self-consciousness, he bared his naked form and dove off the stern of the yacht. Bronzed. Godlike.

'Well . . .' Nicole Graziani grinned slyly, raising her shades to assess matters. 'The man who has everything really does have *everything.*'

THE DAYS BLED TOGETHER, PLEASURE BLURRING the edges between one experience and the next.

They toured Greco-Roman ruins in Paestum—wandered amid the temples of Hera and Poseidon. Gianni arranged to anchor the yacht offshore and travel by speedboat to a beach in Praiano, where a nightclub—the Africana Famous—had in recent months been built into the natural caverns overlooking the sea. Their party of eight entered a dim space, eyes adjusting to the lilac glow of chandeliers hung between stalactites. They squeezed into a circular booth cut into the rocks, joining the glitterati in their dark suits and shifts, smoking an endless stream of Fumos. Coolly watching a scandalous floor show—African dancers covered in warpaint gyrating to primal drums, one tormenting a woman in a leopard-skin bodysuit. She sprawled submissively beneath their shields and spears. Patrons looked on, swilling champagne in the smoke-thick cavern, pulsing with percussion and the sultry wail of a saxophone.

Marella felt Gianni pull her close, holding her tight through a tender bossa nova. She gripped his jacket—which smelled faintly of suntan oil—as they danced. The tempo quickened, and Marella found herself spun into Mario's arms for a cha-cha, then Benno's for a mambo. She watched over their shoulders as Gianni took his turn partnering Lee, then Nicole, then joined Jackie at the table for a cigarette. He pulled Mrs. Kennedy back onto the floor when an Italian rock-and-roller took the stage, and they danced the Twist, hips swiveling with subtle allure. The space was packed. Feverish. The music played on and they continued in an intoxicating whirl of partners passed back and forth until they collapsed at a rock-carved table to recover. At a quarter past four they descended the steps to the beach, where they piled into the waiting speedboat, motoring back to the anchored *Agneta*, singing—

'Volare! Wooooaaaah-ohhhhh! Cantare, whoo-ohhhh-ohhh-ohhh!'—into the clear night sky. A mythic sky, endless, on the cusp of day.

THE NEXT MORNING ONE OF THE SECURITY BOATS delivered the stack of morning papers.

JACKIE AND L'AVVOCATO: WILD NIGHT IN PIRATES' DEN!

'Oh dear,' Jackie sighed.

The smoky nightclub. The African floor show. Bodies on the dance floor, pressed close amid the haze. Their party entering and exiting the Africana Famous.

'But where *were* they?' Marella asked, perplexed.

Benno studied the photographs. 'They must have been in the club. And on the terrace.'

'I didn't notice them.'

'They have their ways. Telescopic lenses. Hidden cameras. Built into lapels, or briefcases. Even into the beehives of female accomplices.'

'I suppose—' Jackie said, halting in her fashion, so that one was never quite certain if a statement was finished or not, '— that's the end of that. We should head back to Ravello.'

Gianni grabbed another paper—**GIANNI E JACQUELINE IN AMORE**—crumpling it in his fist. 'Damn these vultures to hell! We *won't* change our plans! We'll sail to Capri as planned,' then, to Jackie, 'You still want to see it, yes?'

'Well— I did *so* want to. And to perhaps get some of those divine palazzo pajamas—I *do* admire your choice, Marella. I'd love to take a pair back home.'

Marella smiled. 'I'm sure the Countess would be delighted.' The Countess, their dear friend Irene Galitzine. The Russian Chanel. Her pajamas-as-evening-wear were *facevano furore* all across Europe. Countess Galitzine lived in a rented Medici villa on the isle of Capri.

Gianni rose with purpose. 'So it's settled. We sail on! Let them try and stop us.' As he strode out to make arrangements, Agent Hill's speedboat arrived. Gianni waved him aboard.

Hill made his way to the gallery, where they were lingering over coffee.

'Good morning, Mr. Hill. Join us. Would you care for some toast?'

'Thank you, but I've eaten. Mrs. Kennedy.' He handed Jackie a telegram. 'This arrived for you this morning. From the White House.'

Jackie beamed, tearing the envelope open as her cohort began to discuss morning plans.

'Marella,' said Benno, 'I'm keen to photograph the Faraglioni rocks when we hit Capri. Care to join me?' They'd formed a bond over the past week, Marella having reminded Benno how much he loved experimental photography, removed from the bread and butter of society image churning; Benno having reminded Marella of a world that she had lost touch with these nine years.

Nicole was debating with the Radziwills, 'I know we've *done* the Green, but shouldn't we give the Blue Grotto a whirl . . . ?'

'Jacks . . . ?' said Lee, noting her sister's expression. 'You all right . . . ?'

The color had indeed drained from Jackie's face. She looked to Lee, handing her the telegram. 'From Jack.' She rose and left the table. Lee read the message and set it back down, scampering after Jackie. Stas snatched the paper and read it aloud.

Four words, crystalline in their sparseness:

MORE CAROLINE. LESS GIANNI.

MARELLA ARRANGED A PICNIC (chicken terrine in Amalfi lemon aspic) while Benno gathered their camera equipment. Nicole, snorkeling gear. When they departed around noon, the Radziwills were already stretched out in the sun. Sandro and Mario were at their chessboard, having resumed a game from the afternoon before. Jackie was nowhere to be seen, having spent the morning in her cabin.

As Marella, Nicole, and Benno climbed into the auxiliary boat and started its motor, Gianni, floating a short distance from the *Agneta*, swam up to see them off.

'Last chance, *Avvocato*!'

'*No, grazie*, Benno. I've had enough photographs for the time being.' Then, grinning at Marella, '*Divertiti, angelo.*' He blew her a kiss, and backstroked toward the yacht.

Motoring on, the Grazianis and Marella found themselves gradually drawn into waters so blue, the sky skewed violet by comparison. Looming before them, three jagged, sculptural rock formations rising majestically from the sea. The Faraglioni.

'They have names, you know,' said Marella, for whom they'd held a special magic since girlhood. 'The large one is Stella, star. The smallest, Mezzo. And in between, Fuori. Some say these are the very rocks from which the sirens might have crooned, luring Ulysses and his men.'

Benno gave a low whistle. 'Well . . . one can see how the poor bastard would have been tempted!'

As they drew closer, Nicole shimmied out of her sundress and slipped into the water. Marella and Benno reached for their cameras. Fuori gave the impression of movement, though when one looked closer it was in fact lapis-tinted lizards crawling across the craggy surface. Marella held the box of her Rolleiflex at waist level, looking down at the image in the frame. She positioned it at an angle at which the jagged silhouette resembled a woman's breast, the negative space of liquid consuming the form like a hungry mouth.

THEY RETURNED LATE THAT AFTERNOON, Nicole exhausted from her swim, Marella and Benno satiated from a rewarding artistic outing. Just in time for the cocktail hour.

'My kingdom for a Negroni . . .' Benno enthused, flopping down in a deck banquette beside Lee.

'Well, you'll have to mix it yourself. Gianni's not back yet.'

Marella joined them, kicking off her sandals, looking out to the waters below. 'Is he out for another swim? We didn't pass him coming in.'

Lee yawned. 'He went ashore.'

'Oh . . . ?'

'With Jackie. And Mario.'

'Without the rest of us . . . ?'

'Well, Gianni thought it would do Jackie good to get out. She wanted to buy some palazzo pajamas like yours, so he took her to Countess Galitzine's.'

'I thought we'd discussed *all* of us going to Villa Vivara,' Marella said, forcing a smile. 'I'll make the Negronis.' As she left to fetch supplies she turned back. 'Did they say when they were coming back . . . ?' This with practiced calm.

'I assume in time for dinner?'

And yet cocktail hour came and went. No Gianni. No Jackie. No Mario.

Marella knew the third member of the expedition party was designed to lend their absence the appearance of innocence. Darkness fell and still the wayward threesome had not returned. The remaining guests were getting restless. They had planned to motor in to the island for dinner. And yet now . . . How might one hope to coordinate a rendezvous?

'Shall we just dine on board?' Marella offered, after Lee and Nicole had mentioned hunger pains, despite having depleted a tray of antipasto.

'*Nooooooo!*' came the collective whine. 'I *do* so want to go ashore now. Shall we?'

Various schemes were tossed out. They could take the auxiliary boat. Stay a night at the Quisisana, the hotel of the moment. They could surely find the missing trio in such a small enclave? Or at the very least be prepared to form a search party to descend on Countess Galitzine's Villa Vivara in time for breakfast? The surprise element of this plan pleased them enormously, especially Lee and Benno, who began to whisper conspiratorially. Each disappeared to their cabins to fetch overnight bags, while Marella stayed on deck, staring up at the stars.

'But Marella darling, aren't you coming?' they asked, as Stas and Benno sent the steward to start up the *motoscafo*.

She shook her head, braving a smile, as she had so many times before. 'I think I'll stay here. I feel certain they'll return, and I wouldn't want Gianni to worry,' waving away their concerns. 'Besides, I have a bit of a headache from being in the sun all day. I really would prefer to stay.'

'No!' they protested. 'You must come!' they cajoled.

But she would not be persuaded, so the party clambered into the tiny boat and motored toward the lights of Capri, as Marella stood waving on the *Agneta*'s polished deck.

When they'd gone, she went to the galley, having long sent the staff to their berths. She made herself a simple pasta, which she found—sitting alone in the salon—that she had no appetite for. She poured a glass from the decanter of wine breathing at the center of the table set for nine. She checked her wristwatch—well past midnight. She took her glass and wandered back up to wait on deck, reclining in a lounger, in time falling into a fitful sleep.

She dreamed she was in a rowboat on inky waters, pulled by a forceful current. She looked to see the figure of an Italian princess with honeycomb hair, luring her toward the first of three jagged rocks. A low, melodic voice pulling Marella's vessel ever closer. Another voice joined in from the second, as the lapis-tinted lizards crawled across the cragged silhouette of a buxom stone goddess. From the third, a breathless voice—halting, eager. Merging in a siren's song, drawing Marella closer, ever closer to the perilous rocks—

She woke with a start. Alone. The old panic a cleaver in her chest. She again checked the time: well past two. She paced the deck, muttering to herself, to the heartless stars—

'Wretched Marella! Why these sighs? This anguish! He's yet *again* betrayed me. Played me for the fool. The loyal wife who waits, who forgives. But still . . .'

She had a flash of the lines around his eyes when he smiled, as if radiating from two equal points. Of the lone patches of silver hair in the sea of black. Of the ease with which he bore his bronzed skin, his delicious physicality. The thrill of the possible she felt every time she watched him enter a room and lingered long after he'd left it. And as ever, she softened. The swell of warmth and love for him returned, as it always did, and he could do no wrong.

She retired to her stateroom, where she undressed and crawled into sheets of cool Egyptian cotton. Monogrammed with her initials, entwined with Gianni's. She knew that she would forgive him. Despite the dull thrum of anguish, the secret yearning for vengeance. For all were outweighed by one simple truth: When she gazed upon his features, her heart still thrilled.

It was well after four when she heard it. The low growl of a speedboat, increasing in ferocity as it neared.

The sound of *L'Avvocato* returning.

Her heart felt it might break through her heron's breast, beating in time with the motor, just outside the porthole. Then . . . silence. Footsteps above—Two sets? Three?—followed by the muted tones of . . . strings? The baroque plucking of a—was it a lute?

Marella slipped into a robe and tiptoed up the stairwell to the deck above. There she hung back, watching from the shadows.

A lone musician sat on the prow, plucking at a mandolin.

A few feet away, there they were, forms merging in the moonlight. Gianni, holding Jackie close. Bare feet shuffling against the polished deck, dancing to the quiet strains of the mandolin. Jackie was wearing a pair of Countess Galitzine's palazzo pajamas in pale green silk, shimmering like a mermaid's tail in the reflection of the moon-bright sea.

Marella held her breath as Gianni whispered something into Jackie's ear, though she couldn't be certain what. She thought she saw Jackie nod, but she may well have been tossing her chestnut hair, a habit she was as prone to indulge as the baby voice and halting speech. Marella thought she saw the mandolinist's gaze meet her own across the divide, with what she *might* have interpreted as an expression of compassion.

It was there that Marella left them, just before dawn, dancing beneath the *Agneta*'s claret-colored sails, which billowed gracefully in the breeze.

THE NEXT MORNING SHE FOUND GIANNI alone on deck, eating the rest of her pasta from the previous evening. He grinned at her . . . then, finding the gesture unrequited, resumed his ingestion.

Marella approached, sitting down beside him.

'I suppose you're angry.'

She shook her head in reply.

'I took Jackie to the Countess—for those ridiculous pajamas.'

She nodded.

'And then she wanted to see the Number Two nightclub, so we *all* went—the Countess, Mario, Jackie and I—meaning to stop briefly. But of course you know how those places are. By the time we left, the waters were too choppy to return right away. Dangerous . . .'

Again, she held his gaze.

'Well, dammit! Say *something*!'

Marella hesitated, then leaned in, placing her head for a brief moment in his lap. He ran his fingers through her short curls. She lifted entreating eyes.

'My love, may I ask something of you?'

'I knew it. You're angry. You want to make a scene.'

'My darling, I'm no longer angry. It's pity that I feel. I no longer care where you were, or with whom. Doesn't matter. I no longer remember your lies. It's just a favor I want to ask.'

'What is it you want—a gold leash on which to keep me close?'

'Don't laugh at me.'

'Laugh at you? What for! What do you want from me, *angelo*?'

'That you change your ways. That you slow down.' It was the first time she'd asked anything of him in a serious way. No crying,

128

no yelling. Asking. Gianni stared at her, taken aback. Then he started to laugh—a defiant, boisterous laugh.

'Good for you, *mio amore*! Keeping me in line!'

'*Please* don't laugh.'

'Good for you!' He threw his head back with mirth.

'I'm worried . . .'

'We're fine, *angelo*.'

'No—I'm worried . . . for *you*.'

He sat, silent, a shadow from the blood sail passing over his countenance. Marella rose, and—in an unexpected gesture— Gianni grabbed her hand. He placed it over his heart and held it there. And in that moment, he seemed to Marella ageless and ancient at once. He looked to her like that lost boy, orphaned by speed; the beautiful satyr, kissed by Dionysus' lips; a very old man, for whom the definition of hell would be dying alone. She felt, hand on his breast, what made his heart beat. *Velocità! La bella vita! The glory of humanity!*

And in that moment she knew. To change him would be to diminish the very thing she loved most in him. 'Ah!'—barely audible, Marella released an exhalation of breath. She stood for a long moment, feeling the beating of his heart, his hand holding hers. Finally he squeezed her palm, then released it.

'Now come. Let me eat. And if you wish, eat with me.' He lifted his fork, twisting a ribbon of pasta around it, passing it to her.

Marella resumed her seat at his side. She took the fork, pouring two glasses of wine. They sat, wordlessly. Sharing a meal, watching the new sun crest the horizon.

CODA

IT WASN'T LONG BEFORE THE RUMORS began to surface—salacious ones.

Ones we take little pleasure in repeating, save to refute them, and certainly—let us be clear—these in no way reflect our *personal* views.

Rumors of an Agnelli envoy being flown back to Washington to retrieve Jackie's diaphragm. Or did they say it was sent direct, care of Air Force One?

Truly vicious whispers over the years, by the most callous of shit-stirrers. John John looking more like Gianni than Jack Kennedy. (We blush to admit that we each paused to count the gestational months, and were relieved to find that the timing simply didn't add up.)

Those in the Radziwill party have invariably denied that anything untoward took place.

'Jackie was devoted to Jack,' Benno has insisted. 'She was all about Caroline on that trip. Waterskiing. Making spaghetti. Real maternal stuff.'

'Gianni wasn't interested in complications,' Mario, who knew *L'Avvocato*'s habits well, has concurred. '*That* would have been complicated.'

'Preposterous,' says Lee, lighting a defensive cigarette when we quiz her over lunch. But then we've known Lee to bend a few truths in her time, especially when it comes to her sister.

Of course the most dangerous of rumors can be traced back to Truman, who is the only one apart from Lee who knew all the parties well and thus claimed to speak with authority.

'Oh, *trust* me,' Truman would say, a few Negronis in—usually his segue into such indiscretions—'I *know* what happened that August on the Isle o' Capri! I wasn't there . . . but I have it on *very* good authority.'

When his source was demanded, he batted those flaxen lashes.

'Noooo! A stool pigeon I is not—I keeps my sources to myself!'

When we'd give up—*All right, just tell us!*—he'd lower his voice, almost to a whisper, so confidential was the intelligence.

'Weeeeullll. Let's just say that juuuuust before dawn, on the thirteenth of August, Mrs. Kennedy received a *proposal*.'

A marriage proposal? We'd look perplexed.

'Well, of *course*, honey. I wouldn't sully my tale with any other kind!'

But they were both already married!

Truman would fish the orange—'the healthy bit'—from his Negroni, insisting, '*Lee* was mid-annulment . . . I *told* you about the Pope on a speedboat, to whom Gianni flashed his package.'

It was a priest—not the actual Pope.

'Perhaps *another* Barnacle Bouvier was gunning for Vatican services.'

But Jack Kennedy was alive at the time! And still a sitting President!

He'd grin, sucking the pulpy orange from its peel.

'I couldn't begin to speculate. I's just knows what I'm *told*.'

FOR ALL TRUMAN'S EFFORTS, the strand of buzz we most enjoyed took a surprising slant.

The following year JFK made his own presidential visit to Italy.

Like Jackie before him, he charmed local leaders to common men; visited the Pope and caused a paparazzi frenzy. Yet there was one night of his visit that remained, officially, unaccounted for. It is known that he rented a magnificent villa at the foot of the Alps in Lake Como . . . a short drive from Turin.

It is said that he dismissed the staff, awaiting a highly confidential guest.

The locals still speak in hushed tones of a Fiat car pulling into the grounds, a heron-like woman with an exceptionally long neck behind the wheel.

A woman who looked a great deal like Donna Marella Caracciolo di Castagneto Agnelli.

When asked years later if it had been her, if she had arrived to spend an evening alone with President Kennedy, Marella would shrug, cryptically.

'Perhaps. Perhaps not. I really can't remember.'

W ORD LATER GETS AROUND THAT TRU has taken special care to
mail Babe a copy of the *Esquire* edition the day before it
hits newsstands.

It arrives first class in a brown Manila envelope, he having
paid extra for the service. He's tucked a note inside, penned on
the Tiffany stationery Babe had helped him select: eggshell correspondence cards, with a dapper navy monogram.

For My Beautiful Babyling, always my muse. Your Tru.

The envelope goes unopened, lost in a stack of mail, when
Babe spends the morning at Sloan Kettering—needle-pricked
and pumped full of chemicals—then the better part of the
afternoon at Kenneth's for a full servicing: facial peel, brows
arched and nails lacquered in an attempt to still feel human.
She misses having her hair done; these days she hides the
duck-fuzz she has left beneath chic, silk turbans—or bespoke
wigs, masterfully styled, which she carries off so gracefully a
stranger would be hard-pressed to know that anything was
wrong.

She summons the strength that evening to host the Guinnesses
for dinner, but finds she tires before the meal is served and
retreats to her bed.

The envelope is thus discovered early the next morning, as
Babe sifts through the neglected mail. When she sees Truman's
brief missive, she's delighted by the gesture and beams with
pride as she always does when he sends her his work. She takes
it into the oak-paneled dining room, opens it to the page he's
carefully marked with a gold paperclip, and begins to read, over

the little she can stomach of her sectioned grapefruit and espresso.

At first she is amused, chuckling at his cleverness, placing her and Bets next to Jackie and Lee and other recognizable faces, in a setting we know so intimately. La Côte Basque. Haunt *de rigueur*. How funny to be cast as a 'background artist.'

The more she reads, however, the more she begins to feel a tightening in her chest . . . the grapefruit sticking in her throat. From the second paragraph, Babe knows that this is bad. As Tru's ventriloquism-show gets going in earnest, his Lady Ina dummy is given Slim's catchphrases. Regurgitates her cadences. Her details appropriated, down to her pet lunch order—Soufflé Furstenberg—the spinach, the custard, the specially sunken yolks.

It's clear that Jonesy is an idealized version of Truman, captured by Lady Ina and forced to dine and gab—she having been stood up by the Duchess of Windsor.

The others are easily guessed, an eeriness in their thin disguises: faces concealed with cheap dime-store masks that could snap with the snip of a string. The Ann Woodward bit strikes Babe as particularly vicious, but nothing like what Babe feels are shameless shots at Slim. Slim, whom Truman so adores!

Slim—in reality recently split with Husband Number Three, His Lordship Kenneth Keith. Babe knows how much Slim loathed that whole English horsey set. She had too much pizzazz for foul teeth and fox hunts. It simply wasn't a match. Keith was dull, dull, dull. The opposite of Slim. We'd all commented on it— *How could she stand it?* (What had gone unsaid is the very fact that Truman has so cruelly pointed out in print . . . It was obvious to anyone why Slim lasted as long as she did—*At least she wasn't alone.*)

Babe is stunned to find that Tru has painted 'Lady Ina' as a champagne-guzzling wreck by the end of her Jonesy lunch, sobbing into her soufflé, confessing fears of aging and dying on her own. She has Slim's height and breeziness. Carries Slim's Bulgari compact. Refers to Papa Hemingway, to whom we all know Slim was close. The likeness is uncanny. Then there are the digs about Coolbirth being '*fortyish*,' on her way to Mexico to end yet *another* marriage. Worse still, he paints the Coolbirths as a stodgy English prick and crass western broad—two people who barely tolerate one another, whose split is instigated by Lord Cool, who rejects Lady Ina while she's stuck beside him on a transatlantic flight, stuffed full of booze and Thorazine. Most heartbreaking of all is the vulnerability Truman foists upon her.

Slim must have discussed these fears with him, after what happened with Leland . . . having kept her secrets close for years (while telling *ours* in their place, we're quick to note, indulging in a moment of bitterness).

For Truman to single Slim out in the wake of a divorce as someone needy, as sour milk, past its expiration date . . . Babe thinks the breach unconscionable.

How could Truman say these things?

As Babe reads on she can't help but note that the prose is lewd as well. Gone are the honey drawls, the croaks and squeaks and cicada drones. Gone, the voices of these things from whence he came, the music that shaped his prose.

Truman has always had a salacious side, but *this* reads as pornographic. An ex-lover of Ina's is mentioned, a photo of whom she keeps tucked in a copy of Dinesen's *Out of Africa*, an author Babe knew Slim to love, she having met her through Truman on their famed trip to Copenhagen. The image depicts said lover with his member exposed, posing for the camera. A lover Ina fondly identifies as 'Dill' on the back of the snapshot.

And then there is the Sheets business.

The moment Babe reads it, she feels in her bones that it's Bill. Despite her Good Wife pretense, she does know that Bill is who he is. More than she lets on. Far more than Bill is aware of . . .

Years earlier Babe had found evidence of a love affair—not Bill's usual passing bit of tail, but a proper fling. There were—of course—dozens, but this is the one Babe uncovered, rifling through Bill's desk. There were jewelry receipts. Hotel bills. So cliché they seemed like evidence from a cheap B-movie.

There were letters from the girl, who clearly thought her position more secure than it had been. When it ended—Bill having feared she was becoming too attached—she flung herself from the nineteenth floor of a third-rate hotel, leaving a note for him in her room, thanking him for his generosity, without the faintest trace of irony.

Babe felt the bile rising in her throat as she read it. She'd heard about the girl in the papers, who made her grisly exit front-page news, though they'd kept Mr. Paley's name out of their reports, as had the New York Police Department. (It's been whispered there were generous 'donations' made to editors and precinct chiefs, courtesy of the network.)

Babe had of course phoned Truman right away. He arrived within the hour to find her chain-smoking L&Ms, filling three open suitcases on the bed with carefully folded clothes.

One look at her bloodshot eyes and he knew.

(Actually, Truman had known all this before . . . He had introduced Bill to the young lady in question, had helped arrange the hotels, even selected the jewelry. He'd told us he had, the little two-faced pimp . . . Of course this Babe knows nothing of . . . It would kill her if she knew.)

'Oh, Babyling—What do you think you're doing?'

'Leaving. I can't do this anymore. I just can't—I deserve better. I deserve more.'

'Sweet-pie. You deserve the world on a solid-gold stick. And guess what? You got it.'

Tru had gestured in the manner of a Renaissance jester to the Park Avenue palace around them.

Babe shook her head, taking a deep drag, dumping a stole into the nearest case. A stray lock of hair had escaped her neat bouffant. She pushed it from her eyes, uncharacteristically frazzled.

'I have nothing.'

'Baby, you have everything. Everything there is to have.'

'I don't have love. And that's all that matters.'

'But darling, you do! You have me.' Confessor, confidant, he opened his miniature arms to her and she fell into them, weeping on his shoulder. Truman stroked her hair, smoothing the silver strand back in place. 'Listen to me . . . I love you, Barbara Paley. I love you more than life itself.' He leaned in and kissed her forehead, with the most exquisite tenderness.

How she wished this was enough to make a marriage. If only she loved Bill half as much as she loved Truman . . . If only Bill loved her at all.

'Babyling. You must listen very carefully. You, my angel-girl, have ascended into the clouds of heaven. And you're gonna stay there. Come hell or high water.'

Babe stared at him, listening, his graveness commanding her attention.

'You are Mrs. William S. Paley—goddess. Bill didn't create her. *You* did. You're a glorious work of art. And I'll love you. I'll love you forever.' Babe sank back into his arms, quiet as he stroked her hair. 'Darling, just think of being Mrs. William S. Paley as a job. The most wonderful job in the whole wide world. And remember—you have the one thing that's better than love . . .'

Babe turned her head to meet Tru's eyes.

'What's that?'

His thin lips had curled into an infectious smile.

'Power.'

AFTER BABE HAS PLACED HER EARLY CALL to Slim (the lapse in protocol acceptable in a crisis), she phones Bill at the office, something she hardly ever does. She greets the CBS switchboard operator by name, inquiring after her children—then waits for Bill to answer, enduring an anesthetizing muzak rendition of 'Satisfaction' as she holds.

When he comes on the line, his voice is clipped—'Paley.'

'Darling?'

'Oh, hello, Baby. Everything all right?'

'Yes, of course . . .' A pause, while Babe fingers the glossy pages.

'Can it wait till tonight, whatever it is? It's a hell of a day here, trying to hammer out this scheduling and—'

'Has anyone *said* anything to you today . . .' Babe interrupts him, something she almost never does, '. . . about Truman?'

No reply.

She can just picture him in the high-backed swivel chair she'd selected for his office, an Eames for Herman Miller, pausing to read a memo, or to open an envelope. (*Or* receive oral favors from the interns in the office, or so the rumors go . . .) Classic Bill. Always juggling ten things at once. It was seldom she ever had his full attention.

Babe, undeterred, persists—'*Truman*. Has anyone mentioned anything?'

'What? No. Baby, can't this wait?'

'Has anyone asked you, today . . . about *bed sheets*?'

The line goes ominously quiet. She hears shuffling in the background, the clean slice of a letter opener splitting a seal. Then—

'I have no idea what you're talking about, Babe. Why would anyone ask me about Truman or bed sheets? And the two in the same sentence seems more than a little implausible, wouldn't you say.' He laughs, but it rings hollow.

'What about *Esquire*? Is anyone talking about that?'

Bill, irritable now, 'Look, Babe, I've got a dozen meetings on my plate. I don't have time for phone games. I'll see you at home. Be good.'

The line goes dead.

'Be good,' Babe thinks. If anyone needed to 'be good' it seems to Babe it's Bill who warrants the behavioural warning.

WHEN BILL COMES HOME EARLY THAT NIGHT (nothing short of the Second Coming) and with flowers (something he never thinks to do), Babe knows not only has Bill read Truman's article, but that he is—without question—the model for Sidney Dillon.

And if Bill is Dill and Slim undoubtably Ina . . . could that part be true as well? Has her whole life been a sham? In the span of nine pages Babe finds herself questioning the three individuals she's most loved and trusted for over twenty years.

As the truth sinks in, she can't decide who she's more angry with—Bill for the transgression, Truman for writing it down, or Slim for knowing and not telling her.

WE'LL LATER LEARN THAT TRUMAN sent a copy of his *Esquire* tale to Bill's office as well, marked to The Sheets with an identical golden paperclip.

Bill had opened it and skimmed the piece while Babe was on the line, he'll later tell Slim, as they commiserate over their shared Scotches in a hidden bar along the street from the St. Regis.

'Lady Ina' and 'Sidney Dillon' are indeed old friends.

They've always shared a chumminess, shared *a lot* more than that . . . But this Truman business has renewed a deeper kinship they haven't taken the time to nurture in ages.

'I can't believe the little shit would have the balls to go there,' Bill grumbles to Slim, in an out-of-the-way booth in outer Siberia.

'I can't believe he used *me* as his fucking mouthpiece, the sick little fuck.'

Bill pauses, two rounds in. 'Did *I* tell him that goddamn story or did *you*?' he suddenly thinks to ask.

'At this point, who the hell knows?' Slim shakes her head, at a genuine loss to remember. 'I swear I'll never speak to him again.'

A vow. Resolute.

'Oh, *I* will,' Bill assures her. 'There's more than one way to skin a snake.'

Slim tosses back her drink. 'I'll tell you this—if he was doused in gasoline and set on fire like my poor little Buddy I wouldn't pause to piss on him. He's dead to me.'

TRUMAN—A SAFE DISTANCE AWAY in Los Angeles, having made his temporary getaway— attempts to ring Babe from the West Coast, only to be told that she is 'not home' whenever he calls.

He tries Slim next, who simply hangs up at the sound of his girlish voice.

He gathers his nerve and rings Bill at his office, and is a little more than surprised when he's put through.

'Paley.'

'Bill . . . ?' Truman's voice comes out more tentative than he'd planned.

'Truman.' Neither friendly nor angry—*utterly* neutral.

Unable to read him, Truman weighs his options.

'I was just calling to say hellooooo, and that I've missed you both.'

'Hello, Truman.'

Then silence.

'How's Babyling . . . ?'

'Fine.'

'Ohhh, good. I was worried—not having heard from her . . .'

Silence.

'Soooooo, just wondering if you got the story that I sent you . . . ?'

'Yes. I believe I did.'

'Well, I sent one to *both* of you—so you could each have your very own copy.'

Silence still.

'Did you read it yet . . . ?'

'No, Truman, I don't believe we got around to it.'

Truman can hardly believe his ears. This is the *last* thing he'd expected. He shifts back and forth in his socks, jigging with impatience in his living room, a postmodern Rumpelstiltskin. It won't be too long now—we feel certain—before he makes a beeline for the bar cart.

'Well . . . when do you plan on reading it . . . ?' he asks, need creeping into his voice.

'Actually, Truman, I think someone must've thrown it out with the trash.'

'Well, I can send you new ones—personally!'

He jigs through the excruciatingly long pause before Bill delivers his cool blow—

'Truman, my wife is a very ill woman. We simply don't have time for such trivia.'

Thwack! Like a javelin to the chest, wounding with indifference.

'Your *wife*? You mean *Babyling*! Bill . . . it's *me*, for gawd's sake!'

Bill's satisfaction may as well have whooped and hollered, so resounding is his silence. (Slim will later concede that Bill's plan was *genius*, withholding the attention the arrogant little shit expected as his due.)

Finally—'Truman, I really must go. I have a very important call to take.'

Click.

The line goes dead, leaving the great author feeling very small indeed.

HE WRITES BABE A LONG LETTER from his trailer on the set of a third-rate film with an all-star cast, where he finds to his dismay that he cannot manage to play himself, the skill for which he'd been hired. (He really is dreadful, we'll concur, watching the cringe-worthy results in cinemas months later.) He carefully pens a plea explaining his tale, comparing it to Proust (to whose œuvre he'd introduced Babe in cozier times) but his missive goes unanswered.

He writes another, inviting her to lunch. Again no reply.

A third is returned-to-sender, unopened, the contents of which we cannot hope to know.

Deafening silence.

Gun-shy after the Bill call, he begs his darling Jack to telephone Babe on his behalf.

Babe has always had a soft spot for Jack, and Jack for Babe in turn—a fact of which Truman's well aware. She admires his steady calm, anchoring Truman to earth, weathering two decades' worth of storms— the angst, the art; the other toxic men, of whom Babe did *not* approve. She always felt for Jack, knowing that even the steadiest partner on earth could not hope to contain Truman's restiveness. Lord knows Jack has tried . . .

So when her maid says, 'Mr. Dunphy . . . ?' Babe accepts the call.

'Babe, I'm asking you—for me. Please. *Please* talk to Truman.'

'Oh, Jack,' a catch in her voice. 'I'm terribly sorry—I love Truman. Love him with every ounce of my being. But after what he did . . . Bill and I—we just can't.'

'He thought it was *art*, Babe. What he did with *In Cold Blood*. Reportage as fiction.'

'These were people's *lives*, Jack . . . People who trusted him.'

'He's a writer! You *knew* that. Writers write what they know. And he knows you better than anyone.'

Babe doesn't reply. She thinks she can hear static from another line . . .

'I'm begging you.' Jack takes a breath and gives it one last shot. 'You're the love of his life, Babe.' Neither bothers to argue. She knows that Jack is right. 'We both know this will ruin him.'

There is a long pause, which Babe silently weeps through, trying to compose herself. She doesn't want him to see her weakness. *Can't show it—can't . . .*

Finally, steadying her voice—'Oh, I don't know, Jack. Let me talk it over with Bill.'

After she hangs up, Jack watches the last of the evening light fade to darkness through the window, bracing himself to tell Truman that they've failed.

JACK CANNOT TEMPER HIS RAGE when Slim renounces the boy.

'Honestly, Truman. After all you did for that girl . . .? Fuck her.'

Thus Truman enlists one of his faceless, toxic beaux (. . . beaux we've declined to bother with—even in happier times. Beaux who have bruised and bloodied the boy; beaux unworthy of his talent and our company, with whom we refuse to engage) to act as an intermediary.

141

When Slim receives a call from one such gentleman, she, with her usual bluntness, makes it perfectly clear that there isn't any point.

'I'm on my way out. Whadda you want?'

'Look, Slim. Truman understands that you're very upset.'

'Truman understands right.'

'He thought you would think it was funny.'

'Well, I don't.'

'Do you really think Lady Ina was you?'

'I think that's exactly who she's supposed to be.'

Slim can suddenly hear it—breathing on the line. A third party, listening in.

Addressing him directly—

'And Truman . . .?'

The breathing faults as the culprit holds his breath.

A tiny voice, hardly more than a whisper—

'Yes, Big Mama?'

'You're not forgiven.'

And with those three words, the last she will ever speak to him, Slim hangs up the phone on her beloved Truheart, cutting him from her life like the cancer he's become.

TEN

1958

SLIM

FANDANGO

NOT SINCE BILLY WOODWARD WAS GUNNED DOWN by his trophy bride in Oyster Bay had Manhattan been so mesmerized by a single domestic scandal.

After all, dramas of this scope don't come along every day. The usual trysts—yawn. This season's splits—shrug. But a drama with an extended, star-studded cast, spanning five cities in three countries—and all that fuss for just three little people! The disproportion alone enthralls.

Who could tell what would touch a collective nerve. What might inspire New York's jaded bystanders to haul themselves from the passivity of the bench and root for one team or the other. Camps have been chosen, bets placed, favorites fiercely supported.

Most of us declare ourselves 'Slimites'—the term naturally coined by Truman. He has also given the ordeal a name, tired of the generic phrase previously employed in genteel circles, who heretofore referred to the unfortunate sequence of events discreetly as 'Topic A.'

Truman's christening is far more colorful: 'the Hayward–Churchill Fandango.' *Olé!* Especially clever, we agree, given that Slim was in Spain, oblivious, when the theft occurred.

In her absence, Tru has declared Babe the leader of the Slimites, taking the forefront defending Slim's position. Babe was Slim's best friend after all . . . and the guilt must be eating her alive. Frankly, the whole messy business has caused quite a *situation* among the Cushing sisters. Babe and Betsey, that is, Minnie wisely choosing to steer clear of her younger siblings' entanglements.

Not to confuse Babe's sister *Betsey* with Slim's pal *Betty*, as in Bacall. As in the film star, stage name Lauren. Aka Mrs. Bogart. The recently *widowed* Mrs. Bogart . . .

Both Bet-*sey* and Bet-*ty* had been unwitting catalysts in the whole chain of events, though both through entirely innocent requests.

If only Betsey hadn't promised to host the former Mrs. Churchill. If only she hadn't pawned the obligation off on Babe. Any number of factors could have altered the outcome.

Had Truman been in town that night, nothing untoward would have taken place (and how often can we say *that* about Truman?!)

'Did you know,' Tru would enthuse, delighted with his cleverness at the whole naming business, 'that quite *apart* from being *the* dance du jour with aristos back in the day, *Fandango* has a figurative meaning too? It's considered a synonym for: A. a quarrel, B. a big fuss, or C. a brilliant exploit. Can you believe that—?! Now don't all *three* just sum up what happened to Big Mama to a T . . . ?' His smug grin would widen and he'd slurp his sangria, satisfied. (We have to agree this is apposite, especially the 'big fuss' bit . . .)

If only Slim had kept her eye on the prize, looked after her own interests. But she was trying to be a friend. She's like that, Slim. Salt of the earth. There for a pal, no questions asked. So when Betty decided, a year after Bogie's death, that it was time to scrape herself off her terrazzo tile and live again, who better than Slim to orchestrate her resurrection? Slim, who had created her persona in the first place.

'You have to go, Nan,' Leland had agreed. Leland never called Slim 'Slim' as Howard had. She was Leland's 'Nan.' A vestige of the Nancy she'd long since left behind, in the ashes of her childhood in Salinas. 'After what she's been through, Betty's not asking much.'

144

Slim took his face in her hands and kissed him hard. She'd only just returned from four weeks in Russia with Truman. Yet there was Leland, so gorgeous about her turning around and packing her bags yet again. He'd always been a prince about these things, Leland. Most of the husbands kept shorter leashes.

'It's only a week. You can meet me in Paris and we'll head to Berlin from there.'

So it happened that Slim found herself in Spain with Betty, and Papa, when the Fandango began. And by the time she could hear the rhythmic clack of the castanets, the death rattle of the tambourine, the dancers in question were already a blur, whirling beyond her grasp.

THE PHONE RANG AT TEN FIFTY-FIVE, ON CUE.

Slim, carrying an armload of garments from her closet for review, raised the receiver from its Bakelite cradle.

'Morning, Truheart,' she answered, not bothering to question the caller's identity.

Ten fifty-five—Truman's morning work break.

'You're having lunch with me, Big Mama.'

'Can't.' She held a linen sundress to her Saluki frame, the fabric's buttery hue matching the light streak in her hair almost exactly.

'Why *not*?'

'Packing.' Tone firm.

'A girl's gotta eat.'

'I've got a lunch date.'

'With *whom*?'

'Shipwreck Kelly.'

'Well, cancel him.'

'I can't. We've been set for weeks.'

'You *can*, Big Mama. And you *will*.'

Slim laughed in spite of herself. His bossiness could be oddly endearing. She'd gotten used to it over long weeks on Siberian trains, where they'd fallen into the rhythms of an old married couple. 'And why,' she challenged, 'would I do something so ratty?'

'You're gonna cancel because your Truheart needs to see your shining face. And besides, you know you'll have a much better time with me than with dullsville Shit-wreck Kelly!'

'You know, you *are* Satan.'

'With horns and a pitchfork, honey! But really, Big Mama, you *know* I'm right. Humdrum or hellion . . . who wouldya rather?'

'Where?' (Relenting . . .)

'21. I'm simply craving those scrumptious little pot pies. We'll go incognito . . . a booth in the bar room, tucked back in a corner. No one'll even know we're there.'

'Fine.'

'Goody!' She could almost *hear* him smile.

'Rat.'

Slim replaced the receiver. She felt a twinge of guilt as she fished her phone book from the vanity drawer, flipping to the K's for poor old Shipwreck's number, summoning a cough, preparing to feel under the weather.

BY THE TIME SHE'D SETTLED INTO A BOOTH next to Truman in the bar at 21, Slim couldn't have been happier to have changed her plans. They whispered beneath the jumble of antique toys hanging precariously from the ceiling, tucking into pies, slurping mojitos through straws.

'So I suggested Madrid. All she needs is a good dose of fun.'

'And maybe a matador or two . . . ?'

'Big Mama's guide to taking bulls by horns.'

'Or whatever appendage is handy . . .'

'Bottoms up!'

'Here's hoping . . .' Truman grinned salaciously. Then, lifting his glass, motioning an ancient waiter for another round—'Oh, Mr. *Weissssss* . . .'

Beating Weiss to the table (his tortoise pace an accepted feature of the establishment) was Babe, sailing into the bar room in a light mac, shaking droplets from her umbrella.

'Hallo, Babyling!' Truman beamed, then, calling to the server—'Make that three, Mr. Weiss!' They exchanged a round of pecks as Babe removed her scarf, tying it absently around the handle of her handbag. She slid in next to Slim, fixing her with entreating eyes.

'Slim darling, I'm in *such* a pickle—and you're the *only* one who can help me. I know it's a bit much to ask, but may I borrow your husband for a night . . . ?'

'Come again?' Slim hardly concealed her amusement.

Timing impeccable, Weiss reached the table balancing a round of mojitos. Truman plucked a highball from the tray, taking a long suck through his straw. 'Well, well. Luncheon just got a helluva lot more interesting!' He winked at Slim. 'Now, would Shipwreck Kelly have given you *that*? What did you have in mind, Babyling? *Ménage à trois*, or an even swap—?'

Babe swatted Truman with her menu. 'Not for *me*. Well, I guess it is for me, in a way . . . and Betsey.' She rolled her eyes, a gesture that tended to accompany Betsey's name.

'Incest to boot?! Baby, I didn't think you had it in you! Though I must say, I wouldn't have pegged *Betsey* as your type.'

'Truman, please remove that mind of yours from the gutter.' Turning back to Slim—'*Technically*, it's for Pam. Churchill.'

'Pam Churchill?' Slim frowned, puzzled.

'Seems she and Jock were close friends in London during the war—'

'Of *course* they were,' Tru chipped in gleefully. 'So were Misters Onassis and Agnelli . . . and Misters Harriman, Kahn, and Rothschild—oh! and Eddie R. Murrow—'

'Ed's just a rumor,' Babe swiftly corrected. (Tru and Slim exchanged knowing glances otherwise.)

'But what on earth does *she* have to do with *us*?'

'Well, now that Betsey and Jock are playing cross-pond ambassadors, it would seem they've renewed their old friendship. Apparently it came up over dinner that Pam would simply *love* a holiday in New York.'

'*Naturally*.'

'And Betsey offered to host her, knowing full well she had no intention of coming home. So guess who it falls to . . .'

'Baby sis. Christ, what a pain.'

Babe poked at the muddle of mint in her mojito, peeved. 'It *is* a hassle, especially *Europeans*. The last batch we took in wanted their sheets ironed. Hand-ironed! Anyway, I told Bets I'd do it—I mean, what else could I say?'

'*NO!*' Slim and Tru bellowed in unison.

Babe smiled. 'But we know I'd never do that, don't we.' She took out her cigarette case, lit two L&Ms and passed one to Slim. 'I agreed to the *minimum*. I'll throw her a dinner at Kiluna on Friday, then drum up theater tickets for Saturday, which is hopefully where *you* come in,' she nodded to Slim. 'Sunday she's on her own.'

'I'll have Leland pull house seats. *King and I* or *South Pacific*?'

'Either. More important, since you'll be in Spain with Betty, and Tru in Verbier with Jack, I was wondering if Leland would mind terribly joining our group as Pam's escort? Just for the play on Saturday—I wouldn't *dream* of putting him through that dreadful dinner! I know it's a bit of a busman's holiday, but I have to find someone willing to sit with her for the two hours between curtain up and down before we can ship her back to wherever she came from.'

'Leland wouldn't mind.'

'Are you *sure*? I know it will be frightfully dull.'

'Anything for a pal,' said Slim, true to form.

'When does Leland leave? To join you?'

'Betty and I'll meet up with Papa in Madrid, *avec* bride *número cuatro*—'

'*Puh-leeeze,*' Truman groaned. 'One of the great closet queens of our time!'

Slim, ignoring him. '—Then we're off to Paris. Betty'll leave to film in London, and Leland and I will head to Munich to meet the Baroness.'

'The Baroness . . . ?'

'Von Trapp. Nun-turned-nanny. Snagged the father, fled the Nazis. She's written a memoir about their singing litter in lederhosen. Leland thinks there's a musical lurking in there somewhere. We're going to negotiate the life rights.'

'I've always thought those SS boys could be whipped into a *marvelous* chorus line,' Truman posited, poking two bread rolls with fork-and-knife, staging his own version of Chaplin's Dinner Roll Dance, manipulating the doughy 'feet' into a goose-stepping series of high kicks, to a jazzed-up rendition of 'Deutschland über alles.'

'Oh, Tru.' Slim shook her head, snickering at the notion.

'You really are too much.' Babe, shielding her eyes with her hand.

They sipped their mojitos, indulging a peal of guilty laughter.

SLIM FELT A RUSH OF WARMTH WASH OVER HER as she walked into the hotel suite at the Ritz in Madrid.

A sensation curiously reminiscent of the shock she'd felt walking into the surf at Matador Beach, hurtling exposed skin into the most deliciously salty of breakers. An 'involuntary memory,' as Truman would have told her, launching into a characteristic explanation of Proust and madeleines.

Whatever the trigger, the mixture of shock and delight transported Slim for an instant from the Ritz in Madrid to a beach in Malibu. Enjoying the tingling she knew would cling to her skin—a secret, carnal saltiness that could be tasted on her flesh long after she'd dried. The faintly briny perfume of seawater beneath an evening gown.

That saltiness was Leland all over, lingering on her skin like a tantalizing secret. Perhaps it was the scent that made her think of Hay, which led to an endless chain of memory.

For even before she and Betty entered the room, the perfume beckoned. Not the clandestine oceanic fragrance of memory, but a sweet, floral one, wafting into the hallway, beneath the tiniest crack in the door. Slim pushed the portal open to reveal a room filled with white flowers. Sculptural orchids. Freesias. The Little Gem magnolia, Truman's favorite, the whole of the South in seven waxy petals.

It was Tru who'd introduced Leland to them at Petrov's Florist on Sixth Ave., gushing—'Now, Big Daddy, you've just *gotta* buy one of these for Big Mama. They're the crème de la crème. Just *smell* that . . .'

Leland had leaned in and inhaled, with a sommelier's judgment, the fragrance of the creamy saucer-bloom. Milky. Spicy. Heaven.

Truman, who simply loved to elbow his way into the wooing process, was famous for his taste, all the more appreciated by men of taste themselves.

'And get a load of those leaves! They're like flowers in themselves!' He touched one's stiff, deep-green surface. 'Leathery and glossy—the most divine mix of hard and soft. Just like Big Mama.' He stroked the bronze, fuzzy underside wistfully. 'Do you happen to know that Little Gems are some of the first trees to lift the veil of winter? Nina kept these, everywhere she lived, in tiny pots, even out on her crummy old postage-stamp fire escape when she was still Lillie Mae, before she met Joe. She loved them on account of their flowers being the first to grace the bare branches of spring,' he added with a sad smile. 'You know they start out pretty scrawny, but they eventually get as big as grandifloras . . . it just takes them a little longer.'

Always one for a pitch, Leland had flagged the florist and ordered a dozen.

'Noooooo, Big Daddy—you only need *one* of these,' Truman jumped in. 'That's how precious they are. Big Mama can pin it in her hair . . . beautiful, that paper-white against the gold? Afterward float it in a soup bowl filled halfway up with water. Trust me, Big Daddy, there's something magic that happens when they get wet. There's nothing quite like the scent of wet magnolia.'

Leland had repeated this to Slim as he presented it to her that evening, encased in its plastic coffin. How he'd caught the glint in Tru's eye, and, with a laugh, pulled out his wallet.

'Truman—enough. Sold.'

THERE WERE BOWLS OF FLOWERS NOW, filling the hotel room, jockeying for space amid the hothouse of white petals.

Slim and Betty dropped their handbags on the sofa by the door, taking in the scene with the delight that had been its objective. A card sat on an oval inlay entry table. Betty picked it up, fishing her thick black-framed glasses from her pocket. Jarring, Slim always thought, to see the screen goddess with the bookish specs, removing the celluloid chill that belied her actual warmth, reminding those who'd known her all along of the gawky Betty Joan Perske before she'd been neatly packaged into 'Lauren Bacall' (Betty being too homespun and Perske sounding too Jewish).

It was Slim who had spotted her, while standing in a grocery line in Santa Monica, in March of '43. Slim had been arrested by the image of a girl not unlike herself. Lanky, blonde. A severe, no-bullshit gaze, a directness that when coupled with uncultivated beauty could be construed as intimidating. The girl stared back at her from the magazine rack. Waiting . . .

In a smart navy suit in the foreground of the frame, 'BAZAAR' emblazoned above her. Behind her, a frosted door bore a scarlet cross—the shadow of a nurse passing behind the pane as if through a film of gauze. The girl seemed to be waiting in a hospital foyer. The message was clear—Give Blood, Help the Red Cross, it's the patriotic thing to— —

Yeah, yeah, Slim thought, unable to take her eyes off the girl, who would, to be fair, command anyone's attention. Nobody's thinking of blood or war—or anything but those eyes. Piercing, belying their years. Unapologetic. Emanating a scrubbed-clean, healthy glow, but with the dangerous hint of a panther prowling beneath. Slim felt she was looking into a mirror.

'I'VE FOUND YOUR GIRL,' she told Hawks that night over dinner.

'Which girl . . . ?' he asked, uneasy. Though the marriage was new, his philandering had not tempered. Slim guessed he feared she'd discovered the girl in the commissary, who she'd known about for months. Or Dolores Moran, that bimbo Howard had cast for an unspecified film, in an unspecified role. Slim could guess what her role would be, and when the affair was known around town, many a crowded table at the Derby had found themselves weeping with laughter at her impersonations of her husband's lover, changing her name from Dolores Moran to 'Dollar-ass Moron.' It was Slim's way— make 'em laugh, no matter how you cried.

'Your *girl*. For the Bogart picture.'

She'd pulled the folded fashion rag from her bag and passed it to Hawks, at the tail end of another meal soured with his lies. While his initial response was unenthused, the minute he saw those eyes gazing at him, he grabbed the magazine, studying it closely. Slim lit a cigarette, enjoying her cleverness.

'I called Mrs. Vreeland. Found out who she was. One Betty Joan Perske.'

Howard wrinkled his hawk nose. 'Well, *that'll* have to go.'

'I dunno . . . I kinda like it.'

As Slim tapped her cigarette ash and refilled her dwindling manhattan, she watched Howard see what she herself had spotted . . .

'My God. She's *you*.'

'Who did you *think* I'd found?'

Howard looked up from the glossy page, on guard.

'Look, Slim, I have no idea what you're—'

Bored, Slim leaned in, predatory, kissing his lips, if only to stop the lies.

Howard pulled back, startled. It had been a long time since they'd kissed like that. A long time since she'd been rough with him. Slim had learned early on that's what turned Howard on—violence. Fight then fuck. That was his fetish. Just looking at his films, wasn't it obvious? Shouldn't she have watched a few more of them before throwing in her lot? Barbed banter, a slap, a punch, then the leads tumble into bed. That was Howard's idea of seduction.

Well, give 'em what they pay for.

INT. HAWKS HOUSE — DINING ROOM — DAY

Slim shoves her tongue deeper into his mouth, giving his lower lip a good bite as she exits. Howard pulls back, bringing his dinner napkin to his lips, blood seeping through the clean, white linen.

HAWKS
What did you do that for?

SLIM
I've been wondering if I'd like it.

HAWKS
What's the decision?

SLIM
I don't know yet...
(they kiss again)
It's even better when you help.

She steps away, recovering her smoldering cigarette, sucking in a long drag to erase the taste of the well-done T-bone Howard had inhaled for dinner.

SLIM (CONT'D)
I'll be out back. If you need me, just whistle.

HAWKS
Slim...

SLIM
You know how to whistle, don't you, Hawks?

Sly smile playing at the corners of her mouth.

153

SLIM (CONT'D)
You just put your lips together… and blow.

As she turned to leave, she could almost see Hawks spinning
the exchange into a scene for Bogie and the razor-eyed Miss Perske, who, sitting down with her mother to a soggy pastrami
sandwich at the Formica table in their Bronx walk-up, had no idea
that her life was about to change.

Slim opened the back door of the prim Colonial that she had
designed, based on the set for Hawks' *Bringing Up Baby*. God,
how he'd loved that fake house, and Slim had, in the early delu-
sional days of their marriage, thought that a replica transported
to the Bel Air canyons would set the stage for the notion of happily ever after. Especially a house that bowed to Howard's vanity,
reconstructed by his own scenic artists, who were even so bold as
to incorporate the hopeful cliché of the white picket fence.

Slim looked around the suffocatingly traditional facade of the
home she'd come to love all the more, knowing it was temporary.
She knew what the next plot in her script would be. And she'd
achieve it while Howard was preoccupied, per plan, with *To Have
and Have Not*—a story she'd help him convince Papa to option.

Ernest had objected, pushing the Spanish book instead, *For
Whom the Bell Tolls*. Hawks had failed to understand it.

'Give me your worst piece of work—the absolute turkey. With
a rewrite and Bogart, I'll make it a hit!' he had boasted to Papa,
while shooting pheasant in Sun Valley.

Slim's gaze had met Papa's in that moment around the camp-
fire. She'd rolled her eyes and Papa had laughed. Slim thought
Papa's *Bell* his best work yet and told Howard so. But then Howard rarely listened to Slim.

Not like Leland would . . .

Leland, Slim's 'Hay.' Her second-act hero, waiting in the wings
to enter the scene, offering armloads of pallid blooms.

Yes, Slim knew, the timing was perfect. Howard would be
consumed with her doppelgänger, Miss Perske, who Slim had so

generously scouted for him. Obviously he'd seduce her, with the ever-ready excuse of the director-showing-the-starlet-how-to-play-the-scene.

There was no way of Slim knowing that she'd chosen at random a woman after her own heart. Betty would not play casting-couch games with Howard, as it turned out, but have the gumption to fall madly in love with her co-star. Had Howard known, he would have picked another ingénue.

Slim couldn't know that she had plucked a lifetime friend from the grocery stand in Santa Monica. Couldn't know that Betty Perske-turned-Bacall would become Bogie's 'Baby,' whose own babies she'd see born, whose hand she'd hold as Bogie, in a decade's time, would die the most gallant of deaths. For months riding down each evening in a dumbwaiter (lacking the strength to take the stairs) for cocktails with her and Leland, with Leland's old flame Kate and Bogie's best friend Spence. The Inner Circle. The only ones allowed to witness the harrowing process of Bogie's decay. Slim couldn't know that she'd clutch Betty's arm moments after Bogie's labored breathing ceased, a single squeeze communicating all that they had shared.

All she could think as she stood in the gloaming was that there couldn't be a better moment to make her exit from the role of Mrs. Howard Hawks.

Slim found herself musing, as she stamped her cigarette into the flagstones with the heel of her espadrille, that her only regret would be that she'd never get credit for all that dialogue.

'TO MY TWO EXOTIC BLOOMS—LOVE LELAND.' Betty read the card aloud, in the hothouse of the Spanish Ritz.

'Sweet Hay,' Slim smiled, proudly.

'What a prince,' Betty flattered.

'What a prince,' Slim agreed.

After Slim had disappeared into her room to unpack her case, had rung Papa and arranged to meet for sangria, pre-corrida, this being Papa's passion *du jour*, she rejoined Betty in the sitting room.

She found her by the window in one of a pair of club chairs, the second empty beside her, the dying light hitting her severe profile at just the right angle.

Betty sat holding a bouquet of starburst lilies, looking into middle distance.

Slim approached, kicking Betty's calf gently, flopping into the chair beside her.

Betty smiled at Slim, cradling the lilies, tears welling in her eyes. 'These were in my room.'

Slim looked to the graceful blooms, their significance registering. 'Casablancas . . . Get it . . . ? Isn't Leland lovely.' And with that Betty crumbled, weeping into the sleeve of the mackintosh she hadn't yet removed.

Slim grabbed her, pulled her close, and didn't let her go until the tears had ceased.

A DRINK WOULD FIX EVERYTHING, Slim assured her.

Well, maybe a couple of drinks . . .

They were on holiday after all—and not just any holiday. This was a resurrection. They were already well oiled from a pitcher of sangria, sipped overlooking a sand-swept square, by the time Papa arrived. The fruit was bruised and the wine hard, but it went down a treat.

Betty looked to Slim like that nineteen-year-old girl she'd first known—even younger now, perhaps, her butterscotch hair swept into a girlish ponytail and her face bare, nose freckled from the sun. For the first time since her world had fallen to pieces, Betty looked happy. It had been ages since they'd laughed, simply for the pleasure of laughing.

When Papa approached, entourage of matadors in tow, he bellowed Slim's name across the plaza, 'MISS SLIMMMMSKY!' She smiled as he made his way to her, taking her hand and kissing it, whiskers tickling the back of her skin like the bristles of a soft white porcupine.

'How are you, Pap . . . ?'

'My Slimsky.' He touched her golden hair covetously.

She nodded to Betty behind her. 'Meet my pal.'

Papa fixed his cloudy eyes on the sunburnt Betty Bacall and Slim saw him, for the first time since they'd met—nearly two decades back—turn his gaze from her to another. He looked at Betty and fell hard, as only Papa could. And, to be fair, for the better part of the afternoon he loved her with unwavering devotion.

'Mrs. Bogart.'

'Mr. Hemingway. Call me Betty,' her throatiness at odd contrast with the girlishness.

'Ernesto,' he replied, a grotesquely boyish grin emerging through the leathery folds of his weather-beaten face. 'At last we meet.'

'I feel that we have. Your little book changed my life. I've already had your words in my mouth.' As ever with that voice, the most innocent line seemed to pulsate with innuendo. Slim watched with satisfaction as the scene unfolded, Betty opening and blooming like a Casablanca.

Papa chuckled. 'Much as I'd love my words in that mouth of yours, I'm afraid I can't take credit. That was Miss Slimsky. Hundred percent.' He cut his eyes to Slim, a conspiratorial wink. 'Slimsky, forgive me. You and I both know we're destined to end up together . . .'

'Spoken for.' Slim raised her left hand, bearing the delicate band Leland had slipped on her finger in a modest ceremony on the Paleys' back lawn at Kiluna, nearly a decade before. Babe had set a beautiful luncheon table with gazpacho and crab salad and cold salted beef, and they'd dined al fresco around a table for eight, the tiny wedding party toasting the newly minted Haywards with chilled champagne cocktails.

In reply Papa waved his own wedding ring, as if to cancel her argument. 'Not for long you're not . . . Ten years is about your matrimonial run, isn't it?'

'You're even fewer than that.' Slim shoved him, playfully. He pulled her into a brotherly kiss that lingered a breath longer than comfortable. Slim pushed him away, ever so gently, and Papa cleared his throat.

'As I was saying, you and I will grow old and die together—you just don't know it yet. In the meantime, I'm sure you'll forgive my infidelity, for this ravenous creature is in dire need of attention.' He turned back to Betty. 'Mrs. Bogart, have you ever faced a charging bull?'

Betty grinned. 'Not that I can recall.'

'Well, I have. Let me tell you what it's like, to look mortality in the eye . . .'

And taking her arm, Papa launched into an elaborate explanation of the corrida and its rituals, and all about the *mano a mano* pairing of Luis Miguel Dominguín and Antonio Ordóñez, the two great bullfighters of the day, about whom he was writing—which naturally, Slim mused, came full circle back to Papa.

'*Quelle* fucking *surprise*,' she could hear Truman groan, and smiled.

AT THE PLAZA DE TOROS they were joined by Mrs. H, *número cuatro*: Miss Mary, who never had taken to Slim. It seemed Mary could never forgive that whether Mrs. Hawks or Mrs. Hayward, Slim had come before her, had outlasted wives and lovers alike, and thus held a special place in her Ernest's heart. She shook Slim's hand coolly, appraising her length and leanness and her maddeningly sun-kissed hair—the color her husband had forced her to dye her own.

Papa didn't help matters, insisting he sit between Slim and Betty in the stands, enveloped in all that blondness, as if flanked by two trophies of exotic game: a pair of butterscotch panthers curled on either side of his thick, bearlike thighs. Miss Mary, none too pleased, attempted to squeeze in past Slim, when Papa bellowed — —

'What do you think you're doing, woman?'

Mary stammered something about her seat, her view, and blinked back tears as he banished her to the far end of the row.

Sitting apart, her tight little mouth quivering in martyrdom, she shot a look of blame in Slim's direction, as sharp as the picadors' lance-points that pierced the bull's flesh in the ring below, leaving gaping cuts like a series of open mouths.

If Slim had wanted Betty to drink deep, they'd achieved it in grand style, swigging cherry brandy from a suede flask they passed between them, squirting the potent liquid from its leathery bladder. The more the brandy flowed, the more Slim watched Betty relax, woozy and oozy, leaning against Papa's strong arm, while Miss Mary sat so rigid Slim worried that the fourth Mrs. Hemingway might shatter and break into a thousand lethal shards.

They'd lingered in the cantina over steaming plates of paella, the scent of saffron mingling with crustacean brine. To Slim's delight, Papa spent the better part of the meal leaning over, whispering into Betty's ear, the latter laughing throatily at his efforts.

Slim had been corralled by Luis Miguel Dominguín, attempting to unburden his troubled soul in a hybrid Spanish and English—something about an ill-fated affair with Ava Gardner, who he'd met when cast as the matador Romero in *The Sun Also Rises*. The words 'stormy' and 'fiery' were repeated in both languages, which didn't surprise Slim in the least. Luis Miguel was not Ava's first matador, but he *was* her first matador while Mrs. Sinatra.

Slim had it on good authority—Frank had told her this himself over a shared cigarette beneath a tangled set of hotel sheets during the one weekend they spent together in the desert, when Leland was out of town. Three stolen, sweat-soaked nights . . . Slim wasn't proud of it, but there it was. She considered it a one-off. In ten years of marriage, surely Leland had done the same . . . ?

Between the Avas and *tempestuosa*s and *ardiente*s, Slim noticed Miss Mary—again relegated to the nub end of the banquet table—rise, seizing the moment when Papa lumbered off for a piss or a fight or a combination thereof.

Mary walked calmly toward Betty, sliding into Papa's empty place beside her. Tipsy, dizzy, in love with the world once more, Betty beamed at her. With a terse smile, Miss Mary held out two clenched fists.

'Mrs. Bogart, I have something for you.'

'Oh, Mary.' Betty purred. 'How kind.'

Indicating her fists, Miss Mary urged, 'Go on. Pick one. Left or right?'

A wave of girlish delight flashed across Betty's face. Hesitating a moment, she pointed to the right hand of the offered pair and waited with anticipation.

Miss Mary's lips twitched into a nascent crescent moon, as she uncurled her fingers to reveal a gleaming silver bullet resting in her palm. Slim and Betty stared at it, stunned sober. Mary leaned in close . . .

'That's what you'll get if you ever lay a hand on my husband.'

'Betty . . .' Slim rose, protectively.

Miss Mary whirled around. 'Care to play the other hand, *Miss Slimsky* . . . ?'

She dropped an identical bullet from her left fist onto Slim's plate, where it landed with a muffled clink on the discarded mound of prawn shells.

BY THE TIME SLIM AND BETTY crossed the threshold of the Ritz— this time in Paris—they'd had quite enough swigging from foul brandy gourds. Enough big game and men's men, enough severed bull's tails and *tormentas* and *incendios*. They were happy to shed panther skins for ladylike sheaths—grateful for pearls and bath salts and proper glassware.

So it was with the pleasure of the familiar that they walked through the marble lobby, tipping scarlet-capped porters who wheeled their luggage ahead. As they took their keys and turned toward the lobby lift—still laughing over the madness of nearly being shot, skinned, and roasted on a spit by Miss Mary, a tale they'd embellished on the flight back to Paris—they found themselves accosted by a monocled concierge, waving a slip of paper.

'*Pardon* . . . Madame 'Ayward?' he called, handing Slim a pink 'message' notice. 'Just to inform you—Madame Churchill's car waits outside.'

Slim frowned. 'There must be some mistake. We didn't hire a car.'

'*Oui*. But Madame Churchill has made her car available for Madame 'Ayward's use.'

After the requisite trade of *merci*s the concierge took his leave. Slim and Betty exchanged befuddled glances.

'Pam Churchill?' Betty raised an eyebrow. 'As in Aly Khan and Stavros Nicharos and Élie de Rothschild and Averell Harriman Pam Churchill?'

Slim nodded, bored. '. . . and Ari Onassis and Jock Whitney and Gianni Agnelli . . .'

'I didn't know you and Leland knew Pam.'

'We met her once at Babe's. I must say I couldn't see what all the fuss was about.'

'I'm surprised that Babe would have her . . . *you* know. Around Bill.'

'Pam took her shot at Paley years ago,' Slim said, dismissing the notion. Then, almost as an afterthought—'Truman knows Pam.'

'Truman knows everybody.'

'He lunches with her occasionally—I think to come away with the most appalling dirt!'

'Such as . . . ?'

'Last week he told a story to a packed table at the Colony,' Slim grinned at the memory, '—spilling the beans about Pam's hysterectomy, claiming that her doctor pitched it as a form of birth control.'

'No!'

'Yes! Of course Tru launched into an imitation of Dr. Womb, who reportedly said after the procedure was over: "Well, little lady, we've taken away your baby carriage . . . but we've left you your playpen"!'

'Only Truman,' Betty chuckled. 'Poor Pam!'

'Poor Pam,' Slim agreed, as far as she could be bothered.

THAT EVENING SLIM AND BETTY settled into the curve of the Ritz Cambon bar and ordered a pair of gimlets.

In no time, another concierge appeared, clutching a stack of message slips the same sickly lipstick shade of pink, bowing ever so slightly as he retreated.

'What in fresh hell . . . ?' Slim grinned, tossing them onto the bar, sipping her celadon cocktail. Betty pulled eyeglasses from her evening bag, focusing on the first of the rosy papers.

'*Mrs. Churchill requests Mrs. Hayward ring her. Number listed.*' She flipped to the next. '*Mrs. Churchill would like to invite Mrs. Hayward and guest*—that would be me, presumably—*to her pied-à-terre, where she's planned a quiet supper.*'

'Jesus Henry Christ! Skip to the last . . .'

'*Mrs. Churchill* very *much hopes to receive Mrs. Hayward and guest for dinner—reply requested.*' Betty removed her glasses, taking a swig of gimlet. 'Seems *someone* has an admirer.'

'Why all the interest in "Mrs. Hayward"? I barely know the woman!' Slim laughed. 'I mean, I *suppose* she must be grateful that I loaned Leland out for the evening . . .'

'You what?!'

'Babe asked me if Leland might pull *Pacific* house seats and join their group, wheeling the sad-sack broad around New York for an evening. Tru was in Verbier with Jack, and Babe was in a bind . . . Leland did it as a favor to me, and I was doing it as a favor to Babe, who was doing it as a favor to Betsey—'

Betty chuckled, 'Helluva lotta favors.'

'Well, what can you do with an Extra Woman?' Slim motioned the barman for another round. 'It's a bit of a pain in the ass, if Tru's not around to do the honors.'

Betty drained the dregs of her glass in silence.

Slim touched her arm. 'Betty? What is it?'

'Nothing I haven't thought of before.' Her gray eyes watered as she removed a Lucky Strike from her cigarette case, tapping it on the metal surface. 'I've been part of a pair since I was nineteen. Now that Bogie's gone, am *I* an Extra Woman . . . ?' She lit her smoke, inhaling deeply, holding it in drooping fingers, like Bogie used to do.

'Don't be ridiculous. You'll always be Bogie's baby. And you'll move on, when you're ready, and be Mrs. So-and-So. And if you choose, Mrs. What's-His-Name.'

'I won't be Mrs. Anyone but Bogart.'

'Because you chose Bogie and he chose you. I was *there*, remember?' They shared a nostalgic smile. Slim considered. 'The terror of being an "Extra Woman" is that no one's *chosen* you.'

'Like Pam Churchill.'

'Exactly.' Slim plucked a cigarette from Betty's case and lit it. 'They may toy with her. Support her. But mark my words—nobody *marries* Pam Churchill.'

The barman deposited another round of gimlets, with them a telephone, attached to the wall with a cord the length of an unrolled ball of string.

'Pardon, *mesdames*. But I have Madame Churchill on the line for Madame 'Ay-ward.'

Slim grinned at Betty—'Now this is getting farcical.'

THE NEXT EVENING SLIM AND BETTY arrived promptly at Madame Churchill's Left Bank apartment for dinner, as summoned. The butterscotch panthers were in exquisite form—Slim in ivory jersey, delivered from Grès atelier, Betty in black Dior.

Opening the door to greet her guests, Pam Churchill struck Slim as being the human equivalent of meat in a butcher's window, *slightly* past its prime. There was something of the premature matron about her, something musty and stale. Her bouffant hair seemed a choice someone twice her age might have made—and her dull crêpe dinner dress evoked Blitz-era thrift. One could hardly picture this cozy, rosy woman as the seductress of lore, but who knew what fetishes she satisfied behind closed doors. Perhaps Pam played the role of governess in a sensible brassiere and nursery-apron, and spanked the most-powerful-men-in-the-world, punishing them for their naughty thoughts. Slim could hardly look at Pam without snickering—she certainly couldn't meet Betty's eye.

'Mrs. Hayward!' Pam enthused, pulling Slim into an unexpected embrace.

'Mrs. Churchill . . .' Slim returned the gesture, but only out of courtesy. She noted that Pamela's palms were warm and slightly moist.

'This is my dear friend Betty Bac— —'

'Yes, of course—Mrs. *Bogart*,' Pam interrupted, taking Betty's arm solicitously. 'I'm *terribly* sorry to hear of your loss. Do come in and tell me all about it.'

Pam led them through a foyer, where she'd taken care to order an enormous arrangement of white flowers. In contrast to the rather garish, faux-rococo decor, the flowers were clean and simple—the only thing in the fussy brothel that provided the eyes a respite.

After they'd settled down to an intimate table for three, a downtrodden *femme de ménage* served the first course—vichyssoise, an odd choice for fall, barely edible. The topic of conversation floated from shared acquaintances to general chatter—about Paris, London, New York. Turned out Pam had simply *loved* Leland's play. *Adored* Mary Martin—and Leland was *so* kind to take them backstage. Their group had decamped to Sardi's afterward, and Leland was *so* thoughtful to have introduced Pam to Misters Rodgers and Hammerstein—and Yul Brynner to boot! She simply *must* see *The King and I* when next in town.

'I'm so pleased you had a lovely time,' Slim said as her untouched vichyssoise was removed and a sliver of *saumon au gratin* set in its place. She could tell in an instant that it was cooked to death—how Leland would hate that! They hardly ever ordered salmon when dining out, anticipating this common misstep.

Leland was a sensational cook—more skilled than most restaurant chefs, Slim loved to boast. It was his habit to make late-night suppers, just for the two of them, after the requisite rounds at Sardi's and El Morocco and the Stork, and wherever else one went after the curtain went down on any given night. They'd return, often as late as three, and Leland would don his apron and indulge his passion for exquisitely prepared meals served on clean white plates, with clean white napkins, and clean white candles on the table. As Slim looked down at Pam's Rothschild china, with its patterns of fowl and insects and tangle of botanicals vying for space amid the scraps of food, she missed the simplicity of Leland's clean plates.

From the next room a phone began to ring . . . and ring. Unrelenting. Finally, after a mime-show of 'ignoring' the interruption, Pam looked apologetically to her guests.

'Will you excuse me, ladies? I *am* expecting a transatlantic call.'

'Of course,' said Slim.

'I'll only be a moment.'

'Take your time,' Betty assured her.

As soon as their hostess left the room, Slim looked to Betty and the two fell into a fit of silent chuckles, which they muffled with their dinner napkins: a messy, paisley linen.

'Who do we think it is? Gianni?'

'No! He and Marella are in Rome.'

'All right . . . Élie de Rothschild?'

'Possible. Highly possible.'

In hushed tones, like unruly schoolgirls, Slim and Betty ran through the list of candidates for the caller, narrowing it to exactly three tycoons, until, after a brief absence, Pam returned, round cheeks rubicund. An air of satisfaction wrapped around her like a cocoon.

'My apologies.'

'It's quite all right,' Slim and Betty, in unison.

'It's astonishing,' Pam blotted her dewy upper lip with her serviette, 'how *clear* cable calls are nowadays! One can hear New York, for instance, as if the person's in the next room!'

Betty cut her eyes to Slim, satisfied, she having put her phone-contender money on an heir to a Wall Street banking fortune.

'Where were we . . . ?' Pam was saying. 'Oh, yes! Babe. Babe is lovely. What a delightful soul. Fragile . . . but delightful. *Bill*, on the other hand . . .' She laughed a little too knowingly. 'Well, Bill's certainly a *handful* . . . I can't imagine *that* marriage is easy!'

There was something about her tone that Slim didn't care for. She couldn't quite put her finger on it, but she allowed herself to wonder if the enterprising Mrs. Churchill had indeed had a second go at Bill Paley. Perhaps Babe had sensed it, and that's why she'd wanted Leland to join their party—reinforcements against an all-out Churchill invasion?

Always one to have a pal's back, Slim smiled politely at Pam, defending Babe by turning the topic to marriage in general. 'I suppose any marriage has its challenges.'

'And are you happy in your marriage?' Pam leaned forward, all the more fascinated.

Slim sipped her wine, considering. Why should she tell a stranger about the pressures of a decade of till-death-do-us-part? About the life of a wife of a theatrical impresario, who stayed out each night till the wee hours. How even if you stayed out together, you were never alone. Not except for a stolen three-o'clock supper here and there, the only time you might stand a chance of harnessing his attention. Even then, the talk was of shop, shop, shop. This actor. That composer. Those returns, that flop . . . Sure, it looked shiny on the surface, but the specter of failure was palpable.

Why should she tell a stranger that she often felt like an underpaid nanny, saddled with three headcase stepkids? That every time the phone rang she felt a stab to the gut, wondering whether it might be the nut-bin about Billy, or the hospital reporting that Bridget had yet again attempted suicide, her seizures having made life unbearable. Why tell a stranger, thought Slim, that her own poisoned womb managed to lose fetus after fetus, like a plot from a third-rate horror script both of her husbands would've barred from production . . . ? That all she really wanted was to give Leland a child—a *normal* child, to make up for the defective ones whose eyes he couldn't bear to meet. Slim wasn't about to tell Pam Churchill—with her stale-cream-puff hair and garish plates—such complex truths.

Instead she simply said, 'I guess no marriage is perfect.'

Pam looked at her curiously, as if watching the most *fascinating* performance, hoping to glean something from it. 'Whatever do you mean . . . ?'

Slim heard her own voice, a detached, vague one . . .

'Well, I suppose one could argue that a case could be made for living alone. Free of responsibility. From the realities of a partnership.'

Pam smiled, sympathy creeping into her tone. 'Yes. Being an Extra Woman does have its advantages.'

Over the next hour, Slim and Betty soldiered through the dessert course (tarte Tatin, store bought) and—when cognac was offered—feigned just the right number of graceful yawns (claiming jet lag) to bring the dinner to a merciful end. They rose, thanking their hostess profusely in an effort to hide their ennui. Pam followed suit, turning first to Betty with the special smile reserved for widows, one that offered a sickening combination of condolence and condescension.

'Mrs. Bogart, *bon courage*! If there's anything else I can do for you while you're in Paris, please don't hesitate. We Extra Women must stick together.'

'Thank you, but I leave for London tomorrow.'

'Ah! Business or pleasure?'

'Filming.'

'My, how glamorous.'

'A gal's gotta work.'

'Pity we won't see more of one another,' said Pam.

'Next time,' Betty vowed, though Slim knew her well enough to know there wasn't a snowball's chance in hell. With that, Pam fixed her eager gaze on Slim, taking her arm in a conspiratorial manner, leading her into the foyer. 'And you, Mrs. Hayward? Can I do anything for you?'

Slim shied ever so slightly from her grasp, though not enough for Pam to notice. 'No, thank you. Very thoughtful, but Leland arrives tomorrow.'

Pam nodded, accepting the information as a given. 'Yes, of course he does. I hope you won't mind, but I've taken the liberty of preparing a little dinner in your and Leland's honor . . . I do so hope you'll let me. Just a few close friends. Very intimate.'

Slim willed the edges of her mouth upward, the corners rising into a polite grin as if being pulled by invisible strings. But while the grin cooperated, the words refused to follow.

'And afterwards, I have tickets to a play that I thought might be amusing for Leland to see.' Before Slim could respond, Pam quickly added—'In return for his generosity in New York. I'm still dreaming of *South Pacific!*' She proceeded to hum a few off-key bars of 'Some Enchanted Evening' while Slim stared, speechless.

'I'll have to check with Leland of course.'

'Of course. I am so indebted to Leland—and Bill . . . and Babe,' she added, almost as an afterthought. 'And to you of course, for loaning me your husband.'

'Yes. Well. It was our pleasure,' Slim said as she and Betty inched toward the exit.

The solicitous Madame Churchill fetched their coats, all but helping them into them.

It was not until they'd said their goodnights that Slim noticed it, resting on a table just to the side of the door . . .

A single Little Gem magnolia, floating in a bowl, wet and fragrant as Truman had promised Leland it would be, almost a decade before.

'GODDAMN LYING BASTARD HAY . . . Two-timing goddamn bastard!' In the taxi Slim erupted into a profanity-soaked diatribe, a red-hot stream of fears and insults combined. Betty laughed outright.

'*Leland?* With that frump of a hausfrau?! When he has *you?*'

'But the fucking *magnolia*—!' Slim sputtered.

'Coincidence.'

'*Really?*'

Betty considered, then dismissed a more sinister explanation. 'Absolutely. If anything, she was trying to impress you. She tailored a whole goddamn evening to your tastes! White flowers, white candles . . .'

'But not white plates,' Slim couldn't resist. 'God, was that china not repellent?'

'Tasteless.'

'Put me off the whole goddamn meal!'

'As if the meal needed any help.' They laughed at the awfulness of bland vichyssoise, not quite chilled enough. Of salmon not quite warm enough, despite having spent ample time in a pan, yielding desiccated balsawood flakes. 'God, how Leland would have *loathed* that!'

'Precisely. He'd loathe *her*—her whole fussy, frumpy, fading-English-rose routine! New York must've been hell, schlepping *that* around.'

'You really think?'

'Leland's a gent. A man of taste—of *drama*. In you he has the whole package. The razzle-dazzle.'

Slim smiled at her appreciatively.

'Pam Churchill,' Betty continued, 'wouldn't know dazzle if it knocked her out of her loafers!'

They snickered at the notion, and for the first time in hours Slim breathed easier.

WHEN LELAND ARRIVED THE NEXT MORNING, an hour after Betty had departed for her flight, Slim was relieved to find he was his old gorgeous self. So adorable, in fact, she banished any lingering doubts about Little Gem magnolias from her mind.

The laughing eyes, clear and blue as a summer sky. The tributaries of lines at their edges. The collegiate crew cut, rendered no less boyish by the salt and pepper flecked throughout. Wearing a wide grin, arms filled with three dozen paper-white roses—his other floral staple.

Not just any roses . . . Bourbon Boule de Neige, their special varietal.

After they had set up housekeeping in Manhasset on the North Shore of Long Island, they planted beds of them outside every window. They took pleasure watching them grow beyond their playful, tinted edges, bursting into unlikely white snowballs in the thick of the August heat. Two blooms linked by a single stem, flourishing together.

'Oh, *Hay*!' Slim's eyes welled with tears.

She pressed against him, crushing the roses between them, bringing her lips to his.

'Don't tell me my Nan's getting sentimental on me'—his voice graveled and warmed from countless cigarettes. He kissed the wet patches on her cheeks, then the droplets that clung to her lashes. 'What's with the waterworks?'

Slim laughed through her tears, at the unadulterated joy of his presence. His arms felt like home—as if the walls of the hotel suite had vanished, and with them the months (the *years*, if she was honest) of fretting. Gone were the asylums in which Billy and Bridget Hayward atrophied, their childhoods lost in a never-ending round of pills and shocks and seizures. Gone were the hospital wards that had become a fixture of their marriage, where Slim spent years grieving half-formed offspring, an endless hemorrhaging of blood and tissue and hope.

What a toll it had taken. Slim had weathered these heartbreaks alone, while Leland faced his own. Beneath his unflappable veteran's exterior, insecurity festered. As Leland had entered his fifties, he had confronted a rare thing in his career: failure.

Before the recent string of successes there'd been an equal run of flops, followed by a spell as dry as a drought in the Mojave.

'You're only as good as your last hit, Nan,' he'd say when she attempted to bolster his flagging ego. She had tried to be there for him, but Leland's instinct was to retreat into his cave and lick his wounds in solitude, for which Slim, by her own admission, had little patience. She had taken care of him in a superficial sense . . . But if she was honest, she'd resented it. Hence her weekend with Frank . . . and maybe a few more like it. She hadn't always been 'dazzling,' as Betty so generously put it. Being away from Leland for nearly six months—first with Tru in freezing Russian wastelands, then with Betty in Paris and Madrid—had made Slim think. What would she be without her Hay? Hadn't they weathered the worst of the tempests and survived them? Were they not still hanging on by the same stem, worse for wear, dormant even, but poised to blossom again and again? There was nothing but Leland. They'd have a second act now, after the unfortunate interval—if luck decreed, a third.

She raised her tear-stained face to his, beaming.

'I'm just so happy to see you.'

She kissed him as they tumbled onto the sofa, sweeping white blooms and stems aside, all hands and limbs and mouths, consuming each other as they had when they were ten years younger and ten years hungrier.

AFTERWARDS THEY LOUNGED TOGETHER, limbs entwined, matching Ritz bathrobes wrapped around their nakedness. Leland laughed as Slim told him, over a pair of Scotches, about her odd encounter with the attentive Madame Churchill. As ever, Slim provided a bang-up impersonation of her overzealous hostess and when she informed him of the encore invite, she was mildly surprised when his objection wasn't more fulsome. By a second round, he actually posited that it might prove 'entertaining' to turn up.

'Entertaining in what way . . . ?'

'Oh, you know. She'll put on a show, at the very least.'

'What did you make of her, in New York?'

'Well, she's a character,' Leland answered, as if sharing a joke only they could appreciate. Slim breathed an exhalation of something like relief. She laid her head on his broad, bare chest, her fingers smoothing the graying hairs that peppered its surface.

'Was it awful, my darling . . . ?'

'Utter hell.' Leland reached beyond her for his tumbler. She added a handful of ice from the bucket and took a sip after him. Their lips met again, sharing the sting of the cold Scotch between them. He brushed a strand of hair from her face, tucking it gently behind her ear. 'You know I only did it for you.'

'I know. You're a prince.'

She curled deeper into his embrace, inhaling his scent, with its top notes of bay rum and tobacco—more intoxicating to Slim than a thousand Boule de Neige roses and Little Gem magnolias combined.

THAT EVENING AS THEY ARRIVED AT LA CHURCHILL'S pied-à-terre, Slim was surprised to find that Pam's 'intimate supper' was actually anything but. There were twenty guests waiting just to meet the famous Haywards, arranged at tables of ten, set with the garish Rothschild china, place cards stuck in the bills of gold-plate mallards at each setting.

As Slim followed her husband to the hostess table, Pam stepped in, playfully steering her toward the other.

'Now Slim, as much as I'd love to keep you to myself, I cannot deny my friends the pleasure of your company. Would you mind presiding over our second table?'

What could Slim do but accept? She was introduced to French poet after French painter after French politician, each with French wives, who appeared to be Frenchified versions of Madame Churchill. As she later slogged through a stodgy soufflé course, moving from bad to worse with tournedos of grayish, well-done beef, Slim—marionette grin lifted high—did her best to blame the language barrier for the unspeakably dull conversation.

'So, Madame 'Aaaaay-ward . . .' began the poet who, Slim noted, lacked the H-in-Hay to an even greater degree than your average Frenchman, 'Pamela tells us you are, 'ow shall we say . . . *une femme indépendante*.'

Slim, catching the gist, replied, 'Well, yes . . . I suppose I am.'

A boucléd politician's wife, sporting a neater version of Pamela's cream-puff coif, all but sneered, 'But what does *Monsieur* 'Ayward think of this? *Il dois se sentir seul, n'est-ce pas?*'

Again, Slim grasped enough to smile politely as she sawed through her wodge of meat.

'Mister 'Ayward is *très heureux* . . . He's simply elated.' She leaned in close to the politician, and the painter beyond him. '*Je suce sa queue*,' she informed them sweetly.

As the Mesdames Pâte-à-Choux gasped with horror, Slim chuckled to herself, having memorized such an off-color phrase in every language precisely for such moments. She'd learned from dearest Truheart—if she hadn't known it already—the handiness of shock value.

'Big Mama,' Truman had told her on more than one occasion, 'you should know how to "suck a cock" in every tongue. French and German and Spanish and Italian . . . *Trust* me, honey. It's a very useful phrase! Now let's review them again. Repeat after me: *Je suce sa queue* . . . *Ich seinen Schwanz lutschen* . . . *Me chupan la polla* . . .'

As the French matrons recovered from her bombshell, Slim looked across the room, hoping to catch Leland's eye with their *I've-got-a-tale-for-you-later* look.

But Leland seemed absorbed in whatever story Madame Churchill was regaling the male faction of her table with, while their wives picked sullenly at their over-steamed vegetables.

LATER SLIM WOULD CLAIM SHE'D DEALT NOBLY with the dinner.

She certainly prevented further discussion of the 'Ayward marriage, yet she couldn't escape the feeling that her dinner companions knew more about her domestic affairs than she cared to contemplate. After a chocolate mousse possessing all the lightness of a Zeppelin, the company departed for the theater. To Slim's dismay, it wasn't just the Haywards and Madame Churchill attending the performance at the Théâtre Hébertot . . .

It was the whole goddamn bunch. All twenty close, personal friends. *Vingt amis.* Naturally, Pam explained apologetically, their party would have to splinter into smaller pairings, as 'it was impossible to secure tickets in such a *large* block.'

Large block is right, thought Slim. Not such an 'intimate party' now, is it, Madame Rat?

As they entered the lobby, Slim saw, to her horror, what they were in for: *A Long Day's Journey into Night. En français.*

Sweet Jesus on a stick, it had been painful enough in English!

She steeled herself for *quatre heures* of tedium, taking comfort that she might at least slip off her shoes and run her stockinged toes up Leland's leg. Grasp his hand beneath the playbill and feel his long fingers stroking her palm in the darkness—

'Now Slim, you'll *certainly* need a translator, and *Pierre* has insisted that he do the honors.'

The journalist at her table—the one diner who had looked upon her with new-found appreciation after her *'queue'* bombshell—smiled at her, baring a row of smoke-stained teeth.

'. . . And *I'll* interpret for Leland,' Pam decreed. 'It will be fascinating for you to see how it translates, Leland.' She took his arm (practically *seized* it) as Pierre offered Slim his. She managed to meet Leland's gaze as he was led away by Mrs. Churchill. He gave Slim a shrug, followed by a wink. Small consolation for four hours of O'Neill under enforced separation, but she'd take what she could get.

The house lights flickered. Usherettes steered patrons to their seats with flashlights. As Slim was escorted to her row, she noted a parallel beam indicating Mrs. Churchill and Mr. 'Ayward's seats, exactly three rows behind her. As Slim sat waiting for the lights to dim, she could hear Pam's laughter hanging in the air, a stale, ringing echo, like a siren's wail. She was a siren all right, La Churchill—Slim was now sure of it. Half woman, half vulture, luring unsuspecting impresarios to their doom with slightly off-key renditions of 'Some Enchanted Evening' with the very purpose of flattering the fragile egos of the men who produced the ditties in question.

Now that she'd identified the precise beast she was dealing with, Slim vowed she wouldn't let her guard down again. She willed herself to look ahead, staring numbly at the space before her. Aware, with every breath, of the theft taking place just three rows behind her back.

PULITZER OR NO, THE *JOURNEY* CERTAINLY TOOK IT OUTTA ONE.

Slim had hoped to make a hasty exit as soon as she was reunited with Leland, but when their hostess proposed the *briefest* trip to a nightclub, Leland pressed Slim's hand in commiseration, yet politely accepted the offer. In the taxi en route, Pam squeezed herself in between them, insisting that they each have a window from which to watch the lights of Paris fly past. Slim was starting to see how she played things, the canny Mrs. Churchill.

She noted how thoughtfully Pam touched Leland's elbow, pointing out marquees winking offerings of interest. Voice an even drone of English finishing-school polish, punctuated—with startling regularity—by tinkling gales of laughter. Enough to strike a man as musical, yet ring false to a woman.

For her part, Slim couldn't tear her eyes from Pam's upper lip, tripping over that truly unfortunate line of cuspids, concerned that it risked sticking permanently to the enamel. Yet with each phrase, the tenacious lip managed to hitch itself free, just in time for the next. Between all this and those ingratiating smiles, the poor woman must have been exhausted by the end of an evening. You had to hand it to her, she *did* make you look. Perhaps that was

Mrs. Churchill's trick—get them fixated on the mouth, then gobble them up whole.

LELAND AND SLIM NUZZLED AT A CORNER TABLE in the nightclub, watching a burlesque dancer. She relished his strong fingers gripping hers, feeling his breath on her neck as he whispered in her ear—commenting, predictably, more on production values than the titillating nature of the performance. The buzz of the alcohol and Leland's nearness made Slim feel generous toward her French drinking *compagnons*. That was before the floor show cleared and the dance floor opened—where, by the third *hour*, Slim began to grow testy. She craved the comfort of silk sheets at the Ritz, missed the pleasure of crawling into them *avec* Leland, feeling his bare toes tickling hers, slurring their way through an evening's recap as they drifted off to sleep. Waking the next morning to room service trays, resuming where they'd left off.

At Leland's cajoling she joined him for a cha-cha, then retired to the bar. The O'Neill was catching up with her, and if denied bed she at the very least intended to get as loaded as the tippling Tyrones. The French *amis* possessed boundless reserves of enthusiasm for sambas and rumbas alike. When Leland offered Slim his hand for yet *another* cha-cha, she shook her head.

'Sorry, kid. I'm out.' She kicked off her heels and propped her feet on the chair opposite, wiggling her toes to restore feeling. 'Can we not just get a taxi for Chrissakes?!'

'Sweetheart, we wouldn't want to seem ungrateful.'

Slim muttered in a low voice, 'How fucking grateful do we need to be . . . ?'

As if on cue, Madame Churchill made her solicitous approach, bearing yet another pair of martinis. In a seamlessly choreographed movement, Pam deposited the drinks on Slim's table with one hand, offering the other to Leland. 'Mr. Hayward, as your wife is taking a breather, perhaps *I* could tempt you onto the floor?' she inquired with an encouraging little tug. Leland pecked Slim's cheek before following Pam into the sea of bodies.

Oh sure, Slim thought. *What can he do with that but oblige?* She had a sudden, vodka-blurred memory of something Truman had told her, after lunching with Pamela at La Côte Basque the previous spring. He said he'd asked Pam her secret—was she especially brilliant in the sack?

'*Precious*,' Tru reported he had squealed, 'what are you doing to all these *men*? Do you know something *I* don't . . . ?' He said Pam had shaken her head, sagely.

'It's nothing like that,' she'd assured him. 'Look, I meet a man. I sit next to him. I *listen* to him. And the next day, if I feel that he's game, I go to Cartier and have a cigarette case engraved with a personal note inside, based on our conversation. I send it around, and what can he do? He *has* to respond.'

Slim, vaguely interested at best, had filed the anecdote in the dusty recesses of her brain. Perhaps she should have paid closer attention . . . Truman, she recalled, had seemed impressed less with the act itself than with the price tag.

'*Cartier*, Big Mama!' he had enthused. 'Who do you think picks up *that* tab?'

Through the thick haze of Gitane smoke and palpitating samba, Slim thought that she must remember to check Leland's pockets tomorrow for cigarette cases inscribed with 'Some Enchanted Evening.' Slinging back yet another round, she scanned the crowd for the bobbing cream-puff coif. Pam wasn't difficult to spot, incandescent and matronly at once, tilting her double-chins upward to Leland.

Slim's Hay held Madame Churchill's beefy upper back as she stumbled through a tango, she laughing her siren's laugh through white incisors, upon which her upper lip sat balanced with precarious joy.

IT HAD ALL FADED INTO A MILDLY DISTRESSING DREAM by the time the Haywards reached Munich.

They eagerly anticipated meeting the Baroness von Trapp, in whose story they'd spotted narrative pay dirt. Perhaps it began with Hawks, all those years ago, but after two husbands in the biz, after combing through dozens of scripts, studying countless sets, costumes and budgets, Slim had become an inadvertent pro. She had, over the years, proven herself all the more valuable for having no agenda apart from that of taste; opinions dictated by gut. From the start she believed the von Trapp story would be the vehicle to revive Leland's career (before *Pacific* and *King and I* beat it to the punch). Now it seemed a luxury, to be at the top of the game and still want more. This would mark the end of their worries, and the beginning of retirement. Not that Leland would ever *retire*—it wasn't in his genes. But he might work from desire rather than need. Now that he no longer needed to *prove*, now that the children were grown, they could finally set about the business of making one another happy, which Slim had resolved to prioritize.

With the vision of these Valhallan days ahead, she made a point of being doubly charming to the Baroness von Trapp, who served them tea and *stollen*.

When Leland presented the offer of a five percent share of the show, the Baroness disappeared into another room. Leland raised a peppered brow to Slim, who casually nibbled her cake. The Baroness returned and disappeared several more times until Leland leaned in toward Slim, hissing, 'Does she have a team of lawyers in there or is she phoning each of the seven von Trapp kids individually?'

Slim suppressed a laugh as the Baroness returned, wearing a grave expression. Leland rose, removed the contracts from his briefcase, and took the chair beside hers.

'Baroness. Where were we . . . ?'

'More tea, Frau Hayward?' asked the Baroness. Leland and Slim waited patiently while the Baroness refilled their cups, humming a Schubert lied in a clear, melodic tone. As she served another plate of *stollen*, Leland resumed his pitch:

'Misters Rodgers and Hammerstein are on board. Lindsay and Crouse will write the book. And one of our finest musical-comedy artistes, Mary Martin, would like us to express personally how honored she'd be to play you. She . . .' He trailed off when the

Baroness lifted a serene palm. Leland and Slim waited, like chastened children silenced in church by Sister Maria.

'Herr Hayward. As I mentioned, I do nothing without first consulting the Holy Ghost.'

Slim watched, amused, as Leland maintained a neutral expression. 'And . . . ?'

'Well, I've spoken with him and now he says he wants *ten* percent.'

Slim saw the smile play at the corners of Leland's mouth. The Holy Ghost would get his percentage and the Haywards would get their hit. She'd later admit that she admired the Holy Ghost's ballsy tactics, adding that he was, in fact, better than most theatrical veterans at the art of negotiation.

Returning home triumphant, no sooner had their plane hit the tarmac at Idlewild than darling Jerry Robbins bombarded them with yet another project to add to their stable of hits: *Gypsy*, based on the memoir of striptease artist Gypsy Rose Lee. Leland simply couldn't say no. Sure, he'd be busy—swamped, no less. But Leland was a workhorse, thriving on chaos.

And so the Haywards resumed their usual pattern of work, entertaining, and being entertained. Saturdays were Babe's nights. Formal gatherings. Evening dresses and dinner jackets. Low music and four-course spreads. Sundays were Slim's—barbecues and fish fries. Tiki torches, lounge records, and sundresses and capris. Boozy afternoons of strip croquet—an article of clothing forfeited for each poor shot.

Slim and Babe had long ago agreed upon this schedule, to avoid conflicting invitations, and had, in doing so, solidified their bond.

With Leland consumed with work, and travel behind them, Slim blocked out a week in her calendar to sneak away to the Maine Chance health spa in Tempe to drop a few pounds. Christmas indulgence on top of rich European food had begun to take their toll. One couldn't very well be stuck with 'Slim' as a nickname and fail to live up to the promise.

Leland grasped the added inches lustily, biting her thigh. 'I'll take you whatever way you come, Nan Hayward.'

'You like a fat wife, do you?'

'You're the sun and the moon and the stars. That's all I know,' he replied.

HE CALLED HER THREE TIMES A DAY while she was at Maine Chance, steaming and starving. He told her how desperately he missed her, how home wasn't home without her. Slim smiled on the other end of the line, and said she'd see him soon. Lying beneath an infinite desert sky in the middle of nowhere, she sensed how profoundly Leland was the center of her own small universe. She wanted to tell him—face to face, staring into his kind, azure eyes—that he was the sun and the moon and the stars for her as well, the constellation around which she revolved.

Slim canceled her traditional Sunday barbecue the day she returned to Manhasset.

Even for her casual shindigs, it had been too much to organize from Tempe. Besides, she'd been looking forward to an evening in with Hay. They'd open a bottle of Château d'Yquem— 'The wine that never fails to get a man laid,' Leland often chuckled. Toss a baguette and cheese onto a tray, with cornichons and salty Parma ham—god, how good it would be to *eat* again! They'd tuck into their cold supper and chilled wine. They'd talk and kiss and laugh, and she'd tell him what she had realized in the desert on her own. That she wasn't—now that they were reunited—going anywhere. Not with Tru. Not with Papa. Not with Betty. She was *his*. That she never, ever wanted an 'I' without a 'we.' That they, the glorious Haywards, added up to one lovely shimmering 'us.'

When she walked in the door and set down her bags, she called his name. She proceeded down the hall to their bedroom, unbuttoning her silk blouse and stepping out of her skirt as she went. She found him sitting on the bed, on the phone. He looked up, smiling, motioning her near. Sweet Hay, Slim thought, warm with fondness for the familiar. She crawled panther-like across the bedspread, curling into his lap. She studied his face, reaching up to stroke his jawline.

'Yes, that's fine,' said Leland, wrapping up the call. 'Yes. Seven o'clock. See you then.'

He hung up, setting the phone aside, leaning down to give Slim a kiss. She purred happily, closing her eyes. He nudged her—'Hey, kid. Where're your clothes?'

Slim motioned with a limp gesture to the hallway. 'Won't need 'em for days. I don't think I'll be moving from this spot—except to walk to the kitchen and back. And maybe, if I'm feeling really ambitious, I'll venture out into the garden and lie there stark naked.'

She pulled his face back to hers. He pecked her cheek, gently nudging her upward. 'Well, as much as I wish that was the case, we gotta get a move on.'

'Whatever for?'

'We're going into the city for dinner.'

'What? . . . Why?'

He rose. 'I'll run you a bath.'

Slim sat up, groaning. 'But I just got in! And it's Sunday! *We* have the dinners on Sundays! What kind of rustler would dare tread on our patch?'

Leland had moved into Slim's closet. 'The white Mainbocher or the yellow?'

'Neither.'

'Nan. C'mon.'

'Which is it? Von Trapps or *Gypsy*?' She followed him into their dressing room.

'Which is what?'

'I'm assuming a mandatory dinner in Manhattan is related to some form of business crisis. Is it Slippery Strippers or Loose Lederhosen?' she joked, dipping a toe in the bath.

'Actually it's neither. It's Pam. Churchill.'

Slim stared at him blankly. 'What?'

'Pam Churchill's in New York, at the Carlyle, and she's invited us to dine.'

'Why?'

'I think to welcome you back to town?'

'To welcome herself, more like . . .' Slim, with a sudden chill, reached for a dressing gown, covering her body, aware that Leland had said nothing about the ten pounds she'd managed to shed. 'Call her and cancel.'

'No.'

'Why not?'

'Because she asked us and it's a small group and I said that we'd come,' Leland persisted.

'I'm not about to go into town and have dinner with Pam Churchill!' Slim snapped, losing her famous cool. 'I *just* got home— I haven't eaten a *morsel* in days. I certainly don't want her gray meat and rubber soufflé! I want to stay in, sit with you, walk in our garden, and eat *your* cooking.'

Leland faltered, then retreated to his own closet, returning with a necktie. Slim frowned as he knotted it in the mirror.

'What are you doing?'

'Well, if you're not coming, I guess I'll just have to go alone.'

And with that Slim knew she had no choice.

She disappeared into her closet and reemerged minutes later in a flowing black pantsuit, hair pulled back tightly in a bun, more dressed for a funeral than a dinner. Dabbing a pat of scent behind her ears, she walked past Leland, leaving the bath untouched, faucet dripping into the steaming water.

SLIM WONDERED, AS SHE AND LELAND WAITED for the door to be opened at La Churchill's Carlyle penthouse, which of Pam's many benefactors was footing this particular bill. (Rumor had it that she'd had another go at Élie de Rothschild. Who they *say* provided that noxious Parisian pied-à-terre after their *first* split—though others claim it was Gianni. That *both* left her high and dry when she'd issued ultimatums. And those were just the usual suspects. The suite could have been hired by any *number* of mystery men.)

Slim had stonewalled Leland in the taxi, so resentful was she that he'd allowed their reunion to be disrupted. She hadn't even had the chance to spring her great surprise. She had decided in Tempe that what they needed, what they had earned, was a second honeymoon. Not a pilgrimage with friends, not a business venture. Not a visit to an asylum to see a Hayward offspring, or to a hospital to lose one. Just a month, just the two of them. Slim and Hay. No interruptions. She'd worked out the logistics. Once *Gypsy* was cast, they were free of commitments. They could fly first to Paris, stop briefly in Madrid, then spend the rest of the summer in Venice. She had even wired to arrange a month-long rental of an apartment in the Gritti Palace. Her big reveal would have to wait, thanks to—

Slim practically winced as the door opened to reveal Mrs. Churchill's eager face. Looking almost identical, in her new habitat, to the matron Slim had last encountered in Paris—perhaps a bit chubbier, a bit rosier, the thickness of her arms curling around a sleeveless shift she had no business wearing.

'Slim! Let me look at you.' Pam stepped back and appraised her in the manner one might assess a child returned home from summer camp.

It was over her shoulder, locked in that suffocating embrace, that Slim saw it: an entire foyer, practically stuffed to the rafters with white roses.

And not just any white roses. . .

Special roses. Rare ones.

Her roses.

At least five hundred dollars' worth of Bourbon 'Boule de Neiges.'

Slim walked to one and touched it, just to make sure its velvet petals were real, not some nightmarish hallucination induced by seven days of starvation in shriveled desert plains.

She turned to Pam, looking directly into her dull, bovine eyes.

'Where did you get these?'

Pam smiled, lip curling with satisfaction. 'Oh, I don't know . . . Someone sent them?'

Slim shifted her gaze to Leland, who smiled, innocently.

Pam slipped into hostess mode. 'Slim, may I tempt you with a cocktail after all that abstinence? Leland tells me it's just been *dreadful* for you.' She brushed a hand across his lapel as she moved into the body of the suite. In passing, in that prim English-rose tone, coated in familiarity—'Leland, you know where the ice bucket is. Be a dear and refill it, won't you?'

Slim looked to Leland, shaking her head. He took a step toward her.

'Nan . . .'

'You son of a bitch.'

Then, like any seasoned pro, Slim entered the dinner theater and put on one helluva show.

SHE'D NOT MET HIS EYES the remainder of the evening.

She had been perfectly civil, perfectly polite. No one could fault her there. At the end of a surprisingly uneventful dinner of chicken roulade over rice—perfectly acceptable pinwheels of blandness—Slim had thanked her hostess and walked with Leland to the elevator.

It wasn't until they'd hailed a taxi in front of the Carlyle, after they'd traveled for a good half hour in silence, that Leland cleared his throat.

```
INT. TAXI — NIGHT

Leland's voice cuts through the silence—


                    LELAND
        Nan, I think I better tell you, before
        Truman or some other goddamn gossip does ...

                (a beat, then—)

        I've taken Pam Churchill out a few times
        while you were away. No big deal.
```

> SLIM
>
> Well now.
>
>> (a bitter smile)
>
> *That* should have been your opening line.
>
>> LELAND
>
> Come on, Nan. You know you're the only
> woman I've ever really loved...

He reaches for her hand, but Slim turns away. She
stares blankly out of the window, watching the
lights of Manhattan fly past in a blur.

IN EXACTLY FORTY-EIGHT MINUTES and fifty-seven seconds, the taxi
pulled up in front of the Hayward house in Manhasset. Slim waited
until Leland had paid the driver and they walked safely back
inside. Waited until she'd wandered numbly down the hall, shedding the black pantsuit, leaving it lifeless on the carpet like the
shed skin of a missing corpse.

Waited until she had stepped into the bath Leland had drawn
for her hours earlier, the water now as chilled as the pond beyond
their garden.

Waited until he'd predictably called from outside the door
that he was 'going out to get some air'—she suspected as far as
the pay phone by the corner shop to ring the thieving Mrs.
Churchill. Then, lying back in the icy bath, Slim began to sob.
Silently, so that no one might hear her, even though the house
was empty.

After an hour she emerged, shriveled, flushed dry, ready to
patch the gaping wound that was her future.

CODA

OF COURSE WE'D EACH SPOTTED PAM in various boutiques, brazenly
looking at wedding china.

We were sitting at lunch at Le Petit Jardin, in a circular booth, watching the maître d' flambé our spinach salads with cognac from a rolling cart at the head of our table, applauding when the alcohol ignited in an impressive burst of flame.

The dining room was a delightful play on a Mediterranean garden, with lighting that changed hues and intensities to simulate the lifespan of a day in the indoor botanical space. Early lunch, it was a pale sky blue, deepening gradually over the hours to a rich sunset shade. We all acknowledged this was terribly effective, and found ourselves stretching our luncheons over multiple courses, just to enjoy the shifting atmosphere.

It was at that moment that we saw Pam cross the room, carrying a large hat box from Bergdorf's. A few Tiffany bags as well. Of course we could only guess what *those* might contain—

'Can you *imagine*? The audacity.'

'To register before the body's even cool?'

'Surely Leland wouldn't possibly consider *that* . . . ? Over *Slim*?'

'Well, we do know what she's like, *Mrs.* Churchill . . .'

'And what *they're* like.' (Implied: The Husbands.)

'We certainly know she goes for the brass ring each time.'

'They do love that English peaches-and-cream routine—'

'The governess fetish . . .'

'Perhaps Leland's had too much *Sound of Music* on the brain . . .'

'That *has* to be the Balenciaga . . . The white one? The one in the window on Fifty-eighth? It's the only hat that would take a box that big.'

'Do you remember what she used to look like? *Before*. She wouldn't have known a Balenciaga from a Barbour, for Christ's sake.'

'I remember seeing her in Capri just after the war, and instead of wearing, you know, appropriate slacks and espadrilles—she had horrid lizard brogues and the *gaudiest* dirndl skirt . . . Not the first clue! Within one year of meeting Gianni, she's suddenly wearing Chanel this and Dior that, and the most stunning of jewelry . . . ?'

'Well, of course! She's the only woman Gianni ever spent money on.'

'And that's not to mention the *parting* gifts. That extortionate apartment in Paris—don't *dare* tell Marella!'

'Don't forget the *Bentley.*'

'He couldn't even fob her off with *Fiat* stock!'

We cackled at this, a little too loudly. A little too . . . *collectively.* Pam turned her head, looking at our table from across the room with a curious expression.

'Oh God—she's seen us.'

'Well, of *course* she's seen us.'

'Shit. She's waving.'

'Just smile and wave back . . .'

We did so, making an effort to smile across the room to a woman that we loathed, each of us waving. One or two of us even tempted fate with a disingenuous air kiss.

'Bitch.' This through teeth clenched into a smile.

'She can't come over. There isn't any room.'

'She could pull a chair up . . .'

'Well, we'll just have to have another cart-dish to keep the path blocked.'

We looked to the maître d' as he plated our salads, placing them around the table with a nod and an 'Enjoy, madame' for each of us.

'And we'll have six fettuccine carbonaras as well—baby size.'

'So fattening! We can't!'

'It keeps the cart here . . .'

'*I* heard she'd had Christie's around to appraise the Haywards' collection.'

'She can't do that! The deal's not sealed yet—frankly, she got closer with Gianni.'

'Even if Leland was so idiotic, she *can't* just start taking Slim's things!'

'State of New York. Equal division of property.'

'Well, my cook heard it from Slim's cook, confirmed by Delores who's friendly with Brooke. They *say* Pam's been in residence in Manhasset the whole time Slim's been away.'

'*No!* For how long?'

'Ever since that goddamn *South Pacific* with Bill and Babe.'

'Does Slim know?'

'Of course she doesn't know! Do you think Slim would keep quiet over that? Pamela Churchill—living in *her* house?'

'She never should have gone to Europe to help Betty.'

'What do you mean? She was being a friend!'

'Darling Slim.'

'Salt of the earth.'

'Always there for a pal.'

'Do you want to know the *worst*?'

'Go on!'

'You have to *promise* not to breathe a word to another living soul . . .'

We all swore, solemnly. (A promise we'd keep until the next lunchtime sesh, when we'd make others promise the same. We maintained a shared delusion that any of us could ever keep a secret. Try as we might, there was always someone we'd find that we *needed* to tell.)

'The cook says that Pam has gone through the house with sheets of red stickers—you know those 'sold' dots they use at charity auctions? Well, the Hayward *cook* says that Pam has gone around and stuck those on everything she wants Leland to get in the divorce.'

'*No!*'

'Furniture, paintings, the whole lot.'

'Isn't she vile?'

'Wretched woman!'

'Poor Slim!'

'I could just punch Leland in that great big jaw of his.'

'But I've always *liked* Leland so . . .'

'Not anymore.'

'Agreed.'

'Still . . . It's not over yet.' This had been hopeful, on all our parts.

'After all, nobody *marries* Pam Churchill.'

And as the maître d' returned to prepare the carbonara that we didn't really want, that we'd only ordered to prevent the foul Mrs. Churchill from pulling up a chair, we watched the light fade a shade darker in the simulated gardens at Le Petit Jardin, and we pondered what kind of woman thinks to put red stickers on another woman's treasures, and sighed a breath of relief, knowing how close each of our belongings had come to that same pock-marked fate.

ELEVEN

1960

SEPTET

THERE WAS A FINAL TWIST IN THE FANDANGO that involved us all.

Slim was lying in bed, wallowing. Frankly, missing Leland. It was still early days, and she hadn't completely accepted it was over.

The phone rang just before nine, something that's seldom done, as we say. Her heart leaped as she scrambled for the receiver—*Leland*?

'Helloooooo Big Mama,' the caller chirped.

Truman, whose voice she was happy to hear. If it couldn't be her darling Hay on the line, she would prefer the caller be Tru than any other.

'Morning, Truheart. Why so early?'

'Weeeuuullll, I've got a *very* special lunch all planned for you today, and I just had to get hold of you to make *sure* that you can be there.'

'Where?'

'The Colony. Trust me, Big Mama—I can't tell you anything else about it, but I *personally* think I've come up with something really stupendously special.'

WE LATER LEARN that he had given us all slightly different time-lines, in order to stagger arrivals.

Slim was the first, as per Truman's arrangements.

She entered the lobby, greeted warmly by owners Gene, then George: Of all our lunchtime haunts, the Colony took the cake for service, and while a popular business lunch spot for the gents, George and Gene knew *precisely* where their bread was buttered. One o'clock onward was known as the Hive, 'Queen Bees' reigning in the majority.

'Hello, Miss Sleeem. What beautiful Dior you wear today.' George kissed both her cheeks in the European style. Slim did look lovely, in a white crepe pantsuit with a low neckline.

'Thanks, George. I'm meeting—'

'Meester Truman—yes, he is expecting you. He has planned something *most* special. I think you all will like it very much.'

'All of us who . . . ?'

'He says it's for heeeezz Swans.'

'Ah. And how many "Swans" is he expecting . . . ?'

'Oh, I cannot say—that is Meester Truman's surprise. He awaits you in the bar.'

He motioned toward a Moorish door to the left of the lobby, which Gene held open for Slim to pass through. He offered a slight bow, not being quite so Continental as George.

'Afternoon, Mrs. Hayward.'

It still pained Slim to hear that name, no longer hers.

They continued into the bar room, where Truman sat, looking *très* cat-ate-canary, grin widening as she approached.

'Here, darling, I've already ordered you a little something. Marco's made you a Colony Special . . .' He slid a martini in front of her on the bar.

'Okay, Truheart. What gives?' She perched on the stool adjacent, studying his expression. 'I just *know* that you're up to something. You look *far* too pleased with yourself not to be.'

He batted his lashes, assuming a thick Southern accent. 'Why, Ms. Slimsky, I haven't the foggiest notion why you'd *imply* such a thing.'

'Who's coming? George already spilled the beans it's not just us—which I'm more than a little peeved about, by the way. I dragged myself outta bed to be with *you*. I don't need a group.'

'Babe's coming.'

'Oh, well, that's all right. If it's just Babe.'

'And maybe just a *few* others . . .'

'Mmm. We eating in here?' She motioned the bar area, set with twenty-some-odd tables. Since the Duke of Windsor proclaimed he actually *preferred* to eat in the bar, it had become all the rage.

'Oh Lordy, no! I have a table all set. In the *main* room. This is a *formal* luncheon.' Truman looked at his Cartier, strapped to his wrist. 'Goodness, the time! Bring that with you. We'll go on in, I think. We wouldn't want to miss anything . . .'

He took Slim's arm, cozying up to her while leading her back to the lobby.

George pushed open the portal to a long, rectangular space, burgundy and cream in tone, lit by cut-glass chandeliers and flickering candelabras. The dining room was heaving, chatter galore . . .

Yet the moment Slim and Truman entered the space, a hush fell over the crowd. All eyes turned to assess the new arrivals. Conversation and silverware suspended, and for a breath of a moment, it was as if time froze—a ritual that would repeat itself in varying degrees for every new arrival. The diners watched with added interest as George led them to a circular table, which had been specially placed in the prime location. Set for twelve, much to Slim's dismay.

'Looky here, honey,' Tru enthused to Slim. 'The choice spot. The holiest of holies.'

'Fucking Christ, Truman! Do we even *know* this many people?'

'Now, Big Mama, it's good for you to be *sociable*.' He pulled a chair out for Slim beside his own. The table was exquisitely set with the finest linens, clean white china, and antique silver. Hand-calligraphed menu cards sat at each setting, and at six of the twelve places, tiny, individual bowls, a fresh-cut gardenia floating in each.

Slim looked to her host, brow raised. 'No Little Gems today?'

'Nah—I thought we'd shake it up a bit. Gardenias are what Lady Day wore in her hair, and trust me, they smell *heavenly*.'

And as if on cue, in walked Babe. Same ritual: the silence from the other diners, the assessment. Mumbles of approval.

Babe, reaching the table, oblivious, pecked Slim's cheek, then Tru's.

'Oh Tru, this really *is* lovely.' Looking closer at the menu cards. 'Ooooo, Quails Colony! My favorite. And Slim—look! Your crab bisque!'

'Why do you think they're there, Babyling? I've picked *all* your favorites. Now, Big Mama, do you want me to pin your gardenia in your hair? Clean white always looked so *right* against the gold.'

And with that the door swung open once more, revealing Marella. Truman called to her from across the room, '*Benvenuta, Uno!*'

Marella looked perplexed to see Slim and Babe, clearly misunderstanding that her invitation was not, in fact, *à deux*. Over the next ten minutes, the group expanded to include first Gloria, then C.Z., Truman delighting at each arrival.

Small talk commenced, Tru telling Marella and Gloria all about Verbier, about which snow bunnies had been spotted with strapping instructors skiing off-piste on the backside of Mont Fort. Babe babbled on about some special fertilizer she'd bought for the beds at Kiluna. C.Z. offered an alternative—elephant dung she'd procured from the animal handlers when Barnum & Bailey's Circus had come to town. Slim alone sat silent, unable to get Leland out of her head. Eventually Marella leaned over to Truman and asked—'Vero, why are we a party of six at a table for twelve?'

'*Pazienza*, Uno . . . *pazienza!*' And with that he checked his watch and looked eagerly toward the entrance. 'It won't be long now . . .'

'Won't be long until what?'

'Until our guests of honor arrive . . .'

'I thought *I* was the guest of honor,' said Slim.

'Nope. You're the most *important*, but not the "of honor." Let's just say it's more of a *dubious* honor in this case . . .'

We—and Slim—stared at the empty chairs, then to the door again.

It was then we each saw Truman's mischievous grin widen as the door swung open, and diners froze forks, knives, and conversation, poised to assess . . .

And there she was. None other than Mrs. Churchill. The infamous Pam Churchill. The newly–wedded Mrs. Leland Hayward. The *non-Slim* Mrs. Leland Hayward. The slept-with-all-our-husbands Pamela Digby Churchill Hayward, in her wide Balenciaga hat.

We can't remember which of us, under our breath, said, 'Oh, Truman!'

Which of us said, 'How could you?'

From Marella, a low curse, uttered in Italian.

We do know that Slim sat tall, shooting Pam a look that could freeze the Sahara. We know that we felt composed and settled—a strong flock. A unit of solidarity. Babe squeezed Slim's hand beneath the table.

We have a vague memory of Truman's face, flushed with delight—a spectator watching a tennis match, swiveling back and forth between wronged wives and husband-hunter.

Our prevailing memory is the look of sheer panic on Pam's face as she was forced—in front of not just *us*, but fifty other tables, boasting the most powerful faces in Manhattan—to either retreat, or make that long walk of shame across the packed eatery, in which one might have heard a feather fall.

By the time she reached our table and claimed her empty spot, beads of sweat had formed around that cotton-candy hairline, and on the upper lip, pooling above what we all agreed were truly unfortunate cuspids.

For most shit-stirrers that would have been enough, but given Truman's talent for public humiliation, no one was surprised (except perhaps Marella) when the last guests appeared.

Our husbands. Mrs. Churchill's co-conspirators.

One by one, Loel Guinness, Bill Paley, and Gianni Agnelli arrived, forced like Pam to make the interminable walk under the watchful eyes of the Colony. They stopped on the way to our table, pausing to shake important hands along the route. Aware of being observed, they moved with studied swagger. They kissed the cheeks of most of us around the table—with the noted exceptions of Truman and Pam, whose gaze they were careful to avoid. They laughed particularly loudly and talked with amplified zest, all the while checking their watches, plotting their escapes. Each sat for all of five minutes before making their excuses of needing to return to their various offices.

Throughout, Truman kept up the role of the bubbly host, chatting about anything and everything in a thin attempt to disguise what he was really doing . . . trotting Pam Churchill out in front of Manhattan's finest and branding her with a big husband-stealing scarlet 'A' in the marketplace of the Colony.

Finally—after the Husbands had made their excuses and begged off, one by one, the backs of their suits sheepishly receding, no matter how they pretended otherwise—Slim said to Pam, coolly, 'So. Is Leland not joining us . . . ?'

Tru, for his part, quipped, 'Oh Big Mama, *trust* me—I invited him.'

Pam, perspiration weeping under our collective gaze, said in a clipped voice—'Leland decided not to come.'

Slim—in that droll Betty Bacall tone, the tone that Betty got from Slim—'Well. That seems to be the one smart decision Leland's made of late.'

PAM LEAVING FIRST WAS A GIVEN. The rest of us divided into pairs, Babe and Marella heading toward Kenneth's on East 54th, C.Z. and Gloria to Erno Laszlo on West Broadway, hoping to wing appointments. Enjoying the post-mortem at the Colony bar, Slim and Truman washed down a pair of Marco's special martinis, jabber fueled by absinthe and gin and a feeling of triumph. They giggled recounting the faces of each of the wayward husbands, and even went so far as to ponder what Leland might have done—and what he would say when he heard of the episode.

'Truheart,' said Slim through riotous tears, 'there's a special place in hell reserved for souls like you . . .'

'Yeah, but the point is . . . didn't you have fun, making her sweat?'

And Slim, for the first time in weeks, realized that she had.

They laughed so, spurred by martinis and mirth, that Slim could almost forget that the disgraced Mrs. Churchill Hayward had the one thing she most wanted, never to be recovered.

Her sweet, darling Hay, who she'd never stop loving.

WHILE THE REST OF US SAW this little Colony episode as nothing more than a naughty bit of fun—something to bolster Slim's flagging ego, something to end the battle that had been waged in New York since the whole ridiculous Hayward–Churchill Fandango began—*Marella* saw it as something more sinister.

'Perhaps it's my English, but when Truman told me all these years that I was his *Numero Uno* swan . . . I didn't know that he called all of us the same.'

'What do you mean, darling?' asked Babe as they waited for a taxi.

'He said it was because of my neck—it being so long. I thought that was just what he called *me*. I hadn't realized it was just a word that he used . . . for us *all*.'

'I don't think that means anything, really.'

'*Cigni . . . Troppi cigni.* Too many swans.'

TWELVE

1954

LAMENTATION

THE BOY IS TWENTY-NINE when his Mama leaves him for good.

She's tried to cut and run before, has left and returned so many times, in fact, when he finally realizes she's gone away in earnest, he thinks it another of her wolf-crying stunts.

It's four days past New Year's, just after the confetti has been mopped from the gutters in the damp Champs-Élysées—where streamers are trodden underfoot, clinging to stilettos like strands of soggy seaweed.

He is in Paris, with Jack.

His Jack.

He is in love—wildly so.

After all that searching, to think that love could be so effortless, so constant . . .

It makes him want to pinch himself, he so can't believe his luck. He refrains, however, for fear that in doing so he might alter things—that perfection might suddenly vanish.

They've just left Sicily, where they rented a house on a craggy cliff, where each spent mornings writing, then wandered, separately more often than not, down to the ocean to swim. They'd taken turns going to the market while the other reclined on the beach. They reconvened at midday and prepared simple lunches of olives, ripe tomatoes, and fresh-grilled redfish.

'When two people are as close as *we* are,' the boy will later report, 'you don't need to be together every second. You're together even when you're not.'

Afternoons were devoted to writing—Jack working on a play; the boy in the early stages of inventing a girl called Holiday Golightly. Part Nina, part Bang-Bang Woodward—an amalgamation of about a dozen girls he knew. Perhaps closest to the truth, Holly is the Siamese twin of her creator. Those of us who know him will find we cannot read her without hearing his Southern squeal speaking her dialogue, a whimsical hillbilly. A genuine phony—a wannabe, hanging on the fringes, who, like the author himself, turns to visits to Tiffany's to escape what they both call the Mean Reds.

The Mean Reds are infinitely worse than the blues, and something the boy knows well—although Jack has cured him of the malady almost entirely. His deep voice, bare chest, and the sure shuffle of his footsteps have replaced silver breakfast sets and alligator wallets as tonic.

The boy has committed himself to fiction once again, having just finished writing *Beat the Devil*, the Bogart picture—*saving* it more like, ever the pocket Merlin, Nelle having spotted perhaps his greatest talent early on. He'd been asked by Big John Huston to work his magic on a picture with no script, flailing its way through production. The tow-haired scribe was sent back to his monastic room each evening to create the following day's scenes from scratch. This he achieved 'by the hair on his chinny chin chin'—though we later tell him the expression rings false, he being far too prepubescent to grow facial hair of any sort.

It was a gig he couldn't refuse, for it paid him enough to bankroll Nina and Joe—the ability to do so being something he wants badly.

Having met and charmed the matinee idols of his youth, the boy was pleased to have infiltrated their meteoric sphere. He was the film's mascot, never failing to regale both cast and crew with outrageous tales, whose veracity they doubted, but whose invention they admired. He earned the reluctant acceptance of Bogie and Huston, who came to respect their pint-sized scribe for his capacity to out-drink the whole damn bunch, as well as for his astonishing physical prowess.

Having beaten Bogie in an arm-wrestling challenge, the boy is feeling every inch the man his Mama always wanted him to be. He has—all five foot three of him—managed to rassle the great Bogart to the ground, inflicting a week's worth of bed rest.

She'd love that detail . . . it's macho after all.

'*Nina*,' he plans to brag to his Mama, 'I overpowered *Bogart*. I took that poor, sweet man down in a bet. For all his tough-guy facade, he's an absolute *pussycat*.' (Of course we've all heard different figures—two hundred seems to be the median take, but his Mama's indifference requires the fudging of figures for impact.)

When he phones specially to tell her this, a few days before Christmas, he fails to reach her. Christmas comes and goes without a call, but this isn't unique. The boy has spent more Christmases without her than not. She usually sends a present in a box, wrapped in foil-paper, mailed to wherever he might be—tweed suits or bow ties or smart new swimming trunks—but this year he knows not to expect this.

It is *he* who sends *her* boxes now, or envelopes stuffed with cash. Money she needs to maintain her sham of a life; money that will keep her clinging to the final rung on the ladder of Café society, after the others have snapped beneath her.

His stories, once rejected by the *New Yorker*, have long since become the objects of an ongoing tug-of-war between publications.

Better still, he's found love with a kind man. A man who is as present as Nina has been absent. Jack—a man's man. The kind of man his Mama always wanted *him* to be.

'Jack was *tout droit* when we met—straight as an *arrow*, honey. He was married to a *terribly* lovely girl—Joanie was her name. They were in *Oklahoma* together—dancers in the chorus, of all goddamn things! And inseparable, until she ran off with another chorus boy while Jack was fighting the Jerries overseas. Well, that just smashed that big ole heart of his into a thousand little bits. He was never gonna love again . . . until he found *me*.'

The boy's Mama even likes Jack—as an entity unto himself, that is. When first introduced she flirted with him shamelessly, as she had with all of Truman's lovers. He's her perfect specimen. Rugged good looks, in an 'everyman' way. Freckled Irish skin. Auburn hair. A strong-set jaw and rich baritone. And Nina *does* love a man who can dance.

Her only beef with Jack, in fact, is the fact that he could ever take an interest in her son in that way. She refuses to believe Jack is anything more than her boy's 'close friend.' When her own friends argue otherwise, Nina's quick to insist, 'Jack was *married*, for Chrissakes! As for Truman, all he needs is to find the right gal and settle down.' When pressed—after a coupla Scotches—Nina will slur, 'Look, I know what he *is* . . . But there are plenty of queers who marry nice girls.'

THE PHONE GOES AT SUNRISE in the room at the Hôtel de France et de Choiseul on the rue Saint-Honoré.

The boy and Jack are sleeping, limbs entwined.

Jack fumbles for the phone, reaching past the boy, who disappears beneath the bed sheets. When he hears Joe Capote's thick Cuban accent shouting on the line, Jack passes the phone along, wordlessly. It's hard to make out what Joe's saying on a good day, but now he sounds sauced beyond sense.

'Joe . . . slow down,' Jack hears the voice beneath the covers plead. 'I can't— What about Nina . . . ? Joe . . . Listen to me . . . Just put her on the line. I'll sort it all— What—? Gone? When will she be back?'

Then:

'What do you mean she's *gone* . . . ?'

It's then that Jack feels the boy's body begin to tremble against his torso when he— —

JACK RECALLS BEING UNDER THE DRILL when the call comes—a sad fuck with a root canal.

He returns from the dentist to find the boy sitting on the Big-Bed, hanging up the phone. He looks to him, eyes wide. Frightened.

'My Mama's gone away, Jack.'

He begins to weep, but his tears refuse to come. Jack sits down beside him, wrapping his muscular arms around the stunned little creature.

As if in a daze, the boy assures him, 'Don't you worry. It's *okay*. She's done this before, and she *always* comes back, sooner or— —'

IN A VARIANT TALE, THE BOY HIMSELF REMEMBERS arriving back from a walk in the Jardin du Luxembourg, icicles hanging from the trees like shards of Baccarat. He returns to find a telegram at the Hôtel de France et de Choiseul from Joe Capote.

When Jack returns from the dentist, he finds the boy curled in a ball on the mattress, still wearing his winter overcoat. He's been crying, but he's calm now.

'Nina's gone,' is all he'll say at first.

Jack lies down beside him in the bed and holds him. Then Jack hears him repeating a soft incantation, almost a lullaby:

'I've got money. She didn't have to do it . . . I've got the— —'

STILL ANOTHER TELLING BRINGS a *series* of calls from Joe, who, no sooner than he hangs up, rings back again. He cannot comprehend that she really is gone, and needs to hear the boy's high, melodic voice, his Southern cadence, if only to be reminded of his Nina, to fill the void left without her.

'Just *talk*,' Joe tells him on the transatlantic call.

The boy removes his glasses and rubs his brimming eyes, causing them to overflow, staining his cheeks with the damp.

'What do you want me to say, Joe?'

'It doesn't matter. Say anything. Tell me a story . . . Tell me some gossip from the old neighborhood. I don't care what you say—I just want to hear your voice.'

'Okay.'

'But Truman—?'

'Yes?'

'Keep talking. Keep talking, because if you stop, even for a second, I'm afraid I'll fall apart.'

And so the boy, with a catch in his voice, begins to tell Joe Capote all about a hillbilly girl called Lillie Mae from Monroeville, who had scrapped and scraped to leave the little ole country town, who transformed herself in a willful feat of self-creation into Joe's exotic Nina.

WHATEVER THE TIMING, IT IS CERTAIN that it happened in those first days of the new year, when the boy is summoned home to see his Mama one last time.

Jack resents the hell out of her. It's just like Nina to drag him back, just when he's finding his wings.

A plane ticket has been purchased and the boy has packed his grip. It's arranged that a bus will collect him at the Hôtel de France et de Choiseul and drive him to the airport. His Vuitton suitcase sits by the door, a tag tied to its handle specifying 'NEW YORK' as its destination.

He sits on the bed's edge, staring at nothing in particular. He cradles his dog close to his chest—the one he'd purchased for himself once he became successful. Since no one ever made good on their promises, he had to take matters into his own hands. It's the boy's first English bulldog—a puppy he's christened Charlie J. Fatburger.

'Now Charlie, you'll be a good boy for Jack, won't you?' the boy whispers in his ear.

Charlie fails to reply beyond a steady, listless panting.

Jack is in the bedroom when the night maid enters, stumbling over the suitcase by the door. He hears her ask the boy—in heavily accented English—'*Alors!* Monsieur, 'oo is going to New York . . . ?'

The boy's voice—soft, forlorn—'Me. *I'm* going.'

202

He sounds tiny—even tinier than he is. The boy's persona is usually so much larger than his physical being, one forgets how small he actually is.

When the concierge rings to announce that the boy's transport has arrived, Jack carries his case downstairs for him.

It's a freezing day in Paris, the temperature having dropped to three degrees Celsius. The boy shivers in a second-hand jacket, still holding his pup close, telling him in dulcet tones what a fine boy he is.

The driver takes his case, leaving him to say his goodbyes to Jack, who, in his stoic way, nods as if imparting the courage the boy lacks. He nuzzles Charlie Fatburger's lumpy neck before placing him, with great care, into Jack's arms. And without another word the boy climbs onto the bus, taking his seat among the empty ones. It starts to snow, the exact moment the bus pulls away from the curb, a gust of icy wind propelling him toward the airport, to the plane that will take him all the way across the world, back to New York City.

Later, we'll think this is just the sort of indulgent, gothic detail the boy enjoys adding for impact and doubt that it had happened . . . but Jack, who is never one for embellishment, has sworn to those of us he deems worthy of conversation that it was indeed the case.

For once the boy doesn't need fiction to garner our sympathy.

HE DOUBTS WHAT HE'S BEEN TOLD until the moment that he sees her.

He feels certain they've gotten it wrong, and expects that when he walks into 1060 Park Avenue in his new Italian suit, plum silk waistcoat, and polished patent shoes, looking every inch the dandy, that Nina (a few Scotches in) will give him a scornful once-over and insist that he go change.

'Who do you think you *are*,' he's sure she'll challenge, 'Oscar-frigging-Wilde? Now be a doll and pop off to your room and get yourself dressed proper. I've had your Brooks Brothers pressed and laid out.'

It's not until he's arrived at the barren apartment (she and Joe having been forced, by altered circumstances, to sell possessions in his absence in order to pay their creditors). Not until he's donned the conservative blue Brooks Brothers suit she's always favored—'Now *thaaaat*'s classic,' she'd drawl with sickly-sweet approval when he'd worn it under duress. Not until he's seen her all laid out at Frank Campbell's on Madison and 81st, Manhattan's finest funeral parlor, for which he has footed the bill—she lying in the casket, in her one *real* Chanel suit, which she'd saved up for months to buy.

It's not until *then* that it becomes a reality.

The boy braces himself as he approaches her coffin, prepared to encounter the features he's studied so closely all his life. The long face, the porcelain skin. The honeyed curls, set at the beauty parlor in an arc around her face, like a halo dumped on its side.

When he brings himself to peek, the boy is startled to see not his Mama, but a woman much older than the Nina he'd last battled months earlier. Her hair, no longer its carefully maintained blond, is streaked with gray. He'll later learn that she'd been forced to cancel her salon trips—an indulgence she and Joe could no longer afford. Still a spring chicken, just shy of her forty-ninth birthday, Nina's graying hair makes her look a woman of sixty or more.

'Why didn't you *tell* me?' the boy will demand of Joe as they hunch over a pair of bourbons, their fourth—or fifth?—round in a dive bar off East 56th in the blur of days to come. 'Nina *loved* her hair . . . I could have *paid* for that.' Joe will shrug, having existed in a permanent bubble of grief-stricken drunkenness for days.

Serene in her coffin as she never was in life, her complexion is preserved with the mortician's thick pancake base, lending her countenance a smooth, if slightly waxen sheen. (She'd have enjoyed that detail—calling it 'a dewy glow,' something she'd read in a magazine.) Her lips—thinner than the boy recalls, thanks to the stress of her troubles—are painted their signature red, though it now seems a smear of unnatural color.

A thin, crimson flatline.

The boy stares at her as if examining a stranger.

Later, when he attempts to piece together her final days, Eleanor Friede—the friend she had lunched with the week before her death—will tell him a story that nearly severs his grieving heart. Eleanor will recall it having been close to Thanksgiving rather than New Year's, but county coroner records prove otherwise. They had been to the Plaza, the venue Nina (like her boy) loved above all others. They were seated in an out-of-the-way table in the Oak Bar, practically in the *kitchen*. Nina ordered modestly—a side salad and a single slice of bread, foregoing the rich delicacies she once had relished as lunch fare. The Plaza's cognac chicken hash yet another luxury axed with all the rest. Besides, the hint of booze might have tossed her right off the wagon. She refrained from ordering even a thimble of wine, she having been off the sauce for almost six months. She chain-smoked a string of Trues and guzzled cups of coffee.

'Tragic, really,' Eleanor would muse. 'We used to *love* a three-martini lunch, the pair of us. Hell, we'd start before noon, when we thought we could get away with it. But there Nina sat that last day—drinking coffee after coffee after coffee. She had the shakes—I dunno if it was the tremens, or all that caffeine, or plain old jittery nerves. But she wasn't herself, that's for certain. I should have known . . . If only I had *said* something. If only I'd *intervened* . . .'

Nina had confided in Eleanor about her recent trip to Cuba, where Joe had hoped to earn the dough to save his wanted hide. The authorities had circled like a kettle of vultures around Joe's pending fraud case. He had been convicted on three counts and was facing fourteen years in Sing Sing, unless he could manage to pay back the hundred grand he had embezzled from employers. Cuba was a last-ditch effort to drum up the demanded sum, but that, like the rest, had ended in failure. Nina had said the trip would either make them or break them, and it seemed to have done the latter.

She'd thrown one final shindig, months before—had bragged she'd give li'l ole Park Ave an evening it wouldn't forget. She'd made a list of all her society friends, and either circled their names or drawn an X through them, carefully weighing the transgressions of each. She'd planned for her party a Mardi Gras theme— made gumbo and po' boys and beignets stuffed with cheese as offerings. But when word got around that Joe was Sing Sing bound, the guests had failed to come. Nina had sat on a rented chair in her vast, empty apartment and with head in hands had grieved for all that she had lost. She'd almost cracked the glimmering nut that was the great goal of her life; she had *nearly* become a society lady. But fate intervened and tossed Lillie Mae right back into the penniless gutter she'd worked all her life to escape.

Eleanor will report that after plates were removed at that last lunch at the Plaza, Nina pulled a compact from her pocketbook, along with a tube of lipstick. Her signature red—which the boy forever equates with sugared kisses and tin fire engines, bought by a con man called Daddy.

She'll say Nina dug a tiny lip brush from her cosmetic bag, which she used to scrape the last of the lipstick from the tube, down to the *dregs* of the dregs. She painted her lips with an unsteady hand and laughed, sadly, 'Well, that's the last of *that*. Gone with the rest. *Kaput*.'

'So get another—we're walking right past Bendel's.'

'Can't.'

Truman will listen as Eleanor recalls—

'I did say to her, "Nina, for Christ's sake, it's just a tube of lipstick—anyone can afford a tube of lipstick . . . !" She looked at me in a curious way, looked right through me and said— "*I* can't. It's over."'

The boy will shake his head, still trying to wrap his brain around it all. How had he missed it? Had he known, he would have sent her *crates* of lipsticks—cherries and scarlets and juicy candy-apples, mailed all the way from Paris, paying extra postage for first class.

He sheds tears when her birdlike body is all laid out at Frank Campbell's funeral parlor, covered in hundreds of glorious calla— —

'BUT WHAT *HAPPENED*?' THE BOY ASKS JOE as they take turns sitting in the few chairs left at 1060 Park after the funeral. The mourners have reconvened in the empty space, after she's been cremated—burned to a crisp, to the consternation of her few remaining Bible-thumping relatives.

'She told me to get the hell out, so I did,' is all that Joe can offer. He himself seems unable to comprehend the loss—the burden of explaining it proving too great a task.

From what the boy pieces together, asking around the wake, his Mama, in her last few weeks, had fallen off the wagon. She had hit the bottle once again, the pressures of her ruin too much to stomach sober. She found she so relished the taste of that long-banned Mama-juice, she imbibed it like spring water. As was her habit when on the sauce, she'd have a glass too many and tend to pick a fight, with the closest person she could lay her hands on.

With Joe, whom she still loved with a lava-hot passion, her rage would fixate on his roving cock—between his Latin temper and Nina's jealous rages, they proved a lethal cocktail when shaken.

That last night in question, Nina's brother Seabon had come to stay, his wife in Bellevue for a tonsillectomy. The siblings had been drinking since mid-afternoon, starting, innocently enough, with lunchtime Bloody-Bloods, moving onto the dicier realms of Scotch.

As Seabon tells Truman, when cornered at the wake: 'When Joe got home, Nina thought she smelled perfume on his collar. He'd leaned in to kiss her, see. She accused him of being the low-level rat she knew him to be—a no-good cheating *sonofabitch*.'

Joe had waved the white flag of the failed businessman's button-down, which he stripped from his paunch as he retreated to the boy's old room. Nina, itching for a showdown, had followed him, and Seabon in turn had followed her.

'Don't you pretend with me, Joe Capote,' Nina'd reportedly hissed, climbing into Truman's old bed, leaning over him. 'I know where you go at night, you sick, whoring spic! I had you followed. Yeah, that's right—followed by a *gen-u-ine* private dick. And he tells me that your cock-a-doodle-doo has been up to no damn good!'

Joe had rolled away, placing a pillow over his ears. Nina ripped it from his grasp (Seabon says . . .), enraged by her whole god-damn life. 'You're so thick, you're not even smart enough to know to hide the evidence—I found pecker-tracks on your undershorts, for Chrissakes!'

Joe sat up, awake, trembling with rage.

'That's immoral, Nina, to go through a man's private things. You're a nosy, vicious bitch!'

'And you're just a no-good cheating waste of space.'

'I'd *never* go through your things,' Joe shot back.

'I had cause,' she insisted, unable to remember whether this was true or not.

Seabon later tells the boy that he had driven Joe to the only hotel he could afford, the West Side YMCA, while he himself had proceeded on to his office in Queens, to sleep on a pull-out sofa. Sometime while they were gone, Nina managed to consume another half-bottle of Scotch, which she used to wash down a fistful of Seconals.

There is evidence that she'd changed her mind before it was over. Beside her lifeless body—which Joe discovered when he returned just before dawn—was a princess telephone, off the hook, Nina's motionless hand posed as if reaching out to grab it.

'Who was she trying to call?' Truman breathes.

Who *had* she attempted and failed to call in those ebbing final moments? A doctor, to undo her own damage? Joe, to say that she was sorry? Or her boy, whom she loved and resented in equal measure—the son she never asked for, whose persona shamed her as much as his talent made her proud? Had she reached out to call for their help? Or to tell them each to go to hell for spoiling her vision of a life they had denied her? Or had the phone merely fallen when she toppled unconscious, bumping into an object she never intended to grasp?

Neither the boy nor Joe will ever know the answer, that being something Lillie-Mae-Nina-Faulk-Persons-Capote would take with her to the grave.

THE PHONE RINGS sometime during the wake at 1060 Park. Joe, who has been drinking so steadily he can hardly stand, lumbers to answer it.

'Capote rezzzzzzzzzz . . .' Joe, on the line, garbled. 'Herald *who*...?... I don't know any—Circumstanzzzes...? NO suzzzzzzspicious ... Yeah? Well, whadda *you* know about it?'

The boy hears Joe's voice rise and knows what the call must be. The vultures, circling.

'Look here, you lowlife hack—you got alotta nerve, calling here, interrupting a family'zzzzzzz—Yeah, Truman Capote'zzzzz—'

The boy rushes to intercede. 'Hang up, for gawd's sake! Hang *up!!*' he screeches at Joe, who drops the receiver like a hot potato.

LATER, AFTER THE GUESTS HAVE MOSTLY GONE, the grown boy sits on his Mama's bed, still in his Brooks Brothers suit, the jacket of which he refuses to remove—as if by wearing something she loved he might magically conjure her back. He's playing her favorite ragtime records on the old gramophone with its fraying needle, over and over on loop.

Each mourner tiptoes in to comfort him, sharing a memory of the last time they saw her. One recalls Nina staring into the windows at Tiffany's at dawn in a decades-old evening gown, drinking cold coffee from a cheap Styrofoam cup.

'It was hours before they opened—I don't know what she was doing there,' the witness ponders. The boy smiles to himself through his grief.

At last, something of the Nina that he recognizes . . .

'She was escaping the Mean Reds,' he says. His book not yet published, the term is something he shares with his Mama alone—and she's not around to appreciate the reference.

WHEN LATER ASKED WHAT HAPPENED to his Mama, the boy's stock answer is 'pneumonia.' Sometimes it's 'rapid-onset cancer.' Other times a heart attack or seizure took her out.

Nelle alone can tell that he's lying—she knowing the boy well enough—and vows to, over time, learn the truth of Nina's passing.

He is careful who he shares this with, the secret of his Mama's death having become his most valuable of playing cards.

It's not until a year later, when he meets the one that *should* have been his mother, or lover, or both combined, that the boy tells the real tale. (We mean Babe, of course, Nina's exit having paved the way for her entrance.)

To some who have no means of fact-checking, he tests the waters with a bolder lie: 'My Mama was murdered, you know.' Depending on reactions, he'll either leave it at that, or quantify: 'She was killed by the people who shunned her. They slaughtered her, in cold blood.'

In retrospect it's clear that's when he decided to blame us—even though we'd not yet met him. Even though we'd never clapped eyes on Lillie-Mae-Nina-Capote.

He's looking for a scapegoat—a criminal to condemn—and he's decided that we're it. All of us—the privileged set—who robbed him of his Mama.

And perhaps it was then that he had his great idea . . . to seek us out. To befriend us. To punish us for a crime we hadn't the faintest idea we'd committed.

To make the whole damn class of us pay—for our money and our manners and our celebrated names, whether to the manor born or married in and up.

To make all of us regret—no matter how long it took—taking his Mama away from him for good.

THIRTEEN

1975

GLORIA

CORRIDO

PERHAPS THE PERSON MOST INCENSED by Truman's *Esquire* slaughter is the one who it hurt the least. Gloria has been in an absolute state since 'La Côte Basque' hit stands, we cannot help but note. Gloria, who was spared from harm. Gloria, who wasn't mentioned once.

We can't begin to comprehend her reaction, but then we've never been able to comprehend much of what Gloria thinks or feels.

We first detect her ire when lunching at that very spot not long after the brouhaha. Occupying our prime table, which we wouldn't *dream* of relinquishing for the sake of a half-baked fiction. (If Truman hoped to scare us away from the best lunch in town, he's got another thing coming . . .) Having settled in for a nice long session, we rehash the facts once more.

'I mean *honestly*. Can you *believe* the things he said about Paley?' rants Babe, pushing wilted spinach around with her fork. 'And *Slim*, for goodness sakes!'

She cuts her gaze to the co-aggrieved, as Slim coolly sips her martini.

Gloria listens, impassive; ingesting the facts along with her *homard Thermidor.*

Babe is the first to notice a lobsterish flush that creeps into Gloria's cheeks, matching the crustacean on her plate almost exactly. Mistaking the color for a sign of solidarity, Babe places a hand on her arm. 'Oh darling, I just knew you'd understand. And trust me . . . had he done it to *you*, I'd be livid too!'

Gloria retracts her limb from Babe's grasp, scooping the last of the lobster from its shell.

'Who says *I'm* not next . . . ?'

'Well, I certainly *hope* not. Count your blessings you escaped this debacle.'

'There's more coming,' Gloria snaps. '*Much* more. Six hundred pages at *least*.'

Mumbles of assent: 'Yes! I've seen them—'

'I've *heard* them—'

'He's read me snippets—'

'A parcel, wrapped in brown paper—'

'—carefully tied with string,' Gloria completes the phrase, oddly comforted. 'I'm sure that I'm next. That he's saving me for the leading role in his next installment. This *Kate McCloud* whom he speaks of . . . ? I fear that will be me.'

We stare at Gloria, and more than one of us spots something in those dark doe eyes of hers. She's feigning fear, feigning concern. Yet lurking beyond is something else . . .

It's rage.

She lights a cigarette, a Sobranie Black Russian.

'I know I'm next. I just *know* it. I *have* to be . . .'

We each nod, sipping our soups, offering words of consolation, trying to comprehend why anyone would long to be the subject of Truman's vicious slander.

WE'VE NEVER REALLY *KNOWN* GLORIA. Likely never will.

We know her of course—as one of us.

We have lunch at the Colony every Tuesday, at Basque on Thursdays.

We meet at Kenneth's, for hair-sets and saunas—at eleven on Mondays and Fridays.

We've sailed the Adriatic on board the *Seraphina*, the Guinnesses' three-hundred-ton yacht, alternating with the Agnellis' *Agneta*, a sailboat by comparison—splitting summers between the two.

We're frequent guests, when in Palm Beach, not only at C.Z.'s Artemis estate, but at Gemini—Gloria's seaside showplace. So immense as to be divided by an interstate highway, splitting oceanfront and lakeside-facing wings. We've walked the underground tunnel between the two sides, admiring the rococo furnishings Gloria's chosen to distract from the steady stream of traffic whizzing overhead.

We've dined at her Paris town house on avenue Matignon, and her Waldorf Towers pied-à-terre, where she makes sure that the vegetables she serves are even *smaller* than Babe's. 'Practically *microscopic*,' as Tru would note.

Marella sees Gloria when they overlap at their respective Swiss chalets—the Guinnesses' Villa Zanroc 'just a simple farmhouse,' or so its mistress claims, nothing like their château in Normandy, which few of us have seen.

Perhaps we've come the closest to glimpsing the *real* Gloria at her house in Acapulco. The space itself reflects her stark simplicity, her elegant lines. Composed of stucco, smooth and white, cool to the touch on a humid summer's day. Palapa roofs calling to mind indigenous huts, beneath which we loll, only rousing ourselves to indulge in the exotic fare we've come to love: the tamales in their corn-husk wraps, the tang and brine of ceviche.

The tequila flows as freely as the chatter, and we hear a thickness return to Gloria's cadence as she slips back into the skin of whatever girl she once had been. While we aren't sure who that is exactly, we spot glimpses of her in the candlelight, over tables scattered with paper flowers, an explosion of primary hues.

'It's easier, actually, to have *six* houses than one,' Gloria's been known to boast—especially to the press. 'You just hop on a plane and ¡hecho!—your life is there; no need to pack.' (It's rumored she and Loel keep full wardrobes in each locale—from winter furs to evening dress to *trajes de baño* for dips in the sea.) 'I just can't imagine how hard it must be to only run *one* household. Who could possibly spend twelve months in one place?'

We know for a fact that this is bullshit. It's not the tedium that keeps the Guinnesses on the move, but desire to stave off the taxman. We've heard our husbands say so often enough, and Bill and Gianni and Winston in particular would know the details of such things, they being in Loel's orbit as pillars of business and industry.

We've heard Truman tell us flat out—'Sugar, they need to stay on the run or risk paying through the nostrils. Gloria notates in her diary when they've hit their limit in such-and-such, and have to flee to so-and-so. I wouldn't call it *fraud* per se . . . But they're a pair of high-class *bandidos*!' Who but La Guinness could make tax evasion seem adventurous . . . ?

Yes, we know her as one of our own, but we've never really known her beyond that which she's allowed. We've had to subsist on the rumors, and of those there has always been feast enough to gorge to the point of sickness.

She was born in Mexico—that much is certain. Her clipped speech is seasoned with a soupçon of *picante*. The voluptuous vowels. The slight trill of R's rolled languidly on the tongue. She walks with the faintest trace of sway in her slender hips. Suggesting the promise of curvaceousness, if falling short in fact. We envy her mane, a shade so black it glistens with undertones of navy—blacker than we could hope to achieve with Kenneth's master colorists. She wears her hair pulled back in an immaculate twist—which would read far too severe if sported by the rest of us.

We've cobbled together other bits and pieces:

That she was born Gloria Rubio—sometimes Alatorre.

When is another matter. She's the oldest in our midst, by a decade at *least*, we suspect, though she's managed to shave it down to a four-or-five-year difference.

That she grew up in Guadalajara—*or* the bustling Mexico City. Sometimes along the coast of Veracruz.

That her father was a journalist, her mother a seamstress—though there have always been whispers of origins less salubrious.

Babe, who loves Gloria as much as she loathes her—the press having lopped them both together as 'the goddesses' of the age—is the first to defend her when under attack. Yet we've each heard her mutter in moments of vexation, in the wake of the one-upsmanship that Gloria practices with zeal—'You do *know* that she started life as a shill in a Mexican nightclub . . . ?'

Truman, who'd been generally present for such flares, would simply laugh with glee.

'But Babyling dear, it was much more than that! She was a *compañera de baile paga!*' We'd stare at him blankly. 'A *taxi dancer*, honey! The menfolks pays theys fares, and off and away theys goes!'

'Precisely,' said Babe, satisfied. 'One step shy of a prostitute.'

'You have a problem with prostitutes?'

'Frankly I don't care what she does with her nether regions. But why not be honest about it? Why can't she just tell the truth?'

'Ah, but isn't one's story its own *special* truth . . . ?'

Babe's eyes would meet his and she'd smile. Slim, less convinced, would take a drag from her cigarette—'A bullshit artist.'

'*Storyteller,*' Truman would correct. He'd lean forward, conspiratorially. 'Haven't you ever *heard* of a *corrido?*'

'A what?'

'A *corrido*, darling. Why, it's Gloria in a nutshell.'

'Corrid-*aaa* . . . ?' Slim would venture, recalling her Hemingway exploits.

'*Corrid-oooooo.* A folk ballad, *en la tradición Mexicana.* An homage to heroic deeds. Epic. Lyrical . . .' (the final condition suiting him most of all) '*narrative.*'

'In other words,' Slim confirmed, 'a bullshit artist.'

'Or . . .' Truman would rhapsodize, 'something much finer. Something much more rare.' He'd nibble a cocktail onion, thoughtful. 'If one can appreciate the *form*.'

Of course Truman could hear it, the strum of the guitar, the brass of the mariachis, battling for supremacy. But most of all, the guttural voice, rising beyond the chorus. Ragged and rich, a contralto more masculine than feminine, ripened in wood and smoke and peat.

A primal wail, asserting her identity.

EL CORRIDO DE GLORIA GUINNESS

Listen, my dear Diablito—
Listen, beloved one,
To the *corrido* of Gloria *y* Rubio.
'Fore La Guinness's life had begun.

Born the humble daughter,
Of a left-wing journalist pa—
A child of the *Revolución*—
And a zealous laundress ma.

She was nineteen (maybe twenty?)
In that June of 1933.
She had traded her plaits for ebony waves,
And raised her skirt-lengths with glee.

She lived in a tenement *cuarto*.
Shared with her family of five,
Set 'round a fetid courtyard,
Surrounded by other tribes.

On a sweltering midsummer's evening,
In the port slums of Veracruz,
She painted her lips *cereza* red,
Reinventing herself as Man's Muse.

At a makeshift mirror of broken glass
She rouged kaleidoscope cheeks;

Through the crack in an airless window
The stench of the wasteland reeked.

But somewhere beneath the shit and the sweat
She detected a delicate scent:
A bougainvillea's fragrant blooms,
That firmed her resolve as she went.

Slithering into her thinnest dress—
A white of filmiest gauze—
She tucked a flower into her hair
And left the room without pause.

'Where are you going?' she heard her ma shout
As Gloria slipped through the door.
'To the dancing hall, to earn my way out—
I'm a partner's delight on the floor!'

She progressed through the sticky stillness,
Down littered streets toward the hall,
Where beneath the flickering street lamps
The loitering men would catcall—

'Come with me, angel from heaven . . .'
(There were other proposals more lewd.)
She brushed past them and haughtily onward;
She hadn't the time for the crude.

Into the smoke-thick dance hall she marched,
Assuming a worldly-wise role;
That she'd never been far beyond Veracruz
Would never occur to a soul.

She passed by the ticket-booth window
Where men waited to finance their way,
To be given a snake-coil of tickets,
For dancers they fancied to pay.

Girls lined the sides of the ramshackle hall,
Waiting to be asked to dance.

Some of them listless, some of them keen,
Desperate to reel in their chance.

Men hugged the bar—every shape, age, and creed—
Skittishly nursing their booze.
They paid for the pleasure of guaranteed luck—
Just a matter of which gal they'd choose.

But when Gloria Rubio stepped out on the floor,
'Twas as if the whole room ceased to breathe . . .
They watched as she moved with the sway in her hips,
Dancing alone, as to tease.

She roused them from stagnancy onto their feet,
With seductress's man-luring charm,
The big fish lined up, ten pesos a dance—
Each eager to next take her arm.

There were strapping young bucks, smug in their brawn,
Who pulled her close, gripping her tight.
There were shy, quiet types with rough calloused hands,
Who avoided her eyes in sheer fright.

There were men far too short who came up to her breasts,
Men far too tall or too wide,
Men who had stutters or walked with a limp,
Men who had secrets to hide.

Her irked sister dancers looked on in a huff,
Accepting her discarded cargo—
Swearing that once the night's chits were cashed in,
On her they would form an embargo.

It was late in the night that Gloria saw him—
A gringo-fare, standing apart.
He was dapper and lean, by decades her senior;
His impassiveness fluttered her heart.

She decided that moment that he'd be her 'take,'
And crossed the floor, meeting his eyes.

He stood still and watched as she circled around,
Pressing him flush to her thighs.

'*¿Cómo se llama?* Señor Guapo?'
He stared, and again she said—'Name?'
'Scholtens,' he answered, 'I'm Dutch—new in town.'
And he told her he made sugarcane.

Gloria smiled as she led him to dance,
And in stillness together they clung;
As the dancers brushed past and boleros blared on,
She knew she had reached the first rung.

'Honey—*¡Dios mío!* A *sugarcane* farmer?' Truman had squealed when he first heard the tale.

He was parked in a booth across from Gloria, in their *muy propio* spot—a place they went to be alone. To share secrets, where there was no fear of anyone they knew inhabiting adjacent tables. No well-bred ears to overhear even the filthiest of rants.

The Howard Johnson's diner in Queens. Sometimes the one on the Jericho Turnpike, New York State Route 25. They called these expeditions 'slumming it,' for indeed no one they knew—their partners included—would be caught dead in such a place.

On the occasion in question they'd chosen the Turnpike location, as Gloria took care to be particularly discreet. She didn't mention Señor Scholtens *ever*, or the fact that she'd once been his Señora. But there was something that Truman had told her that inspired her confession. About his own Mama and her ambition to marry her way out of Podunk, Alabama. How a man named Arch in his slick suit with his fancy speech wooed her with talk of New Orleans.

'My Mama realized pronto that my Daddy didn't have *dos pesos* to rub together. On their honeymoon he ran outta *dinero* and hadta ask *her* to pay. Lord, she was just sixteen! So she did what any scrapper would—she went in search of bigger fish, the pursuit of which ended up killing her.' And then—as if making a declaration of the purest form of love—he said, 'You'll be my *new* Mama, now that mine is gone—my adopted *Latina* ma.'

'*Su madre adoptiva*.' Gloria had smiled.

'*Mamacita*. You know my Mama would've given her teeth to be *just* like you . . . She tried so hard to be Cuban, to pawn herself off as *Nina*, but she couldn't run far enough from scrawny ole Lillie Mae, from her hicksville hillbilly past.'

It was then Gloria chose to tell him the Ballad of the Dance Hall.

Of the wedding to Señor Scholtens, a husband she'd taken great pains to erase.

A husband she'd marry in less than a month and leave in no more than six. He'd been right to question the sugarcane, Truman—though he was wrong about the farming.

'He was no farmer, Diablito—but a factory manager.'

'Not much better!'

She nodded in agreement. In fact, it haunted her still.

The stench that never left her. The stench that reminded her always of what it was like to be trapped. She had imagined that a house would be all she'd ever need. Anything to escape the *patios de vecindad*, with its slapdash shacks in the midst of courtyards stuffed to capacity; ten people in a single filthy room. Gloria Rubio thought anything must be a step up from neighbors on top of neighbors—*vecinos asfixia vecinos*—two hundred to a courtyard with their flies and racket and waste. What she hadn't banked on was the stench of the cane.

Sugarcane, as it turned out, was anything but sweet. Instead the smell the plant emitted was one of relentless putrefaction. The stench of sugarcane came to represent to the new Señora Scholtens the very scent of death. She could envision herself taking her life, spiking a drink with poison from a bottle, perhaps falling asleep in the bath. She stopped herself for fear it might take days or even weeks for her corpse to be discovered, subsumed by the rot of the plant.

Señor Scholtens doused himself with aftershave, yet once the noxious fumes of sugarcane found its way into her nostrils, it's all that she could smell on him. Beneath his impeccably scrubbed fingernails, in the follicles of his mustache, seeping from his beautifully cologned pores, she always detected the acrid scent of decay.

She knew she had to flee before it took her with it.

One evening as he slept, his bestially stinking perfume lingering on her skin, Señora Gloria Scholtens sat at her vanity, silently applying her rouge. Darkening her lips the color of *sangre*. Quietly rising and slipping into the second skin of an evening dress. Stealing into the night, lured by the sultry triple-pulse of boleros and finer aromas in the night air.

She knew that she'd find a cabaret. Knew that she would saunter to a table, enjoying the eyes of the opposite sex upon her. She knew that she would sit alone, her fine profile tilted high. She knew a well-dressed man would eventually summon the courage to buy her a drink, and she would feel her power return to her, as she accepted with a smile.

She could feel the tempo of the music inside her picking up in pace, brightening in tone, exploding into the next movement of— —

Hark, Diablito! The City of Lights!
On a crisp Paris midwinter's eve!
Where Gloria Rubio—again on her own—
Proved how much a poor girl could achieve.

While rivals were clad in jewels and couture,
It was said that she bore regal carriage—
'Be she milliner's shop girl or nightclub hostess,
She'll make a fortuitous marriage—'

'Wait, Mamacita! What *year* are we in?' Truman interrupted, this time treading water at the circular swim-up bar in the Villa Vera Racquet Club pool. Licking salt off the rim of his margarita, Acapulco Bay sprawling gloriously beyond. Beside him, Gloria, perched on a chlorine-submerged barstool, shaded by dark glasses and a red sun hat.

'¡*Paciencia!* I'm getting there . . .'

'And weren't you *already* married? To Mister Sugarcane?'

'Maybe I was,' she allowed, sipping her hibiscus cooler, fingering a decorative blossom in her glass. 'Maybe I wasn't. It was so long ago, I really can't recall.'

'And how did we get from Veracruz to France?'

'Via Mexico City? Or was it New York—? I can't remember which.'

'You're quite an unreliable narrator, you know.'

'*You're* one to talk, Señor "*Busybody.*"'

Truman beamed with appreciation. 'Touché, Mamacita. Touché.'

'Now listen, *pequeño niñato*,' quipped the spirited *corridista*, as the narrative shifted to its next evolution; its heroine to her next incarnation.

She was barely a day over twenty,
In December of 1935,
Yet she'd ripened and seasoned beyond her years
As if she'd lived multiple lives.

The inscrutable Gloria Rubio
Gave them cause for widespread debate:
In France as a genteel student?
Or courting a darker fate?

Some thought her a Mexican leftist,
Fleeing political rage,
Escaping her father's assassins,
For slander he'd typed on a page.

She now hailed from Guadalajara
(Veracruz wiped from the slate),
Shrouded in mystery, free of her past,
The ideal candidate for a mate.

Some claimed she was secretly wealthy;
Gold stashed in Swiss bank accounts;
Some disagreed, yet turned a blind eye
When she wed a von Fürstenberg count.

They moved to Berlin in late '36
And here's where it gets a bit hazy . . .
Whispers of dangerous 'friends' on the rise,
Though 'the Countess' would deem such talk crazy.

The slander was scattered (whatever the truth)
'Midst the smart set during the war—
'Gloria Fürstenberg—"Traitor" and "Spy"!'
The Countess no more than a— —

'*Whore?*' Truman suggested, sucking on a papaya, spitting
out the seeds. Gloria splashed pool water in his direction. 'Well,
sugar—get to the nitty-gritty! *Was* you working for the Nazis,
or wasn't you?' Gloria sipped her cooler, silent. 'Because Slim's
friend Aline—now the Countess of Romanones—she was spying
for the Allies in Madrid during the war, and she says she knew
you *quite* well . . . And that you were working for the other
side . . .'

She stared at him, expressionless.

'*Chismoso*,' she spat, turning and swimming toward the stairs.

Her companion dog-paddled after her, nipping at her heels.
'Well, of *course* I'm a gossip! But that's not why I'm interested!'

She emerged from the pool, like a glistening Aztec goddess.
'Why, then, *are* you interested? If not to run tell Slim and Babe
and the other *tipas* . . . ?' Wrapping herself in a towel, reclining
in a chaise beneath a palm, she tilted her hat-brim, blocking him
out.

'*Because*, Mamacita, I'm interested in your *story*.' He
stretched out in the twin chaise beside her, drip-drying in the sun
as she eyed him with suspicion. 'You are the most intriguing
woman I know. You're like an epic heroine—but better, because
you've actually *lived*.' This seemed to placate her. 'I, Truman

Garcia Capote'—he only used 'Garcia' around Gloria— 'solemnly swear I will not tell a living, breathing *soul*. Cross my heart and hope to die.'

'Doubtful.'

Suddenly he lowered the pitch of his voice, dropping all affect. 'Please. Someone should know—whatever you went through. And I'd be honored if it was me.'

She stared at him, then surveyed the Club clientele warily. As if the bikinied bathers with their golden tans or the daiquiri-swilling swells might house a mole in their midst.

'All right,' Gloria said to Truman. 'But not here. Not now.'

THAT EVENING, IN HER OWN TIME, she told him. In the privacy of her *casa* high above the bay—beneath the domed palapa that mimicked the huts of Veracruz. She resumed, in husky, lyrical incantation, the tale of her next incarnation.

Her most mythic of ballads—that of the Wartime Waltz.

To neutral Madrid, two children in tow,
The Countess von Fürstenberg traveled.
With the Count shipped away to the cold Russian front,
The marriage had all but unraveled . . .

'Why "unraveled"?' Truman asked, his voice hushed. Reverent.

Gloria paused. For a moment, silence; the gentle chorus of cicadas on the breeze.

'I loved him, Fürstenberg . . . I truly loved Franz-Egon. I thought he was what I'd been searching for. In those saloons and dance halls, on my feet so many nights, so many hours, they'd bleed with the effort. Me leading. Luring. All those bodies . . . Never a fit. From the moment I met Franz—at *Le Bal des Petits Lits Blancs* in Paris—*he* led. He practically lifted me off the floor. I thought, *This* is it. The last big fish I'll ever have to hook!'

'And then . . . ?'

'We married in London, moved to Berlin, had the children . . . We were wildly in love. It seemed too perfect to last. Turns out it was.'

'What happened?'

'The war.' She lit a Sobranie and sat back in her chair. 'He was stationed in Russia—the Fourth Panzer Division. And from the moment he left I was sick with worry. That he'd be killed, or I'd hear he'd gone missing. That he'd lose those beautiful limbs of his. That he'd never come back . . . I wrote him a letter a day for a year.'

'And him?'

'A bit at first, then . . . *silencio*.' Eyes enormous. Anguished.

'Darling.'

'I started to imagine he had died. I pretended that I was a widow, just to get through the days. Knowing was better than not knowing, even if I invented it. I think I started going quietly mad. I really did think about ending it all, perhaps even killing . . .' She trailed off. 'I needed to find some scrap of myself—to recover even an ember of what used to burn inside of me. I needed to do something to force myself to live again.'

'What did you do?'

A shade of a smile in the half-light.

'The one thing I knew how to . . .'

'Twas on the Eve of Saint John, in late '42,
Countess Fürstenberg sat at her vanity;
The reflection stared back, an expressionless blur,
As she pondered the state of her sanity.

She painted her lips a cardinal red,
And slipped into black satin gown;
Round her neck hung a noose of the finest of pearls,
As she left for a night on the town.

A taxi she took to the streets of Berlin,
In search of a palace of pleasure.

Charlottenburg's nightclubs of old had been shut;
There were Party-backed venues to measure.

Each eve out she ventured, dressed to the nines,
To dance on the edge of the flames.
Manically festive, adrift in the whirl,
Befriending a roster of Names . . .

Why shouldn't she mix with high-ups in the Party,
If favors were theirs to convey?
For each small advancement, each freedom she gained,
Her dues Countess Fürstenberg paid.

The festivities raged, savage parties each night,
Champagne and dancing she'd found;
They reveled and sang and they flirted and drank
To forget the world crumbling around.

Nothing could stop the indulgence they craved,
Not even the bombs when they fell.
An explosion would rupture the dance for a breath—
Then the revels continued in hell.

It was here that our Gloria met the big fish,
The ones who'd provide her way out.
For her favors, safe passage and visas they'd give,
While she made the most of their clout.

Her fame spread through the Reich as one they might trust,
She dining with Himmler and Goering,
Even Herr Hitler was struck by her charm,
He— —

    '*Hitler?*' Truman couldn't help but interrupt. 'Mamacita, are
you telling me you dined with the Führer *himself*?'
    'On occasion.'
    'Look, I'm as big a fan of the *manner* of telling as anyone . . .
But I'm simply *dying* to know. Were you actually a *Nazi spy*?'

Gloria took a final drag from her Sobranie, stamping it into an ashtray.

'I did what I needed to do. To get out. To get my children out. Berlin had grown dangerous. We couldn't stay there. So I did what I've always done. I made myself attractive. I charmed the right men. I let them fall in love with me.'

'Who did you work for?'

'All of them. General Wolff of the SS provided my exit permit. The Spanish ambassador, my visa.'

'And the others? What did they provide?'

'Safety.'

'In exchange for . . . ?'

'Sometimes a dance, sometimes more. Just like the old days.'

'Did you smuggle secrets?'

'I suppose, but I never knew what secrets I shared. I was given a dress shop in Madrid. Bespoke designs, by appointment. Let us be clear—it *wasn't* a dress shop. It was fitted with a transmitter in the back room. When I received a coded message, I sent it along to Berlin.'

'To the Gestapo?'

Gloria nodded, suddenly far away. Picturing still nights in the Plaza de Colón, lingering at sidewalk tables over glasses of sweet vermouth. Of cobblestone streets down which lovers strolled, fingers entwined. Of the tiny boutique in the Calle de Hermosilla, its showroom displaying elegant frocks. Bolts of finest silks and handcrafted lace, so cost-prohibitive they could only serve to deter actual customers. Of its rickety stairs leading to a hidden chamber, with its wires and code boards; of its enormous transmitter radio, linked to SS headquarters. Of the heady circles in which she had run, the fêtes and balls and cruises. Of the men that she'd dazzled—more often seduced—in order to access their secrets.

'Mamacita . . . ?' Her reverie broken by Truman.

'Yes, Diablito?'

'Did you kill anybody?'

'Not that I know of. But that doesn't mean it didn't happen.'

And with that Truman rose and came to sit beside her, patting her arm. She poured them each a glass of mescal, which they sipped in silence, save for the ongoing thrum of the cicadas.

WHAT FOLLOWED WAS PUBLIC KNOWLEDGE. She'd proudly disclosed her *post*-war history to anyone who asked, for even her failures confirmed her ascent. She'd climbed too high to ever slide back down, and she didn't care who knew it. These more recent facts she'd shared with Truman early on, over countless luncheon tables— from cheap diners to Le Cirque. From the decks of the *Seraphina* to the slopes of St. Moritz. Poolside, at her various houses. Ringside, where they smoked cigarillos and chattered as Cassius Clay battled Sonny Liston in six rounds of grit and grace. Where Gloria could be found, so might her disciple, feeding off her tales.

And thus, Diablito, peace was restored,
On May 8th, 1945.
The Count returned home, to find his wife gone—
She had done what it took to survive.

She had met an Egyptian, eight years her junior,
A penniless prince she would marry,
But three years of scrimping and saving in Cairo
Proved too heavy a burden to carry.

Two years had passed when she caught her last fish,
The banking and brewery heir,
He was already married to one of her 'friends'—
Though she felt little conscience or care.

'My husband loves boats and I cannot bear them,'
Her friend made the mistake to confide.
'Gloria dear, be a doll and go with him?'
(Never dreaming he'd pick a new bride!)

So the Countess-turned-Princess ascended once more;
Loel Guinness's arm she'd adorn.

He purchased her passport and war dossier,
And the famous 'La Guinness' was born.

CODA

GLORIA SITS IN A BOOTH IN THE ROADSIDE Howard Johnson's, waiting.

The New Jersey Turnpike location. Absurdly remote, but she can afford to take no chances. She has taken the liberty of ordering. She knows what he'll want, he being a creature of habit. Besides, she means to make this quick.

Say what needs to be said. Make a clean break.

The waitress approaches with a tray, placing dishes on the table, one by one.

'All right, hon, that's two clam chowders, a chef's salad for you, and for your friend . . .' She glances at the empty space opposite— at the unoccupied half of a turquoise vinyl booth.

'The jumbo fried clam special,' Gloria confirms.

'You want me to keep this under the warming lamp?'

'No, thank you. I'm sure he'll be here shortly.'

'Enjoy.'

As the waitress retreats, the bell attached to the chapel-style door jingles, announcing a new arrival. Gloria is shocked to see how much weight he's put on—the bloat. Far too much for that midget frame to carry. He raises a hand when he spots her, his face alight with hope. Yet from her impassive expression he lowers it sheepishly.

He joins her in the booth, which makes a farting sound as he slides across its slick vinyl surface. She laughs in spite of herself.

Babe would never dream of laughing at such a thing. She'd flush at the crassness. Marella would, without question, fail to understand. Slim and C.Z. are earthy enough to get it, but their humor tends toward the biting (Slim) and the verbal (C.Z.). Per Bouvier trademark, Lee, like her sister, lacks a sense of humor altogether (though both would argue otherwise).

As Truman scooches into the booth another inch, again toots the sound, causing them both to snicker. Blessedly breaking the ice.

'Hello, Mamacita,' he says, taking in every detail of her face, as if seeing it for the first time. Offering, as a gesture of contrition, a careful smile . . . feeling his way.

'Hello, Diablito.'

Silence.

Then, hardly daring to hope—'Are you speaking to me?'

'*Here* I am.'

'Are you speaking to me anywhere else?'

'No.'

'I see.' He covers his disappointment, turning his attention to the food. 'Oh, look! My favorite! Clams *dos* ways!'

'And a dry martini. I knew that's what you'd want.'

'That's because you know me.'

'It's been a long time. *Demasiadas comidas . . .*'

'One can never have too *many* lunches.' He sips his drink, watching her. 'Are *you* mad at me, Mamacita?'

'Yes.' She stares at him with cold, resentful eyes.

He frowns. 'But why? I didn't write anything about you! Not a peep!'

'*Exactly!*'

He stares at her, confused. 'But—'

'You knew all my stories! *My* stories! You could have had greatness. Danger. A rags to riches tale. Instead you're worried about which *puta arrogante* bled on Bill Paley's *sheets . . .* ?'

'I thought—I thought that I was sparing you.'

'Thanks a lot.'

'I wanted—to teach Bill a lesson. For Babe's sake . . .'

'And you thought she'd be all right with this? Diablito, you certainly don't know Babe.'

'I thought that I did.'

They sip their chowders together in silence.

'Darling,' Truman asks, lost in thought, 'do you remember the Clay/Liston fight? The sixth round?'

'Of course I do.' She softens slightly at the memory of a carefree age—when life still possessed the ability to surprise.

'Everyone said there was no way that brash li'l loudmouth was gonna get anything but massacred after all that talk. And then . . . he didn't.' He smiles, wistful.

Gloria looks at him, shaking her head. 'Oh, Truman. *Pequeño bastardo!* Did you really think you could get away with writing that . . . ?'

He pauses. 'I knew they'd be mad . . . But I thought that they'd come back.'

'Well, *that's* not going to happen.'

'I know that now. I can see.' Then, with eyes full of terror, part confession, part appeal, '*Se me fue le mano.*'

Gloria nods. 'Yes, Truman. You went too far.'

Pleading—'Mamacita . . .'

'Yes?'

'Forgive me.' Then, hushed . . . '*Perdóname.*'

She falters, moved by his earnestness.

'I'd like to, Diablito . . . but I can't.' His eyes well with tears. Gloria dabs a napkin at something in her eye. 'It's just that Loel, being so close to Bill and Babe . . .'

He nods. 'I understand.'

'It's just—I've worked too hard to get here. I can't go back to . . .'

As her voice trails off, Truman reaches across the table, placing his tiny hand atop her long one. 'Honey. You listen to me . . . I *understand*. We're hustlers, the pair of us. You do what you gotta do to survive.'

She covers his hand with her free one, cradling his trembling fingers in the nest between her own. They sit in this manner for another half an hour, at which point they rise, he places a tender kiss on her cheek, and they exit through the steeple of the chapel of Howard Johnson's.

They pause, standing still in a sea of station wagons in the parking lot. He takes a long look, as if preserving the memory of her face for posterity. Then nodding, he turns away, walking to the pay phone, presumably to call a taxi.

Suddenly she calls back—'Truman?'

'Yes, Mamacita?'

'Why didn't you use my stories?'

'Because I promised you I wouldn't.'

'Ah.'

Then, with a devilish grin—'But don't you worry, honey. There's plenty more where that came from. I might just write like a butterfly, sting like a bee . . .'

He gives her a wink, and in doing so allows a tear to fall.

They diverge in the crowded lot, going their separate ways.

FOURTEEN

1978

VARIATION NO. 7

H E LIES SUPINE ON THE SPARTAN DAYBED, pencil clutched in hand, half-heartedly musing why 'lying' and 'supine' constitute tautology, when they happen to sound so right together.

His brain often values rhythm over logic—cadence over correctness. Although in this case it might be argued that the repetition serves, he being doubly guilty of lying, in both factual and horizontal senses.

The pencil is one of his trusty Blackwings—weapons which, for the most part, have rarely failed to serve him.

A yellow legal pad rests on his chest, the color of well-made hollandaise. Not the congealed yellow sludge at the local corner diner. The pale, silky sort, custard-hued, impeccably prepared at Oscar's American Bistro at the Waldorf.

The unblemished yolkiness of the page stares back at him. Relentlessly sunny. Mocking him with its cheerfulness.

He wonders why his limbs won't budge. Wonders who has slipped the poison into his Orange Drink. He wills his arm and Blackwing to flutter, concentrating with all his might on this single isolated act. He'd always insisted that a person could make anything happen if only they focused on their most treasured of desires.

Yet try as he might, the pencil lies dormant, the hand that grips it paralyzed.

His mind is very much alive, racing; thoughts tripping over themselves in a futile rush for preeminence. Spinning into violent tarantellas of nouns and verbs, a blur of images, locked in a whirl of jewel-toned adjectives.

'Of *course* words have *colors*, sugar,' he'd have informed us, exasperated by our ignorance. 'Just like a palette of paints. Some words positively *simmer* in the reddest of reds. Others offer a gulp of azure, like a clear country stream . . .'

Stream . . . or was it a creek? Is there a difference? He thinks he remembers that there isn't, the difference being determined by whatever slob once named them, if they were ever named at all. No—creeks you wade in. Streams you swim.

He has a sudden flash of a crystal *creek*—wading through its gentle current, herringbone trousers rolled to his knees. They're the eggshell ones his Mama sent two birthdays back, and the only reason they still fit is 'cause his shrimpo legs refuse to grow.

He's twelve now, but, much to his dismay, he still *looks* ten.

He shuffles bare feet over the stone floor of the creek bed. He can see Nelle scampering up the bank ahead of him, but he lingers, enjoying the slickness of their polished surface against the soles of his feet.

'*C'mon, Truman!*' he hears her shout through the mile-high reeds. Before he can answer, he spots it . . . the serpentine form, ribboning through shallow water.

He freezes—as that's what he's been taught to do. He's learned such things from reading tales of young Indian braves, left to fend for themselves in the wild. Or perhaps his Daddy imparted this pearl, the one time he turned up to take his boy fishing. Perhaps they'd lounged on the bank over a picnic of pimento sandwiches, watching the riverboats glide past, imagining stowing away on board together—the boy as a tap dancer, his Daddy as a poker champ.

Perhaps his Daddy had assumed a knowledgeable air and said in a voice firm but kind, 'Son, you ever see a cottonmouth, you just stay right put. You play possum, and you can fool that poor snake clean outta his scales.' He might have polished off his cheese and crust, chasing the last morsel with an icy lager, letting his boy try a swig too, as that's what men do. The boy might have nodded, filing the information away for just such a moment.

Or maybe that longed-for chat never occurred ... Maybe it's as pie-in-the-sky as the Gulf Coast beach trips his Daddy'd promised him, tempting with visions of fresh-caught shrimp in a silver bucket that they'd peel and eat themselves, dipped into jiggers of remoulade. They'd visit places with exotic names—Pensacola. Panama City. Galveston and Naples—just like in Italy. His Daddy could sell the skin off a rattler, and his tales of seaside paradise had his boy in a lather. He'd practically leaped with joy in his new swimming trunks, as he rushed to the porch to await the arrival of his Daddy's Cadillac. He had his knapsack packed with garden spades, which would work a treat for building castles made of sand. He'd thrown in a couple of books, appropriately themed. He figured he and his Daddy could take turns reading *Treasure Island* as they lay in the sun, getting brown as matching butternuts. It took three long days, waiting on the porch until Cousin Jenny insisted he come inside for his dinner, before he learned to treat such coastal jaunts as fiction.

Maybe it was the tales of Mohawk braves after all, but he'd been assured by someone that cottonmouths only attack under threat. He forces his body to freeze, standing still as a totem pole, straining to look just as stoic, despite the tom-tom thumping of his heart. All he *now* knows is his Daddy or Hiawatha—whichever's responsible for the lousy advice—got it dead wrong. They should have told him to run, *run!* as fast as his little legs could carry him, which would likely have served him well, the boy being the fastest runner in his class. Instead he stands, feet-pads suctioned to the riverbed floor, watching the longest water moccasin he's ever clapped eyes on swim toward him, mouth agape, revealing its cotton-white insides—white as the gauze that would one day encase the heads of the four Clutters in their coffins, masking shattered countenance in thin, filmy shrouds.

Oh, that snake knows he's a live thing all right, aiming straight for him, sinking hypodermic fangs into trembling flesh.

What follows: a blur. He hears his own cry—an out-of-body howl.

Nelle—or is it his Faulk Carter cousins?—older boys with rural builds, raised strong on collards and buttermilk—scoop his tiny frame in their big capable arms, and scale the creek bank with him slung over their shoulders. They run through the cedar forest, all the way to the nearest farmhouse, leaving a trail of blood behind.

Just like his grown-up counterpart lying on the daybed in the house in Sagaponack, unable to lift neither pencil nor Orange Drink, the last vestige of sensation drains from the boy's pint-sized limbs. He feels the venom pulsing through his veins, robbing him of motion.

The Faulk boys carry him up the porch steps and into the house, where they drop him onto the farmhouse table like a sack of potatoes. Mrs. Walter slides aside the roast she's been basting, and with a country wife's efficiency, examines the wound. Looks hard into his dilating pupils. Without skipping a beat, she strides out the porch door, toward the chicken coop. In a flurry of feathers she grabs one by its scrawny neck. Returning to the kitchen, she removes a meat cleaver from the butcher's block, and maneuvering the flapping fowl close to her patient's lower extremities, raises the blade. Unable to lift his head, he feels himself flinch, though his features, well into septic shock (or so he *says* . . .) register nothing.

He braces himself for the chop, imagining his altered life with an amputated foot. Wondering what it will be like never to run or skip again . . . whether he'll need a crutch or wheelchair to get himself back and forth to school, or whether he'll take to his bed for good, just like old Marcel had done.

The cleaver comes down on the table's edge, severing the chicken's head. Mrs. Walter squeezes its open neck, smearing thick, hot blood directly onto the two puncture marks on his ankle, swollen five times its natural size.

By this point, Mr. Walter has fetched the snakebite kit from the recesses of the hall cupboard which the missus waves away, trusting the wisdom passed down between old wives over modern science. 'That fancy doctor's box won't help this boy,' she assures him. 'Ain't nothin' better to draw out the poison than fresh chicken blood.'

'Baby, I almost *died* that day,' he's since recalled, spinning the yarn to anyone who'll listen. 'But that farmwife saved my life with her remedy. Mr. Walter drove us home in his wagon, with me lying limp in back with my cousins, who slit the throats of three more cocks in wire cages, just to keep me going.' We thought this sounded both medically and logistically improbable, but who were we to argue? When first told the tale, we appreciated such verbal *truth-flexing*, as we came to call it. As he himself put it, they weren't exactly lies per se . . . they were simply the truth made more interesting, for entertainment's sake. This we could forgive, for there was a peculiar romance to Truman's lies. Part pageantry, part poetry. Mesmerizing.

'I was paralyzed—completely *paralyzed*. I couldn't leave my bed for *months*. Let me tell you, 'cause I know from experience . . . there's just nothing more excruciating than *wanting* to move and not being able.'

Back on the daybed, Blackwing in hand, he *wants* to move— at least as far as the nightstand for a top-up on his Orange Drink.

He feels the venom coursing through his veins. Only this time, the serpent is invisible. No milky eyes, no gauze-stuffed gums. But it's there all right . . . he senses it.

O revered creator! Reviled destroyer! Show thyself!

He manages to will his head to turn. He looks to see his reflection in the sliding closet door. Mirrored, left slightly ajar. His image split in its seam, kaleidoscope-divided. He stares at himself, at once repulsed and intrigued. He reminds himself of Lucian Cole and John White, the colored farmhands in his sideshow in Monroeville. His 'Siamese twins,' separate forms hidden behind a suit-draped hat rack. Likely both long dead, Cole and White, the boy being at *least* fifty-three himself by this point. As he contemplates this calculation, his tongue lolls in repose at the side of his mouth, fracturing into two sets of prongs in the mirrored door.

Suddenly he sees it . . .

He's the thing with the poison . . . a mutant, two-headed snake. One body, dressed in a single silken caftan, its slick fabric shimmering like wet scales in the glass.

It was the caftan Yves, in Marrakech, had insisted that he have, as a souvenir of his stay at the Villa Oasis, so that he might retain a relic of Saint Laurent bohemia. We'd all smoked hashish and lolled on ottomans under the stars. We drank vast quantities of Moroccan mint tea, and champagne laced with rose water. We grazed on fruits and pistachios and were nourished by the sound of our own laughter. Yves had worn a caftan. Marella, Lee, and Gloria wore caftans—though Gloria insisted on reclaiming hers as a Mexican striped djellaba. C.Z. and Slim eschewed caftans, the former thinking them impractical, the latter dismissing them as pretentious.

Tru and his beloved Babe had procured identical caftans, his borrowed from Yves, hers purchased in the souk to match. One evening they had swayed together in a hammock in the gloaming, whispering confessions in one another's ears.

'You know, Babyling, you really *are* my one true love,' he said, inhaling the fragrance of her scalp with drowsy appreciation—a mixture of jasmine and the smoke of Turkish cigarettes, bought for a lark in the market. She smiled and nuzzled close. Their bodies, in their matching robes, seemed to merge. Another mythic Hydra—perhaps what has triggered the memory.

And then he said the thing he'd told her twenty years before, that very first day aboard the Paleys' plane. 'You can tell that you're really in love when you don't have to finish one another's sentences.' They were beyond friendship now. Beyond lovers or spouses.

She nodded. They swayed a bit longer, basking in that truth.

After a long, fortifying silence, Babe pulled away—a shy, grown-up ingénue, speaking with the earnest weight of truth.

'I think . . . you're the only person in the world who could ever really hurt me.'

Taken aback, he looked deep into her eyes and vowed—and we genuinely think that he meant it—'But I'd never, *ever* hurt you.'

She considered this, tilting her lovely chin to the side, tracing his own protruding jawline with her almond-shaped nails, as ever buffed to perfection. We knew she loved his face, loved its awkward angles, its elfin eccentricity. She loved the vestiges of the beautiful baby doll he once had been, long before she knew him. She loved his eager expressions, so desperate to succeed, with their hungry eyes and dazzling smiles that warmed gelid drawing rooms with their very presence. How he'd injected life into the flatline monotony that was the circuit. Unlike Marella, who was uneasy being one of the over-feathered flock, or Lee, with her need for exclusivity, Babe adored his talent to love each of us differently. Filling the gaping holes in our lives, born of our own mistakes. Swaddling our particular fears, bolstering singular egos. Babe saw this care as the ultimate gesture. To take those of us whom life had grouped together—perceived (whether worshiped or reviled, or treated with indifference) as one indistinguishable whole—and discover the remarkable in each of us. As much as we'd each like to have been, and competed amongst one another, jostling for preeminence, we each quietly accepted that Babe was Truman's favorite.

'I love you more than anyone in the world. Never, *ever* would I hurt you,' he repeated, as she finished tracing his jaw with her fingertips.

Turning her face to the fading sun, she sighed, ever so slightly— or held her breath, it's unclear which. 'Well, you're the only one who could. Not Bill. Not the Others . . .' (By the *Others* we aren't sure if she meant Bill's women or us.) 'Only you.'

Truman replied with what he continues to incant in sloppy confessionals over six-hour luncheons, holding his rare companion captive, bearing reluctant witness to his catechisms on the subject of his passion for Barbara Cushing Mortimer Paley. He states his most devout of intentions, which he hopes, in his heart of hearts, might still one day absolve him:

'It would kill me to hurt you. I swear I never will.'

She smiled at him, sinking deeper into his arms.

'I know, my darling. But you could.'

They swayed a half-hour longer, until they were enveloped in darkness.

Across the courtyard, lanterns were being lit, one by one, their stained glass flickering like varicolored fireflies. It was Babe who broke the silence, breathing in the fragrant night air, a sweetness lingering on the breeze.

'Heliotrope,' she exhaled, in that moment of contentment. 'You know it's my favorite?' Then, upon reflection—'Does heliotrope grow in Morocco?'

'Not a clue, Babyling. Not a *clue.*'

'Heliotrope . . .' she repeated with a kind of wistfulness, picturing—we feel certain—her garden back home at Kiluna. 'I suppose I must have imagined it.'

Far away, he hears his own voice, though his lips in the hammock have ceased to move.

'*STOP it . . .*'

He envisions Maggie, in the desert at Thirst's End, raising her head at the sound of a phrase she recognizes. He knows this can't be real because Maggie had been put to sleep late last year. Her hind legs were paralyzed, just like his had been before the chicken blood. He had Jack drive her to the vet; he just couldn't bear to do it himself. How he had wailed when she'd gone. He threw himself on the floor, pounded his fists, and sobbed until he just couldn't sob any longer. He still begins to weep when he passes another dog on the beach, walking with its master. He's had bulldogs all his grown-up life, but now he cannot think of getting a new one. He cannot bear to lose another living thing he loves.

'I swear I'll never hurt you . . .'

But you did, Truman . . . didn't you?

He sometimes thinks he hears Maggie barking in the dunes outside the house in Sagaponack, hears her howling at the moon, on the ridge where he scattered her ashes.

I swear I'll never hurt you. I swear I'll never— —

'JUST FUCKING *STOP*!!' He bolts upright to find himself shouting.

Not to Babe, who, no longer speaking to him, has been in recent years reduced to a beautiful memory. Not to us—for while he can hear us, he cannot see or place us.

He starts to say more, but laughs at his foolishness. What would be the point? Memories cannot respond. Nor can invisible voices, should they choose not to cooperate.

He feels a surge of life shoot back into his limbs, healed by reluctant defiance. Lazy as he is, he'll run a goddamn marathon if it saves him from living in memory.

He leaps from the bed with renewed, if manic, energy. A last desperate attempt to rescue himself from the wreckage of his thoughts, from the debris of his homemade bombs.

He slides his feet into a pair of moccasins and descends the steel spiral staircase into an open-plan living room. The stairs are freestanding—and painted cobalt blue, along with the floor, which lends the pleasant illusion of walking on water when he's had a few too many.

He's knocked out the upper walls himself, creating a world of height and light. Bookshelves flank a white bricked fireplace, rising two stories high. An equally tall picture window dominates one wall, yielding a panorama of sand dunes beyond. We've noticed on the shelves—among his prized paperweights and picture frames filled with mementos of former allies—more copies of his *own* books than those of other authors. Upon further examination it becomes clear they're translations of his works into various languages, making his output appear more prolific than it's been. We haven't had much time to notice, it must be said, Truman having kept Sagaponack to himself, preferring to entertain at his U.N. Plaza digs—his salon in the sky. His Hamptons hideaway is preserved as his separate world, one he shares with Jack, for whom he bought the cottage next door, covered in roses and grapevines. He had presented Jack with the deeds to both houses, slipped into the wafer slits of a butterfly-box. Jack once told Babe it was the most generous act he'd ever known—Truman's gift of security.

Their secluded compound is meant to be a temple to their art, though Jack's steady, noble output exists in the shadow of Truman's brilliance, his own small books hardly ever noticed.

Yet from what their neighbors report, Truman spends the bulk of his time of late making trips to the local liquor store. Or sitting for hours at Bobby Van's restaurant in the one-street Bridge-hampton hamlet. The waitresses know to bring him BLTs or grilled cheese sandwiches—clam chowders on Thursdays, when it's soup of the day—and to keep refilling his OJ-and-ice, pretending not to notice when he adds his own hooch from a bottle poorly concealed in a brown paper sack. He's never without his black doctor's bag, from whose recesses he draws a series of pills, which he lines in a row on the Formica table. His 'vitamins,' he tells them, mistaken in his assumption that the waitstaff have never seen a Quaalude.

They look the other way, for, like us, they've fallen for Truman's charms. Just as he's done with each of us in turn, he flatters their hungry vanity. 'Gladys, those gold hoops are simply *marvelous*! Wherever did you find them?' or 'Have you ever thought of getting a perm, Madge? A Botticelli halo around your gorgeous face . . .' or 'Goodness, Ruthie, but you have such regal bones! My *clooooose* friend Mrs. Vreeland ought to put you in her magazine!' (Of course Diana had been sacked from *Vogue* nearly a decade before, but Tru's Long Island Galateas neither know nor care. They're simply happy to be made to feel attractive in their ill-fitting uniforms, after an eight-hour shift.)

In the house in the dunes, he wades through the blue planks into the kitchen—where a window above the sink reveals the surf, mere paces beyond. He opens the refrigerator, studying its contents, torn between options. There's a leftover baked potato filled with caviar that he made and found he had no appetite for, several days before. There's an egg that he could scramble, but thinks better of such effort. He spots a jar of horseradish—a flash of inspiration. Since there's no one to consult, Jack being in Verbier and Mags in canine heaven, he imagines approval of a fortifying liquid brunch.

'That's what *I* thought,' he says. 'A Bloody-Blood it is.' (Lest anyone judge, it could be worse . . . On particularly low days he turns to his Power Shake—a banana, splash of milk, and half-bottle of bourbon, swirled in a blender and sipped from a straw.) He removes a pitcher from the cabinet, filling it with a generous helping of Stoli, ready on the counter. He adds horseradish, Worcestershire and the dregs of a carton of V8. Finally he dumps in cubes from an ice tray, stirring the mix with a jiggle.

He opens his special cabinet, where he keeps his hidden treasures, acquired over time. A pair of Hermès ashtrays, an estate-sale score he'd bargained for, long before he had a pot to piss in. A Dodie Thayer soup tureen, shaped like a head of lettuce. A set of Baccarat goblets—his favorites, which he only brings out for special occasions. He holds one to the light, admiring its aesthetic perfection. Then, with a sense of purpose, he pours a Bloody from his pitcher into the glass, having decided today is one such 'Occasion.'

He has a plan he means to execute, and that alone is cause for celebration.

'*Na zdorovye*,' he quips, toasting the ghosts in the ether.

He returns to the living room clutching his glass, collecting a white princess phone from its perch on the stairs. He drags its exceptionally long wire across the space to the armchair by the fire—a Salvation Army rescue which Babe had helped him re-upholster in a rich marigold velvet. It's looking worse for wear, but it reminds him of her, so he wouldn't dare alter it.

He gingerly sets his drink on the hearth, reaching for a wooden keepsake box, from which he draws his battered black book. Inside, in his spider-like scrawl, he's written hundreds of names and addresses—his constellation of contacts, gathered over decades by the most diligent of star-catchers. Locations spanning the circumference of the globe, from Kansas to California to the breadth of the Continent. Manhattan to Majorca to Monroeville and back again. He flips lovingly through the pages, running his fingers over the fading ink, pausing at several names of folks he particularly misses.

After our jilting, he'd made a special trip to Tiffany's and bought himself a brand-new address book—fine alligator leather, clean pages full of promise. He enjoyed himself thinking of the names that he would add—the new friends he was sure he'd acquire, to make up for the loss of old ones. He even had the shop girl wrap it specially, in robin's-egg paper, tied with a white satin bow. He thought it would cheer him to open a present, pretending someone else had thought to give it to him. When he unwrapped it that night, sitting cross-legged on the floor in his U.N. Plaza study, he found, strangely, that it brought him little joy. The alligator leather failed to enchant as it had in its former milieu. No longer did its masculine scent titillate with newness. Nor did its blank pages seem a new beginning, as they had in the sanctum of Tiffany's. Instead, they just felt empty. He placed the book back in its box and returned it the very next morning, unused.

Outdated or not, his *old* book gives him comfort. No matter that many of its luminaries are fading or have flickered out altogether. No matter that most of those still burning bright wouldn't deign to return his calls, or answer his cards or letters . . .

How many of us still think of you? How many names in that book still care?

'You know,' he says aloud, to no one in particular, 'the Chinese word for star is *xīng*. They have their own separate universe, divided into mansions.'

A third . . . ? A fifth? Or even less than that . . . ?

Placing his hands over his ears, he continues to orate. 'They're grouped into Four Symbols, all mythic creatures. The Azure Dragon of the East, White Tiger of the West—'

How many of those names give a flying fuck what happens to you now?

'The Black Turtle of the North and Vermilion Bird of the South—'

At least before, you inspired our fear. Now you just have our indifference.

'That Vermilion Bird, the *Southern* one, is stronger than you think. A fierce red phoenix with five-toned plumage, eternally covered in flames, rising from the—'

Don't flatter yourself, T. You're not a phoenix or a two-headed serpent. You're at best a little ole common gutter snake. Just a pissant rug rat from Monroeville, shit-scared as ever.

'Oh chickadees, you have no idea what more I have in store for you! Not the first clue what I have left in me . . .' In defiance, he flips through his addresses. 'Trust me—I'm just getting started!' He finds the desired number. Dials. And in that reptilian hiss we've all come to loathe over time, he braves the receiver.

'Missss-ter Clay Felker, *s'il vous plaît*.' Then, delighted at the receptionist's apparent recognition, 'Why *yeeeeessssss*, this *is* Mr. Truman Capote calling . . . How are *you*, sugar?' (A career girl, we suspect—fresh out of Vassar? Eager to flatter her way out of the secretarial pool. *Doubtful she's actually read what you've done . . .*)

He presses on. 'Well, that's just marvelous. Will you see if Mr. Felker might have a sec to spare . . . ? Yes, of course I'll hold.' He rises, crossing the room, an energized prowl between seating options—precisely what the mile-long cord had been rigged to facilitate. He tries a wicker side chair, then, thinking better, settles into the supple leather Chesterfield facing the window. He watches a gull glide past as a voice comes on the line.

'Truman! This *is* a surprise.' Like a warm rumble of thunder, that resonant bass, heralding the storm.

'Hiya, Clay.'

'How're things?'

'Oh fine, fine. How's life treating you, back at chez *Esquire*?'

'Can't complain. How's the masterpiece?' Then, with a laugh as robust as the rest of him, 'You done yet?'

'*Weeee-ulll*, I wouldn't say I'm *done*. It's an endeavor of epic proportions, after all. But what I *do* have,' he pauses both for impact, and for a sip from his Bloody, 'is the *final* chapter.'

'Oh?' Tempered intrigue from a seasoned pro.

'Yup—I'm working backward now. Last chapter to first. And boy, is it a *gasper*.'

'You don't say.'

'Clay baby, I'm calling with a little business proposition.'

'What've you got for me?'

'I've decided it's time for another sneak peek—a fresh round of ammunition, just to keep 'em running.'

Silence from Clay, playing it cucumber-cool.

Truman continues, rising from the sofa, on the prowl once more, beginning to enjoy himself. 'Seeing as how my last *Esquire* outing had such an *explosive* impact, I just couldn't bear to offer this new bit to anybody else. That's why I'm calling you personally.' (Silence still.) 'Hello . . . ? Clay . . . ? Cat got your tongue?'

The pause, one assumes, is strategic. As we say, even the great Clay Felker—patron saint of New Journalism—must have his interest piqued.

If gossip was art to Truman, it was copy to Clay—the stuff of the Big Story, the one that made his readers squirm with the discomfort of its gaze, yet compelled one to read on nonetheless. If anyone could see the art in Truman's madness when it came to *Answered Prayers*, Clay would be the man. While outwardly opposites in every regard—one looking up at the world at barely five foot three, the other towering over it, well over six feet tall—they were both part of the same special breed. Outsiders both, Gatsby-esque idealists.

Oh yes. Truman has an instinct—even as others are failing him—that the bold and mighty Felker might be his last great hope.

'So . . . ? What do you think of my offer?' Truman returns to the sofa now, unused to the pause in proceedings. 'Need I remind you how *looooong* the public has been waiting for this chapter—the last chapter of my magnum opus, twenty years in the making . . . ?'

From the other end of the line, an intake of breath, then—

'Well, of course, Truman, we'd be very excited at the prospect of running the chapter. Very excited indeed.'

'Goody. I just knew that you would be. I'm delighted, Clay. Simply over the— —'

'But you know we'll have certain conditions . . .'

That's straightened his spine. The Great Author bristles at the unfamiliar sting of *conditions*. 'Such as . . . ?'

'I want to read the story first.'

'And . . . ?'

'That's it. I just want to read it.'

It's Truman's turn to fall silent.

Clay continues, 'It's not that I don't think that it will be great. You always deliver, when you deliver. There's just been a lot of buzz. Alotta talk. About delivery dates you haven't met. Advances already spent . . . Hell, Random House is already out seven hundred grand in blue-chip stocks alone. Fox three-fifty for the film rights, before they recouped their down payment.'

'*And—*?'

'Look, Truman. You know as well as I do how big this thing will be . . . But if we're going to throw our hats into the ring, I wanna make sure we'll still have our heads when it's over.'

'All right . . .'

'I'll be in the Hamptons over the weekend. Gail and I have a house about two miles from yours—in Wainscott. I'll ride my bike over on Saturday.'

'First things first. How much are you boys at *Esquire* willing to pony up . . . ?'

'How much you asking?'

'Forty-five grand.'

'How many words?'

'Who's counting?'

'Ballpark.'

'Thirty thousand, give or take.'

'Give or take?'

'Dollar fifty a word—'

'A dollar.'

'Thirty-five thousand. Total.' Truman stands firm.

'Done,' Clay accepts.

Truman slides the rest of the Bloody down his gullet, crunching the last sliver of ice between his teeth. 'Maaaarvelous. I'm dancing a jig as we speak.' (In reality he's lying flat like a slug on the Chesterfield.)

'Saturday then. Ten a.m.'

'Breakfast with *Esquire* it is.' He sets the phone back in its cradle, heading for the kitchen for a refill from his celebratory pitcher.

AT THE WEEKEND, CLAY PEDALS the two miles west to Sagaponack. Traveling along this stretch of the South Fork, he can't help but note how much its remote fields and overgrown reeds evoke the starkness of Truman's Kansas prose and wonders if that's why the author feels at home here.

Arriving at his destination, Clay walks his bicycle up the winding drive to a weathered-plank beach house. He leans the bike against a gate and approaches the back door, as instructed.

He'll later admit to confidants that his heart was racing as he approached, breathless with the anticipation of seeing a scrap of the fabled *Answered Prayers*. Of *course* he wanted the goddamn chapter. He'd been dancing around this debacle for years. The three extracts under previous editors were the biggest thing to hit *Esquire* in eons—practically since its inception. He could hardly have imagined a better way to kick off his tenure as editor-in-chief.

Clay knocks on Truman's door. Waits. Checks his watch, knocks again. Only the sound of the brisk September wind, whistling through the marsh brush.

He makes his way around to the front window and peers in through the glass. He can just make out Truman's silhouette, stretched out on the sofa, his protuberant stomach rising and falling in a blue terrycloth bathrobe. Black sleeping mask covering his eyes. Cautiously, Clay gives the pane a gentle tap. When this appears to have no impact, he knocks more fulsomely, until finally he's pounding the glass, calling Truman's name. The beached whale stirs, pulling off his mask, startled by the apparition.

The Truman who eventually opens the portal a crack is bleary-eyed. Muddled. A breath shy of catatonic.

'Morning, Truman.' Clay reaches for the screen-door handle, opening it gently. 'May I . . . ?' Truman recoils like a pint-sized Nosferatu as the opened screen exposes him to what is, in actuality, very mild sunlight.

'*Claaaaay.* I've got the most *excruciating* migraine. Really. It's like someone's stabbing my eyeball with an ice pick. I've taken enough Percodan to fell a yak . . . I mean an oak . . . See? I'm *reeeally* not making sense right now. I simply *must* lie down . . .'

He starts to shut the door, but Felker blocks it with his loafer.

'Look, Truman, I can see you're under the weather, and we can certainly postpone our chat. Why don't I just take the manuscript with me to read over the weekend and we'll touch base on Monday? Sound like a plan?'

'I'm afraid that's just not possible.' Truman presses fingers to his temples. 'I have to type it up first. You see I always write my early drafts in longhand, *excluuusively* in longhand, and my sorry chicken-scrawl isn't legible to *anyone* but me.'

'But Truman, we had a—'

'Yesssssssssbut . . . the headache. See you tomorrow.' And with that he pulls the door shut, leaving Clay Felker to pedal back to Wainscott empty-handed.

As Clay will inform the wagging ears of Manhattan's finest watering holes, he didn't hold out much hope of hearing from Truman again—the next day, week, or otherwise.

So imagine Clay's surprise when there's a knock on his door the following morning. It's 10 a.m., sharp. Clay, his partner Gail, and stepdaughter Maura are sitting around the breakfast table, reading the Sunday papers. Gail looks beyond Clay to the back door of the cottage.

'It would appear you have a visitor.'

He turns to see Truman's aging cherub face in the pane. Pressed against the glass, watching their family tableau with wistful fascination. Rosy-cheeked, pink V-neck pullover to match. A (comparative) picture of health. He brightens as Clay approaches, opening the door.

'Greetings and salutations!' Truman practically trills. Then, with a raffish grin—'Well, don't look so surprised, Clay. I *told* you "I'll see you tomorrow," didn't I?'

He's holding a brown paper bag, a plastic container of sweet buns peeking from the top. '*Oh, what a beeeeautiful mor-nin', oh, what a beautiful day* . . .' he sings a snippet of Rodgers and Hammerstein as he shuffles past, setting his bag down on the table.

'Truman, this is my stepdaughter, Maura.'

Truman beams at a pretty twelve-year-old girl, who smiles shyly over her comics.

'Well, aren't *you* an absolute doll. Nice to make your acquaintance, Maura.'

'And you remember Gail . . .'

'But of course! The brilliant Ms. Sheehy! I'm a *huge* fan. I simply loved that *New York* piece you did about the prostitutes— "Redpants and Sugarman"? To brave a pair of hot pants to get their *stories* . . . Now that's what I call undercover! You know I used to see those working-gals, drinking Brandy Alexanders at the Bear and Bull, or loitering in Lexington in those darling little shorts—honey, some were so short, they were pos-

itively gynecological! To hustle the *Waldorf*, of all places . . . !
And to write about them like you did, to capture their fragility,
their quiet desperation . . .' He pauses with a flicker of what
can only be described as recognition. 'It was something quite
profound.'

Gail smiles. 'Well, you're more than welcome to stay for breakfast *now*.'

'What can I get you, Truman? Cuppa coffee? Grapefruit juice?
Eggs on toast?'

'Some grapefruit juice would be *divine*—but only half a glass.'
He opens his brown paper bag and presents the container of sweet
buns as an offering. 'These are for you. Baked fresh at Bobby
Van's. They *almost* taste like beignets.' As Clay pours his juice,
Truman reaches further into his bag, procuring a bottle of vodka.
As if it's the most natural thing in the world to carry a liter of
liquor to one's editor's family breakfast.

'*Molte grazie*.' This as he breaks the cap seal and fills the negative space of the juice glass with Stoli, then tucks the bottle back
in his bag, taking an exceptionally long sip.

Maura's eyes widen. Clay and Gail exchange wary glances.

'Are you sure you wouldn't like a coffee? Or something to eat?'
Gail slides the container of sweet buns toward him.

'Oh, no thank you.' Tru pats his paunch. 'I'm watching my girlish figure. This'll do me just fine. In fact it's so *nice* to have a
change from my Orange Drink. I haven't had a Greyhound in *ages*.
Oooooooo—actually, do you know what you *could* get me? Some
salt.'

Maura jumps up to fetch the shaker, delivering it to the dubious guest.

'Why thank you, Maura. Do you know that if you add salt to a
Greyhound it becomes a Salty Dog? My Mama and Daddy used to
love Salty Dogs. They drank a pair each night, at four on the dot.
They'd set up deck chairs in our yard in Monroeville and imagine
themselves on a pleasure cruise, bound for exotic locales.' (*Perhaps they did . . . but certainly never together*.)

'*Speaking* of stories,' Clay cuts in, shutting the Truman-show down with that stentorian voice. 'I hope that there's a manuscript in that bag of yours, along with all the rest.'

'Clay baby, I told you, it's a *chapter*. The last chapter—'

'—of your magnum opus. Yeah. May I read it now?'

'Of course!' Truman reaches into his grocery bag, though only to remove his Stoli bottle for a top-up. The gesture is too quintessentially Truman not to be done for effect. Like a sleight-of-hand magician who thrills at reaching into a top hat, teasing his audience with anything *but* the promised rabbit. 'The thing is, I didn't have time to finish typing it up. I was so down for the count yesterday, you have no *idea* . . . I just couldn't concentrate to save my life.'

'Ah.'

'However, you *do* know that I have ninety-four percent recall.' Modest for Truman—he usually goes for ninety-six. 'So I just thought I'd pop on over and give you the chapter *verbally*.'

'Verbally,' Clay repeats, with a poker face that could rattle Nick the Greek.

Yet Truman doubles down, undeterred. 'Every character. Every moment. The whole enchilada. By the time I'm done, you won't need to *read* it. 'Cause you'll have *lived* it.'

He adds another dash of salt to his Dog and takes a bracing sip. He sets his glass down, starting to come alive. Eyes flashing with adrenaline. Truman is built for such moments.

As he's always said, he simply *loves* to talk . . .

'Weeee-ull . . . It all begins and ends with Kate McCloud. We've met her before, if you'll recall, in my first chapter, "Unspoiled Monsters," and in the subsequent chapter that bears her name.' He allows himself a satisfied snicker. 'Lordy, but hasn't *that* kept 'em on their pedicured toes! They're all terrified that Kate is based on someone real—which she *is*—and that that someone just *might* be them. But back to Kate, and P.B. Jones, who you'll recall is my narrator.'

'*You*, in other words.'

'I never said P.B. was *me*.'

'I think it's pretty tough after "La Côte Basque" to imagine him being anyone else. If it walks like a duck and quacks like a duck . . . He's even writing a book called *Answered Prayers*.'

'Oh sure. There's a *part* of P.B. that's me . . . but there's a part of him who isn't. The things that have happened to him, the things he's *done* . . . These things, thank God, have never touched me. But trust me, he's always a breath away. He's who I *might* have become, had one piece of the puzzle been different.' A pause, removal of glasses, rubbing of eyes. 'You see, P.B. *is* me . . . But he's also someone else. A beautiful, terrible boy who never stood a chance.'

As he turns to the succor of Stoli, Clay realizes who Truman's hinting at. The one person whose very loss has haunted him, hanging from his neck like a golden albatross. The man whose crime and death inspired Truman's gifts to unimagined heights. The loss he cannot shake.

Careful to coax rather than spook, Clay ventures—

'So P.B. Jones is a hybrid of you and Perry Smith . . .'

A hush descends on the table. After a moment Truman meets his eyes. Nods.

'Author and killer. Janus-faced twins. Them's us.' He replaces his glasses, and with a breath he relaunches—'*Sooooooo*. If Jonesy is our eyes and ears, then Kate McCloud's our muse. We first meet Kate when P.B. does, in Paris at the Ritz—'

'And the *new* chapter . . . ?'

'I'm getting there . . .'

'Truman, I've read "Kate McCloud."'

'Maura hasn't.'

'You're pitching *me*!'

Feeling Felker's impatience, Truman speeds ahead.

Aside, to Maura, 'Honey, all you need to know is that they'll all live happily ever after. They'll go to hell and back, they'll journey to the center of the earth, they'll battle monsters of every variety, but they'll have a happy ending.' Then, musing, 'The first and only I shall ever write. An ending as cool and clear as a summer stream. A boy . . . a beach. A dog, bounding over the dunes. A man and a woman, swaying in a hammock, ever so gently. It's how I've always wanted to end a book, in a flash of filmic images. That's what this will be, and I promise you, it's heaven,' his voice wistful. 'But we couldn't possibly know that's where we're headed, when we begin . . .' A beat. Then, shifting the mood to one of fanfare—

'Which brings us to my *FINAL* chapter: "Father Flanagan's All-Night Nigger Queen Kosher Cafe,"' he proclaims, enjoying the shock that flashes across their faces.

'Jesuschrist-and-godalmighty.' Clay shakes his head. *'That'll* have to change.'

'But sugar, it's a *metaphor*.'

'For what?'

'The end of the line. The last stop on the train. The final depot . . . We all know a Father Flanagan's, even if we know it by another name. It's where you're dropped off in a taxi when there's nowhere left to go. It looks like hell, but we'll find it's quite the opposite.'

'Well,' says Clay, starting to lose the plot. 'When you have something *written* . . .'

'I told you, it's *written* in my *mind*. Let me just paint you the opening scene.'

Clay flicks his eyes to Gail, then sits back in his chair.

'Okay, Truman. Floor's yours. Convince me.'

Truman rises, dramatically, sly smile twitching at the corners of his mouth.

> T.C.: It's a sweltering midday in August. We open on the illustrious address of 550 Park Avenue, in an apartment on the thirteenth floor—home of our heroine, Kate McCloud.
>
> She lies in bed, *certainly* supine, propped on a pile of pillows, her auburn waves splayed across their surface. She's startled when the phone rings just before noon. It simply isn't done.

She's being pleasured by her lover, the gentleman in question lapping her twat with the fervor of a husky with a peanut-butter bone—'

CLAY: *Ohhhhh*-kay. Maura . . . skedaddle.

MAURA: I know what oral sex is, you know.

CLAY: How?

MAURA: School.

CLAY: (to Gail) We're paying for this?

T.C.: It's really one teensy detail. And it's about as racy as it gets . . .'

CLAY: What's the rest about?

T.C.: Quiet desperation, just like Gail's Waldorf gals. And love. And heaven, eventually.

CLAY: All right. Get on with it.

T.C.: So. To resume . . .

On the nightstand, the phone begins to ring. *Brrrrrrrrrring! Brrrrrrrrrringg!*

Like a contortionist Kate twists around, shimmying toward a phone on the nightstand, retrieving the handset with surprising dexterity.

Before she can answer, a voice: 'Kate? Katie, dollface . . . you there?'

Lost in the sensations of her own supple flesh, Kate fails to respond beyond a steady, listless panting.

'*Kate!* It's me—*Zip*! Pick up!' On the line, Jerry Zipkin, shameless social moth, who both looks and sounds like a human bidet.

Despite her lover's ministrations, Kate manages to steady the sound of her voice to a timbre of practiced ennui. 'Hello, Jerry.'

'Thank *God*. You're there. I was about to hang up. I'm out here on the coast, doll—California—and I hafta ask you a favor—I need you to check on Maggie.'

'Who?'

'Maggie—Margaret Case. Your upstairs neighbor.'

'Mmmmmmmm, maybe you should ring her. I'm sort of in the middle of something.' She glances down to her lover's head, moving back, forth, and sideways. He's working so hard, it seems impolite to stop him.

'Yeah, but I got you on the line now, and I need you

to go and knock on her door.'

'Who?' asks Kate, stifling a gasp.

'*Maggie*, Kate! Your *neighbor*.'

'Jerry, I don't really know Miss Case,' she tells Zip, uneasy.

'Oh dollface, call her Maggie. You should know her. She's a wonderful woman. But I'm worried about her. I haven't been able to get ahold of her all weekend.'

'Maybe she's on vacation, Jerry. People do go away in August...'

'Yeah,' says Zip, impatient for his reveal. 'But you don't know what *I* know ... I got a call late last week from Diana, who's in Paris. You know Mrs. Vreeland, don't you? *Everyone* knows Mrs. Vreeland. Well, she told me the most *appalling* story...'

Silence, except for a rumble of thunder and a soft patter of rain. Kate looks beyond her lover to the window, delighted to find that a summer shower has commenced.

'So, Maggie's worked at *Vogue* for half a goddamn century. They called her the five-foot terror. Scared the hell out of everyone. Well, according to Diana, last Thursday Maggie arrived for work, as she's done six days a week for forty-five years. She entered the marble lobby and rode up in the elevator, per usual. As she was sitting at her desk—the same desk she'd had for over four decades—there *apparently* came a knock on the door. Maggie looked up from her contact sheets to see two young men in coveralls.

Miss Case? We're here for the desk.

'Well, you can imagine poor Maggie's confusion.'

But this is my desk, Maggie said. *There must be some mistake.*

Sorry, Miss Case. Avoiding her eyes. *There's no mistake.*

The men moved the desk away from her, dumping the contents of its drawers into a cardboard box. They removed the art from the walls, leaving pristine white squares where the sun had bleached the paint around the frames over time. Throughout, Maggie sat quietly in her desk chair, holding her cup of coffee, long gone

256

cold.

Excuse me, Miss Case, one said when they were done. *We're gonna need the chair too.*

'Can you imagine anything more cruel? To do this to an eighty-year-old woman, who had worked in that office longer than the rest of them had been *alive*?'

'God,' says Kate to Zip, for there's really nothing more to say.

'So you can see why I'm worried about poor Maggie. I've been ringing and ringing her. Your concierge confirmed that at least half a dozen moving boxes arrived and were delivered to 16A. He also said that her maid has been in and out twice since Thursday, but said he's not seen Miss Case leave the building.' Jerry pauses. 'Listen, Katie, I know you like to keep to yourself and stay out of people's business . . . But can you *please* go knock on Maggie's door and check to see if she's all right?'

And it's then—as if on some sort of ghoulish cue—that Kate sees it.

A form, falling past the window, falling with the sheets of gentle rain, seeming to take an instant and an age at once. A mackintosh billowing above what appears to be a mannequin—catching the air, parachuting above.

A body suspended for the briefest of moments in space against an overcast sky, buoyed by khaki wings.

A flash of platinum-gray. A glint of gold.

Then—nothing. Just the rain.

Kate reaches down, burying her fingers in her lover's hair, gently stopping his movements. She rises from the bed and walks naked to the window, steeling herself for either the mythic or the macabre, she isn't sure which.

She fights the instinct to look down, instead looking upward, into the restless sky. Hoping to see an exotic khaki bird soaring toward the heavens, having reversed its trajectory. For a brief, shimmering moment she believes that this fate is possible. Seeing nothing beyond the inky clouds, Kate looks down, where in the courtyard below, Miss Margaret Case's lifeless body lies on the pavement, surrounded by the manicured gardens that the residents of 550 Park each contribute sixty dollars a month to maintain. Wearing a Burberry raincoat, clutching a ladylike handkerchief.

Shattered, yet neat as a pin.

The rain cleansing her motionless form.

Kate stares at it for a moment, then walks back to the phone. She picks up the handset, from which she can hear Zip honking away—'Hello? Kate? Katie? You there?'

She sits on the bed. Lights a cigarette. Runs a hand through her auburn hair.

'Jerry . . . I've found Maggie.'

Truman pauses, checking in with his audience. Three sets of spellbound eyes leave him confident enough to milk the silence.

'Did she really jump out the window?' Maura asks.

'Yes. Technically it was a suicide. But she died of a broken heart. You know, I think about the people who might have happened to look out of their windows the moment that she jumped. What they were doing . . . What seeing *that* might have done to them. Had Babe Paley, mere blocks away at the St. Regis, seen a body fall, would she have thought of the unfortunate young lady who'd done the same when Bill jilted her years earlier? Would Slim Keith, but a few blocks further west at the Pierre, have even looked up from her paper and Scotch? I've given Maggie Kate McCloud to bear witness, but what if nobody saw her fall? What if no one witnessed her mackintosh filling with air in that brief moment of weightlessness before reality struck and the poetic gesture became nothing more than a tawdry mistake?

'I think about who found her on the pavement outside 550 Park—they say it was a gardener, arriving to trim the hedges, but Mrs. Vreeland swears it was her maid. I think about whoever cleaned up the mess that a perfectly buttoned coat couldn't begin to hide.

'And finally I think about what must have gone through Maggie's mind on the way down. What flashed through her brain as she fell with the rain into nothingness? Did she think of her girlhood, dancing Charlestons? Of first loves and last kisses, or drinking Singapore Slings?

'Or did Maggie Case think of Azurest, where *Answered Prayers* will end? A tranquil place on Long Island, with clam boats and scallopers bobbing in the water. Families on beaches with black and tan faces, basking in their own private paradise. Or of Father Flanagan's all-night cafe, where we'll all wind up in the end?'

(Smiling to the Felkers ...)

'I *do* wonder.'

And with that he dumps the last of the Stoli into his glass, polishing off his bottle.

'It's a knockout, Truman.' Clay, getting down to business— 'When can I expect it? I'll run it as the cover.'

'Soon ...' Truman replies cryptically, nibbling a scrap of sweet bun. 'I just have to tighten a few screws. Thirty-five grand still okay?'

'Thirty-five grand,' Clay confirms.

Truman beams his thousand-watt smile, pleased as punch with the outcome.

LATER, LAST DROPS OF GRAPEFRUIT AND STOLI depleted, they call him a taxi and watch him totter down the sandy path to the road. He stops dead in his tracks, staring with disbelief at the name of the cab company, emblazoned on its flank—'Hedge End Cabs', which Truman in his bleariness reads as '*Hope's* End.' He hesitates, as if pondering whether he'd like to take the ride or not.

The Felkers watch the driver take his grocery bag and help him into the backseat; they see him wave at them in the window, and wave back from the porch. Afterward they head back inside and begin to clear the breakfast table, plates caked with dried yolk, four hours after the fact. (Truman had, as promised, orated the remainder of the chapter as he glugged, plus 'previews' of two more.)

And it's there, over a sink filled with suds, that Clay confesses to Gail, she washing, he drying—'You know, he could've asked six figures for that goddamn chapter and I think I would've considered it.'

'Really.'

'Oh yeah. Thirty-five grand's a bargain . . .'

Gail completes the sentence for him: '. . . *if* it exists.'

They finish the dishes in silence, lost in their separate thoughts, in their own sacred visions of Azurest.

FIFTEEN

1978

BABE

ELEGY

AFTER A LIFETIME OF ENTERTAINING, she throws the luncheon to end all luncheons, the crowning achievement in a career of relentless hospitality.

She is both here and not. We can feel her presence in the most minute of details as we approach the line of white-coated waiters, gloved hands offering trays of Babe's favorite Pouilly-Fumé de Ladoucette. Another corps of servers emerges with champagne flutes, passing one another in a careful pavane, maids carrying plates of quivering aspic. The choreographed steps of the wait-staff are something we observe with gutted smiles and splintered hearts, expecting nothing less from her.

During the long prelude to this day, she had discussed each choice with us as we came and went, together and alone, sitting at her bedside in those last molasses months. As ever, sipping our gimlets and Vespers, nursing our Scotches and hangovers, as Babe continued to chain-smoke her darling L&Ms, taking what remaining pleasure there was to be had in them; a moth courting the fatality of the flame.

Without leaving her room, she planned her final send-off.

'*Two* menus?' we'd exclaimed, taking our turns looking at the thick stack of lists, the sketches and clippings, the recipes written in her tidy script.

She'd stared at us, as if we were the most impossibly ill-prepared of creatures, and replied without a trace of sentimentality—'Of course!

One if I die in winter, one if I die in spring. One couldn't possibly serve the same spread.'

She had gone in summer, as it happened. On the 6th of July, the morning after her sixty-third birthday, dressed in an imported lace bed jacket, her bald head concealed beneath an elegant satin turban. Mask of perfection intact.

She herself had seen to that, her last act of exertion having been the careful application of her Face. With a shaky hand she darkened her lashes and colored her lips to match the cinnabar console she'd prized in her collection. She'd set her makeup box on its varnished surface for the last time and drifted into a morphine-induced reverie, walking—as we are now—through the visions of the al fresco picnic she was so determined we enjoy. Realizing a June departure was likely, she had tweaked both menu and tables-capes to reflect the season. Centerpieces of Chinese porcelain bowls, brimming with black cherries. Tray-passed lobster salad, served in cucumber cups. As we stroll the manicured gardens of her beloved Kiluna, past its lush dell and pristine beds, we can almost see her in her wide straw sun hat, gloved hands covered in dirt, turning the soil, planting the seeds for next season's azaleas. Pruning, digging, taming vines and flowers in a way she failed to tame her ungrateful children. Shaping shrubs and hedges with garden shears, watching with pleasure how they complied, in a way that Bill and his roving eye never could.

We picture the pleasure with which she'd walk us through the blossoming flowers, proudly pointing out her favorite, the dusty-lilac *Heliotropium arborescens*. We can smell their faint vanilla scent now, as we sip our champagne and ingest the loveliness of the Eden she'd created over decades. Meticulously planned hedges and flowering trees, sloping down to a tranquil oval pond, which Babe spent hours sitting beside.

The last time she had the strength to walk the dell unchaper-oned, she happened upon a man admiring the property. People often wandered the woodland glen and got turned around. She told us she smiled at the man, who smiled back. They exchanged hellos and chatted briefly about the grounds. As they were parting, he pulled a business card from his pocket and handed it to her. She recognized the name—a local real estate shark, known for buying up land in Manhasset, building suburbs of cookie-cutter boxes on its unblemished greenery. Realizing she'd been flattered into a dialogue with the enemy, she handed the card straight back.

'Now you just run along, Mr. Builder Man, 'cause they're gonna carry me out of here feet first!' (Babe found herself channeling Truman's Southern cadence for the rebuff.)

We feel her in the gentle breeze, think we hear her silver laughter in the rustling leaves of the twin linden trees, as we overhear more than one dolled-up mourner whisper, with a glance in Bill's direction—'*Poor* Bill. He must be so *lonely* . . .' Barely concealing their designs.

Inside, the house is brimming with flowers, as if the gardens had been extended indoors. In the famed red-lacquered dining room (from which Truman cribbed the concept for his own), an abundance of cut stems rise from cloisonné vases, each floral variety hand-picked by Babe at Petrov's on Sixth Avenue. She was eager—this being her last shot—to make selections she thought might inspire surprise. Unusual choices. Memorable ones. Ranunculi in a deep oxblood, a dead ringer for Babe's favored nail varnish—a bloom she loved for growing more complex as it unfolded, layer by delicate layer.

She'd always loved the architectural nature of cherry blossoms, but Bill made such a fuss when they shed. 'What's all this pink shit?' he'd grumble at the sight of a dusting of petals on a table or sideboard. Babe had selected them with grim pleasure at the thought that she would not be around to either hear his complaints or hop to, tidying the mess.

Of course it's Slim, Babe's first lieutenant, who has executed her battle plan, down to the last detail. And between her devotion and their long-standing friendship, it shouldn't be surprising that it's on *her* arm Bill chooses to lean. We've commented on it before, the ease with which Bill and Slim seem to interact, although on this occasion both appear so raw, even the most cynical of us refrains from voicing a hint of speculation. We know how deeply both had loved her, how both had—while being the two most taxed by her oft-maddening perfection—depended on her as a vital piece of their very souls. Both must be flailing, wondering how a day might pass without her there to soften their sharp edges. They sit beside one another, Slim and Bill, each staring into middle distance, thighs brushing. Hardly touching the Poulet à l'Estragon, swimming in wine and cream.

In earlier, happier days, when Babe had fallen in love with the dish in the bistros of Montmartre, Slim had joked that it sounded like 'chicken à la *estrogen*.' Whatever one called it, they narrowed the best interpretation to one unassuming establishment—Le Moulin Joyeux, to which they returned time and again. The key to the dish, they'd determined, was the faint aniseed of the tarragon, though Babe suspected it had as much to do with the varietal of wine. As means of confirmation, she cajoled the recipe from the chef de cuisine at the bistro in question. Bewitched by the beauty of *les femmes américaines*, the smitten chef had written both ingredients and instructions on the back of a picture postcard Babe procured from her handbag. A photograph of a gargoyle perched high atop Sacré-Coeur—a winged creature with an extraordinarily long neck and severe expression. Babe had sent one to each of us, writing that its extended features reminded them of our own. Slim, smoking beside her at a cafe table, had taken her pen and added an 'X, S & B' for each. Babe had retained one gargoyle for herself and one for Slim—and kept her recipe incarnation for years in a French cookery book. It was this dog-eared postcard that Slim passed along to the battalion of luncheon chefs, so that they might get the Poulet à l'Estragon *dead* right. (The pun was Babe's, and yes, it was intended.)

From time to time Bill gropes for Slim's hand and squeezes it, as if needing reassurance that they're still of the corporeal world. Babe herself must have detected their closeness, even assumed it would flourish in her absence; that Slim would slip seamlessly into her place within days of her bucket-kick, adding Mr. Paley as the fourth in her line-up of husbands. In fact she'd assumed they were already at it. Both had earned their louche reputations over the decades. Why should *now* prove the exception? We'd all seen her lose her temper with Slim of late in ways she never had before; we'd noticed the narrowing eyes across her down mattress, as if trying to decipher precisely what Slim may or may not be guilty of. When we'd tried to broach the subject of such moments with Slim, she simply dismissed them with breezy resilience.

'That's the morphine talking. Not Babe.'

Still, for all their closeness, Babe must have had her hunches, for she left a telling message in the meticulously selected bequests, which she had taken great care to detail. She made a master list recording the obvious, for fear that her mind was slipping. Listing, one by one, those who she mustn't forget to remember: her family, closest friends, her secretary, and household staff(s). Her retinue of beauty gods, from her hairdressing team at Kenneth's (who now cut and color her wigs), to manicurists, facialists, and her stylists at Bendel and Bergdorf's. Her Pilates jocks, decor gurus, and terribly overtaxed chefs—to whom she leaves a bit extra, knowing what they'll inherit with Bill, when she's no longer present to mediate.

In the months prior to her departure she had itemized and cataloged her wealth of possessions, designating a recipient for each. Writing names, gifts, and their values on lined index cards that she filed alphabetically for easy reference.

She had hesitantly asked some of us if there was a specific piece of jewelry that we fancied—an item from her vast collection that particularly caught our eye. In some cases we brushed this aside, uncomfortable speaking about her inevitable demise, or the prospect of taking Babe's things. Others had answered quite plainly, justifying their forthrightness as honoring Babe's wishes. Gloria had been perfectly clear that she coveted Babe's ivory and tortoise jewelry casket. (We bet she did, at three thousand, five hundred bucks!)

In other instances Babe asked us each in confidence what we thought the others might like. A Chinese porcelain box, adorned with vines of primary shades (worth at *least* a thousand) had been set aside for C.Z.; we congratulated ourselves on the suggestion, as we knew it would remind her of their shared passion for gardening. Mrs. Vreeland receives the gold and white enamel Fabergé powder box that Truman long admired. He used to toy with it on Babe's dressing table, sitting faithfully by her side, watching her apply her Face, brushstroke by brushstroke, with all the fascination of watching a geisha do the same.

In fact, not only does Babe fail to leave Tru even the smallest of tokens, she leaves explicit instructions that he is not to be told of her death—he can read about it in the papers with the rest of the masses—and *certainly* he's not to be invited to her luncheon, so painstakingly planned. She's worried the little bastard will try to weasel his way in, appealing to Bill or Slim in a moment of weakness, asking C.Z. to plead the case on his behalf . . . saying that he always loved her, that he'll be 'bereft without his Babyling,' that he 'couldn't bear not to have a last goodbye . . .' bullshit, bullshit, bullshit. Truman's at his finest in heightened moments of drama, and Babe has been careful to ensure, as a last act of defiance, that he not steal her thunder in what will be her final, glorious exit. She's even threatened Slim and 'Old Bastard Paley' in her morphine-haze that they'd best follow her instructions, as she'll 'be watching' . . .

Perhaps, as we say, she meant to assert her lasting omnipresence in more realms than one, for it's clear that, whether opiate or instinct-induced, she suspected Slim and Bill of a long-term dalliance. This Babe made clear in her bequest left to Slim—a pair of Japanese ceramic crab tureens, worth a measly two hundred bucks. To her dearest friend of thirty years?! We wonder if Babe was trying to communicate something more significant in her choice of that which *could* suggest infidelity; a veiled reference to more than a guileless crustacean. Still, Slim remained unfazed, and would in fact take pleasure serving bisque in the crab tureens at many a dinner to come, thinking of Babe with unmarred affection as she ladles portions.

IT IS SPRING 1978. We know this because last week was Easter.

This being April, Babe is still alive, though not entirely and not for long.

She's made the eccentric decision to move into her closet-cum-dressing room, where she sits propped against an Empire campaign bed she's had moved into the space, nesting contentedly, surrounded by her things. There's a vanity across the room, and shelves upon shelves housing everything from her wardrobe to handbags to stacks of beautifully wrapped packages, arranged in a still-life tableau. The packages have been her project these last weeks; since the arrival of her jewelry from Chase Manhattan, she having turned to the business of personalizing bequests. All were delivered to her dressing room lair, where she's sat for days, meticulously wrapping—taking breaks for drags from either her cigarettes or oxygen tank as needed—priceless jewels that used to be locked in vaults, preparing them to be dispersed into the world, which Babe thinks a more pleasing fate for them.

She's totaled the value of her estate: the jewelry, fine art, and furniture, the furs, gowns, et al.—not to mention the stocks and bonds, of which she holds many; a hefty chunk of CBS shares, acquired before they were valuable. She's calculated that it comes to something in the region of eight million. Eight million dollars. Is that worth a life she fears that she's only *half* lived? Can one put a price on such choices?

These have been the questions she's asked herself as she's filled out her notecards, determining what will happen to her life's worth when she's gone.

Through this process, fighting the pain of her body betraying her, carefully wrapping each gift, she has selected the exact shade of paper she knows that each of us favors, or ones that she identifies with us. Slim is always yellow—sun-kissed, golden. C.Z. is blue—free association with Boston blue blood? She can't recall the reason, but C.Z.'s a pale ice blue, where Marella is cobalt, conjuring visions of the Adriatic. Gloria is any one of a rich palette of greens, palm leaves and key limes and ripe avocados. The bold Diana Vreeland is of course crimson red. Truman *would* have been orange—a bright Hermès hue, a shade darker than his Orange Drinks. But fuck Truman. He isn't getting a present, as she's made explicitly clear. For each gift she takes the time to construct a farewell missive, written on her engraved correspondence cards. For each she notes the name of the recipient on the envelope, seals it, then ties it to the box with a ribbon, knotting the bows several times for good measure.

She wills herself the strength to drag her emaciated form from the campaign bed and makes what feels like the long pilgrimage to her dressing table. Here she sits, lovingly fingering items scattered across the surface, fingers straying to a silver brush, a family heirloom which she keeps on display. She notices, in its fine boar bristles, strands of her graying chestnut hair, left from the last time she had need to use it. She pulls a tuft out and turns it around, studying it like a curiosity in a sideshow exhibition. Looking in the mirror, she unwraps the silk charmeuse scarf she's skillfully twisted around her head in a makeshift turban. Removing it, the silk sweeps against her bare scalp, a rare sensory pleasure.

'It's simple,' she can hear a voice saying, tone coaxing. 'You just lean forward, cover the back of your head with a towel, slip the cap off, then twist the front bit up till it stays . . . like so!'

Her own voice. And then another—an octave higher—the voice of a child.

'I don't want to swim.'

'But darling, you *have* to want to *swim*. All children want to swim.'

Babe is transported back to a cabana, just off the beach at the Hôtel du Palais in Biarritz. She's here with Kate, a girl of eight, wearing a striped bathing costume. She has Bill's features and a blunt Buster Brown bob, low bangs hanging to her eyes.

Standing before her, Babe is marvelous-looking in a white beach romper, strapless. As glamorous as the little girl is plain. She is demonstrating how to wrap one's hair into a towel, removing a red bathing cap underneath.

'See how easy? Now you try.'

'No, thank you,' says the girl.

'Go on . . .' Babe coaxes, handing her the towel and cap.

'NO!' The girl throws them back, defiant.

'Darling,' Babe regroups, speaking slowly, with the exaggerated patience adults are so often guilty of inflicting on children, 'I know that you don't want to swim, because you're afraid everyone will see . . . But I promise you they won't. You'll wear your bathing cap, then you'll cover your head with the towel—then we'll come back here and fix everything. I promise.'

The girl shakes her head.

Babe resorts to bribery. 'You know the Madame Alexander doll you said you had your eye on? Well, if you try just this once I promise we'll get it for you . . .'

Now the girl is listening. (She is, after all, her father's daughter.)

'You promise?'

'Cross my heart.'

Reluctantly the girl takes the bathing cap from her mother.

She reaches up to her haircut and pulls it off, revealing a bald head beneath. Above her eyes where her bangs once hung, a complete absence of eyebrows. She quickly slides on the bathing cap, attempting to pull it low. Babe removes an eyebrow pencil from the makeup bag in her straw beach tote. She leans in, filling in the spaces, drawing Kate a plausible set of brows, as long as one doesn't look *too* close.

'There we are,' Babe smiles. The girl furrows her new brows, concerned.

As if reading her mind, her mother reassures, 'It's waterproof.'

She holds up a compact mirror so that the girl might check her appearance. She seems satisfied, even giving her mother the concession of a shrug. 'It's okay, I guess.'

'You look gorgeous.' (Both must know this is pushing it.) 'Now, after you've had a lovely day, you'll do the towel trick, then we'll come back here and put your hair back on—perfect.' She tucks the child's-size wig into her beach bag, safe from view, as they open the cabana door to a breathtaking seascape.

BABE NEVER REALLY STOPPED BLAMING HERSELF for Kate's condition.

Three years earlier, on a rare *vacance en famille* in Cap d'Antibes, one evening Babe noticed a great deal of hair coming out in Kate's brush, when detangling her locks before bed. The next morning Babe examined her pillow *and* the bath drain to find the same: clusters of brown hair, shed from Kate's shoulder-length bob.

Day by day the hair continued to fall. First in tufts, then in clumps. By the end of the holiday, the child was completely bald.

In a panic, the Paleys took her to every specialist in Manhattan.

Alopecia universalis, they were told. Incurable. Cause unknown, but thought to be associated with severe stress.

'Stress?' Babe had cried. 'But she's *five*!'

The specialists couldn't be sure if the strain of having her favorite nanny sent packing had played a part (for while doting on Kate, she beat the older children), or if her parents' frequent absences contributed to her malady.

For *our* two cents we always thought it a bit bizarre that Babe and Bill moved their combined brood—her two, his two, and their two—to a separate house on the grounds of Kiluna, apart from the main residence. Of course, any of us can agree children are more enjoyable seen than heard—and even *that* can wear thin. But to throw those kids together in a separate house, practically in their own world . . . We'd never dream of telling Babe this, but we wonder if perhaps the youngest Paley simply couldn't take the strain.

While a cure was sought and shrinks were hired to help confront the shock of it all, nothing could be done to reverse the process.

Babe ordered Kate the finest wigs money could buy, and took her to Kenneth's to have them cut and styled in a private room, as if this were perfectly natural.

Now it is Babe who goes to Kenneth's wearing her wigs, to style hair that isn't hers, to cut tresses that aren't really growing, if only to maintain the ritual.

In her St. Regis closet dressing room, Babe lowers her scarf, setting it down on the vanity. For the first time, when she looks very closely at her reflection, she can see a shade of her younger daughter in her own weary expression. Feeling for the first time in years—perhaps ever—a genuine pang of empathy. Something like recognition.

She grips the vanity edge, rising with some difficulty. She makes her way back to the campaign bed, to her index cards and catalogues, where she opens her planner to the final list of endowments. She removes the cap from her fountain pen and adds a name to the end:

> Kate Paley: Schlumberger turquoise necklace, six hundred diamonds; gold coral Panos choker; painting by her uncle Jimmy Fosburgh entitled *Mittens*.
>   Sum total: $30,500.

This listed just below where she had previously been crossed out, Kate's resentments and rebellions pardoned.

BABE THINKS A GREAT DEAL, IN HER FINAL DAYS and hours, about the last time she managed to venture out into the world, before the protracted vigil at the St. Regis commenced. The memory is significant for being the last time she felt truly herself—when her health rallied, which of course meant the last time we were able to foster, with reason, hopes for a full recovery.

It was on board the Guinness' yacht—last June, where Babe sat for hours, soaking in the sun. For the first time she could recall, since the initial bout of pneumonia that led to her diagnosis, she found that she didn't feel ravaged. Nothing was expected of her. No badgering to join the expeditions to various ruins that Gloria once forced her guests to partake in. No pressure to read a book, the days of 'improving' oneself with culture having waned. There were no demands, apart from the collective desire on behalf of her fellow passengers that she might feel a little stronger each day, but even that ceased to be a requirement.

She was able to sit from sunrise to sunset on the deck in a lounge chair, doing nothing more than staring out at the sea or up at the sky. Appreciating the turquoise shimmer of the Mediterranean. Feeling the breeze kiss her skin. Listening to the foreign cadences of the sailors on various boats in the ports in which they anchored, wondering what their lives must be like. Did they have happy marriages? Offspring? Were they fulfilled in their vocations? Was their life overall worth more than their monetary value?

She'd watch the light in the sky fade up or down, running the gamut from grapefruit to onyx. She'd survey the stars at night, no longer bothering with known constellations.

It was the *unknown* that now held her interest.

Though it was summer, she hid her skeletal frame in oversized knits, not wanting to shock her companions. She had one piece of luck in that her face remained largely unchanged, so while the rest of her wasted away, from the neck up she still looked like Babe. She wore the same Valentino cashmere five days running, simply because it was comforting. She no longer cared what others thought. She had to chuckle recalling a time when such things mattered. When she and Gloria were at the height of their unspoken rivalry. She remembered as if it were yesterday those consecutive summers, decades before, when Gloria famously hoodwinked her.

'What's the dress code?' Babe had asked her on the phone while packing for the annual Guinness-hosted cruise—ten days on the Adriatic.

'Oh Bebé, it's very intimate, *very* low-key. Just a few close friends. *Relajado.*'

Babe had arrived with cases full of cotton slacks and palazzo pants and white blouses, the occasional shirtdress thrown in for good measure.

Awaiting cocktails in a pair of dark blue jeans, striped *marinière*, and jacket with nautical buttons, Babe was perplexed when the female guests, one by one, emerged from their cabins in evening dress. She watched, gobsmacked, when La Guinness floated onto the polished deck—'Oh my, I'm the *last* to arrive'—in a strapless Balenciaga gown, flamenco hem trailing behind. Clinging to Gloria's frame like a second skin.

Truman, always one to appreciate a good shit-stirring, was delighted by the mischief of it all. Chewing an olive from his martini, he'd leaned in and enthused—'Well, Babyling, she's certainly trumped you there!'

The next summer Babe took no chances. She brought three suitcases full of meticulously chosen ensembles. Structured gowns, smart suits, tailored dresses that showcased her slender form. The first evening Babe pulled out all the stops, proving an absolute vision: an extraordinary Dior in two shades of pink, a deep raspberry floor-length skirt, topped with a plunging neckline—skin-toned, which lent the illusion of nakedness. From her lobes hung a pair of morganite drops; her hand was swallowed by an enormous black-diamond cocktail ring. Paste, of course—by Kenneth Jay Lane, king of the costume fake. This element was Babe's private joke, testing to see if La Guinness might notice. But when Babe materialized on deck, dressed to the nines, she found Gloria & Co. lounging on cushions, in jeans and T-shirts, barefoot. To make matters worse, dinner was revealed to be baby-back ribs that one ate with one's hands, spreading a sticky russet sauce over everything in sight. As Babe sat, overdressed, feeling faintly ridiculous, quietly fuming, Gloria sweetly offered, loud enough for the length of the deck to hear—

'Why, Bebé, that's the most beautiful dress you're wearing! It makes me wish *I'd* thought to dress up too! But I would be simply mortified if you got sauce on that divine crêpe de chine . . .' Then, a mischievous smile playing at the corners of her mouth, 'Would you like a bib, darling? I'm sure we can rustle something up.'

'Trumped again, Baby! Guinness: two, Paley: zip!' Truman had kissed her cheek and roared.

Their last cruise to St. Tropez bore no trace of the former quietly waged battle for preeminence. Gloria couldn't have been more solicitous, bringing Babe items the former knew the latter particularly loved. A pot of Moroccan mint tea on a tray with a Turkish delight on the side. A margarita on the rocks, salt lining the rim. A single oyster on a plate, resting on a pillow of shaved ice—just a taste, as Gloria knew Babe lacked the appetite for more. Babe savored the lingering minerality, like a single silver penny on her tongue.

When Gloria returned to collect her plate, Babe had taken her hand and held it.

Gloria sat down in the lounger beside her.

Babe looked to her. Smiled . . . to which Gloria nodded.

They sat in this manner, Babe and Gloria, for the better part of the afternoon, watching the sun dip below the horizon.

ON THE DAYS WHEN BABE CAN MANAGE (and they're growing fewer and fewer) she forces herself to dress and go and visit her oldest sister. Sick as she is, Babe reasons that Minnie is even worse off, and feels it the duty of the younger sister to care for the elder.

Minnie has been through a terrible time, having just lost her husband Jimmy to cancer as well. If one didn't know better, one could say that the Cushing girls' illnesses appear to be contagious, were it not for Betsey and her irritatingly glowing health, flaunting her lack of cancer like a pageant trophy. Now, apartment empty, her days numbered, Minnie confides she is terrified to be facing the same curtain Babe is, all on her own.

They have a silent pact not to discuss Truman, who Minnie refused to shun. They have so little time left, neither sister can bear to waste it arguing about anything. All might have continued in this fashion, with his name never passing their lips . . .

But for one rainy afternoon, when Babe and Bill ring Minnie's bell at her East 64th Street apartment. They're hardly on speaking terms themselves at this moment, the Paleys—Babe having managed to give Bill an earful in the taxi about some transgression or another. As they wait, he attempts to take her arm, to make peace post taxi-rift.

'Darling, I was only saying that I don't understand why you can't just consider *talking* to Dr. Berman about—'

'Oh fuck off, Paley.' Babe shrugs his hand away. She rings the bell again, growing concerned at the lack of answer—then knocks. 'Minnie?' she calls through the door. She's relieved when she hears from within a surprisingly cheery '*Coming!*'

A moment later, the door opens to reveal Minnie, a dowdier version of Babe, wearing a far less effective wig—closer to Kate Paley's childhood Buster Brown. Smiling like Babe hasn't seen her smile in ages. Holding an innocuous-looking highball of orange juice.

'Babe! Billy! *What* a *surprise* . . . !' she giggles, embracing them. 'Come *in* . . . We're just having the most *marvelous* chat.'

'"We" . . . ?' Babe looks wary.

Minnie opens the door, leading them inside, wobbly. The Paleys follow her down an entry hall lined with Jimmy's paintings, opening into the living space.

And there, perched in a wing chair in a striped sweater and cap, is Truman.

Babe freezes in her tracks; Bill places a protective hand on the small of her back.

'Hello, Bill,' says Tru, as if nothing is wrong.

'Truman.' Bill. Clipped.

Tru turns to Babe. Softer—'Hi, Babyling.' He manages a weak smile, daring for a moment to hope. Eyes locking as they always did, communicating without speech.

Please. Please forgive me.

Babe says nothing. Just stares.

Minnie beams, clearly several Orange Drinks in. Delighted by what seems, from her perspective, a long-overdue reunion. 'Well. Here we all are! Come sit, Babe.'

She pats a place on the sofa beside her, opposite Truman— kicked back like a pasha in Jim's old wing chair.

It occurs to Babe that she hasn't seen Minnie this happy since Jimmy's death. Her sweet face—poodled though she may be, thanks to *him*—moves Babe in a way she hadn't expected. As much as she would have insisted she would rather be burned at the stake than sit in the same room with Truman after what he did to her, now that it's upon her, she finds she cannot bear to deny her dying sister this one moment of happiness, simply for the sake of her *own* heartbreak. And so it is for Minnie that Babe perches stiffly on the sofa.

Truman looks to her, eager. 'Can I get you something, Babyling?'

'No, thank you,' she replies, civil.

'You sure . . . ? Coffee? Tea? *Orange* Drink?' He attempts to raise a playful eyebrow.

'No, thank you.'

'How about a Bloody-Blood? I know how much you love my Bloodys . . .'

Bill takes over. 'Actually, Truman, my *wife* . . .'

There it is again—'my wife.' As if Truman hadn't known her better than *Paley* ever could. Bill feigns clearing his throat, just to have the pleasure of repeating it—'My *wife* is on a number of medications for her illness, which is quite serious. She's been advised by her doctors not to mix medications with alcohol.'

Minnie, likely on the same medications, happily sips her Orange Drink.

Truman looks to Babe. Eyes wide. Concerned.

'How *are* you, Babyling?'

'Fine, thank you.' Like ice. She can't help it. She's never loved and loathed anyone so much in her life. It kills her to be distant, but she can't bear to trust him in the way she once did. She doesn't have the strength to scrape herself off the floor again, in case of another — —

Out of nowhere, Babe feels short of breath. Her heart—it feels like someone is taking a cudgel to the center of her chest. *Can't . . . breathe . . . .*

Oh God . . . is this it? Is this what it will be like, after all she's . . . . . .

'Babe?' says Bill, concerned. He goes to her—*'Babe?!'*

Her face red. Tears stream down her cheeks as she coughs. And *coughs . . . . . .* God, the fucking *pain . . . Truman . . . . !* she cries out, in silence. She looks to him—their eyes lock.

He hears her. It still works—the old telepathy.

Truman leaps up, but Bill is there, rubbing her back, shouting—'Barbara, what do you need?!'

He doesn't know how to help you, Truman says wordlessly.

'Babe?' Minnie too rises, frightened off her Orange Drink cloud.

Babe sees Minnie's oxygen tank across the room. Her eyes meet Truman's . . . then she flicks them toward the tank. In an instant, Truman has bounded the length of the room and back again, delivering the air to Babe in what seems an instant.

She chokes in the oxygen, panicked gasps, punctuated by coughs.

Throughout, Babe's eyes stay fixed on Truman, who silently reassures her.

Gradually shallow breaths come, then deeper ones.

In and out . . . in . . . sssssssssppppppp . . . and out . . . hhhhhhss-seew . . . sssssssssppppppp . . . hhhhhhhhhhhhhssseew . . . for several minutes, until her breathing returns to a regular pace.

He sees it happen: As her breath calms, her eyes begin to cool again.

He feels her receding.

Babyling . . . his eyes plead. *Can you still hear me?*

From her expression, he knows that she can.

Of course I can hear you, Truman . . . but I'm choosing not to listen.

She sits back against the sofa, as Bill fetches a glass of water.

Aloud Truman says, 'Are you all right . . . ?'

When Babe speaks, it's *over* her voice, rather than *in* it.

'I'm fine, now. Thank you for asking.'

You're safe with me—not him. I'll take care of you.

You, Truman . . . are the last person in the world that I'm safe with.

She stares not into his eyes, but through them, and he knows that he has lost her.

FOR THE REST OF THE HOUR-LONG VISIT they chat. The William S. Paleys, the eldest and youngest Cushing girls, and their twisted little cherub—he who fell from paradise.

When later pressed, none of the individuals in the room that day could say what it was they talked about. When the company rises to depart and Minnie walks them to the door, Bill, Babe, and Truman venture out into the vestibule. They're all smiles as they turn to wave at Minnie, who watches them make their way to the elevator bank. The triumvirate of old.

As they turn toward the closed doors and Bill punches the call button, the smiles disappear. All three stare straight ahead. Lost in their private thoughts. Dreading, with every fiber of their beings, the ride in that claustrophobic car down thirty-nine floors to the lobby.

What if I break down? What if I break down in front of you? the little shit says silently, willing Babe to hear him. He turns his gaze toward her . . . But her graceful profile doesn't move. Doesn't turn to catch his eye. Chooses not to. One of the last choices she'll ever have.

She continues staring straight on, waiting for the doors to open.

After what feels an interminable wait, Truman panics when the door *dings* open. The Paleys move forward, but he doesn't budge. Feet suctioned to the hall carpet. They step into the elevator and turn coolly to face him—they inside, he out.

'Oh, mercy me!' He feigns shock. 'Don't you know, it's only *just* come to me—I left my wallet behind at Min's. I'll just pop back and get it.'

Bill presses the 'hold' button, with a sigh of irritation.

'No, no, Bill. No need to wait—I wouldn't want to hold you up! You have to get our beautiful girl home to rest.' Again the old familiarity, the chumminess. He waves them on, flashing a mega-watt smile.

Babe stares at him, expressionless.

'Fine, Truman.' Bill releases the hold button. 'Take care.'

Truman shifts his eyes to Babe, anxious.

Please, Baby. Please—

You're the only one who could hurt me.

And in that lilt of a breath before the doors close, a muscle twitches in her bourbon-colored eye. He thinks he sees a tear gathering, spilling down an expressionless cheek, mask of neu-trality in place. This just as the doors close, and she disappears from him forever.

IT'S JUST AFTER EASTER, when she's moved into her dressing room, that the dreams of Kiluna begin. The more Babe retreats from the world outside, the more she fixates on her house and its grounds ... feeling, as she told us on our visits, that her gardens are calling her back to them.

Her life seems increasingly distilled to such absolutes, which no one who knows her dares challenge. She seems to relax into the knowledge that the end of her life is near, secure in the last things she wants from it.

As summer approaches, she begins to mention wanting to see Kiluna one last time. Of wanting a final pilgrimage.

We've dreaded this day, for we know that it heralds the finality we've each been avoiding. Bill refuses to consider any suggestion of a finite end, still making phone calls to specialists the world over, in search of experimental cures, the wildcards that still might save her.

But Babe has insisted, and Bill can't bear to refuse her.

SHE MAKES HER FAREWELL JOURNEY in June, when the blooms still retain the newness of spring, yet have had time to flower to full, glorious fruition.

Kiluna's sunken lawns prove as magical as remembered, their fresh-cut grass tickling her nose. She appreciates the hay fever, the sniffling and eye-watering, for they help conceal her tears. She enjoys the series of sneezes that before would have seemed an inconvenience, but now serve to remind her that she's still alive.

A golf cart is procured to drive her on one last survey of her sloping, verdant space. When they reach the pond, eldest son Tony lifts her from the cart and carries her down to the bank, where she sits for a very long time.

After several hours absorbing every detail, sounds and fragrances heightened, colors taking on a saturation even more pronounced than usual—a brightness almost blinding in its intensity—Babe turns to her children and nods. She even manages to give Bastard Paley's arm a squeeze of thanks—a shard of residual affection.

They drive the golf cart back to the house and after a simple dinner of sandwiches which Babe declines to eat, they make the long drive back to the city.

When she returns to the St. Regis, Babe moves out of her special closet lair. Back into her bedroom, with its tangle of Moroccan vines and pillows of jade-plumed lovebirds.

And in the weeks she spends awaiting the inevitable, she remembers that in her gardens the heliotrope remains as fragrant as ever, its lilac inflorescences turning their rows of delicate flowers toward the sun.

CODA

SITTING DOWN TO BABE'S FINAL LUNCHEON, served on the portico at Kiluna, we reach for napkins folded into the shape of calla lilies, cross-pollinating sculptural floral centerpieces on the linen-draped picnic tables (her one nod to tradition), and we think of the streamlined bouquet she'd clutched as she married Bill Paley in a modest ceremony, careful not to call attention to her Waspishness or his Jewishness, or to their dual divorces.

We're transported through her Poulet à l'Estragon to Paris in the Fifties, when we were thirty years younger, at the height of our beauty and vigor.

We agree with Babe, the varietal of wine in the sauce is as vital as the tarragon. We think we detect the citrus and vanilla notes of a Rhône Viognier.

Babe had chosen a soufflé for the last dessert she'll ever serve, a rich, bitter cocoa, spiked with Grand Marnier. Beautifully presented, piping hot, in individual ramekins, a jigger of cream on the side.

'Not everyone cares for cream, you know,' she would have informed us with authority. 'Best to serve it on the side, so that everyone has options.'

And when we lift our spoons from the bubbling pots of soufflé chocolat, we can almost taste her loneliness in its lightness, her disappointment lingering on our tongues, as we savor its perfection.

SIXTEEN

1978

VARIATION NO. 8

H E LIES ON HIS CHESTERFIELD, flipping through the Sunday *Times*, enjoying himself, perspiring in the summer heat. Truman's always been a bit of a newspaper hound.

He's expanded his range to include all the New York dailies, plus darling Kay-Kay's *Washington Post*, for while he doesn't give a hoot about politics, he likes to support his friends. He takes the *Garden City Telegram* to keep up with the Midwest doings of his Kansas bunch and, to his own chagrin, the *LA Times*—written by 'Moron Zombies with the purpose of sucking the last braincells of other Moron Zombies,' according to Tru. Best to prepare for the apocalypse.

When he's spent long stretches of time in Europe, the papers have proven a lifeline to the world he left behind. When he and Jack were in Taormina for nearly a year, Truman would make the journey each afternoon down to the tiny newsagents in town, to whom he had arranged to have a *New York Times* sent each day.

He has the papers delivered to Sagaponack and Verbier when he's in residence, and puts them on hold when he leaves. At the U.N. Plaza, Sidney the doorman brings his subscriptions up and leaves them on his doormat each morning, in a neat, pleasing stack.

He can yak your ear off about which journalist worked for which editor, for which publication and when. He is a student of fonts and typesets. He's picky about his layouts—and don't get him started on headlines! He can sniff a gimmick caption a mile away, and holds a particular disdain for 'punny' ones. For while

Truman is the first to lean toward flights of fancy in his speech—or fable in his fiction—he's a bit of a purist when it comes to his journalism.

He feels a special kinship with the world of newsprint, we believe, because he is, in a strange way, indebted to it. It was, after all, the *New York Times* that gave him the subject for his masterpiece. He'd been horizontally reading his paper in bed, per routine, when he saw it:

> HOLCOMB, KANSAS, NOV. 15 [1959] A wealthy wheat farmer, his wife and their two young children were found shot to death today in their home. They had been killed by shotgun blasts at close range after being bound and gagged ... There were no signs of a struggle, and nothing had been stolen. The telephone lines had been cut.

He had paused. And for a fraction of a second, he found that he could hardly breathe. Just from that tiny piece, he *sensed* something ... The germ of a story.

There was more in the blurb, but not much. Three hundred words in all. But that was enough. Truman had instincts for such things. He had been searching for the ideal subject to apply the techniques he had been turning over in his mind—journalism as art; fact as fiction.

But this is beside the point—the *point* is that without that newspaper clipping there would be no *In Cold Blood*, and without *In Cold Blood* there would in essence be no Truman.

As he lies reading his *Times*, he reaches to switch on a standing floor fan, which rustles the papers as it oscillates, blowing cool air toward his damp skin.

Truman knows it's July because it's just been the Fourth. And no one living by the sea could avoid it, with the constant reminders of fireworks being shot off from boats at every turn. He smiles a pained smile each time he hears one, thinking of how Maggie would howl, circling the dunes, convinced that something was wrong. Poor Mags was not here for the *pop! pop!* explosions three days earlier—this being his first Independence Day without her.

Too upset to stay at home alone, in a house with no Jack and no Mags, he had called a Hope's End Cab and taken it to Azurest. He dined at Ouisie's, one of his regulars, ordering fried shrimp and okra, and a side of crisp hushpuppies. All drenched in cornmeal and dropped in hot oil. Truman knows that it's bad for him—but Truman does a lot of things that are bad for him these days. Jack *hates* him eating all that fried shit—'It'll clog your arteries, Truman. That's a heart attack on a plate!'—but he reasons it's a holiday, and Jack, increasingly in Verbier, isn't here to see what Truman consumes.

He sits alone on the shore, pondering the nature of pyrotechnics, listening to a jazz band further down the beach play mid-tempo swing versions of patriotic tunes, lending them an injection of much-needed soul. The smoky voices make him wistful for Lady Day—gardenia in her hair, covering the bald spot where she singed her scalp with a curling wand. The term 'curling wand' he associates exclusively with Southern gals (they calling it a 'wand' as if endowed with wizardly magic; Yankee girls reduce it to an 'iron,' as if grooming was a chore). The thought of Southern gals makes him homesick. He remembers reading his stories out to Nelle and Sook in the old farmhouse kitchen, sometimes making them up as he went, having Nelle take dictation. He thinks of how Sook loved his high melodic voice so much, she was happy to hear him read *anything* aloud. He has a vision, as the fan blows cool air onto his face, of Sook, sweet, gentle Sook, settling into her rocking chair with her sewing, waiting for him to read her the Obits. He can almost hear her down-tilts in the old rocker as she smiles and nods and mends a pair of long johns. He finds himself flipping back to the Obituary page, pondering if he should read one aloud for old times' sake . . .

It's then that he sees it.

First, her face. Her unspeakably beautiful face.

For a moment he thinks he's made a mistake, that he's flipped to the society section by accident. He thought she grew lovelier with time, for while any pretty young thing can turn heads just by flaunting their youth, Babe ripened and blossomed—or blossomed and ripened—with age. As ever, he's mesmerized by her image, to the exclusion of all else.

It's then that he bothers to process the headline:

BARBARA CUSHING PALEY DIES AT 63; STYLE PACE-SETTER IN THREE DECADES GONE.

PHASEN DE TRAUER.

They say that the first stage of grief is denial.

The 'they' we refer to is technically Kübler-Ross—Dr. Elisabeth—whose five-step field guide for battling the Grim Reaper's harvest was all the buzz at our dinners and luncheons ten years back. Most of us at least had a quick skim—enough to feign authority. From this we know her famed five stages—denial, anger, bargaining, depression, acceptance.

PHASE EINS: VERWEIGERUNG (DENIAL)

TRUMAN STARES AT THE WORDS, which simply can't be real.

He knows that typesetters *do* get things wrong and are forced to print corrections on a special page in the next day's issue. If not a prank, surely a mistake . . . ?

He frantically unwraps the other dailies, hoping to find no trace of Barbara Cushing Mortimer Paley, smiling serenely from their pages.

It will take rifling through the *Post*, the *Journal*, and the zombified *LA Times*, flipping frantically back to the Obits, meeting her photographic gaze three more times, the fan ruffling their pages, before he realizes that it *might* be true.

Phase Zwei: Zorn (Anger)

'HELLO, SUGAR . . . I'D LIKE TO SPEAK with Mr. William S. Paley, *s'il vous plaît.*'

This we can hardly believe. He's had the audacity—the bald-faced *audacity!*—to ring up Bill's office at CBS?! On today of all days?

'May I ask who's calling?' A receptionist, voice thrumming with cordial indifference.

He hesitates before he commits, wondering were it not better to use a clever pseudonym, in the hopes that his call be connected. (Not that he could begin to disguise that pipsqueak voice of his—so it's not *really* a feasible plan.)

'This is Truman Capote,' he states with a note of defiance.

'I'm sorry, Mr. Capote. Mr. Paley is out of the office.' Does he imagine it, or does her voice chill ever so slightly?

'Well, when do you expect him back in?'

'I couldn't say, Mr. Capote. Mr. Paley has taken a personal leave of absence . . . To deal with a family matter.' Miss Fort Knox.

'Well, honey, I *know* that. That's the very *reason* I'm calling.'

Silence.

'I'm calling *about* the family matter.'

Silence still.

'I'm a friend of the family. A very *close* friend . . .'

Even the secretary must read the papers, Truman. Even the secretary would know that's no longer true . . .

'I am *calling* about the memorial for Mrs. Barbara Paley. Could you tell me when and where it's to be held?'

'I'm sorry, Mr. Capote. I can't disclose that information.'

'What do you mean, "can't disclose"?'

'That information is of a private nature. It's for the family to convey those details.'

286

'Well, can I have an *address* where this top-secret event happens to be taking place, so that I might, at the very least, know where to tell my florist to send an arrangement . . . ?'

He hears her hesitate.

Then—'Look, sweetheart, I was Mrs. Barbara Paley's very best friend in the world.' (*'WAS' being the operative word* . . .) 'I just need you to tell me if they're going to be at the St. Regis or Kiluna.'

'I'm terribly sorry, Mr. Capote. But I just can't disclose—'

'Can't—? Or *won't?*'

'Sir—'

'*Siirrrrrr,*' aping the drawl in her accent. '*Siirrrrr?* I'm not your Daddy, for Chrissakes!'

'Sir, I'm afraid that your *tone* is not—'

'Tone?! My *tone*? Look, you smug little bitch. I just need to know when and where the memorial for Mrs. Paley is gonna be held. Now, are you gonna *tell* me what I need to know, *provide* me with the information that I seek, or am I gonna have to ask to speak to your superior?'

'I'm sorry, Mr. Capote, but there's no one else to speak with.'

'Oh *reeaallly*? I find that hard to believe. You're actually telling me that there's *no one* above you? No manager? No boss? No superior to report to?'

'I'm afraid not.'

'*I'm aff-fraid not,*' repeating her cadence exactly. 'So you're telling me that you personally—you, *Mademoiselle Secrétaire*—are the sole person in charge of the Columbia Broadcasting System on this sweltering midsummer day . . . ?'

'That's correct, Mr. Capote.' Oooh. Defiance, no less. *Good for you, Miss Vassar.*

'*That's correct* . . . Listen, pussycat. I find that *very* hard to believe. I think you're an absolute cunt. So *fuck* you and the horse you rode in on—which knowing him as I do, is probably named Mister *Bill Paley* . . . !'

He slams the phone down in a rage.

C.Z. HAS TRIED. LORD KNOWS SHE'S TRIED.

She had spoken to Babe directly, over tea at Babe's bedside, then to Slim over lunch at Vadis. Of course it hadn't worked. Babe had anticipated this move. She knew him too well.

And when Truman phones C.Z. after hanging up on Bill's secretary and begs her to intercede on his behalf—moaning to her he didn't get to mend things when Babe was living; the least that they can do is let him say *goodbye*—she listens in silence to his diatribe.

How it was *Bill* keeping him from Babe. Bill who resented him still for The Sheets. How he had only written the goddamn thing to stand up for Babe, to defend her honor, shaming the husband who failed to see her worth.

Tru tells C.Z. it's likely *Slim*, too. Who he misses and adores, but who we all *know* can hold a grudge—Lord *knows* we know *that*. How she'd rejected his attempts to make amends and was keeping him away from Babe as a sort of vindictive gesture . . .

Babe would have wanted him there, he feels certain. She told him so with her eyes the other day. They of course couldn't speak, because the *others* were there, but he heard her loud and clear. Babe would have wanted him to help her plan her send-off—

Does C.Z. know where it will be, by the way? And when?

He could write a eulogy—or a poem perhaps—? A poem called 'Heliotrope,' after Babe's favorite flower . . . Could C.Z. just *talk* to Bill and Slim? He'd be so good—he'd do whatever they asked. He'd be a fly on the wall, if only they'd just let him be there . . .

C.Z. can't bear to hear the desperation in his voice. She knew what he'd done in *Esquire* was wrong, but frankly, she blamed us for being equally culpable.

'How can you think such a thing? We're the *victims*!'

'We knew he was a writer,' she reminds us, never wavering from this view. 'You shouldn't have told him those things. What did you *think* he would do with all those tales?' Hearing him now, so desperate just to see his Babe one last time, even after she's gone, C.Z. can't help but see Truman as another casualty.

The bargaining is starting in earnest now. No more conspiracies. No recriminations. Just plain, desperate begging.

'Please, darling, may I come to her funeral? Won't you *please* ask Bill? I promise, I won't cause trouble. I swear I won't drink. I swear I won't take anything. No booze. No pills. I just want to *be* there. I think *Babyling* would have wanted— —'

And finally C.Z., unable to bear it, unable to protect him any longer, shouts: '*TRUMAN*—' a harsh edict, for his own sorry good '—*STOP!*'

Cutting into his diatribe, frightening him into silence.

A long pause from her end, he trembling in wait.

'It wasn't Bill. It wasn't Slim.' Deep breath. 'It was *Babe* who didn't want you there.'

And with those words, he feels the earth ripped out from under him, severing his last tethers of hope.

PHASE VIER: GEDRÜCKT (DEPRESSION)

IT'S THE ART EXPERT JOHN RICHARDSON who provides our next curiosity.

A few weeks ago, Richardson tells us that he'd wandered into the Westbury, late one afternoon, having all but missed lunch.

He had just come from assessing pieces in Mrs. X's collection, which took an hour longer than anticipated. Not that Mrs. X had any intention of *selling*, but art experts *do* take a professional interest in knowing who has what pieces and what they're worth, if only for future reference. Of course he was clever enough to call his collectors Mrs. X or Mr. Y when telling tales, something Truman never would have considered. English, debonair, former head of Christie's, Picasso biographer in four planned volumes—what's not to like about Richardson?

The restaurant was eerily calm, in that post-lunch hush that falls between meals, before preparations for dinner. Its dark wood and gents'-club leather booths abandoned. The dining room empty, but for one table, where a lone figure sat, hunched over a glass. Frail, open-mouthed, like a parched bird in need of a drink. Richardson tells us from the posture and the thinning hair, at first glance he assumed it was a very old person. A little old man—or woman? Occupying a dark booth, tucked in the corner. He wondered from the bobbing head if the figure had fallen asleep.

Approaching an adjacent table, Richardson looked closer, recognizing something in the profile, when suddenly the apparition raised its eyes, meeting his gaze dead on. He said he was somewhat stunned to recognize the specter . . .

'Well hello, Truman! Fancy seeing you here.'

He tried to conceal his shock that the figure looked no younger when seen straight-on.

'It hadn't been *that* long since I'd seen him . . .' Richardson tells us in the weeks following, at our own impressive homes, flattering our own paintings. 'A few months at the most? It was at the Fabergé auction in early May. This was July, and he looked ten years older, without question.'

Mouth slightly sloping down on one side. Eyes rolling back in his head. For a moment Richardson wondered if he'd had or was having a stroke. But then the pupils focused from a squint. He picked up the glass containing the remains of what looked once to have been a Scotch on the rocks. Holding his glass at a sloppy angle, he sucked the last drops left.

'Hallllooooo . . .' (searching his brain for the name) '. . . John.' Managing a muddled smile. He waved a hand to a waitress, who from across the room looked frightened. This was not Charming Truman—not even Charming Rat-Assed Truman, paying Gladys, Madge and Ruthie sweet (if slurred) compliments at Bobby Van's in Bridgehampton. This was something with a darker edge, Richardson will later clarify.

It wasn't that the waitstaff was frightened of anything he might do to *them*—to them he was perfectly civil, perfectly polite. It was what he seemed to have in mind for *himself* that scared the living hell out of them. Still, the waitress timorously brought Truman another double-double, handing Richardson a menu.

'Goodness, but I'm peckish! Haven't had a bite all day. I got stuck into a rather extensive collection . . .' He smiled. The specter merely stared. 'So sorry—didn't mean to disturb. Lovely to see you, Truman. Let's lunch soon, shall we?'

This last bit was disingenuous, but really, what else could one say . . . ?

Richardson settled into his own booth, quickly deciding on an omelet and salad, if only to order, dine, and get the hell out.

Then—

'John . . . ? *Whyyyyy* not *now* . . . ?'

Richardson, with a forced smile, 'Sorry?'

'Why don't you come sitttt heeere? Doooo lunch *now* . . . ?'

Christ. The very thing one could not decline—a direct invitation, from a genius no less. A genius teetering on the brink of god knows what.

Concealing his discomfort, Richardson rose and joined him in the corner booth, sitting opposite, Tru tackling the new Scotch at a rather alarming pace.

'So, Truman. Tell me—what are you working on these days?' An attempt at small talk. Best, under the circumstances, to steer clear of the personal.

'Heeeeeee . . .' Truman slurred, 'leeeeeeeeeooo . . .' spitting it out, '*TROPE.*'

'You're working with tropes?' Richardson frowned, attempting in vain to follow.

'NO.' He tried again—lord only *knows* how many whiskies he'd been through.

'*Heeeeeee-leo-trope.*'

'Heliotrope? As in . . . the flower?'

The specter seemed to nod, satisfied with having broken through, adding—his features softening—a single word. 'Babe.'

'Babe . . . Babe Paley?' This like some sort of deranged game of *Password.*

Truman nodded, vigorously. 'Beeeeeautiful Babe . . . Writing 'bout . . . *Babe—Heeeliooootrope.* It'll be a—?' He failed to remember the word he was searching for.

'A novel?'

'No—Short——'

'. . . Story?'

'*Longer . . .*'

'A novella . . . ?'

'YEEESSSSSSSS.'

'A novella about Babe Paley,' Richardson clarified.

The specter nodded—'*Heliotrope.*'

'Interesting.'

'I *looooved* her, you know. I was *in* love with her—*still* in love with Babe.'

'I see.'

'She'zzz having lunch today.'

Richardson frowned, knowing that Babe had passed away the previous week. Naturally he assumed that Truman had his facts wrong. But as we've always said, there's generally a sliver of truth in what Tru says.

'Not Bill . . . Not Slimmmm . . . *Babe* doesn't want me. She'zz the only person who could ever reeeallly hurt me. And sheeeee did.'

'Didn't *you* hurt *her*, Truman? By writing what you did?' Tru's reluctant lunch date allowed himself.

'I did hurt . . . but I didn't *meeeean* to. Meant to hurt *him* . . . One who betrayed . . . Bazzzzztard. Couldn't see her . . . Otherrrnesssss . . .' He trailed off, as if lost in thought.

'Ah.'

Then—

'John . . . you know about *infllooor-essences*? An *inflooor-essence* is clussster of flowers, one stem—branch. Individual flowerzz—each unique . . . But they're ssssstuck together, to the same vine . . . stem. Allllwayzz in a group. Can't ezzcape each other. You see?' He leaned across the table, anxious that Richardson understand. 'Heliotropezz separate, yet ssstuck. Like Siamese . . . or a two-headed . . .'

For a moment (Richardson says) Truman seemed to lose the plot.

Then, as if beginning afresh—'John, you know the name "heeeliotrope" comes from a *veeeeerrrrry* old idea that *inflooor-essence* turn their rowzzzz of flowers to the sun?'

'No, Truman. I didn't know that.'

And as if to demonstrate, Truman turned his own face skyward, angling it to the imaginary rays inside the darkened restaurant, as if feeling the warmth on his toad-like cheek.

Eyes closed. His expression rapturous.

Richardson says he paid his portion of the table's ongoing tab, and excused himself to pop to the gents.

When he returned, Truman was sitting, hunched as he'd first found him, mumbling into his drink, over and over again—*Heliotrope . . . Heliotrope*.

Barely audible.

Heliotrope . . .

Phase Fünf: Annahme (Acceptance)

Ten days after Babe dies, Truman goes on television.

Funnily enough, 'unleashing one's demons in a national forum' isn't mentioned, from what we can recall, in the Kübler-Ross scheme.

His appearance on *The Stanley Siegel Show* has been, oddly enough, planned for months. More airtime booked to promote the as-yet-unfinished *Answered Prayers* to the masses, fanning their fervor, and strange as it sounds, there's indeed been fervor. While we don't live in a particularly literary age, we do live in a salacious one, and people really did *talk* about the goddamn thing.

Someone should have stopped him. But let's be honest: there was really no one left to.

He arrives at the studios, or so our sources say, managing to pop a handful of Tuinal (though some claim it was Thorazine) before cameras roll.

They've propped him in Siegel's swivel chair, neutral beige like all such sets, eyes rolling, tongue lolling. A sick grotesque in a turquoise knit, brown felt fedora askew, waiting for the cameras to roll. Eyes bulging, tongue protruding, he looks like one of Babe's Sacré-Coeur gargoyles—or half of a two-headed snake.

Slimy Siegel *must* have foreseen the shame it would cause—the sheer humiliation. Any host with a conscience would have pulled the plug.

The segment opens on a joke, to which Truman's forgotten both setup and punchline. He then babbles on about *Answered Prayers*, with a bit of Babe—confusing the two—

'And McCloud, Kate, izzzz not who you . . . I never even went to her *funeral* . . . Not McCloud, not real, you seeee . . . The other . . . Wazzn't allowed at *lunch* . . . But I'm writing . . . ummmmmm . . . about *Heliotrope*, you see.'

'Yes, I can see that.'

Sensing his moment, like any bloodthirsty shark, Siegel circles the water, preparing to go for the kill.

'Truman, you told me backstage that you haven't been to bed in forty-eight hours. Is that true?'

'*We-ull*, I've been to *bed*, but not to *sleep* . . .' He laughs salaciously, enjoying his own private thoughts. 'I mean a number of people . . .' He trails off, the thought scampering elsewhere. 'I mean my life is so *sssssstrange*. I'm not *like* other people.'

'Yes, I'm sure of that . . . Can I ask you some serious questions?'

'*Sssss-sure*,' Truman slurs. 'Go right ahead. I feel perfectly—'

'Truman, I need to ask you—are you an alcoholic?'

Truman pauses, processing. 'Ohhhh, my *gawd*,' he says with an air of disdain, as if dismissing the point as trivial. 'I mean *allllcohol* is the *least* of it.' He rolls his eyes to the whites, like a demon-possessed soul. 'I mean, that's just the joker in the cardzzzz . . .'

He keeps touching his eyes, his fingers forming a hook. Scratching an itch that he cannot relieve. He laughs again, and the live audience laughs with him. A Pavlovian response, a symptom of discomfort. But a collective one, allowing Truman to think he's among friends.

'Have you taken anything, Truman? Marijuana? Cocaine? Pills?'

'To-daaaaaay?'

'Yes, Truman—this morning.' Siegel feigns concern.

The cunt, we think, our buried loyalties flaring. Much as we loathe Truman for what he has done, we still can be protective, when someone is taking advantage. The poor little shit is so pathetically trusting, so sweetly clueless when it comes to such moments. Presuming all would want to know what the boy genius has to say.

Frankly, we can spot an opportunist when we see one.

Siegel goes on, playing concerned clinician. Handing him the rope with which to hang himself. 'What's going to happen, Truman, if you don't lick this problem with drugs and alcohol? What. Is. Going. To. Happen. To. *Truman*?' Siegel ends each word with a full stop for emphasis.

Truman stops and thinks for a moment, as if pondering a particularly interesting riddle.

'Weeeeeeeulllllll . . . I supppppose that *eventually* . . . I'll kill myself.'

'Yeeeessssss,' Siegel urges, excited, just feeling his ratings surge.

Tru adds as a hazy afterthought, 'I'll kill myself—without *meeeean-ing* to.'

That's the first piece of non-bullshit Truman has spoken in some time.

And as much as we can't stand who he has become, seeing him crumble on a third-rate morning talk show, it rips our hearts in two.

AFTERWARDS, HE REMEMBERS NOTHING.

He's shown a tape of his appearance, and he's bewildered by his behavior. It's like watching someone else—a person he doesn't quite recognize.

He's *so* distraught, *so* mortified, we're concerned from afar for his safety.

We all remember that Truman has a loaded gun in the drawer of his dresser in the United Nations Plaza. He's always liked to brag about this; he thought it sounded macho.

Several concerned parties (C.Z. chief among them) have contacted Sidney-the-doorman, charging him with the mission of quietly confiscating the revolver Detective Dewey had given Truman as a souvenir after *In Cold Blood* was published, 'with regards from his friends at the Kansas Bureau of Investigation'—afraid he'll now find use for it.

TRUMAN FLEES TO THE WEATHERED HOUSE in Sagaponack, with the excuse of needing to write.

It's all he has left, after all. It's his single, fraying lifeline.

If he can only manage this chapter, this one *last* chapter—he'll turn out seven volumes, surpassing even Marcel.

If only . . . If only . . .

Jack follows, reluctantly, summoned from his secluded haven in Verbier. He returns to their once beloved compound, the deeds for which he still keeps inside Truman's butterfly-box. Returns to the wind whistling in the dunes. He arrives to find newspapers piled up on the lawn. Jack brings them inside when he arrives at the house with his single, well-worn suitcase.

'Truman?' he calls, opening the kitchen door.

Covering the countertops are the remains of the boy's last efforts—caviar jars left open. Ditto horseradish and olives.

Eggs half scrambled and abandoned; a congealed effort at a hollandaise, sickly yellow, the color he'd send back in restaurants. A soup pan of Campbell's tomato—'just like Andy used to paint,' we knew he'd tell Jack—another of clam chowder, both with a film-hardened top. And bottle upon bottle, carefully lining the counter—pills, alternating with vodka, alternating with Orange Drink.

Jack finds him in the loft upstairs, in bed, which he hasn't left in days.

'Truman . . .'

The boy opens his eyes, staring at the tall, freckled man, who to him, in this moment, seems the handsomest of strangers. He knows in an instant to be on best behavior, in order to win his affection.

'Hi,' he says.

'Hi,' says Jack, kneeling at his bedside.

The boy stares at him with rheumy eyes and a dopey smile, shy at this stage of their courtship. Truly out of character, he thinks he'll let this stranger make the first move.

'How are you, Truman?'

'I'm peachy, handsome. How're *yoooouuuuuuu*?'

'I'm okay.'

'Just okay?' The boy can't resist—he reaches out and touches the man's freckled cheek. My God, but he finds him attractive.

'That's about the measure of it.'

The boy's bony fingers stroke the stranger's skin, tracing his jawline, as a pair of almond nails had done to his own jaw in a hammock, he thinks he remembers vaguely . . . Or were they red nails, the color of fire engines, cradling him in a Big-Bed?

'Truman . . . I don't think you're okay.'

'No?'

'No. And I'm terrified that you're not.'

'Thank *gawd*—me too!' Relieved that someone finally noticed.

He leans in close to the masculine face, whispering his inner-most fear—the thing he hasn't told anyone. 'You know, the terror starts in my chest, and then makes its way to my throat ... Some-times I can barely breathe. I think a lot about ending the pain. You know what I mean ... ?' He smiles at the stranger, pleased and relieved to be honest.

What a lovely man this is—how concerned. How very gentle.

And yet ... he's crying. Silent tears, rolling down his freckled cheeks, as if he'd gotten caught in the rain.

'What's wrong? What's wrong, my handsome man?'

'Truman, you don't know who I am, do you?'

The boy focuses all his energy on the beautiful stranger's face. Where has he seen it before? ... He knows that it's familiar. He fixes his gaze at the terrain of the freckles and focuses with all his might—a Herculean effort, if there ever was one.

Suddenly, it comes to him. Pleased with himself for knowing the answer, he takes the face in his hands and stares into a pair of greenest eyes ...

'Of course I know who you are. You're *Jack*.'

Perfectly simple. As if it were the clearest fact in the world.

Handsome Jack weeps in silence. The boy takes his hand and, looking down, realizes that he's soiled his bed, and suddenly feels embarrassed.

'Jack ... I'm so sorry, Jack.' But for what, specifically, he doesn't know.

'*Why*, Truman? Why are you doing this? With all your god-damn *talent* ... Why waste it? Why waste *us*?'

'I do this,' the boy says, in a rare moment of clarity, 'because I can't stand the pain without it.' The man holds him in his strong, freckled arms. They cling to each other in silence, for frankly there's nothing left to say.

LATER JACK WILL GO DOWNSTAIRS and clean the mess in the kitchen after changing the sheets and removing the boy's soiled clothes. He'll bathe him and scrub his scalp and dress him in fresh pajamas. He'll make the boy hot tea and broth and feed him with a silver spoon. He'll sit in a rocking chair by the boy's bed and wait for him to fall asleep, comforting him with his down-tilts.

Truman will look at him and smile, and just as he closes his eyes, he'll see *them* sitting across the room as well, watching him.

One with honeyed pin-curls, lips painted the reddest of reds; the other chestnut-streaked-with-silver and her bourbon-colored eyes, watching as his lids flutter shut.

When he thinks that he's asleep, Jack will approach, squeezing into the single bed, curling his body around the wasted form, careful not to wake him.

'He was tired,' Jack will later say, to those who care to ask. 'So tired. Like he'd stayed too long at the party and now simply wanted to sleep.'

SEVENTEEN

1978

C.Z.

The Rehab Follies

W E ALL KNOW THAT C.Z. (God love her) irrationally loves a winner.

This need to succeed, to help those around her triumph, pervades every area of her life. Whether a sluggish filly in whom she senses a champion racer, or a three-legged mutt that she's rescued from the pound, that stalwart spirit of hers is unlikely to give up on even the most pitiful of cases—which without question explains her attitude toward Truman. Her refusal to drop the little shit is in perfect keeping with what we've always known to be the bedrock of her character. A reluctance to throw in the towel. A resilience that exceeds our own.

Perhaps it's the competitive zeal of the sportswoman within her. Her standing Saturday-morning tennis match is played for points, where the rest of us relish a giggle at the net, whispering about who's standing a bit *too* close to their doubles partner three courts down, pondering if eleven forty-five is a tad too early to get away with a Tom Collins.

She's as fierce a competitor whether bidding at Christie's for an antique writing desk or for yet another stallion to add to the Templeton livery. No mere hobby, the stables boast seventeen stalls, and breeding and training champions is something the Guests take seriously.

'I've always wanted to win,' she laughs briskly when we tease her. Or rather, drawing out her vowels in that flat patrician lockjaw, like an elegant bird with her faintly melodic caw—'Ahhh've aahhl-ways wanted to be a win-*aaah*,' an elongation that might be mistaken by the untrained ear for a Southern drawl, but to those familiar with it undoubtedly heralds the bright, cracked vowels so particular to the Brahmins of Boston.

She's up and in full riding kit before breakfast each morning, exercising her horses. She's likely completed a full day's regimen before the rest of us have made it out the door for lunch. That's another thing we find curious—when she's in New York, in residence at Sutton Place, she's very particular about luncheon. She eschews spots *du jour* and classics alike, having her own list of preferences. There are some overlaps in taste. She adores 21 of course, but we think anywhere with a jockey theme out front might hold a special place in C.Z.'s heart.

Oddly, she prefers the Four Seasons to the usual suspects. Built around a stark geometric pool, in a structure made of glass, it surprises us that C.Z. responds to it so favorably, her own environment dominated by an English manor house aesthetic. Patterned rugs that mask the tread of packs of dogs. Decanters on silver trays, displayed in book-laden libraries. Polo mallets and garden shears and wellingtons caked in mud.

When we ask her the appeal of the harsh glass lines of the Four Seasons' dining room, her eyes look as clear and bright as the materials that compose the space in question.

'Why, *daaaah*-ling, it's so *mah*-dern!'

In fact, C.Z. had managed to spot straight away what the proprietors were aiming for . . . progressiveness. Courting the movers and shakers. Bucking the Gallic trend in Manhattan eateries with a decided shift to *new American* cuisine. But frankly the food was the least of it. It was industry that mattered. The Four Seasons was a place to be seen doing business.

While we were perfectly content being the center of our own *petits univers* at Vadis or Basque or Cirque, C.Z. loathed the stuffiness of the routine.

'Nobody's *doing* anything here,' she'd bemoan on the occasions when she joined us. 'No one's getting on with *life*!'

Really, we'd later confer—*how much life does one need to get on with over lunch?* We've gradually discovered from such comments that C.Z. seems enthralled by the very thing that we detest about the Four Seasons. On our infrequent visits we'd swiftly realized that amidst all that moving and shaking, we were irrelevant there. No one knew that Babe was allergic to peanuts or that Slim loathed sour cream. Not a soul slowed their pace when walking past our table, hoping they might be so fortunate as to overhear a snatch of our conversation.

'My gaaahh-d,' C.Z. had enthused, feeling the energy crackling in the space, which *we* found rather unnerving. 'The things going *aaahnnnn* between these walls!'

'*What* walls?' we'd ask, glum. Just a big, transparent box that made us feel invisible.

For all her traditionalist manners, C.Z. is perhaps the most modern of us in thought. Whatever the shifts in taste and fashion, she embraces them fully, as if a traveler from another age, accustomed to change and accepting it. Lacking in nostalgia.

'The cool vanilla lady.' It's what Truman always called C.Z., and there is something of a regal iciness to her bearing. Yet beneath that very chill, a warmth percolates. For just as she lacks nostalgia, so too does she lack fickleness. Once a friend, always a friend—no matter how far one might have fallen. Once she has committed, C.Z. is invested in you, like one of her champion thoroughbreds. She *waaahnts* you to win.

We knew that she'd stand by him. It didn't surprise us a jot. And we don't blame her for it. Even in his blackest moment, in C.Z.'s eyes Truman has every chance to turn his wreck of a life around—to overtake the pack and reemerge triumphant. And so we knew when we amputated Truman from our lives that she'd stick with him. That she would bandage his stub paws and bolster his wounded pride. She sits at his luncheon tables when no one else will. She invites him to her dinners. She accompanies him to the theater as she's always done, since the first night they met in one decades ago. Maybe, we've thought, it's that plucky, board-treading ethos that's behind C.Z.'s resilience. That as much as sportsmanship has molded her approach, so too has her *brief* time on the stage. (Something we still find hard to believe, knowing her, as we do, in her current incarnation.) A show-must-go-on attitude that Truman of all people understands. He's got the showman in his bones. The razzmatazz of an old vaudevillian.

'I really *did* earn my keep as a boy for a time tap-dancing on showboats with my Daddy. While he was at the card table, I was givin' 'em everything I had! I had a tiny formal suit that my Mama gave me . . . They used to call me Taps-and-Tails.'

We don't judge C.Z. for trying to save Truman after the *Siegel Show* fiasco. But we *do* plan to observe from afar, poised critics— as the one-time showgirl attempts to coax Mr. Taps-and-Tails back onto the boards. To force him back onto the great stage of life.

IT HAD BEEN AN INTERVENTION.

After Babe had died the week before, after the funeral snub, the Guests watched the *Siegel* footage in horror. C.Z. had turned to Winston and said—'Enough's enough.'

Having fought his own battles (with the bottle, in his case), Winston agreed. 'He'll kill himself in a year, if he goes on like that.'

'Ahhlll that talent . . . We have to help him, dahling. Someone has to try.'

That was how Truman found himself snatched from the road outside the house in Sagaponack, stumbling home from Bobby Van's, and bundled into a car. A victim of abduction. How he found himself sitting in the garden at Templeton in Oyster Bay, being berated by a Hitchcock blonde with exquisite legs and a helluva mouth on her.

He'd been placed in the shade of the five yews in the garden at Templeton, in an Adirondack chair that had been moved there especially for him. He thought he remembered yews having special meaning in ancient culture, but narrowed it down to either a symbol of life or death, which seemed too fifty–fifty to risk the exploration. He'd rather admired their sculptural forms, first shaped by landscape architect Russell Page, whom C.Z. had shared with Babe, along with the Duke and Duchess of Windsor. While intended as variegated abstracts, Truman had long claimed to see shapes in their leafy forms, and over pitchers of C.Z.'s orange mint tea he'd spun yarns about the characters lurking within. The tales got even better over Bullshots—cocktails of vodka, lime juice, Tabasco, and beef bouillon, which C.Z. religiously served to Friday-night guests who'd crashed in the poolside cabana, the Guest children's former playhouse turned hedonists' hostel. Saturday mornings it was her habit to leave a pitcher of that unique concoction for her stragglers as she raced off to the Piping Rock Club for her tennis.

While Truman recalled such days with fond nostalgia, on the morning in question his hostess, in an uncharacteristic show of muscle, had refused him anything but tea.

'I must say, Sisssszzy,' Truman whined—though he enjoyed the play of returning her nickname to its origins, when her little brother had tried to say 'sister,' coming up with her now-famed initials instead—'methinks the lady is proving a *rawther* stingy hostess to her guest.'

C.Z., on hands and knees in a nearby flower bed, dug her fingers deeper into the earth. She felt the cool dampness of the soil, the slime of life writhing within. It was here—with the mulch and the earthworms and seedlings and plants—that she was happiest. The simplicity of the task of getting one's hands dirty in order to see results appealed to her. It was straightforward, just like she was. One put the effort in, one diligently tended to one's patch, and the fruits of one's labor would follow.

Pulling a handful of weeds, she rose, brushing the dirt from her gardening togs of T-shirt and short-shorts, revealing her fabled gams. 'This—' CZ informed him, sitting on the edge of his chair amid the yews, '—is a kidnahpping. *Not* a social call. It's an intervention. And he who is the subject of said intervention has no rights to requests. Do you hear me?'

'Yes, boss lady.'

'Good. Now what would you like for your lahst supper?' She couldn't help but indulge him, at least from a *culinary* perspective. He was about to go cold turkey, like it or not. He'd shed the considerable pounds soon enough, without the booze that led to the bloat. Without the pills that made him lose count of the number of meals he'd had in a day. Without the fried comfort foods he imbibed in not-so-secret lunches at Ouisie's Azurest Diner. Institutional cooking and going dry—for good, if the program worked—would sort him out soon enough. She could allow him one last treat.

His pupils dilated with shameless gourmandism. 'Oh, Sissy! Might you happen to have one of those *lovely* baked hams of yours . . . ? The kind with the honey glaze and pineapple stuck on top? And that *divine* macaroni and cheese that you set out on buffets for parties?'

'I think we could rustle up something similaaah.'

'Darling Sis! You do spoil me so.'

'Well . . . Enjoy it while it lasts, bustaah. Because tomorrow starts a new regime.'

'The Mistress of Templeton has spoken.'

'You betcha. Now come on.'

'Come on where?'

'Well, I'm either going to pick the bell peppahs from my kitchen gah-den, or go in and change and go for a ride. Which would you prefer?'

'Honey! Neither!'

'Well, I don't trust you as far as I can throw you. I'd come back to find you half a dozen Orange Drinks in . . . ! So what'll it be? A pleasant trot or help me hahvest?'

'Sissy, why don't you take a little break from me. I just wanna go lie in that warm sun by the pool. I'll close my eyes and pretend

I'm on the most *exotic* of holidays. And I promise—naught but a *water* bottle will pass my lips!'

C.Z. relented, though not before popping round to the kitchen to instruct the staff to keep an eye on Mistah Capote, then changed into jodhpurs and boots and headed toward the stables.

Upon her return in an hour's time, she found Truman dozing like a baby in a lounger, clutching a paisley throw like a security blanket. Beside him on the ground, a chaste bottle of Perrier. It was only later that evening when she'd noticed his slurred speech and increasingly animated tales—coupled with a new-found passion for 'Adam's ale'—that she thought to check the large Perrier bottles he'd been consuming all evening, to find their contents cunningly replaced with vodka, providing undiluted hits of hooch in twenty-three-ounce doses.

Ladies and germs, it is therefore with pleasure that we give you, presented by Mrs. Winston Guest, of the Oyster Bay and Palm Beach Guests . . .

THE REHAB FOLLIES

PROLOGUE

HAZELDEN BOUND

THE PATIENT . . . . TRUMAN CAPOTE

THE CHAPERONE . . . . C.Z. GUEST

ALT: 9,000 FEET
AIR SPEED: 300 M.P.H. (260 KNOTS)
ETA: 2 HRS 55 MINS

They'd flown together countless times over many years. Between first Idlewild, later JFK, and Palm Beach International. They'd flown to Mexico to visit Gloria. To Turin to see Marella. To the Caribbean to stay with his darling Babe.

Truman always enjoyed flying. And as many times as they'd indulged the privacy of the Paleys' CBS plane, or the luxury of the Guinnesses' jet with its Louis XIV furnishings, there was something about *commercial* air travel that never ceased to thrill him.

'I just love those darling gals in their short skirts and capes and their jaunty pillbox hats, pushing their dear little carts—' (Speaking of which . . .)

He turned his head to chart its progress down the cabin aisle. C.Z. gave his ribs a jab with her elbow. 'Don't even think about it, mistah. You're being punished. For lahst night.'

'But Sissy, I *did* say nothing but water bottles would pass my lips! I didn't promise what was *in* them . . .' He grinned sidelong at her . . . a smile she failed to return.

'Truman. It isn't cute.'

'I didn't say it was.'

'I'm delivering you to Hazelden, whether you like it or not, and you're not leaving my sight until a doctor takes you from me personally.'

'Well, darling, we may as well whoop it up while we can.' Leg jigging. Beads of sweat beginning to gather at his temples.

'Oh *nooooooo*. I'm going to deliver you to them sober as a judge.'

'Well, that's just dumb.'

'In what way?'

'If you deliver me to them *sober*, what's there to fix?'

In his self-satisfied grin she saw a shade of the old Truman.

'Oh, Tru. You really need to stop. You'll— —Something ahhful will happen if you don't.'

Her warnings ceased as the drinks cart arrived and an indifferent air hostess in a rubiginous waistcoat and tie asked, 'What can I get you?'

'Two coffees,' C.Z. replied for both. 'Black.'

Truman squeezed her hand, his own trembling. 'Darling, please. Just this once. I'm not feeling so hot . . . It's my heart—I think it's breaking.'

C.Z. studied his face, spotting the terror in his eyes.

'Please, Sissy—just one to calm my nerves.'

Relenting. 'Okay.'

'Sugar,' he looked to the hostess, 'might we have two bourbons with that?'

'Soda?'

'Neat.'

She poured two glasses and set them on their tray. Before he could thank her, or tell her how much he simply *loved* her tie, that it looked just like *Annie Hall*, which was still all the rage, she'd moved on, functionally serving the next duo of passengers.

'Well. I guess one can't expect *panache* on a flight to *Minnesota.*'

C.Z. watched as he greedily took the glass, raising it with two hands to his lips. She noted with dismay how his teeth clattered against the edge.

He drained it in a breathless gulp, and she saw his body calm itself.

'Thank you, darling,' he whispered.

He leaned back in his seat and closed his eyes with pleasure. His body went so still, for a moment C.Z. feared he wasn't breathing.

'Truman—?'

'Tell me a story, Sissy.'

'That's your depaht-ment.'

'No it isn't. We all have stories, darling. And you've got a particularly great one. A real showstopper—in five action-packed acts.'

'Oh . . . ?'

'Of course you do.' He opened his eyes. Reached for her drink . . . 'May I?' When she nodded, he took a demure sip, nursing this one slowly. 'Tell me about Lucy.'

'Lucy?'

'Yes, darling. Tell me all about the beautiful Lucy Cochrane, debutante extraordinaire.'

C.Z. could see where this was going. 'Truman, you know that story.'

'Yes, but I want to hear *you* tell it,' he preempted her sigh. 'Please? Soon I'll be at the Alcatraz of clinics, stuck in those dreadful group chats with Midwestern nobodies droning on about their brute husbands and their kiddies and how they just need a handfulla pills to get through the day . . . Tonight, over this drink, tell me something I *want* to hear.' His tone was so entreating, she softened. As ever, he had her in his tiny palm. 'I'll begin it for you. Our curtain rises on Lucy Cochrane, the ice vanilla debutante. She's the finest debutante Boston has ever seen, except for one small glitch . . .'

C.Z. smiled. 'Lucy Cochrane could frankly give a *rhaaaat's ahhssss* about being a debutante. Lucy Cochrane's biggest ambition in life is to get herself thrown *out* of the social register, once and for *ahlll*.'

And in her expression C.Z. seemed to embody her nineteen-year-old self and to remember the desire for escape.

Act I

THE REBELLIOUS DEBUTANTE

IT STARTED WITH SMALL ACTS OF DEFIANCE.

While crowned the unquestioned celebrant of the '37–'38 season, Lucy—or C.Z., as she was called by her intimates—spent the better part of the parties drinking cocktails from a smuggled flask to supplement the thimbles of champagne, counting the hours until she could return to the stables and ride again. In fact, the only young men in Boston she was interested in were the sluggers of the Red Sox, for whom she rooted religiously, and the Bruins ice hockey team. If she was perfectly frank, Jack Kennedy and that whole Harvard crowd put her to sleep with their flat vowels (not unlike her own, though less musical by far) and their flat chat (something of which she was never guilty). She knew one thing— that her ambitions lay well beyond the suffocating New England boundaries of her birthplace.

She had started to see a handsome young man she met on the beach, stationed in Boston in the Coast Guard. He'd made a couple of pictures in California before the war. A matinee idol by the name of Victor Mature. She'd seen him in three films: as the young romantic lead in the remake of *No, No, Nanette*; a fur-clad caveman in *One Million B.C.*; and a swashbuckling swordsman in something called *Captain Caution*. One night as they strolled along Ocean Pier, Victor had paused, taking her chin in his giant hand. She thought he meant to tilt her face up to his and kiss her in the moonlight, but instead he simply studied her features, turning her profile, assessing each angle. She gazed up into his heavy-lidded eyes (which she could never quite decide whether she found attractive or off-putting), at his lips as full as an ingénue's (or those of a pouting halibut), and waited. Finally, in that deep, throaty, matinee-idol voice he said—

'You know, you've got a face for showbiz, kid. Your jaw is just square enough and your nose short enough. You need that to avoid casting shadows with the lights. Not that you'd need light . . . You're like the moon up there—lit from within.'

It was Victor who first gave her the idea. Not becoming an actress for acting's sake, but acting in order to sully her reputation just enough to render her 'tainted goods' as far as marriage to the 'right' men from the 'right' families was concerned.

Within a month she'd recruited her sister and a handful of debs to join a cabaret on the rooftop of the Boston Ritz. She sang Irving Berlin's 'Blue Skies'—slightly off-key, nevertheless stunning in a pale evening dress that clung to her athletic form, a slit up to her thigh revealing what she'd always been told were a great pair of gams when spied in swimsuits and tennis shorts. It seemed all of Boston dropped in at some point to see what shenanigans the Rebel Debs of the Ritz were up to, and Lucy was enormously satisfied when the Harvard crowd treated her like a fallen woman—or at least a temporarily misguided one. She sped around Boston in Victor Mature's Chevrolet convertible, drinking martinis from a thermos and necking in public.

Her mother was appropriately horrified.

To the Ritz one evening, Victor brought a guest. A lean, dark man with slick hair and a hungry look. He sat at a table at the edge of the floor, studying each of the young ladies with a connoisseur's eye. His intensity made the other girls uneasy, they'd later tell Lucy, but *she* met his gaze without blinking.

After the final song, the sirens joined their patrons. Lucy tucked a stray platinum strand behind her ear and sipped her Brandy Alexander. Victor touched her arm, prompting—

'Mr. Shubert is a producer, Luce. On Broadway. He runs the *Shubert* Organization . . . ?'

Lucy nodded and smiled, which might as well have been a shrug, from her lack of recognition.

'Sweetheart, what's your name? Your given name,' he asked, the hint of a Slavic accent discernible over the din of chatter and swing from the band.

'Lucy.'

'Lucy, you wanna be an actress?'

'Not pahticularly. But I would like to be something.'

'Well, take it from me. You can't sing and from what I can see you can't dance—not that that ever stopped any of the dames in the biz. What I mean to say is that you got no talent. But what you do have is a face. I know a face from a mile away—and sweetheart, you got one. A face to die for.'

Lucy felt her pale cheeks color, but simply took his card.

'Thank you,' she said.

'You call me.'

'I will.'

And she did.

ALT: 28,000 FEET
AIR SPEED: 460 M.P.H. (399 KNOTS)
ETA: 2 HRS 12 MINS

'YOU POOR, DIM CREATURE . . . Did you really not know who the *Shuberts* were?'

'Hahdn't the foggiest.'

'Don't *all* aspiring actresses know the Shubert Organization?'

'Dahling, about the only aspiration I had as an actress was to be good enough to be bahnned from Boston.'

'And did you manage it?'

'I'll say!' She grinned, taking her drink from him and sipping. As Annie Hall wheeled the cart back the other way Truman looked to C.Z., imploringly.

She sighed, relenting. 'It's cold turkey tomorrow, bustah.'

'Cross my heart, sugar.' Flagging the stewardess. '*Miss . . . ?*'

'Sir?'

'*Le même encore, s'il vous plaît.*'

The girl cut her eyes to C.Z., who nodded. The drinks were poured and deposited—C.Z. setting Truman's before him.

'Was it marvelous, darling?'

'Was what mahvelous?'

'Well, the *Follies*, of course. Treading the boards. The Great White Way. Wearing next to nothing with all those peepers gazing on you with lust and envy and absolute *yearning*.'

'I certainly told everyone back home how terrific it was.'

'And in reality . . . ?' He slurped the top of his bourbon with relish.

She paused, allowing her limbs the memory of holding up the weight of an enormous cage structure—batwings extending five feet in either direction, dripping with beads like an overladen chandelier. Balancing atop a nest of curls, an explosion of a headdress on the scale of Mount Vesuvius. Megawatt smile held in place, the muscles in one's cheek spasming with the effort.

'Actually, I was bored as hell! Bored of the costumes. Bored of the lights. Bored of standing, of walking, of holding a pose till my arms wanted to break.'

'But surely you got bit—just a teensy bit—by the showbiz bug.'

'Not even the tiniest nip.'

Act II

ZIEGFELD GIRL

HER CONTRACT WAS EXPLICIT. She was a showgirl—not a dancer.

As Mr. Shubert had spotted, she couldn't dance and she couldn't sing. But she looked radiant on stage. She was billed last, her name in the smallest print. No featured roles, she was the third blonde from the left. Yet she drew eyes.

'The *very* blonde one,' it was said.

'The *society* girl,' it was whispered.

Her costumes, as a rule, were white. White to match the platinum of her hair, so pale it gave the illusion of lacking any pigmentation beneath the stage lights. White pearls, strategically draped to cover scandalous bits, leaving little to the imagination.

The zenith of her evening was shedding the weight of the cages. Wiping the garish red from her lips, slipping back into her comfortable second skin of Harris tweed and moccasins, joining the cast in the bar on West 45th for Brandy Alexanders. Parties were frequently on offer, peopled with far more colorful characters than a Boston Junior League do; not a strand of pearls in sight. It was at a party for the opening of something or other that the man who would stage her next act would make his entrance.

It was high atop the city, at the Rainbow Room on the sixty-fifth floor in Rockefeller Plaza. Walking into that glass sphere in the clouds, she felt as light and fizzy as a human champagne bubble—monochrome hair and evening dress sustaining the illusion.

She had heard all about the rotating dance floor, cleverly linked to a Wurlitzer organ, which cued lights that changed colors according to the tone and mood of each song.

The band was in full swing in the brilliant glow of a golden, syncopated foxtrot. A rosy rumba followed, and a fiery crimson cha-cha, until the tone chilled into a pale blue waltz. It was then that he made his approach. Notably handsome, with high cheekbones, chiseled features, and a trim beige mustache. Politely cutting in, taking her in his arms. She smiled, a distant, formal smile, placing her long fingers on his broad shoulders.

'Well, good evening,' she said.

'Good evening,' he replied, his lips barely moving.

'Mahvelous, isn't it?'

'What, specifically?'

'This is the first dance that's a cool color.' And indeed they were surrounded in an ice-blue luminescence, as if bathed in moonlight. 'I prefer them—cool colors. Don't you?'

'Why is that?' The corners of his mouth teasing vaguely toward a smile, revealing traces of deep-set dimples beneath prominent cheek bones.

'Well, I suppose it suits my temperament. After all, there's only so much heat a girl can take before she wants a tall glass of wahter.'

It was then that he smiled in earnest and she saw what his severe expression had been hiding. Amidst those strong, fine features, a pair of buck teeth, like a cartoon rabbit. Instantly the mystery was replaced with a sweetness. Affability.

'I can believe that. There's something about you . . . even from a distance. I suppose it is a chill. An aloofness . . .'

'Heavens, as bad as that?'

His grin spread broadly, on either side of his buck teeth.

'No, no. There's something else . . . Warm shades, simmering just beneath. It's good. Good to have a bit of intrigue.' The waltz reached its conclusion, and the band transitioned into a rendition of 'Mood Indigo.' As she stepped back, he offered his arms again. 'May I . . . ?' She smiled and accepted them. She liked his rabbit grin. It was disarming. After they'd swayed through the clarinet's plaintive solo he said, 'Name's Darryl, by the way.'

'A pleasure. Lucy.'

'May I be so bold, Lucy, to ask what you do?'

Affecting her best Brahmin accent, 'Now it's a *very* rude question to inquire about a lady's ahhcupation. That's as bad as asking my age, or if I'm divorced or with child.'

'And are you?'

'No. No. Twenty-four. Undetermined. In reverse order.'

'At the risk of sounding banal, has anyone ever told you you have a face for pictures?'

'Yes.'

He laughed at her indifference. 'And who told you that, if I might ask? A teacher? Father? A fella . . . ?'

'Victor Mature.'

'You don't say?' Bucks bared in the now-lilac glow. 'We bought the four years left on his contract with Hal Roach. Paid eighty grand for him. The minute this war is over I—'

'*You* bought Victor's contract? But I thought a studio—'

'Exactly. Twentieth Century Fox.'

'You're Fox?'

'No, Lucy dear. But I may as well be. I'm Zanuck.'

'Ohhh, I see. Yes, I've heard about you. From Victor.'

'I've always said that kid's got the Midas touch. The public loves him—everything he's in turns to gold. But directors don't see it—not yet. Can't get past those looks of his. All brawn no brain, they assume. But I've got plans for him.'

'That's lovely, Mr. Zanuck.'

'Darryl.'

'Darryl.'

'I can spot a star a mile away. Or at least star potential.'

'I suppose that takes a particulah talent.'

'Yes, it does, Lucy, and right now, I've gotta be honest, I'm spotting it in you.'

'Oh.' Nonplussed.

'Yep. How would you like for me to arrange a screen test?'

'Ha.'

'What do you mean, "ha"?'

'Well, to begin with, I have absolutely no talent. Whatsoever.'

'Is that right?'

'I can't sing and I can't dance—pretty good odds I can't act either.'

'And who told you this?'

'Mr. Shubert. Of the Shubert Organization.'

'I see. Which Shubert?'

'All of them.'

'Well, how about this, Lucy . . . Lucy what?'

'Cochrane.'

'Well, how 'bout this, Miss Lucy Cochrane. You fly out to California, take my little test, then we'll see whose instincts are right. I can arrange for Victor to be there, so you'll feel comfortable. Whaddaya say? Doesn't every girl want to be in pictures?'

She shrugged a pale shoulder.

'Next Friday too soon?'

'Well, I couldn't possibly. I have a show, you see.'

'A show? But you said you weren't in the business.'

'I said I was *undetermined.*'

'What show?'

'The *Ziegfeld Follies.*'

'Featured player?'

'Third blonde from the left.'

'Well,' he said, chuckling at her honesty as he whirled her off the floor and toward the bar. 'It really isn't a question, is it? You're coming to Hollywood, where I suspect I'll make you a star. Just like your friend Victor.' And with that he lifted two flutes of champagne from a tray, passing one to Lucy. 'To our future.'

'Well, it's a very tempting offer, Darryl, but as I say, I do have a prior commitment. Perhaps I'll think on it. May I have your card?'

He produced a card from a silver case in his waistcoat pocket. 'Here you are, Lucy Cochrane. You'll call me . . . sooner than later.'

She sipped her champagne, keeping her thoughts hidden beneath that well-chilled politeness. But after two more weeks of heaving the bead-laden birdcages across the stage of the Imperial, a new test of any sort seemed a welcome challenge.

When she picked up the phone in her room at the Ritz and dialed Zanuck's offices, he answered the call with six short words.

'Lucy Cochrane . . . I knew you'd call.'

Act III

ZANUCK'S STARLET

'OKAY, LUCY, LET'S TRY THIS AGAIN,' she could hear Zanuck's voice, off camera.

She stood awkwardly, staring into a void. Nothingness. She could hear rustling behind the camera, could hear the occasional cough. Certainly the whispers, which she felt all but certain were criticizing her performance (if one could call it that—she had her doubts).

They were testing her for a specific role in a specific picture, as they had nineteen times before in the eight months she had been there. Nineteen times she had failed.

The early screen test she'd passed (on her looks). She'd been signed on the spot to a seven-year contract, the very length of Victor Mature's—who she'd since learned half the contract players referred to as 'Manure.' And so began the weeks of lessons. Speech and elocution. Movement. Scene study. She joined the throngs of girls walking with books on heads, they taking the whole process *terribly* seriously. She'd appeal to Zanuck about that, submitting a photograph of herself balancing a five-foot Ziegfeld headdress, with a note attached: *BEYOND BOOKS . . . !* She was invited to all the parties and premieres, had her photograph taken by the publicity department, who played up the

Rebel Debutante angle and chronicled her arranged dates with strapping young contract players who took her to dinners at Musso & Frank's.

'It's only a matter of time—the right thwcript,' Zanuck assured her, the word getting caught in his rabbit teeth. 'It'll happen. I know a star when I see one. *Patience*, my dear.'

But Lucy could see that it was hopeless. She could hear her voice—so wooden. Lacking the sweet languor it possessed in its natural state. She could feel her muscles stiffen, forming a protective armor around her when asked to walk this way or that. Felt the disconnected actions as she lifted a phone and pretended to say hello. She began to dread the calls for a screen test. To dread reading the dull script in the first place, much less learning the lines. She could hardly be bothered choosing her clothes, putting them on, and turning up, that ridiculous clapperboard with its zebra arm clacked in front of her face, then her four minutes—if that—to perform on cue, like some sort of deaf seal?

She preferred to be reading books, not scripts—or, more accurately, she longed to be outdoors. To be galloping through an open field on the back of a thoroughbred, as she had done all her life in Boston. After nine months of failure, Lucy had had enough.

One morning in August, when the heat was so thick one could slice it with a butter knife, Lucy Cochrane failed to arrive at the studio for her elocution class. Her absence was again noted at scene study, where a craggy young man—a poor man's Victor Mature—was left without a partner. Mr. Zanuck was alerted by lunchtime, and—Lucy being something of a pet cause of his—had taken the matter into his own hands. He left four messages with her service, all of which went unanswered. He called her bungalow on Doheny Drive, where the phone rang and rang, for there was no one left to answer it.

She'd awoken that day with a sense of purpose. The stillness in the air carried clarity in its stagnancy. It was as if she knew there was no life in this strange place—this temple of plastic dreams. It was tolerable enough, she supposed, for those who wanted it badly. They could afford patience. They could sit another seven years, watching their potential wither in that lifeless air. But what came to her in the stillness was that this was a hot place—a place of burnings and longings in crimsons and charred orange hues. She was an ice-blue thing. Removed. She never wanted this. It was never her dream, so why waste another moment of life in this place? Contract or no, she wasn't a slave and could not be kept here. As if it was the simplest choice in the world she rose, removed her stacks of twinsets and skirts and short suits from drawers, which she neatly placed in the open suitcase on the guest bed. She walked from the house out into the blazing light and never looked back.

'What do you mean, you're going?' Zanuck had bellowed on the phone when she called that afternoon from a booth in Union Station. 'You're going where?'

'I'm not sure yet.'

'What do you *mean*, you're not sure?'

'I haven't decided where I'd like to be next.'

'Be? Where you'll be? You'll be on the lot by nine tomorrow morning.'

'I'm terribly sorry, Darryl, but I'll be gone by then.'

'Need I remind you that you're under contract?'

'Yes, that *is* a shame—and I'm sorry about that.'

'You'll never work again, if you do this.'

'Well, thank *Gahhhh-d* for that.'

'Lucy honey, listen—'

'Goodbye for now, Darryl. I'll let you know, as soon as I get where I'm going.'

With a satisfied smile she hung up the telephone and stepped out of the booth, going in search of a libation to celebrate her liberation.

ALT: 37,000 FEET
AIR SPEED: 560 M.P.H. (486 KNOTS)
ETA: 55 MINS

TRUMAN TURNED HIS HEAD, looking for the stewardess, nowhere to be found. Left with little choice, he reached in the inner pocket of his linen jacket and pulled out a silver flask.

C.Z. raised a judgmental brow. '*Really . . . ?*'

'Well, dear heart, what was I *supposed* to do, continue to *hide* it and let us go parched? Besides, they'll only confiscate it when they strip-search me tomorrow, so I figure why not live it up now . . . ?'

'Lahst. Hurrah. Do you hear me?' She found him hard to resist when he was Old Truman. Happy, chatty. He had been himself so seldom of late.

'Whatever you say, boss lady. But until such time, would you care for a li'l refresher?'

She pushed her glass toward him on the tray table and he opened the flask, taking the greatest care to steady his hands.

'You know, bustah . . . soon you'll be a changed man. You've *ghat* to be.'

He shrugged in return, taking a greedy sip. '*Got* to? What *for*?'

'Truman, you have great things left to write, my dahling. You're a champion.' Then, with fierce conviction, 'You're a win-*ahhhh*.'

He looked at her, his eyes wide. 'My sweetest Sis, do you really think . . . ? After all that's . . . ?' His small voice trailed away.

She set her drink aside, gripping his arm, shaking him forcefully. 'You, Truman Streckfus Persons Capote, are the greatest writer I've ever known, and you've got more of that left in you. You go and show them—show them all how wrong they are. You make the most beautiful gawddamn piece of ahhhhh-rt they ever laid eyes on.'

'But Sissy. Nobody cares. Not anymore. It's too late.'

'Now you listen to me— It's *nevah* too late to come from behind to win the whole damn race.' She held his gaze until he fluttered his butterfly lids away, looking into his drink.

'Less Truman, more Lucy.'

'Fuck Lucy,' said she who used to be her.

'Sissy—you promised.'

'Oh Truman, it was so long ago. I'm me—Lucy was another lifetime ago.'

'You're both my heroines. She's no less real than you. No less real than Nina or Slim, or Holly Golightly or *Babe* . . .' At the sound of Babe's name his eyes clouded. 'Please, Sissy, more Lucy. She is you and I love you both so . . .'

'Ahlright, Truman. But only this once.'

'So. Where does a gal go after walking out on Hollywood?'

'She picks a place at random.'

'In Lucy's case?'

'Mexico.'

ACT IV

IN VINO VERITAS

SHE WAS SITTING IN CIRO'S BAR in the Hotel Reforma. That much she remembered.

She had chosen Mexico for the sole reason that she had never been there—she had seen an ad in a magazine at Union Station as she sat with her Brandy Alexander and thought that it looked festive. Plenty of sky, of white sandy beaches. Photos of tourists waterskiing and skydiving. Lush hills. Flowers of every variety. She bought a ticket to Mexico City for no other reason than it happened to strike her fancy, and having no one to answer to but herself, she telegrammed home once she'd installed herself in the Hotel Reforma.

It was there she sat one afternoon, sipping a daiquiri, flipping through the racing forms for the Hipódromo de las Américas, that her next role found her. It approached in the most unlikely of forms—a bull of a man in workman's overalls, splattered with color.

'*Buenas tardes, señorita.*'

Lucy looked up from her racing form. '*Buenas tardes, señor.*'

It was an off hour, the bar nearly empty.

'*¿Tu eres americano?*'

'*Sí.*'

'*¿Cómo se llama?*'

'*Mi nombre es* Lucy . . . Lucy Cochrane.' She smiled, vaguely apologetic. 'I'm afraid that's the extent of my Spanish.'

He smiled in return, an open, confident grin. 'Well, we shall see how we get on with my English. May I join you?' His face would have been comical, had his gaze been less sincere. Wide-set eyes at a disconcerting distance. Grooves beneath—permanent bags, too deeply set to budge.

Lucy hesitated. She just wanted to read her racing forms in peace, but she nodded and folded the paper. He called to the barman, '*Una botella de vino y dos copas.*'

She motioned toward her daiquiri. 'I'm fine, thank you.'

'No.' He settled into the leather chair opposite, in a seated position, gut rising almost as high as his chin. Not a bit of him seemed concerned that this might dampen his ability to charm. His dark eyes flashed with merriment. Enjoying his patriarchal show.

'"No"?' she challenged. 'I'm accustomed to ordering my own drinks, Señor . . . ?'

'Rivera.'

'I'm accustomed to ordering for myself, Señor Rivera. And a cool daiquiri was my preference, as you can see.'

'Yes. But. Today, together, we will drink wine.'

'And why should I alter my afternoon plans?'

'Because I am very interesting. And I can see you are very interesting too.'

She laughed, as a gold-vested waiter delivered two glasses and a bottle of Rojo.

'Why wine?'

The big man leaned forward, uncorked the bottle, and poured. Lucy thought his great distended belly looked as if it might pop.

'There is a phrase in Latin in which I happen to hold credence— *in vino veritas*.'

'I took Latin in school but I never paid attention.'

'It means: "in wine, truth."'

'In that case . . .' She lifted her glass to him. '*A tu salud.*'

'To your beauty,' he returned. 'For surely someone so radiant is in possession of health already.' He knocked back a glass in a long, deliberate guzzle. 'So, Señorita Cochrane. You are American. From where do you come?'

'From Los Angeles, I suppose . . . by way of Boston and Manhattan.'

'Ah—I too was in Manhattan. For a brief time.'

'And what were your impressions?

'*Lo odio!* It is full of capitalist pigs, Manhattan. Do you know the son of Rockefeller? Nelson? He commissioned a work from me in his building.'

'You're a painter, I presume.' She nodded to the splatters that covered his overalls.

'A muralist. He commissioned a mural for the lobby of his *Treinta* Rockefeller Plaza.'

'I know it well.' Lucy brightened, recalling the magic of the Rainbow Room's carousel floor, its spectrum of shades. She had a vague memory of a scandal in the press . . . 'Do go on.'

'He knew my work—had seen the kind of thing I painted. Political work. Work with *una conciencia* . . . The work of the people. And he commissioned my services.'

'And . . . ?'

'He shied away from the truth. He wanted me to paint the common man. A portrait of man striving . . . *Man at the Cross-roads*, it was to be called. It was a celebration of technology. Of human effort. A battle of class. I gave him the cosmos . . . the universe. Well, the *rica puta* was much too much a chicken. He ran scared when Lenin appeared in the mural.'

'Appeared?'

'He told me he wanted to be there.'

'And Mr. Rockefeller?'

'He demanded that I change it. I refused.'

'Whatever did you say?'

'I said I would rather see my mural destroyed than ruined by a capitalist *conejillo de pollo*! And so he took his chisels and his hammers to my work. It was shattered into a thousand pieces.'

'I apologize for my countrymen.'

'*Gracias, señorita.* I painted it again. Here, in the Palacio de Bellas Artes. The very next year. I renamed it *Man Controller of the Universe.* Because the universe was in my hands once more.' He lifted his hands where she might admire them. They indeed looked capable. 'I favor the new work. It is bold, as it should be. It captures the chaos of the modern world.' His fat face wrinkled with a wicked pleasure. 'I added yet another portrait that demanded inclusion . . .'

'Let me guess. Mr. Rockefeller?'

'I place him with a young *pedazo de culo* . . . a microscope slide of syphilis hovering just above his head.' He chortled, pleased with himself.

'I would love to see your work, Señor Rivera.'

He refilled his glass of wine, topping up hers in the process.

'Tell me, Señorita Cochrane, what do you make of the portraits on these walls?'

Lucy looked around the bar. Hanging at regular intervals were portraits of women. Sensual portraits. All nudes. Romanticized female forms, for the most part enveloped in floral cocoons. Lilies as big as their heads, some discreetly covering faces, masking the sitter's identity, some draped over the subject's sex. Some bared their bodies, hands laced in their hair, breasts pointed proud toward the viewer. There was something simple in the style of them. Folk art . . . yet seductive.

'They're very sensual,' she said. 'They celebrate the female form in a way that is unique.'

'In what way unique?'

'Well, the style is uniform . . . so at first glance the women seem interchangeable. But . . .'

'But . . . ?'

'When one looks closer, each woman is uniquely worshipped. Their attitudes toward their nakedness come through in their positioning . . . in their relation to the flowers.'

'Well, Señorita Lucy. You have just assessed my work.'

'*Your* work? But you said you were a political muralist.'

'I am also an admirer of the female form.'

'Good thing that I liked them.'

'Señorita Cochrane, one honest critic is more valuable than a hundred false flatterers.'

'They really are quite beautiful.'

'Would you like one?'

'Would I—? Goodness, I would love to have one! But I hardly have a home at the moment to hang— —'

'No. I've not been clear. Would you like one . . . of you?'

Lucy stared at him. Slowly, 'Are you asking me to pose for you, Señor Rivera?'

'Diego.' He attempted to lean closer, a supplicatory gesture, but his balloon gut prevented it. 'I see you, as I once saw the women on these walls, in your purest form.'

'Naked, in other words.'

'You see, I can tell—in an instant—when a woman needs to be painted. When she possesses something I want to immortalize. I know the female form . . . and I know who must be captured for the ages.' He watched as she reached for the bottle of wine, pouring them each a full glass. 'Have I offended you, señorita?'

A smile found its way into her inscrutable expression. 'Would it matter if you had?'

'Not in the least.'

'Well, Diego,' taking a long sip of her wine, 'I think you'd better call me Lucy.'

HE SAW HER, HE SAID, AS AN ODALISQUE. *Odalisca* . . . a concubine in a harem.

While his other portraits in Ciro's were vertical studies, posed upright against surreal bouquets of simple callas, of regional flora, Lucy's would be horizontal, five times the scale. He would design it to mimic the dimensions of the Reforma bar, where it would be hung in pride of place. One glance at *bonita* Señorita Cochrane and the management agreed, for all were in accord that hers was the most beautiful of faces. And while grown men, many with wives and children, they blushed to think of the beauty that Señorita Cochrane's clothing concealed.

Lucy's portrait would be a departure from the folk art tradition of Diego's previous nudes. Hers would be an ode to Renaissance portraiture—a reclining Venus. In the tradition of Titian's *Venus of Urbino* with her classical grace. Of Manet's *Olympia*, with her radical lack of modesty. He even tried to procure a peacock feather fan to replicate the pose in Ingres's *La Grande Odalisque*, but settled instead for a hand mirror as her prop, so that she might see herself throughout the sittings and thus enjoy the process.

For this she traveled to his studio in San Ángel—two houses, joined by a bridge. Modernist structures, a rare sight amid adobes and haciendas. One white and pink (for Diego), one cobalt blue (for Frida, his wife), a hedgerow of cacti and a shared gate between them.

In Diego's studio the streamlined shell of the structure faded in a farrago of traditional Mexican artifacts. *Los Judás* figures crowded around the space, papier-mâché devils of every shape and size. Looming human puppet suits, massive in scale—*mojigangas*, he said they were called. The weight of their giant limbs balanced by the strength of those who wore them brought back visions of the torment of C.Z.'s Ziegfeld cages, which she told him about with a shudder. He'd laughed his robust laugh and his enormous belly wobbled.

'Well, Señorita Lucy, I assure you, posing here will be far less arduous. The opposite of a cage.' He motioned to a sheet of whitest silk, draped over a chaise. Two down pillows awaited her platinum curls like a bed fit for a princess, or a courtesan, or a combination thereof. She'd been given a pale kimono to change into when she arrived. When she rejoined him, having shed her sweater and skirt and stockings and underthings, she saw on the table behind the chaise a goblet of wine. White this time—to match her hair, he'd later explain. He held a goblet of his own, which he raised to her.

'*In vino veritas.*'

She smiled and sipped, enjoying the sensation of the cool liquid sliding down her throat.

'How would you like me to . . . ?'

He nodded toward the chaise.

'I'd like you to be free.'

She slid out of her robe and settled on her side—the left—half turned toward the painter. She could feel the warmth of the sun as it streamed in through the high windows in the space. Watched the particles of dust suspended in its shaft.

'Perfection, Señora Lucy . . .'

'"Señora"?'

'Yes . . .' he intoned with a kind of reverence. 'For you came here as a girl. Now I see you as a woman.' Lucy felt herself flush. 'Do you see the mirror there?' She nodded. 'Take it and look at yourself. See yourself as *I* see you. Clothed in nothing but beauty.'

She lifted the mirror and held it up, studying her own reflection. She wasn't the mutinous debutante, nor the painted actress. She thought, as she studied her face, that perhaps this was indeed Lucy, the woman. Free of expectations, of ambitions. Just a body, a brain, a soul.

'Lucy . . .' the painter called. Almost a whisper.

327

Without moving, she cut her eyes to his and held them until he stood, stretching his giant girth, and informed her there were tamales for lunch.

It was Lucy's gaze—that very image that hung above the bar in the Hotel Reforma, confronting the patrons who ordered their drinks with the sexuality that simmered beneath the cool surface of the reclining odalisque—which Rivera christened *Veritas*.

'AND THAT'S THE PORTRAIT THAT HUNG for years at Templeton—in the *pool house*?!'

'Yes, my dahling. The very same. Frankly, I didn't see what all the fuss was about.'

'You were buck naked, honey. The *Mayflower* maids must be spinning in their graves . . . !'

'Nothing we haven't seen before . . . Two eggs, sunny side up.'

'Oh, but the *lower* half is quite risqué . . . But if memory serves me, wasn't the snatch primly covered with a garland of flowers . . . ?'

'Lilies. Pink Renoirs. They were added *aftah* the fact.'

'And how did this scandalous portrait get from the Hotel Reforma to a pool house in a very private residence . . . ? Do I detect a jealous husband's hand at play . . . ? Is this where the strapping Mr. Guest makes his entrance?'

Her expression softened. 'Winston didn't have a problem—at least he *said* he didn't. He didn't want to traumatize the family anymore than my carefully plotted wayward past already would. He didn't want the Phipps and Churchill clans up in arms over the brazen harlot bride.'

'How much did he have to shell out . . . ?' Truman asked.

'Fifteen thousand pesos. Just about three grand.'

'A bargain!'

'Three grand to buy back the reputation I tried so hard to sully. Ironic, isn't it?'

'Well, let's face it, Sis, you didn't do a very good job in that department. You ended up right back where you started . . . Tenfold! The English banking Guests would make those Boston Brahmins practically *weep* with envy.'

'Hmmmmmm.'

'So you traveled all that way to end up a paradigm of society anyway.'

She smiled.

'No. I traveled all that way to find *home*.'

Act V

MRS. GUEST

SHE SHOULD HAVE KNOWN, she'd later say, that it would have been horses that gave her a life back.

Bored by her acts of rebellion, C.Z.—who had ditched 'Lucy' in favor of her childhood nickname—had made her way back to Boston. She found purpose once more in sport, in the discipline of training. She loved the pungent smell of leather in the reins, loved the soft jangle of metal hardware. She thought the finest of sensations was the touch of a new filly's coat. She had become quite serious in equestrian circles both in dressage and as a jumper. She was passionate about the fox hunt, and welcomed its formal rituals. She was invited to the hunts in Middleburg regularly, where she crossed paths with the then Jacqueline Bouvier, though she never quite took to her, Miss Bouvier being more focused on hunting husbands than foxes. C.Z. was there for the sport itself. Around the tables that inevitably followed the hunts, she preferred to forgo the societal chitchat and speak in numbers and statistics—the odds on racing forms. The pedigree of a Quarter Horse. The score on a polo board.

It was the latter of these that called the attention of the restless C.Z. Cochrane to a *winnah* like herself. She had seen him on the field, in a charity match in Palm Beach. No—it began, one might argue, long before that. She'd heard tell of one Mr. Winston Frederick Churchill Guest (second cousin of the old Bulldog himself), star of the US polo team, considered one of the finest players in the world.

It wasn't until she spotted a man on a magnificent dapple-gray mare that she found herself hoping that he might be the Mr. Guest of lore. A more skilled rider she had yet to see. His strength was apparent—the whack of his mallet would send the ball sailing—but it was his gentleness with the mare, his finesse, that caught her eye. She found herself moving down from the stands to sit on the sidelines to get a better view. In the final chukka, he took the ball from a knock in, maneuvered clear of the pack, drilling an onside shot through the posts from thirty yards to score the winning goal. The crowd erupted in cheers.

As the end bell sounded, he turned his horse's muzzle in C.Z.'s direction. And much to her surprise he looked directly at her—not haphazardly, but with purpose. As if he already knew her.

She would later learn that he had been waiting for his moment. Winston had seen photos in the papers of the debutante-turned-showgirl and had been waiting for his introduction since. Rumor had it, upon seeing her picture he'd said this was the woman he would marry, if he ever had the chance. While such overtly romantic notions made C.Z. uneasy, what she did recognize was a kindred soul. A competitor. A champion.

When he first dismounted and approached her, removing his helmet, sweat seeping through his otherwise pristine white shirt, mud caked to his boots, she felt no timid tremor—this was a mighty quake.

He strode toward her—all six feet four inches of him, hand extended.

'Lucy Cochrane. I've been looking for you.'

'Oh. I . . .' She accepted his hand with a firm grip. 'Everyone calls me C.Z.'

He grinned, holding her hand a beat beyond a handshake.

'Well, then. I'll call you Lucy.'

WITHIN THE YEAR THEY WERE MARRIED, in a Cuban villa, amid the palms and mariposa. The Finca Vigía, the prized domain of Winston's old hunting pal, who was to serve as his best man.

'This,' said Winston proudly, 'is my luminous Lucy.'

'*Encantada*,' said their whiskered host, kissing the bride-to-be's hand, bristling her skin like a white, quilled hedgehog.

Lucy smiled. 'Lovely to finally meet you. Winston's told me all about your adventures.'

'Has Wolfie ever told you about the time we shot a crash of rhinos?'

As he launched into an elaborate account of hunting glory, leading them into a house boasting antlers and tusks as evidence of credibility, C.Z. noticed a woman standing to one side, watching. A bottle-dyed blonde, eyes shooting daggers. As if she'd seen all this before.

They were ushered into a covered portico, the scent of lime and sweet hibiscus perfuming the air. While their host busied himself at a bar cart preparing a round of Floriditas, C.Z. turned to the blonde, who she assumed to be her hostess.

'What beautiful hibiscus. I've not had much luck with them.'

The bottle-blonde smiled, a strained little grimace.

'Well, *Papa* always says— —'

VIGNETTE

ALT: 9,000 FEET
AIR SPEED: 270 M.P.H. (234 KNOTS)
ETA: 11 MINS

'OH NO . . . NOT *THAT* CUNT AGAIN!'

'Now Truman, you wanted to hear Lucy's story. Can I help it if Lucy happened to get hitched at Chez Hemingway . . . ?'

'Do any of you *not* know him? He seems to crop up like a bad penny, just when I thought we were rid of him.'

'Do you want to hear it or not?'

'Not that bit, honey. Not when I'm facing such an *ordeal*. Can't we just skip the wedding and move on to the rest?' He slurped his Scotch.

'Of course, dahling. But the rest is blissfully ordinary.'

'I'd say your life has been anything but *ordinary.*'

'Since Winston came along, it has been—in the most wonderful of ways. I had my rebellion. I lived my other acts. Then I found the role I was meant to play. It's just been a matter of staying the course.'

'Darling Sis, may *I* tell the last bit?'

'I thought you'd nehver ahsk.'

He set his drink aside and thought for a moment. Then, in that high melodic voice that C.Z. had come to love—joining the ranks of Sook and Babe and Marella and even Slim—he began: 'Once there was a cool vanilla lady, who married a handsome lord. She had loved him then, and continued to love him for many years to come. They built a life around their horses and their dogs, both of which they kept in packs. They had a boy and a girl, in perfect symmetry. They wintered in Palm Beach and summered at Templeton, traveling the world in between. Their court was one of mixed breeds, from pedigreed guests—the Duke and Duchess of Windsor, the Maharajah and Maharani of Jaipur—mixed with exotic specimens like Warhol and Dalí—mixed with outright mutts like that awful Truman Capote.'

'Truman, you *aren't* awful—'

'Shush! They all lined up for baked ham and macaroni and cheese, wagging their tails like one big happy pack.

'Even when their lifestyle exceeded their means and they were forced to downsize, not once but *twice*, the lady approached the moves with trademark pragmatism. Each home they called their own, whether grand estate or reduced quarters.

'She put on her old clothes and got her hands dirty, turning the soil. She planted her own vegetable patch. Flowers of every variety. Her hothouses yielded the most glorious of orchids.

'They loved orchids, the pair of them. They treated them like precious jewels—more vital than, for they were living things that required care. Just like children and horses and dogs and friends who couldn't take care of themselves . . .'

'Dahling, you *can* take care of yourself. You just have to *try.*'

'They bought orchids for each other as expressions of their love. Surprising one another with the rarest of varietals. The years passed and the lady still looked like something out of Raymond Chandler. Steely platinum reserve intact, that simmer still beneath—'

'Then one day,' she interjected, picking up the tale once more, 'the lady was out riding, in a field in Oyster Bay, when she approached a broken fence. As she coaxed her horse to jump it, she saw in a flash two rusty nails sticking out of a post. As they went over, the nails tore through her chaps, practically shredding her leg. She looked down to see the blood pouring from the wound, leaving a ribbon of red behind. My *Gah-d*, she thought as she galloped for help. I've done something awful. The wounds were wrapped by the groom, but the blood wouldn't stop, so the lady was rushed to the hospital. She was told she had missed slicing an artery and severing a vein by a fraction of an inch. Twenty-four stitches and two plastic surgeons *latah . . .*'

'Sugar, it *was* grim . . . Thank gawdalmighty it didn't leave a scar.'

'Yes, but you're missing the *point*. The lady was stuck in bed for months on end, unable to ride—unsure if she'd ever be able to *move* again. Unable to walk or run or play tennis. Couldn't leave the house. Nothing but that dreadful *Wahttahgate* on television. The lady was going half outta her skull. She was low. Lower than she'd ever been. She thought that she was through. That the curtain had finally fallen. And who should step in and remind her of her worth?'

He hid a smile in his coat sleeve. 'Aw, Sis. I didn't do nothin'.'

'You did! When I had the idea to write about gardening and feared that I couldn't, you told me, "Sissy dear, you can do anything in the world that you set your mind to." You gave me the courage to write that first book. You gave me another act.'

'Well, no one knows more about making things grow than you.'

'I know a damn sight more than that, so you listen to me, bustah. You're gonna do the same thing. You're gonna have the most spectacular encore those bitches have ev-ah *seen*. You're gonna fight and you're gonna *win*.'

'If you say so, Sis.' He nestled in close to her. 'But before that, how's about one more teensy round for ole times' sake?'

ENCORE

ALT: 0 FEET
AIR SPEED: 0 M.P.H (0 KNOTS)
ETA: LANDED

C.Z. HAD TAKEN NO CHANCES.

A car would be waiting to collect them at the airport.

Two porters gathered their luggage—C.Z.'s overnight bag, Truman's Vuitton cases, découpaged with labels. She insisted they walk on ahead, the porters following, keeping Truman trotting at his chaperone's brisk pace.

They herded him toward a black Lincoln Continental where the driver stood holding a sign: CAPOTE. Truman tried to turn back, yet found himself cornered.

'Sissy,' he said, making an earnest appeal, 'I think I left something behind on the airplane. I'll just pop back and see if the stewardess found it.' He turned back toward the terminal, to find himself blocked by her heavies.

'Not a chance, bustah. You'd be in the nearest bar faster than I could blink.' She took his arm—which she noticed was trembling—and guided him toward the open car door.

'Or on the next plane home . . .' a meek squawk of protest, as he ducked inside.

As C.Z. slid in beside him, she noticed his leg, jiggling at grasshopper speed. She placed a reassuring hand on his knee, and the leg calmed, only to start up again as the driver assumed his position and started the engine.

'Good afternoon,' he said in the rearview mirror.

'Ahhh-fternoon,' C.Z. smiled in reply. 'Hazelden Lodge, please. Center City. 15251 Pleasant Valley Road.'

'Yes, ma'am. I have it here.'

'*Pleasant . . .*' Tru scoffed, under his breath. 'About as *pleasant* as a root canal.' He leaned forward. 'Mr . . . . To whom do we have the pleasure?'

'My name's Louis, sir.'

'Well, Louis, I don't suppose you have a bottle of bubbly in this hearse?' He removed his snuffbox from his coat pocket, selecting two pills at random.

'No, sir. But there's a chilled bottle of Perrier.'

'Are you quite *sure* there's nothing up front? I just have to wash down the *teensiest* of pills, and they're always so much nicer with my old friend—HEY!' he squealed as C.Z. reached over and pried the pills from his hand. She rolled down the window and, to her charge's dismay, tossed them out onto the highway.

'Pahty's over, dahling,' she said, pocketing his precious snuffbox.

He sank, sullen, back into his seat. The leg resumed its grasshopper jig. They drove in silence until Truman finally ventured, 'Sissy?'

'Hmmm?'

'Do you remember when we first met?'

'Of course I do. At the thea-*tah*—the Mahrk Hellingah. On the opening night of *My Fair Lady*. When was it . . . ? March of '56? Or was it May?'

'Wrong, Sissy.'

'About March—or May?'

'About the *venue*. It was not at the Mark Hellinger Theatre. It was in the *bar* across the street. I walked in during the interval, and there you were, standing with Cecil—'

'Divine Cecil—it really was his crowning achievement. The Ascot scene in particulah.'

'There you were in that steel haze of cigarette smoke, an absolute vision. Do you remember what you were wearing?'

'Well, dahling, of course not. Likely whatevah I reached for in my closet.'

'Well, I can tell you, because you outdid even Cecil's Ascot bunch. You had on a simple white column. Not a scrap of jewelry to mar its clean perfection.'

'Main.' She smiled at the memory. 'Mistah Bocher designed that gown. He thought it should be white so it wouldn't compete with all the flowers.'

'Your face was as clean as a girl's, with just the palest hint of lipstick. Your hair was the color of the champagne in your flute, a dry vintage, which you sipped *veeerrrrry* coolly as I approached.'

'Truman, I'm sure you've remembered this wrong.'

'But you did, Sissy! With a chill that could freeze the Gobi! But then when Cecil said, "Meet my friend Truman," and you shook my hand with that warrior's grip, I *knew* we'd get on. And wasn't I right?'

'You were right, dahling.'

He turned to look out the window. Flying past in a blur, rather pleasant scenery. Emerald leaves rustling in trees. A spattering of lakes. The frequent shimmer of water.

'Well, Truman, I must say, this all looks *very* tranquil. Just look at all that *green*.' She stuck her hand out the window. 'Just *breathe* that fresh *air*!'

Truman smiled and nodded, patting C.Z.'s hand. They rode on in silence, feeling the breeze filtering in through the open window.

Then, in a low voice . . .

'Sissy . . . I'm scared.'

'Truman, there's nothing to be frightened of—they're going to *help* you.'

'I'm terrified that—' He pulled himself up short.

'Terrified that what?'

He shook his head and held his terror close.

'Truman . . .'

Before she could say more, he dabbed his eyes with his sleeve and began to hum. A bright, jaunty tune, to which he added lyrics. '*Shaking the blues away, unhappy news away . . . If you are blue, it's easy to shake off your cares and troubles . . .*'

An old *Follies* tune, C.Z. spotted in an instant. She smiled. 'Irving Berlin?'

He nodded. In his syncopated cadence she could hear the jangling of a banjo. The slide of a trombone. '*Telling the blues to gooooo, they may refuse to goooo / But as a rule, they'll go if you'll shake 'em away . . .*' As if to convince himself, he launched with gusto into the bridge: '*Do like the people do, listening to a preacher way down South! They shake their bodies so, to and fro / With every shake, a lucky break . . .*' He paused, as if actually considering the implausibility of the lyric for the first time. The tune fizzled.

'*Proving that there's a waaaaay . . .*' C.Z. prompted him.

When he failed to resume, she belted the chorus, a chipper alto, slightly off-key. (The Misters Shubert always said she couldn't sing.) '*If you would lose your weary blues, shake 'em awaaaay.*' She nudged him—a sharp jab from her elbow. '*Your* turn.'

Truman complied, recovering a cheerful (if manic) energy if only in order to please. '*If you would lose your weary blues . . .*' C.Z. joined in a dissonant crescendo—

'*Shake 'em awaaaaaaaaaaaaaaay!*'

THE CAR STOPPED BEFORE A PLEASANT HOUSE. Arched portico. White columns. Seven steps with iron railings, leading to the entrance.

'Well, this looks perfectly lovely. I don't know *what* you were worried about. Come on. Let's go get you checked in.'

'No, Sissy. You just stay here and wave to me—like I'm going on a cruise.'

'Truman, don't be silly. I've come this far . . .'

'Sis, you don't need to *hand-deliver* me. I can't escape now.'

'I wouldn't put it pahst you . . .'

'I can do this myself. I promise.' He pulled the hip flask from the innermost pocket of his jacket. He grinned at C.Z. sheepishly as he depleted the last of its contents. Then he screwed on its cap and passed it to her for safe keeping. 'I promise . . . that I'll try.'

He kissed her cheek as the driver opened the passenger door.

As he stepped from the car and made the walk up the gravel road, C.Z. leaned out the open window and called to him— 'Remembah, Truman Streckfus Capote, YOU are a *WINNAH!*'

And as if hearing jangling banjos and buoyant brass in his mind, Truman mounted the steps, kicking his heels up in a cakewalk as he went. At the top step he paused to tip an imaginary top hat in C.Z.'s direction before launching into an impassioned tap routine, Time-Stepping and Shuffling Off to Buffalo at the gates of purgatory.

EIGHTEEN

1966

VARIATION NO. 9

COMPOSITION IN BLACK AND WHITE

WE WERE DESPERATE TO STAND OUT.
To be seen as unique. *Singular.*

The worst we could imagine, on such a night as Truman's ball, would be to blend into the crowd, be it our small coterie, or the larger one. The mere thought of being lopped in with anyone—whoever they might be—rankled. We didn't want to be mentioned alongside even those to whom we were closest and thus most often paired: Babe and Slim, the lady and the broad; Marella and Lee, royalty by birth and marital upgrade; Gloria and C.Z., raven and dove. Wretched, the idea of being *compared*. Worse still—compared and found to be lacking.

Ordinarily we didn't mind being mentioned alongside one another. We accepted that we were part of an elite, and while we strove to exist in our own right, it was comforting on some level to know that we belonged. But other times we yearned to be so exceptional that no one—not even Truman—could tag us as one in a flock.

Put plainly, we wanted to *outdo* one another.

The masks proved especially tricky, for they threatened to cover our faces; to conceal our identities. 'But that's the whole *idea*, sugar!' Truman had laughed.

They were a theatrical touch, we had to admit, and one could appreciate the spirit of egalitarianism they promised to promote—'So the doorman might dance with the duchess,' he'd enthuse—but what good was striving for recognition if we were just to be hidden away behind a bunch of goddamn masks? Did that not render us interchangeable—the very thing we were striving to avoid? But Tru had insisted, and we accepted it as the price of admission. Lord knows we enlisted the milliners in the effort, plucking every wildfowl on the eastern seaboard.

'*Masks!?*' Loel Guinness had scoffed from the table of his French château, where he sat finishing his cheese course, at which time he ritually allowed Mister, his prize Pekinese, onto the table to be fed his peppermint. 'Kids' stuff!'

Gloria had tried to sway him, really she had. 'But darling, Diablito says they're the great leveler—that people can mix beyond their usual circles.'

'I don't need to mix beyond my usual circles . . . right, Mister?' Mister wagged his tail, moving down the table to lap from Gloria's water glass.

'But Loel, Diablito will be *so* disappointed. Everyone who is anyone will be going. It's to be the party of the century.'

'Did Truman tell you that? I hope he's half as good at writing as he is at self-promotion,' Loel, who didn't go in for fiction, chuckled.

Changing tactics— '*Gianni* is going. And Stas and Winston and *Bill* . . .'

'Well,' said Loel, pouring a healthy glass of Bordeaux, retiring to the armchair in his study. '*They* can enjoy it. *I'll* be home in bed.'

Gloria, we'd later learn, would console herself for her un-escorted state by purchasing an ebony gemstone mask for an undisclosed sum from a jeweler in Paris, to contrast the white gown of cylindrical crystals she'd commissioned from couturier Castillo, selected for their shared Latin roots. She decided on not one but two chokers to adorn her fragile neck—diamond and ruby respectively. Happy to be absent, for once Loel—*notorious* cheap-skate—didn't quibble.

While striving for *sui generis* in her choice of designer, Gloria was deflated to learn that Babe—quite independently—had chosen

Castillo too. And from the custom department at Bergdorf's no less, rendering Gloria's European purchase meaningless. With perfectionist's assurance, Babe had decided on a column gown of white zibeline, a mix of wool and camel hair. Her only embellishment: a collar of faceted rubies (paste again; she kept the real ones in her safe). She had them sewn into the neckline, descending in regal, Byzantine drops. A high slit lent subtle sex appeal, for, on this evening of evenings, even *Babe* hoped to shake things up.

Of course it was she who helped Truman plan the menu. He was clever in allowing us each to feel invested in different ways, but, as usual, Babe got the lioness's share.

'Babyling, I want a *looong* buffet, served at midnight. And on it I want all the things I love. This chicken hash, first and foremost,' he proclaimed as they lunched at the Oak Bar, '*hashing* out the menu,' he'd snickered.

'Darling, are you *sure*? It's awfully rich for—'

'Of *course* I'm sure! Hell, for one night, I'll serve 'em a heart attack on a plate without qualm!'

'Scrambled eggs and caviar?'

He balked. 'Baby, I may have earned some *dinero*, but made of money I ain't! Thank *you*, but I'll save the big bucks for the bubbly'—referring to the four hundred bottles of Taittinger he planned to order—'which I want to serve in crystal coupes, as round and perfect as Marie Antoinette's tit!' Babe laughed. He grinned. 'What?! That's what they were designed to replicate! So. *Yes* to the scrambled eggs, cut the *trop cher* caviar, add biscuits and gravy. And my *pièce de résistance*: spaghetti and meatballs,' this, smacking his lips.

'Truman,' Babe put her foot down (or tried.) 'You cannot invite hundreds of women to a formal gathering, make them wear *white* and serve them spaghetti and meatballs.'

He considered. 'They have the option of *black* . . .'

'It's a disaster waiting to happen.'

'Bring on the flood.' He refused to bend on this matter. The messy meatballs stayed, though later, when the rains came, we wondered if Tru's so easily tossed-out 'flood' comment cursed his evening from a meteorological perspective.

He proved equally implacable regarding his strict policy of 'NO PLUS-ONES, NO EXCEPTIONS!' He'd already had several 'Extra Men' decline upon learning they couldn't bring dates. He held his ground, declaring, 'I don't want strangers at my party.' (Read: riff-raff.)

Slim told him flat out that this wouldn't do. She was remarried, to Lord Kenneth Keith; still she knew something by this point about the hell of being considered an 'Extra Woman.'

'Truheart,' Slim barked when consulted, 'you cannot, and I mean *cannot*, ask a bunch of grown women to don fucking *masks* and turn up solo at the Plaza! They'll simply refuse. You've gotta allow them dates.'

That's when he thought of the *dinners*.

'Dinners?'

'*Pre*-ball dinners—that way everyone arrives in groups . . . no one's left alone! The Paleys can host one, and the Burdens, and——a handful of others.' He refrained from saying '*Pam* and Leland' for Slim's sake, but that's precisely what he meant and what transpired.

Slim conceded that this plan would work, though she was acting on behalf of Extra Women in *theory*, she having an escort in the dashing Jerome Robbins. Who better to take to a ball than Jerry? Even those of us who loathed dance thought his choreography sublime. And he'd been so attentive to Slim in the wake of the Leland fiasco . . . For all her pretense otherwise, Slim planned for Tru's fete as meticulously as the rest of us, ordering a pair of Galitzine palazzo pajamas, shipped specially from Capri. Oyster silk. Streamlined. Daring. Beneath her sangfroid surface she was giddy as a debutante.

It was Slim who suggested Truman book two bands, he having naturally sought her opinion regarding the entertainment portion of the evening. One for 'social' dancing, one to get down and dirty. They'd settled on Peter Duchin's Orchestra—the most sought-after society band, as his father's had been before it. Peter *knew* Truman's guests—was practically one of our tribe, a fact Tru used to finagle a discount. And for the funk, Benny Gordon and the Soul Brothers of Detroit. (Their fee significantly less, the Brothers charged Truman full rate.)

Lee, Marella, and Gloria had of course been in on the early planning stages—on their yachts and planes the previous summer. They'd been party to the creation of Truman's ever-evolving guest list, laughing at those who offered bribes in the hope of being included. But as the day itself approached, requests became demands. Those who once offered theater tickets and Mont Blanc pens and five-figure checks now resorted to threats. The host found himself bombarded by the excluded *and* the press—chasing him down on the way in or out of his building. 'I was positively *hunted*. One little ole fox and a thousand rabid hounds! I'm *telling* you, they nearly tore my limbs to shreds!'

He'd fled the city the Tuesday before. Only Babe was privy to his whereabouts—which we'd later learn was nowhere more mysterious than his house in Sagaponack—and if any of us absolutely *needed* to reach him, we were told we'd have to go through her.

We accepted this—that if not his guest of honor, Babe would act as unofficial hostess, a preeminence made all the more apparent when the pre-ball guest lists were revealed, the Paleys being given the A-list in a divvying process that was *allegedly* equal. Tru attempted to camouflage this glaring gesture of favoritism by subdividing diners by category: the politicos at Jean (Kennedy) Stein's. The writers at the Lumets'. The Haywards—Leland and Pam—had the showbiz faction, *except* for the obvious omissions. Betty told Slim she'd rather eat nails than sit down to dinner with *Frank* after what *he'd* done to her . . . After a whirlwind hush-hush engagement, the press had gotten hold of their romance. Frank assumed it was Betty who'd spilled the beans and the Chairman got cold feet, leaving poor Betty high and dry. And now he had a *new* Mrs. Sinatra, about as far from gravelly Betty Bacall as one could ever be. A sprite, a *child*! Mia Farrow, younger than his *daughter*, for Chrissakes!

Even Tru knew to steer clear of mixing Slim and Betty with *that* combustible bunch; besides, the butterscotch panthers had made it perfectly clear how they felt about Pam's hapless cuisine. They were thus added to Babe's list, with Truman's other favorites. Agnellis. Radziwills. Vreeland. Beaton. Gloria, *sans* Loel. Detective Dewey and his wife Marie, flown in from Kansas for the occasion. Even Truman and Kay planned to swing by for a drink before returning to nibble on 'a bird and a bottle' in their suite at the Plaza, courtesy of 21.

The only one of us not included in Babe's elite was C.Z, she having been chosen as the 'bone' True threw to a rival hostess who bitched that her dinner roster was something less than glittering.

'Sissy.' Truman had phoned C.Z. in a state. 'You've just gotta do me this one little favor. The Meehan party needs a dose of the old razzle-dazzle.'

'Truman, I could give a raaaht's ahhss where we dine,' she drawled, nonplussed (as he predicted she would). 'It's *your* night.'

Of course C.Z. had approached preparations for that evening-of-evenings with her usual nonchalance. She'd phoned up her *dahling* Mainbocher, who sent a simple design just suited to her taste. Two-tone lace, black skirt, white bodice. Showcasing arms toned from hours with her racquet. Having had her fill of headgear from her Ziegfeld days, the masquerade aspect held neither fear nor thrill, and her white mask—jets of plumes shooting forth like a ring-spray fountain—seemed as natural extending from her head as if she'd sprouted feathers.

As for the setting, Tru used thrift to his advantage. At the center of each table, he arranged to place a golden candelabra, vines twining through their arms. There was not to be a bloom in sight, thus saving himself a hefty florist's bill. In yet another masterstroke, spinning cost-cutting as narrative, the host had been heard to proclaim—'The *people* will be the flowers.'

WHEN THE LONG-AWAITED MORNING brought torrential rain, it seemed the only aspect of the proceedings Truman *couldn't* control was the weather. Even *this* he dismissed as Dionysian intervention, bestowing upon his fête the most dramatic of conditions.

As he checked into the Plaza that morning, he chirped to the bellhops as they carried his luggage up to his suite—'I just *adore* a good gully-washer, don't you?'

And to the Kansas crew when they knocked at his door— 'Maybe it's poor Perry and Dick weeping up in heaven that they're missing all the fun.'

Nobody argued, but it was clear from Detective Dewey's expression that he thought Dick and Perry's souls were operating from below, not above, if the bastards existed at all.

Due to the swarm of private planes arriving on the Sunday, LaGuardia was forced to close its runways to all other incoming flights, leading one to believe Truman had commandeered the very skies. Frank and Mia had flown in from Palm Springs, Gloria with the Rothschilds from Paris. The Agnellis transported the Radziwills and a contingent of aristos from Rome, more space swallowed by luggage than passengers. Just as Gloria and Babe had separately chosen Castillo, Lee and Marella found they'd each commissioned gowns from Mila Schön, though who could know (apart from Ms. Schön) who'd approached her first. Lacking the fervor of the Paley-Guinness rivalry, the Princesses Radziwill and Agnelli could easily see that Lee's mod shift with its patterned silver paillettes could not have been more different from Marella's ethereal caftan. Apart from their creator and iridescent hue, the two shared blessedly little in common.

By midday the host was spotted leaving the Colony, Lee on his arm, looking like the tomcat who guzzled the cream. They'd had a leisurely lunch, joining the crush of ball guests crowding Manhattan's luncheon hot spots. They emerged cool and collected, Lee in a belted coatdress, Tru in a smart gray suit, eyes hidden behind rose-tinted glasses. The duo sailed past an explosion of flashes, photographers shielding cameras from the rain beneath their flapping macs. All shouting Truman's name, demanding details.

'It was the smartest thing he could have done,' Lee would recall, years after contact was severed, on the rare occasion we allowed ourselves to indulge in such topics. '*Not* to run his mouth for once. The less he gave them, the more they wanted to know. Between you and me, I think he was more excited by the *preliminaries* than anything.'

Lee had watched as Truman, who never *could* keep a secret—who loved nothing more than to toot his own tuba—simply smiled when besieged with questions. They shouted. They cajoled. But the boy in the smart suit said nothing; simply kept walking toward a waiting taxi, which he and Lee ducked into, escaping the deluge.

MEANWHILE, KAY WAS ARRIVING AT KENNETH'S, at Truman's insistence.

The Fifth Avenue town house from which Kenneth and his team tamed our locks was a whirl of perpetual motion. Tucking our furs into chilled storage lockers, shuttling us from room to room, bustling us into saunas and out again, laying us out to dry beneath Murano glass chandeliers. In the madhouse of famous heads, demanding elaborate coiffures worthy of Versailles, Kay, with her sensible hair and her sensible shoes, found herself lost in the shuffle. She watched a revolving door of clients entering as women, exiting as mythical beings. Two hours in, she rose and approached the desk, meekly dropping Truman's name. When the haughty desk girls realized that this dowdy out-of-towner was the mysterious guest of honor, they hopped to quick. They bustled Kay into an elevator, ascending to the heavens, leading her to the inner sanctum, doting upon her with flutes of champagne.

When Kenneth finally appeared—having curled hundreds of ringlets in Marisa Berenson's genetically blessed locks—he escorted Kay to his famed chair. A tasteful man in a Savile Row suit, Kenneth stepped back, studying Mrs. Graham's face. Kay felt her cheeks burn under the scrutiny of his gaze, certain he was judging her as a frump. But as the maestro cupped her matronly bob, she felt every bit as alluring as the women who'd sat in that chair before her—Jackie, Marilyn, each of us in turn. Kenneth touched her cheek, proclaiming a sophisticated bouffant just the thing—Babe's height and Lee's sleekness combined.

In an hour's time Kay returned to the Plaza with a plastic net carefully preserving Kenneth's creation (the one that evening of which he remained most proud, he'd later claim). She went straight to her room, where she sat at the dressing table, applying the makeup she seldom wore, having sought the advice of friends in the know.

Just before Truman was due to collect her, she slipped into her Balmain gown.

When the rap on the door came just before eight, Kay leaped to open it.

There he stood—the midget suitor. Dapper in a classic tuxedo, specially made to fit his pint-sized frame. Kay before him in a high-necked robe of ivory crepe, bell sleeves and collar edged in hematite, just like the crusting of gems which topped her mask. Simple, understated . . . yet unquestionably glamorous.

Truman stepped back, placing a hand over his heart. Taking her in as if gazing upon the most exquisite of creations. *His* creation. The heroine he'd cleverly chosen for his tale. The former duckling who stood before him every inch as much a swan as Marella or Babe or any of the rest of us.

'Ohhhhhh, Kay-Kay,' he said in the reverent hush with which he assessed us in such moments, which we knew from experience induced the most extraordinary sensation of lightness. '*Look* at you . . .'

'I haven't yet—not all of it put together. I was waiting for you.'

'Close your eyes,' he instructed. 'It's even better if you close your eyes.' He took her hand and led her to the wardrobe door, where a full-length mirror was mounted. He positioned her in front of it. 'Now ... *open.*'

Her eyes fluttered, sticking slightly from the unfamiliar thickness of mascara. When she saw herself, Truman standing at her side, her eyes welled with tears. 'Thank you, Truman,' she whispered. *'Thank* you.'

His eyes watered too, as if the condition was contagious. He wiped them, scolding, 'Now Kay-Kay, *stop* this nonsense, or I'm gonna hafta redo your peepers!'

THEY SHOULD HAVE BEEN A MISMATCHED PAIR; the extremes of each pointed out the other's imperfections. Tru's diminutive frame rendering Kay a giantess; her height making him all the more gnomish. Yet as they walked into the Paleys' silk-draped living room, where Babe had set candlelit tables, beautifully dressed and amply laden, Truman and Kay—who on any other occasion might have been mistaken for a comedy duo—looked *perfect* together.

For all of our efforts—and we *did* look divine—the host and his guest outdid us. Our tow-haired boy shone more golden than ever before. By some strange spell, that evening he was more alluring than Gianni with his handsomeness and Bill for all his charm.

And Kay ... Good Lord ... *Kay*! She'd transformed from duck to Swan as we never dreamed possible. While she lacked Babe's bone structure or Marella's elegant length, no mere genetics could approach Kay's radiance that night, which simply dazzled with its wattage. For the first time we saw what Truman had seen in Kay, what his kindness and love had coaxed from within. In their presence, our rivalries seemed to melt. Nothing mattered but this evening, this moment. Their success. Success that existed apart from us—the warmth of which we were simply happy to bask in.

Tru and Kay left after Babe's cocktail hour, for he was anxious, he said, to return to the Plaza early. Good thing they did, because what with slick streets and fleets of cars sailing toward the Plaza, they got back an hour later than expected. Their picnic dinner ill-fated, they eschewed bird and bottle for teaspoons of caviar.

Just before they ventured downstairs, Truman approached the mirror in his suite, a simple black domino mask in his hand.

Weeks earlier, en route to the Oak Bar to meet with the Plaza's catering staff, Truman and Babe had wandered past Cartier. The jewelers had dressed a window in masquerade homage, display-ing two masks, side by side, one crusted in black diamonds, one in white. Unable to resist, Truman had popped his head into the store, calling to the salesman, '*Pardon*, honey. But *combien*? *Pour les masques?*'

'Thirty-six thousand, *monsieur*,' the salesman replied. Smug. French. Pleased with the hefty figure. Truman gave a low whistle, then beamed at Monsieur Cartier.

'*Merci* buckets,' he trilled on their way out of the shop. Back on the street, he'd practically skipped down Fifth Avenue, giggling with glee, chanting, 'Thirty-six thousand. Thirty-six *grand!*' Then he stopped short, turning to Babe *avec* mysterious grin. 'That reminds me, Baby. I've got one *teensy* errand to run before we lunch, if that's all right with you . . . ?' Babe had followed him down the block to the windows of FAO Schwarz, whose displays seemed to delight him every bit as much as their Cartier counterparts. His eyes had gleamed as he surveyed the cornucopia of baby dolls and fire engines and bicycles and guns—plastic, of course, though he could never see one without a flash of the Clutters and the years he'd spent pondering why a boy as kind as Perry might've pulled that trigger.

Tamping down such thoughts—for this was a moment of hard-earned *joy*—he had entered the shop as a man on a mission, navigating the aisles like a seasoned pro. He'd paused in the fancy dress section, where he plucked a simple black domino mask from the rack. He had held it to his eyes and turned and grinned at Babe. 'Thirty-nine cents! Take that, Cartier!'

As he donned this simple mask months later, looking in the mirror of his Plaza suite with its flocked wallpaper, studying his own reflection alongside Kay's, he felt, we can only imagine, vindicated. And with that long-awaited gesture the revelries began.

WE ARRIVED AT THE PLAZA in groups, as planned, buzzing with camaraderie. We praised one another's sartorial choices—and were surprised to find that we meant it. There were no *Extra* Women or *Spare* Men. We were more than single, fragile beings, capable of pain or the terror of being alone. We were part of a lovely, shimmering whole.

We piled out of cars ebullient, heedless of the rain, which continued to fall in sheets. We huddled together beneath umbrellas, moving past the crush of photographers and onlookers gathered beyond the barricades, proceeding through the front doors, and along the path Truman had planned for us. We walked through the marble lobby, shaking droplets from our evening coats, dabbing our soggy furs. Pulses beating faster, we followed one another past the graceful Palm Court, up a staircase to the mezzanine and down a corridor, where a camera crew awaited. Who should be granted the TV exclusive but Bill Paley's CBS, broadcasting live from the lobby. This was *drama*, Bill insisted, exploiting the contrast between Haves and Have-nots.

What none of us could have anticipated—as we stepped two-by-two through that arc of an archway and made our way down the long passage—was what would happen when we reached the end. Lee was the first in procession, gliding past white tapers, flickering on either side of an endless hall of mirrors. As she reached the threshold, she paused at the final glass, lowering her head to secure her mask. When she lifted her chin and examined her reflection, something curious occurred. Just as Kay had undergone a transformation from lone duck to one of a bevy, for Lee it was the opposite. In that moment she saw herself. No one else. It was *her* mask, shaped like wings, taking flight. *Her* tawny locks framing her face, tucked behind her ears to showcase diamond drops, which swung like delicate pendulums. There was no Jackie ahead of her or beside her, nor any of the rest of us. Only Lee. And in that moment, a photographer snapped a photo, directly into the mirror, capturing steady kid-gloved hands in control of crystal wings. Lips set determinedly, a breath before they broke into a satisfied smile.

It happened to each of us in turn. As we approached the staircase, drawing us ever closer to Truman's monochrome vision, we shed the collective skin that grafted us together, and slithered into newborn, separate beings. Babe stepped into the cameras' gaze, hurrying ahead of Bill, pulling her white mink closer. Dodging one lens, she moved out of frame, only to skittishly escape another; her lovely head ducked as if seeking shelter from a gale, while Bill, the grinning mogul, shook hands and nodded to colleagues, seasoned media pro. Behind him, Gloria took her time, moving like the dance hall temptress of her youth, indulging the hip-sway, setting in motion the cylindrical beads hanging from her dress, rattling like muted maracas. She moved so languorously, the cameras nearly missed the Agnellis sailing past—Gianni moving at his usual clip, Marella keeping pace. By the time the lenses turned, they only caught the flash of Marella's ostrich plumes, a trail of vapor in their wake.

Slim and Betty hung back, prowling, surveying the scene with big-game savvy. Slim on the arm of Jerry Robbins, who as ever seemed to float, not walk; Betty with Husband *Dos*, Jason Robards. Robards was already looking for the nearest bar, though the panthers hardly noticed, Betty scanning the crowd for that lowlife Sinatra, Slim for her darling Leland.

C.Z. navigated the hall with her usual lack of fuss, dutifully stopping to speak to Charlotte from the *Times* and Suzy from *Women's Wear Daily*—themselves in evening dress, stenographer pads, glasses, and pearls—praising Truman's triumph in her lyrical lockjaw.

'He really is a *mahh-vel*. We're all so damn *proud* of him.'

'Yes, but isn't this a party for Mrs. *Graham*?' Charlotte challenged.

C.Z. smiled. 'Dahling. It *is* a pahty for Mrs. Graham, but don't for a moment kid yourself . . . It ahhhlso is a pahty to celebrate a genuine publishing sensation. Champagne will flow like the Nile—or I suppose in Truman's case like an endless Ahlabama stream.'

She rejoined Winston, taking his arm, climbing the staircase to Truman's Mount Parnassus. They approached the first checkpoint, presenting cards that accompanied original invites—then a second, a table set up just outside the entrance. Ms. Elizabeth Davies sat collecting the cards that had been sent only days before, a final tactic to discourage counterfeiting. She had Truman's master list, but no need to reference it. She had all 540 names memorized—verbatim.

C.Z. greeted her warmly. 'Evening, Lizzie. Any gatecrashers . . . ?'

'Not yet. But the night is young.'

C.Z. noticed a tall, burly fellow guarding the entrance. Sidney, the doorman at Truman's United Nations Plaza, in full monkey suit, wearing a black domino mask identical to Truman's.

'Sidney!' C.Z. enthused. 'You look so handsome. *Whaat* a pleasure!'

'Evening, Mrs. Guest. Two of Mr. Truman's bouncers called in sick, so me and Carmine said we'd step in.' He shrugged, sheepish; far from the bully required for the gig.

'Somehow I think you'd be better at dancing than bouncing.' She bestowed a friendly peck on his cheek, which caused said cheek to color. Out of habit, Sidney opened the door for the Guests, who continued into the ballroom.

C.Z. caught her breath as they entered the space. A dazzling blur of motion. Monochrome images—some static, others a ghostly blur, moving too fast for retinal capture. Too spry for shutter speed and aperture. As her eyes adjusted, flashes of color emerged, all the more vivid for their sparseness: scarlet waiters' coats like the whirl of matadors' muletas. The gold decorative reliefs flecking columns and ceilings, the swags of damask curtain. The jade of the vines coiled like rattlers through the candelabras. It was, she thought, the vision of a writer.

As they waited in the reception line, she could hear him up ahead, that pipsqueak squeal, greeting each guest—'*Well, welcome*, sugar! Thank you *so much* for coming! Have you met my *dear* friend Mrs. Katherine Graham? Now *Kay*-Kay, this is so-and-so . . .'

Duchin's band was in full glorious swing, the dance floor beginning to fill. Homages to luminaries who peopled the room inspired the orchestra's set, as was the custom with such an elite roll-call of guests. They riffed on *Camelot* tunes—which might have been a nod to lyricist Alan Lerner, or for the Kennedy faction; *My Fair Lady*—again for Lerner, or Cecil Beaton, whose Ascot designs had been Truman's inspiration for the evening's theme. The band launched into an upbeat rendition of 'On the Street Where You Live' as the receiving line inched toward their host.

C.Z. found herself recalling a night decades earlier, when a strange-looking boy approached her at the theater bar during the interval on opening night of that very play, minutes after that tune was played. How she'd regarded him with indifference and he'd made up his mind to woo her. The couple ahead moved along and C.Z. stepped into Truman's eyeline . . . Both smiled. No need for words.

'*People stop and stare, they don't bother me . . .*' Truman took her hands and crooned.

'*For there's nowhere else on earth that I would rahhhther be . . .*' C.Z., finishing the lyric, endearingly flat.

'My cool vanilla lady.'

'It's *gorgeous*, Truman.'

'You're a vision. A beeeeautiful flower, like I've always said.'

'You look pretty dahhhn handsome yourself.'

'Aw, shucks,' he beamed.

'Listen—you've gahtta promise me something, *Mistah* Capote . . .'

'What's that, Sis?'

'You *enjoy* this. Every lahst second.'

'Oh, I am, Sissy! *Trust* me.' He grinned.

She leaned in close, brushing his cheek, whispering in his ear—
'There has *nevah* been another party like this and there *nevah*
will be again.'

She winked at him, and he at her before the Guests moved on,
admiring Kay in her Balmain, then advancing into the space.
Corps of waiters circled with coupes of champagne, but they made
a beeline for the *bahhr*, where C.Z. had suggested to Truman
weeks before that he might extend his monochrome palette, by
serving martinis with white cocktail onions and *blahck* olives
rahhther than green. As they watched them being shaken with
factory-line efficiency, C.Z. heard a familiar voice at her elbow—

'Well, well. If it isn't Lucy Cochrane.'

She smelled the cigar before she turned. Recognized the subtle lisp. She had a vision in her mind of a slim man with sandy hair,
rabbit teeth when he smiled.

'Darryl . . .' She pivoted to face him. The only bit that remained
of the man she once knew was the absurd set of gnashers, hidden
beneath the hood of his lip. The hair on his head was white, thinning, and seemed to have migrated to his brows and mustache,
which were twice as thick as they once had been. Gray-tinted
glasses obscured his eyes. She embraced him.

He looked beyond her to Winston. 'This the fella who ruined
your career?'

'I never *had* a career.'

'It was only a matter of time, Lucy. Matter of time.' He extin-
guished his cigar and extended his hand to Winston. 'Zanuck.
Pleasure's all mine.'

Winston gave his hand a firm shake. 'Lucy's told me all about you.'

Zanuck looked surprised. 'I thought everyone now called you
B.C. or A.D. or something ludicrous. I'm pleased to hear that Mr.
Guest uses your given name.'

'He's a keepah.'

Darryl smiled. Duchin's band launched into a gentle swing.
'Give an old man a dance?' Zanuck offered his hand, pudgier than
the last time she'd taken it.

She took a sip of her martini, leaving it in the care of Winston. She followed Darryl onto the floor, foxtrot in progress.

'So. Mr. Zanuck.'

'Miss Cochrane.'

'Mrs. *Guest.*'

'You know I've never forgiven you.'

'For what?'

'For leaving before I made you a star.'

'I think you did just fine,' she laughed.

She followed Zanuck's gaze to the iridescent mass of balloons Truman had hung amidst the Baccarat chandeliers.

'It isn't the Rainbow Room,' Zanuck said.

'No,' she agreed. 'But it's something else.'

He studied her, bringing a hand to touch one of the fountains of plumes that spouted from her head, recalling their Ziegfeld counterparts.

'Third blonde from the left. That's what you told me.' They shared a quiet chuckle. 'You haven't changed a jot, lovely Lucy Cochrane.' She didn't bother to mention that *he* had. 'Have you been happy?'

She looked over his shoulder, and in one panoramic sweep spotted Tallulah Bankhead, Betty Bacall, Henry Fonda—and a dozen showfolk who had spent their lives doggedly chasing the tail of that pursuit. Then her eyes landed on Winston at the bar, faithfully guarding her drink. So stable. So secure. Her eyes found Zanuck's through the charcoal shades.

'*Very* happy.'

He smiled. 'Good for you, Lucy Guest.'

As the song neared its crescendo, Zanuck—in a display of the grace of which he was capable—whirled C.Z. back to the bar to rejoin Winston, who handed her her glass. Beside him, Jason Robards, ordering a double Scotch, Betty and Slim and Jerry Robbins.

'Betty,' Daryl nodded in Bacall's direction.

'Daryl,' said Betty, detached.

With a last look at C.Z., Zanuck made his exit.

'How was that?' Slim raised a brow to C.Z.

'Just a waltz down memory lane.'

'You do know,' Betty said to C.Z., 'you were about the only one Zanuck never tried to maneuver onto his casting couch . . . ?'

'Maybe that explains why I nevah got any pahrts!'

'And good thing you didn't,' Winston draped a protective arm around her shoulder. 'Now, could a poor old husband get a dance in edgewise?'

'*Dah*-ling,' C.Z. intoned, 'I thought you'd nevah ahsk!'

As they joined the masked throng for the remainder of a rumba, Slim and Betty looked on, sipping their martinis. It *was* extraordinary, Slim thought, as she surveyed the scene, to see just how many bigwigs had gone along with Truman's scheme. The *artists* were one thing—they'd show up for the opening of a bus stop. But to see economists like Ken Galbraith, or newsmen like Ben Bradlee, walking past people like— —

It was then that she spotted them.

Slim nudged Betty. 'Incoming.'

At a distance—Sinatra, black cat mask with whiskers, a waif on his arm with butterfly eyes. Heading for the prime table by the stage, claim staked by the bottle of Jack Daniel's set there by the servers, Frank having a devoted following among the waitstaffs of Manhattan. Mia's *Directoire* gown would send whispers round the room of yet another little Sinatra on the way (false as they turned out), though she looked a child herself; saucer-eyed, as if she'd stumbled out of the sandbox.

Betty lit a cigarette. 'As if *that*'ll last.'

As Slim snickered in agreement, they both saw it.

Him.

A beat after Frank . . . *Leland*. Making his way toward Sinatra's table, led by Pam Churchill— Pam *Hayward*. For that's what she was now, no use in denying it. Slim watched her navigate an enormous ball gown, an antebellum monstrosity, with what seemed enough tulle to smother an army . . . Slim turned back to the bar, pleased for the first time to be wearing that goddamn mask, if only to hide the tears. She shouldn't have come. She'd *thought* she was over the theft, even if she wasn't over Hay.

She felt a tug at her arm. Jerry. 'What is this? A funeral? C'mon, Lady Keith.' Ignoring her protests, he took her hand and dragged her onto the dance floor, holding her in his arms. Lovely Jerry—so powerful, yet full of grace. Jerry, who made anyone he danced with look like a million bucks. In appreciation and homage to the broad-of-all-broads, Duchin segued into Rodgers and Hart's 'The Lady Is a Tramp.' Was that all she was, Slim wondered—one of the boys? Was that why she had lost him in the end? She felt their eyes on her—Pam's. Frank's. *Leland's* eyes. She faltered. As if reading her mind, Jerry spun her in a series of turns, just past the stage, whispering in her ear, 'Don't look at them, look at *me*.' He dipped her low to the floor, suspending her in his sure grasp to applause. As Jerry pulled her back into his arms, he kissed her cheek.

Slim felt herself flush at the attention. 'I think I need some air.'

They made their way toward the door, where Truman and Kay had only just finished greeting their receiving line of guests.

Tru scampered toward Slim, pulling her away. 'Oh Big Mama, isn't it all too *beeautiful*?! Come look at *this*.' He led her into a side atrium, where waiters readied the buffet, delivering trays from the kitchens. One station offered breakfast: eggs, biscuits and Southern gravy. Another, the famed chicken hash, aroma of cognac mingling with the tang of spaghetti and meatballs beside it.

'Steer clear of that sauce.' Babe appeared in the archway, joining them.

'Have you come to have it axed, Babyling, hoping I wouldn't notice?' Truman, feigning vexation.

'Just to make sure they had their best servers on the case. And plenty of soda water, in case of emergencies.'

Tru lovingly fingered the paste jewels extending down the front of her white sheath. 'Weuulll . . . if someone trips and spills tomato sauce down the front of you, we'll simply pretend the stains are extra rubies.' Basking in the warm glow of the candle-light, he launched into a jig. 'Oh, aren't we having a marvelous time? Isn't it just the most *wonderful* party?' As he led them back into the ballroom, meeting and greeting along the way, they passed a unicorn in a tuxedo.

'It's *fabulous*, Truman!' the mythical beast enthused. The unicorn lifted his mask, revealing Billy Baldwin, Babe's decorator.

'Billy!' Tru squealed. 'You've simply *outdone* yourself!'

Ahead, two fur cats approached—one black, one white—masks fully encasing the craniums of a fashionable man and woman. ('The de la Rentas,' Babe informed Slim as she plucked a cham-pagne glass from a passing tray.) A giant swan headdress sailed above the sea of bodies—two eiderdown necks entwined. ('Bill Cunningham's wife,' Slim informed Babe, handing her empty coupe to a waiter.) Mink rabbit ears bobbed by, matching a mink-trimmed gown. ('That darling Candice Bergen,' Tru would later divulge, 'in Marisa Berenson's ears, no less! Marisa missed a fit-ting, so Halston gave 'em away!') He relished such tidbits and doled them out in snippets. Scampering ahead, then darting back now and again, Pan seeking his nymphs.

'Honey!' he'd hiss confidentially. '*That* one in the stripes is the one who threatened to slit her *wrists* if I hadn't allowed her to come!'—then disappear once more.

Babe and Slim watched as Truman grabbed Kay's hand, lead-ing her out onto the floor, where the dancers were ablur with motion. Duchin's band was swinging, he leaning down from his piano on high, chatting with friends as he played. In the low light, beads and baubles glistened like stars, forming restless constella-tions, reordering themselves with each change of partner as the orbit of bodies swayed.

Observing from on high, as if rivaling the gods on Olympus, were those guests quick enough to have nabbed one of the half dozen boxes that lined the side of the room, secure behind ornate railings. Babe was not in the least surprised that the Prime of these had been commandeered by Gianni, Stas, and Bill, serving as a base from which Agnellis, Radziwills, and Paleys might operate.

'Whaddaya say, Slim?' Irving 'Swifty' Lazar approached. 'Fancy a cha-cha?'

As Slim peeled off, taking the floor with Swifty, Babe made her way to the curved box where Bill sat tête-à-tête with Gloria. Even *more* solicitous than usual, Babe reasoned, as poor Gloria had been forced to come alone.

Babe joined them, placing a hand on Bill's shoulder. He patted it, failing to break his conversation with Mrs. Guinness—or his gaze from her slender neck, around which her gemstone necklaces coiled like Cleopatra's asps.

The lone photographer Truman had permitted inside the ballroom approached.

'May I . . . ?' he inquired politely, indicating his camera. As they posed Babe noticed Bill lean toward Gloria a fraction of an inch, rather than back toward her. It was Gloria's arm that wrapped casually around Bill's waist as they posed, while the Paleys' four hands remained visible on the table. Both Gloria and Bill had removed their masks, though Babe's white Aldo remained on, adhering to Truman's edict.

'Darling,' Babe said mid-snap, 'where's your mask?'

'Where's what?' Bill, through a set smile.

'And one more . . .'

'Your mask.' Babe spoke through the second shot as well, prompting the photographer to cut his losses and move on to the Agnellis.

'What about it?'

'We're supposed to wear them until midnight, so that we feel free to *mingle*.'

Gloria shrugged, fingering the necklaces that Bill seemed so beguiled by.

'Mine gave me the most appalling headache.'

Bill—'Mine itched.'

They resumed their conversation.

Babe rose, mask in place, venturing onto the dance floor. Finding the first man she didn't recognize, she tapped him on the shoulder.

'Care to take a turn?' she asked, doe eyes batting from behind the mask slits that had been designed specifically to showcase them.

'You *bet*.' The stranger took one look at the masked Mrs. Paley and abandoned prior pursuits. Babe beamed as they drifted past the ringmaster himself, partnering Princess Radziwill.

'You see, darling,' Truman enthused to Lee, watching Babe, approvingly, 'it's all working out, exactly as I planned. That young man could be anybody! A cat burglar . . . an armed guard . . .' He nodded to Luciana Pignatelli, chatting with Marella to one side of the ballroom. She wore a headdress of plumes as well, but in the center of her lovely forehead, just between her eyes, hung a diamond the size of a golf ball. 'You know that Luciana borrowed that baby from ole Harry Winston, who was delighted to let it out for the night, in hopes of attracting a buyer. Six hundred grand is the word on the street, though *I* suspect ole Harry'll charge more than that!'

The orchestra, in homage to their host, launched into a jaunty swing rendition of 'A Sleepin' Bee' from his Broadway hit *House of Flowers*, the lyrics for which the author had composed. Truman danced around Lee, trying out a few of his old tap steps, drawing the attention of the floor. 'Mr. Truman Capote, ladies and gentlemen,' Duchin announced as the crowd applauded. Truman bowed before pulling Lee back into a jaunty two-step.

'Princess dear, isn't this just the most *sensational* party you've ever been to?'

Lee laughed. 'If you do say so yourself.'

The official photographer moved in close, snapping shots of Lee and Tru dancing. The silver paillette waves of her gown shimmered beneath the lights. The author's tortoise specs barely reaching past her shoulders.

'What was I saying—? Oh *yessss*—so ole Harry agreed to let Luciana borrow their sixty carats as long as she agreed to be escorted by their henchmen, and *I* said it was okay by me, as long as they sent strapping ones and they agreed to wear masks.'

Lee looked to see, swarming around Luciana, in a poor attempt to remain incognito, a trio of men in dominos, the bulge of their handguns evident beneath their rented tuxedo jackets.

One of them caught Lee staring, and at the sight of her seemed to forget his duties altogether, moving closer to watch as she danced with the host.

At midnight dinner was announced and Lee and Tru joined the others at the buffet, where Babe felt a quiet vindication as she watched ladies assiduously avoid the spaghetti. Couples paired off as couples tend to do at dinners where seats have not been assigned.

Standing alone in line for the chicken hash, Gloria heard a droll voice behind her:

'Well, he *almost* managed it.'

She turned to find Jack—Truman's Jack, who was hardly *ever* seen at public affairs. He was wearing a tuxedo (which he'd seldom be caught dead in) that suited his lithe dancer's frame.

'Jack!' Gloria embraced him. 'You clean up well.'

'On the rare occasion.'

As the Plaza chefs spooned out plates of the creamy hash, Jack shook his head. 'Heart attack on a plate that stuff. He'll never listen.'

'You can take the boy out of Monroeville . . .'

'Exactly.'

'Where's "Pa"?' (Truman's nickname for Loel).

She gave a brave smile as they moved, plates in hand, through the anteroom. 'Loel said that masks were childish.'

'Can't say I disagree with him. Truman told me mine was vile.' Jack nodded to his discarded mask, a black strip of fabric peeking from his pocket. She laughed as he tossed the scrap into a palm in passing.

As they reentered the ballroom with their plates, Jack turned to Gloria—'Would you do me the honor of acting as my dinner partner? Appears *mine's* a bit preoccupied.' He nodded to Truman, bouncing between tables, too excited to sit.

Gloria beamed, delighted with her dapper plus-one. 'The pleasure, Mr. Dunphy, is mine.'

They chose a table at the back of the room—as far from prime as possible—where they might observe the proceedings with the judgment that bonded them whenever they spent time together, which was infrequent, Jack keeping a rigid schedule, the Guinnesses none at all.

'What did you mean,' Gloria asked, 'when you said he almost managed it?'

'Well, he managed to get the whole damn world here, practically. This "new elite" he's always banging on about, based on merit—on talent, or intellect, or beauty. Point is, he assembles his ideal cast, gets every goddamn one to wear a mask, anxious to see what they'll *do* when they meet, hoping to shake 'em into the ideal social cocktail . . . and look what happens.'

Jack grinned as Gloria surveyed the room, spotting precisely what he knew she would. Tables self-divided by interest, class, or creed. Entertainers with entertainers. Politicians with politicians. Artists with artists. Intellectuals with intellectuals. The actors mixed between stage and screen, the writers fiction and non, but that was as far as it went. The society folk sat apart—dividing and subdividing within, the nomads apart from domestic, and even within that, dividing by region. The Italians stuck together, though Marella and Gianni crossed camps with the New Yorkers and the Swiss. Even the Kansans had a table apart, an elite within an elite for having double status as the products of Truman's fiction. Gloria and Jack exchanged a glance and burst out laughing.

'I've never seen such shameless ghettoizing in all my life!'

'Yes,' Gloria agreed. 'But they have one thing in common, these disparate souls . . .'

Jack smiled, his love greater than his cynicism. 'Truman.'

She nodded, feeling it herself. 'He is quite something.'

'That he is.'

'*Un verdadero original.*'

'I dare say there's never been anyone like him.'

'And never shall be again.'

They sat for a long moment, watching Truman flit between tables, causing even the most resistant of revelers to melt. Basking at their moment in the warmth of his gaze.

'Mrs. Guinness,' Jack rose, 'would you care to cut a rug?'

'I thought you'd never ask.' Gloria grinned. 'We were both, in other lifetimes, professionals, were we not?'

By the time the former taxi and ballet dancers made their way to the floor, Duchin's orchestra had finished their first set of standards and been replaced by Benny Gordon and the Soul Brothers, who from the get-go served their function—providing a 'dirtier funk.' As Tru and Slim had anticipated, the energy shifted, and within a song or two the Brothers of Detroit had Manhattan's elite twisting and frugging away.

Gloria and Jack Shook a Tail Feather, Jack unleashing with an abandon seldom seen in him. (He would later reveal this was the last night he ever danced, rendering the occasion all the more preserved in memory.) Gloria was delighted, not having danced with such *pasión* since a past she'd long erased from record. She shouted over the brass and pounding beats and primal shrieks of Benny Gordon, 'Jack, you really do know how to *move!*'

Truman and Lee Frugged. And Slim and Betty Frugged, sharing Jerry Robbins, who proved a match for even Jack. Lee Frugged so vigorously, her dress shed its silver paillettes, sending them scattering across the smooth parquet floor. Gloria Frugged until the weight of the twin chokers on her fragile neck induced the most dreadful of migraines.

When Benny and the Brothers played the 'Camel Walk,' a downright filthy shuffle, they urged the tony crowd to reject the tame twist: '*Put your hands on yo knees, get a hump in yo back and do the walk, the Camel Walk . . .*' The sight of Mrs. Paley bent low and hunched, revealing the subtle slit that had been creeping up her thigh all evening—not mere beauty, but carnality—caused Benny Gordon to stop singing altogether and stare at Babe with awe. 'WOW. Yeeeessss, *ssssirrr*. That is one *fine* lady.' Emboldened by the flattery, Babe Camel Walked with Jack and Tru and her handsome stranger, who, mask removed at midnight, was revealed to be an editor at Random House, barely out of college. When the Soul Brothers finished their set, they all bowed with reverence to their muse, one Barbara Paley.

Babe walked back across the ballroom, flushed. Tousled. Eschewing the Prime Paley balcony, she took a cool coupe of champagne from a passing tray and wandered out toward the mezzanine.

It was there, alone, that she marveled in what had just transpired. She, Barbara Paley, had been considered *desirable*. Not beautiful. Not stylish. Something else . . . Something deliciously base. The eyes that had fixed their gaze on her were ones that craved. Coveted. The stuff of thirst and need and breathlessness, not tepid *admiration*.

It was then that she sensed someone approach from behind.

Reaching for her.

It would have to be a stranger. Someone who didn't know her, who didn't box and label her. It would *have* to be . . .

But then, she knew his hands.

It was how he *used* to reach for her—before he had stopped without warning.

The hands gripped her shoulders and turned her. She started to speak, but the lips stopped hers. Biting, eager—teeth sinking into flesh. He grasped her waist roughly, crushing the white camel hair of her dress. Her eyes met his, seeing the hunger he'd long ceased to feel for her. A look reserved for his whores.

'Bill . . .'

'Don't talk.'

Again his mouth stopped hers, drinking her breath, as he reached low, slipping his hand into the slit in her dress, running a greedy hand up the length of her thigh.

EXITING THE POWDER ROOM, Marella, accompanied by Luciana Pig-natelli (followed by her armed guards from Harry Winston, who barely stopped short of trailing her into the Ladies) *thought* that she spotted shadows in the recess of the mezzanine . . . though it could simply have been a trick of the light.

The light in the old hotel was dim—dingy, Marella thought. It seemed the kind of place that spirits lurked in corners. She felt guilty to admit it, but she frankly did not grasp the allure of the venue. Used to balls in actual *palaces*, this Plaza of Truman's seemed quaint at best. And placing balloons beside Baccarat? Was it a child's birthday? She loved her Vero, however, and was pleased that this made him happy.

They returned to the Agnelli table to find Gianni and his cadre of *amici* had grown restless. 'Can we not find somewhere that's open to eat properly? And get a game of cards in?' There were debates as they struggled to come up with a venue in Manhattan that would suit their needs. They could think of a dozen in Rome; still more on the Riviera. Princess Luciana was delighted to move on as well, having exhausted Truman's venue in her quest for available men and grown tired of her wardens.

Gianni turned to Marella. '*Angelo*, are you coming, or would you prefer to stay with Lee and Babe and Gloria? I appreciate you might not want to upset your *Piccolo Vero*.'

Marella wanted to ask him to stay, not lose him to a card game. Instead she smiled and said, '*Amore mio*, we haven't danced all evening. Will you dance with me before you go?'

His weathered face softened. 'Of course, *angelo*.' He reached for her hand and led her onto the floor, where Duchin had cooled things down after Benny, providing the contrast Truman and Slim had so carefully planned. The band was playing a slow, sultry ren-dition of Lerner and Loewe's 'If Ever I Would Leave You.' That dreadful *Camelot*, Marella thought, relieved at least that *Jacque-line* had declined Truman's invitation.

Gianni enveloped her in his arms and slowed his pace for her. The restlessness on display moments earlier seemed to be replaced by a tempered calm. She placed a hand over his heart, as she had done before. She looked up at him; he smiled.

'What is it, *angelo*?'

'Your heart.'

'What about it . . . ?'

'It is so beautifully still.'

'*You* make it so.'

She closed her eyes and leaned into him. Truman's simple Plaza seemed, on second thought, the most magnificent of palaces.

'Gio-*vanni* . . . !' a voice cawed, interrupting the moment. Clipped English consonants. Open vowels. Marella opened her eyes to find that Churchill woman, in her ridiculous bell-shaped gown. Part hideous crow, part Victorian matron in mourning.

'Hello, Pamela,' Gianni said genially.

'Giovanni Agnelli. It's been ages—simply *ages*. Hello, Marina!'

Marella nodded, not bothering to correct her.

'Would you mind terribly if I cut in . . . ? Dear Leland wants to leave soon, our whole party actually. And I *did* so want to sneak a quick turn around the floor with an old friend.'

Marella stepped aside, graciously yielding her partner.

'Thank you, dear,' said Pam, upper lip snagging the cuspid. 'I'm sure I'd do the same for you.' As she stepped forward, expectantly, Gianni reached for Marella's hand, pulling her back to his side.

In his pleasing baritone he said, 'I am sorry, Pamela. But I am dancing with my wife.' Perfectly genial. Perfectly polite. So polite, it took a moment for Pam to fully comprehend. She flashed that English-rose smile, gave the tiniest nod of concession, and retreated to her table.

Gianni offered his arms to Marella once more. She stepped in, allowing them to envelop her like wings. He held her gaze and repeated, 'I am dancing with my *wife*.'

Marella rested her head on his chest, against his even heart.

It wasn't 'I love you,' but it was close.

SHE LEFT WITH GIANNI AND THE ITALIAN *AMICI*, but not before Harry Winston's security guards followed them into the corridor and removed the sixty-carat diamond from Luciana's forehead. It was boxed in a velvet casket, then placed in a locked briefcase and carried out of the Plaza and into an armored van by two of the hired guards.

Lee followed them as far as the staircase, making arrangements with Marella for lunch the following day. She waved, then turned back toward the ballroom. Though she'd claim otherwise, she wasn't entirely surprised to find the Harry Winston guard who had been staring at her all evening standing in her path, awaiting her return.

She walked up to him, expressionless.

He studied her through his black domino.

'I'm Lee,' she finally said, but sensed that was a detail that didn't really matter.

She held his gaze as she slid past him. An invitation of sorts. He followed her onto the parquet floor, where they danced in charged silence for the rest of the evening.

At our various luncheons the following week Truman would enthuse:

'Listen, I have it on good *authority* that that Harry Winston watchman was *fou amoureux* with the Princess Radziwill. Poor man simply couldn't take his *eyes* off her. It's a good thing for his two *amigos*, or Luciana woulda absconded with that diamond like a *bandita* in the night!' We'd unearth other unexpected treasures in those lunchtime post-mortems that next week and long after. Yet several stories down the line, Truman couldn't help but return to the topic of Lee, made all the more poignant when we learned she'd left Stas, and hindsight turned to speculation. 'You know,' Tru would lean in confidentially at table after table, 'Lee never uttered a peep, but *I* reckon that was the moment she knew that she'd move on from poor ole Stas. Oh, it wasn't about the watchman per se. It was about something she realized that she was missing and needed. Maybe that's when it hit her that in marrying Stas she'd married a version of her daddy.'

Apart from Lee and her watchman, another couple embodied the promise of Truman's social experiment. Tru felt particularly vindicated that this involved his precious Kay-Kay, who confided in him that the most memorable dance partner of her evening came late in the game. It wasn't George Plimpton or William Styron or Arthur Schlesinger Jr. Not Cecil Beaton or Andy Warhol or surly Norman Mailer, picking fights in his rumpled raincoat.

It was Truman's UN Plaza doorman, Sidney. He had worked up the courage to ask Kay for a dance, which was so pleasant it turned into three. When they parted, Sidney kissed Kay's hand, like he had seen gentlemen do in the pictures, and said with utmost sincerity—

'Thank you, Mrs. Graham, for the best night of my life.'

Kay would later report to Tru that she was deeply moved.

IT WAS TOWARD THE END OF THE EVENING that Truman spotted a woman loitering outside the ballroom, peering in. Plain black street dress. Mousy.

Something about her reminded him of a copyboy from long ago who'd indulged in stolen lunches downstairs in the Oak Bar. Who'd crept up to the sacred space, peered inside, and seen phantasmagorias within. How he would have loved for someone to have been kind to him. To have invited him in . . .

He approached her and smiled.

'Good evening,' he said.

'Good evening.'

'Are you lost, sugar? Can I help?'

The woman looked embarrassed. 'I—I'm so sorry. I just read all about it, you see. And I did so much want to see what it looked like.' She could be his Mama, in her Lillie Mae days.

'Well, come right on in. Would you like a glass of champagne?'

Her plain face brightened. 'Oh yes. Yes, please.'

Truman took her hand and led her into the ballroom. He watched with pleasure as her eyes widened, taking in the scene. *His* creation. A galaxy of supernovae, blinding in their brightness. Beauty and light. His own tiny universe.

He motioned a waiter, who swooped in with a silver tray of crystal champagne coupes.

'It's Taittinger,' Truman said proudly, handing her a glass. 'Four hundred bottles. And I designed these glasses myself.'

The woman nodded, accepting the coupe, from which she took a long sip.

Then, without warning, she threw the rest of its contents in Truman's face. As if something snapped and the lost lamb bared wolfish fangs—'How *dare* you?'

Truman stared at her, stunned. 'But—'

'Four hundred bottles of *champagne*?! You and your rich friends and your excess! What about the hundreds of men who'll come home in a body bag or missing a limb? What about the victims of the bombings in Cambodia? The napalm strikes? Innocent children burning alive? Or the hundreds of homeless just outside those doors? You should be ashamed!'

Truman listened to her diatribe, his face graying. He felt a hand grip his arm protectively, and turned to see C.Z., Sidney the doorman-turned-bouncer at her side.

'Sidney,' she said pointedly, in her stern drawl, 'I believe this young lady has lost her way? Do be a dahhhling and take her for a spin . . . just out those doors and right down the stairs.'

'It's *you* who's lost the way. You're like horrid aristocrats—ripe for the guillotine. And trust me, sister, the revolution is coming.'

C.Z. yawned. 'Oh, I'm sure you're right, dear. But it's not coming tonight before dawn. Ahhfter all, there's a time and place for everything.' And with that she pulled Truman from the wreckage, marched him across the room to a table, where she sat him down and tenderly dried his face with a dinner napkin. Tears streamed down his wide, flushed cheeks.

'Now, Truman. I *cahn't* dry your face if you're just gonna wet it all over again.'

'Oh, Sissy. Am I a terrible person? Have I done something bad?'

'That's not even worthy of an answer.'

'I just wanted to throw a party—was that so wrong?'

C.Z. rose abruptly. 'Get up.'

'No, Sissy. It's ruined.'

'Truman Streckfus Persons Capote. You get your ahhhsss outta that chair and dance with me this instant.' Her tone was so tough he could do nothing but comply. She led him to the dance floor, holding him in her forceful grip.

'Now you listen to me, bustah,' she said as they moved in triple time. '*Nothing* is ruined. Look *around* you. Look at what you've created! All these people . . . The best and brightest of the gahddamn *century*, all here for you!'

'For Kay . . .' he said sheepishly.

'Truman. We're all here for *you*. Because of what you wrote. Because of who you *ahhrre*. You've thrown the best gahddamn pahty anyone has ever seen. An act of creation, like a book or a play or a painting. We're all here because we love you. You, bustah, have *arrived*.'

He looked at her, his little heart nearly bursting with joy. 'Do you really think so, Sis?'

'I know so. And besides,' she grinned, 'you're a gahddamn genius.'

Slim sailed by in Jerry's arms, beaming at her Truheart in passing. Between Jerry's footwork and Tru's champagne, Slim felt as if she were floating; as if the iridescent balloons hanging from the chandeliers had traded places with the floor. She scanned the space, looking for the person she'd most like to share the feeling with. The person she had shared her whole adult life with, identity and all. The person she'd given up so much to resurrect, knowing in her bones that Betty would gladly have done the same for her. She spotted her at a table, alone, Robards having gotten rat-assed enough to have taken a taxi home. Slim suspected she'd only married him to bandage her pride *après* Frank. She was and would always be Mrs. Bogart.

'Jerry . . .' Slim said. 'There's a dame over there who could use a spin with a maestro such as yourself, and not mangle your toes like me . . .' Jerry followed Slim's gaze and gave a conspiratorial wink. In a fluid motion he spun Slim toward Betty's table, exchanging one man's broad for another. Betty looked surprised, but pleased. Slim took her cigarette, smiling. 'Floor's yours. Knock 'em dead, kid.'

From his perch at the piano Duchin spotted Jerry leading Betty onto the floor. A showman in his bones, he knew a 'moment' when he saw it. He stopped the orchestra mid-tune, in order to draw attention to Robbins and Bacall. A few oblivious couples continued dancing as the band struck up the opening phrases of Irving Berlin's 'Top Hat, White Tie and Tails,' but most parted like the Red Sea. Betty and Jerry glided across the floor improvising what seemed the most carefully choreographed of routines. Like the lyric said—they simply *reeked* class.

This is what Slim had wanted for Betty that long-ago summer in Spain. The sheer joy she'd seen in Betty's eyes whenever she looked at Bogart. Life itself! Beauty so profound one hardly dared breathe in its presence.

Lee had pulled Mr. Harry Winston aside to watch with a girlish grin that seldom broke through all that coolness. Gloria forgot the stabbing of the migraine in her eye—healed for the length of the song. Truman squeezed C.Z.'s hand with elation. 'Oh, Sis . . .' he breathed. 'No one could ever forget *this* . . . !' Babe, still fumbling in the dark recesses of an alcove in the mezzanine, would later be told that it was a vision to behold.

When the song drew to its conclusion, the Grand Ballroom of the Plaza burst into rapturous applause. Duchin—knowing to alter the pace in order to spare Bacall and Robbins the tedium of endless encores—struck up the simplest of shuffles and the floor filled again. Betty and Jerry continued to dance, laughing and chatting.

Slim smiled, satisfied. She turned to head for the bar, bumping smack into . . .

'Hiya, Nan.'

Leland. Her Leland. Looking as sharp in a tux as he always had. God. He still had the power to take her breath away.

'Hiya, Hay,' Slim replied, hoping he couldn't see the color rising in her cheeks. What was she, twelve? She'd been married to the man for a decade, for Chrissakes!

'Too bad we didn't spot that chemistry years ago.' He nodded to Jerry and Betty on the floor. 'We coulda made a killing.'

They smiled, taking a moment to ponder all those productions that never were. Then they looked at each other and laughed. Nerves palpable, yet something else . . . *Relief*. Relief to be in one another's company, if only for a moment, if only in passing.

'How are you?' she asked.

'Not terrible. You?'

'Same.'

'So. Two old-timers who aren't terrible.'

She forced a smile. 'Not bad, considering.'

He smiled back. She studied the terrain of lines on his face, the ones she remembered having deepened, new lines shooting off them like unknown tributaries.

'So, listen, Nan . . .' He paused, scratching the nape of his neck, an old tic she knew well. 'We're about to head off.'

Slim felt her heart sink. 'I see. Well . . . Good to have seen you.'

'Frank wants to swing by Jilly's, you know how it is.' He shifted uncomfortably.

'Yeah. As I say . . .'

Overlapping—'But first I thought—'

'It was good to have—'

'Dammit, Nan,' he said, exasperated. 'I'm *trying* to ask you to dance before we go.' He ran a nervous hand through his silver boyish crew cut. His voice softened. 'Would that be okay?'

Slim smiled. Same old Leland. What a prince.

'Okay.'

They walked out to the floor, where Leland, who had yet to dance all night, naturally took his turn at a Duchin homage. Which'll it be? Slim thought. *South Pacific? The King and I?* On the piano's cue, the orchestra began to play a swing rendition of 'The Sound of Music.'

Slim looked to Leland, shaking her head.

'*Really? That* old can of worms?'

'Of all the goddamn shows . . .' Leland agreed.

Nevertheless, she slipped into his formal dance hold and they began a gentle two-step to the soundtrack that had ended their marriage. By the time the medley had moved on to 'My Favorite Things,' the former Haywards had started to snicker, which—when eyes met—couldn't help but break into full, contagious laughter.

'Stop it!' Slim giggled, unable to look at him. 'Let me breathe!'

'You have to admit it's funny—a bit of black comedy.'

'Well, of course *you* think it's funny,' she said, the old playfulness revived. 'You made a killing in returns!'

'Not fair. I gave you a percentage . . .'

'Hay . . . I think the Reverend Mother made more than me in the end.'

They laughed. He held her wrist tight and pulled her closer. Lips at her ear.

'God, Nan, but I miss this.'

Slim felt her breath catch like a faulty hinge.

'Miss . . . *what*, exactly?'

'You. I miss you.' Simply. Frankly.

She cut her eyes up to his.

He paused for a moment. 'I miss *us*.'

'We were pretty great together, weren't we?' Slim allowed herself. She turned her head so he couldn't see the tears. By the time she looked back she'd managed to stave them off. 'Well.' She tried to sound bright. Sunny. 'Not to be.' What she really felt was a hole in her gut that had never gone away. 'I'm sure you're happy.'

She permitted herself a glance and saw it in his eyes. He was as miserable as she was. He tightened his grip and leaned in to whisper in her ear once more.

'There was only ever you, Nan.' There it was, clean as glass. 'You're the only one.'

'And you for me.' Didn't begin to scratch the surface, but what more could she say? They danced on, as Duchin ended his medley with a waltz of 'Edelweiss' that cut Slim to her very soul. She knew he felt it too, as she'd always known when they were in accord. When she dared to meet his eyes, she saw that *he* was the one on the brink—his eyes, still as blue as a hundred clear skies, clouding with rain.

'Hey. What's with the waterworks?' She permitted herself one brush of his weathered face with her fingertips. He allowed himself to take them in his, looking to the finger that once wore the simple band that he had given her, another man's ring in its place.

He held her hand between them for the last moments of the waltz, in the space between where their hearts should have been.

'Just know that I'll love you till I die, Nancy Hayward.'

'It's Keith now,' she reminded him.

His hand strayed to the small of her back, lingering.

'Not for me it isn't.'

As Leland held her and turned her around the Plaza floor to that last love song they'd shared, Slim knew that husbands may come and go but, like Betty, she was a one-man gal, who would never really be any 'Mrs.' other than Hayward.

OF COURSE IT WASN'T REAL LIFE. Slivers of perfection seldom are.

And naturally it couldn't last. We knew as much at the time. But we never dreamed that the fall would be *quite* so great.

We recognize what easy pickings we were. Ripe for the fantasy that Truman peddled. Even then we knew that our heads could be turned by half-truths and enough booze and the illusion of beauty. We knew on some level that it was a fiction, nothing more. One of Truman's finest. He had gathered us all there—his cast of characters.

Maybe he was right when he insisted time and again that his evening was '*not* about *In Cold Blood*, honey!'

It was of his *future* masterpiece that he was thinking, Marella for one is convinced.

'He called us there that night for a reason,' she's told each of us. 'That guest list we watched him construct—it was nothing more than the cast list for his precious *Answered Prayers*. He was assembling his characters, watching us as we played out our own pathetic little dramas. Gathering plots for his *letteratura del pettegolezzo*, poaching our lives as fiction.'

It is a convincing argument. We find it rather stunning to note how many of us were there that night who ended up in his *Esquire* filth, or were slated for the larger opus.

Some of us have chosen to compartmentalize, seeing this as an evening arranged by a Truman who no longer exists, therefore the memory might remain unsullied.

Because of who Truman *was*, that evening will always be perfect—nothing could hope to rival it. But because of who he *became*, it can never exist again. He has taken it with him, and for that, above all else, we can never fully pardon him.

One cannot forgive the tainting of the sublime.

NINETEEN

1961/1972/1979

LEE

MIDNIGHT RAMBLINGS

I T WAS A MILD SPRING EVENING by most accounts—just between Easter and May Day, when the cherry blossoms were losing their leaves, dusting florets like snowflakes onto the pavement. The political set was aflutter, donning their ball gowns and penguin suits. The gentlemen carried mackintoshes, casually slung over forearms. The ladies favored mink stoles which barely covered their shoulders.

It was the Kennedys' first White House state dinner—the first of forty-three, in their brief three-year residency—given in honor of the First Lady's sister Lee Radziwill née Bouvier and her husband, Prince Stanislas.

Martinis were mixed from a bar erected in the corner of the State Dining Room. Butlers made the rounds, replenishing glasses, perhaps with too much efficiency. By the time dinner commenced Vice President Lyndon Johnson had knocked back three or four bourbons. There were bowls of yellow tulips, flown in from afar, cheerful hue reflecting the glories of spring. Jackie stunned in a boatneck shift, cut to a shallow V in the back, Veronese green in hue. Lee wore ecru crêpe. As the evening's entertainment, Pablo Casals played Bach's Suite No. 3. Jackie's designer, Oleg Cassini, hijacked the HiFi and introduced the Twist, which the White House press secretary later took pains to deny.

It was during the after-dinner dancing that it happened.

Jackie was standing in the Blue Room when Gore Vidal, three sheets to the wind, sidled up for a chat. In a gesture one could construe as familial, he placed his arm around her waist. Before he knew it, RFK was behind him, removing the offending appendage from the First Lady's person. 'That sort of thing doesn't fly around here,' witnesses quote Bobby snapping.

The argument moved into the hall, where the two exchanged words.

'Says who?' Vidal had challenged.

'Says *me*. Get the hell out.'

'Don't offend a writer,' Vidal had hissed at RFK, 'without expecting revenge in print.'

Security then asked Vidal to leave, and from all accounts he departed forthwith, but not before— —

IT WAS A CRISP AUTUMN D.C. EVENING, other attendees will recall. Elm leaves littered the pavement, husks sticking like tissue to shoe soles in the damp.

It was at the young Kennedys' third formal White House dinner—given in honor of Gianni and Marella Agnelli, who'd flown in from Turin.

Negronis flowed from the bar, erected in the State Dining Room. By the time the dinner commenced Lyndon Johnson had knocked back five—or was it six?—bourbons. Fires blazed in every room, despite the mildness of climate. There were dahlias arranged in silver bowls, a blend of dusky hues. Jackie looked exquisite, in a Grecian style gown of palest yellow custard. Lee wore fuchsia silk. A military panorama was staged on the South Lawn, after which the guests returned inside, where Oleg Cassini hijacked the HiFi and introduced the Twist.

It was during the after-dinner dancing that it happened.

Jackie was sitting on a settee in the Red Room when Gore —having plucked half a dozen Negronis from circulating trays— made his woozy approach, stumbling from the intake. He touched her bare shoulder, then knelt down beside her and started to chat—something about her mother, whom he proceeded to disparage, despite having hardly known her. When he tried to stand, he found that he needed to steady himself, and did so by grasping Jackie's shoulder, using it for leverage. Bobby appeared behind him, removing his hand and throwing his balance.

Gore followed him into the hallway, enraged. 'Listen to me, Daddy's Boy, don't ever touch me again!'

Bobby laughed. 'And who are you, pal? Yeah . . . exactly. You're *nobody*.'

'I'm a writer,' witnesses say Gore hissed. 'And let me tell you something . . . we *always* have the last word.' It was then that the Secret Service arrived, politely asking Gore to leave, and so he departed with— —

STILL OTHERS RECALL A SUMMER FÊTE, in the sizzling heat of July, when the thought of wearing a monkey suit held little—if any—appeal for the gents. The ladies worried about their bouffants falling, like a series of soufflés collapsing, and feared the perspiration might seep through their silk, creating unsightly rings.

It was at a state dinner, given for the Radziwills *and* the Agnellis in the third year of Jack's term—though already this doesn't add up, as we know for a fact Gianni and Marella spend their summer months exclusively on board the *Agneta*, cruising the Mediterranean.

Cocktails flowed from the State Dining Room bar—Polynesian Mai Tais, served in enormous tumblers, though Jackie had learned to instruct the staff to tepidly top up glasses. (They were encouraged to be less fastidious in their service to LBJ, who was by the third bourbon knocking back iced tea, unbeknownst to him.) The hearths were dormant, though slender tapers in candelabras replicated their welcoming glow. Birds of paradise provided a tropical feel.

Jackie looked divine in a sheath of Nattier blue, wide obi belt at her waist. Lee wore red brocade. A troupe of players from the American Shakespeare Theater performed various works of the

Bard. Jerry Robbins' company followed with a ballet and Oleg Cassini introduced the Twist.

It was during the after-dinner dancing that it happened.

Jackie was sitting on a chaise in the Green Room when Gore—several tankards of Mai Tais in—kneeled to have a word. Some say he leaned in close and slurred something rude—about Jack or Lee or her mother.

'Gore, I think you should leave,' Jackie said, in her wispy baby voice.

'Fine then,' slurred Gore, who rose to stand, tipsily losing his balance. He flailed to steady himself, grabbing for the first thing in reach—which happened to be the knot of the obi belt at Jackie's waist. As he grasped and pulled, he untied it, marring her perfection.

In an instant, Bobby's hand gripped his shoulder, pulling him off Jackie, snarling—

'Who the fuck do you think you are?'

Gore matched his vitriol, firing back—'Fuck you!'

'Fuck *you*, buddy boy! Get the hell out—and never come back!'

White House Security bundled Gore out, where he then proceeded to— —

TRUMAN—WHO HAD NOT BEEN PRESENT the evening in question—usually went for a hybrid of versions when reveling in the tale. Yet while he relished the narrative options when discussing his foe's disgrace, he defaulted—more often than not—to one take in particular, for it was tailor-made for his pleasure, simply dripping in hyperbole.

As Truman told it, that very night he received a call from his darling Lee, eager to dish the dirt. She naturally would have embellished, knowing that Tru fed off such tales like a happy hobo, starving for such morsels.

'*Truman*,' Lee enthused on the line, as she stepped from her evening dress and poured herself a Scotch, 'you'll never *believe* what *I* just saw at *la Maison Blanche . . .*'

379

IT WAS THUS TRUMAN FOUND HIMSELF in the amber glow of Bemelmans Bar at the Carlyle Hotel, telling that very tale to a Cub reporter from *Playgirl*, second-rate skin rag.

'Weeeelllll, you *seeeeeee*, Gore was drunk as a skunk, *quelle surprise*, at a dinner at the White House no less. Lee was there, so I have this on *very* good authority. Gore went right up to Jackie—in the middle of the East Room—and cupped her ass with his rat-paw. He proceeded to insult her mother, whom he'd never met in his *life*! Well, *Bobby*—who always had a thing for Miss Jacks, sis-in-law or otherwise—simply wasn't having it. He picked li'l Gore up, right off the ground, and carried him to the door, where he hurled him out onto Pennsylvania Avenue!' Tru paused to giggle gleefully. 'Isn't it perfect? Poor little Vidal—*bodily ejected* from the White House, never to return?!'

He drained his last sip of martini, popping a gin-soaked cocktail onion in his mouth. 'I'm due at Lee's in an hour. You can walk with me if you like.'

The author and the *Playgirl* Cub had stepped from the Carlyle and strolled down the block, the former *en route* to Lee's brownstone for dinner, the latter tagging along.

'Of course Gore-the-Whore came crawling from the woodwork when Jack was elected President, when their status suited his purposes. He was invited to the White House just once— and was never invited back. Even that, methinks, was generous, given all the smack he's talked about La famille Kennedy . . .'

As they approached Lee's building on the quieter reaches of upper Fifth, the Cub ventured, 'But you began as friends, when you were young, didn't you? You and Gore . . . ?'

Truman looked out onto the leaves of Central Park, taken with their beauty, shimmering like flames, lapping at the branches. It was in such moments that he most loved New York. When he tended to wax nostalgic. In a flash he remembered his youth, when he'd first encountered Vidal. Two young bucks, staking their claims in the Oak Bar at the Plaza. A shared coterie in Venice, not big enough for the both of them. Vying to see who might emerge as leader of the literary pack.

As the cool breeze ruffled Truman's remaining wisps of hair, he shook his head.

'Gore was always harder than me. He'd do anything to claw his way to the top. He'd sell his own mother to the wolves—not that that's saying much. Both of our mamas were drunks. In fact that's the only thing we ever had in common . . . He'd sacrifice anyone to get where he was going. I value the *people* in my life.' And with a tiny shudder at a gust of wind, Truman crossed the street and waved, trotting toward Lee's building.

Little did Truman realize that running his mouth to Mr. *Playgirl* would unleash the wrath of Vidal and his lawyers. Little did we know mere days later—in that fall of '75—that Tru's *Esquire* smut was about to hit the stands; that he was about to betray our trust. Less still could Truman know what Lee had in store for him . . . She who would, in time, give the little traitor a taste of his own medicine, though whether administered with intent, or by accidental overdose, is difficult to discern.

LEE SAT IN A SEA OF PACKING BOXES, the fragments of her life scattered chaotically around her. A cool ripple of velvet draped the walls; the cerulean carnival tent atop which hung the prized work in the Radziwill collection: Francis Bacon's *Man in a Cage*. Stas had bought the painting for next to nothing, to cover the painter's gambling debts. He had given it to Lee when she left him, as generous in defeat as he had been when he'd won her. It had been five years since she'd left Stas, after fifteen years of marriage. A midlife crisis, she supposed it could be chalked up to, though at the time it felt like more. Even the illusion of wealth her dear Stas had provided was revealed, upon his death, to be exactly that. Illusion.

Lee looked to the sparse, modernist figure, trapped in a reflective space within the painting, and felt a certain kinship with him.

She too felt trapped—by increasingly limited options. She thought of Stas as she looked at *Man in a Cage*.

It would have to go of course. She needed the cash that the Bacon could yield—if only she could manage to unload it for the right price . . . Whatever it would take to keep her world afloat, for years now adrift on seas of uncertainty.

'LEE RADZIWILL DESIGNS,' a voice on the line.

'Any calls, Sally?'

'Oh hello, Ms. Radziwill. Yes—Mr. Vidal's lawyer regarding the deposition.'

Lee sighed heavily. Fucking Gore. She'd always *loathed* the little creep, the little that she knew of him, he being related only distantly through their mother's second marriage. She and Jackie had long ago agreed that Gore was bad news—a climber. A snob. A pseudo-intellectual. The single most sinister man she knew.

'And there were thirteen calls from Mr. Capote. He left messages. Would you like them?'

Christ, Truman.

'No.' Lee allowed herself a pause. 'Thanks, Sally. I'll be in tomorrow. Please book lunch at Vadis for noon.'

'Very good, Ms. Radziwill.'

Lee hung up, and fingered a tortoise card case from her collection on the desk. She'd given one to Tru years ago—the most prized in the bunch, a Victorian gem that might or might not have belonged to Oscar Wilde, according to her dealer. She'd had it inscribed, *To Truman—My Answered Prayer.* His eyes had welled with tears and he had held it to his cheek.

'Oh Princess dear, this means more than you could ever hope to know . . .'

Goddamn Truman! How dare he get her involved in his mess! If he wanted to run his mouth and fuck his *own* life, so be it.

But, as Jackie had reminded her, she simply couldn't *afford* to get involved.

TRUMAN—IN HIS OWN ODD WAY—had been in love with Lee from the start.

'Oh, the Princess Radziwill,' he'd gush to anyone who'd listen, 'she's the most feminine creature you'll ever meet—yet she's lithe and tough like a young *garçon*. There's nothing the Princess cannot do. She can act. She can write. She's just so terribly *gifted*!'

If only he'd kept his little trap shut, Lee often thought.

'Darling, we can make you *worlds* bigger than Jackie . . . We'll make you an actress! The greatest star the world has ever seen . . .'

Hadn't he been the one who insisted she was a genius, pushing her toward Everest leaps, when she would have been happy with baby steps? He'd forced her to the precipice long before she was ready. Just because *he* was a prodigy . . . or so the little shit *said*. He had doomed her to fail before she began.

He had not, of late, been the Truman she once knew.

He'd arrive at her house, clutching his black doctor's satchel. He'd sit down to dine, remove a handful of pills at random, organizing them around his plate according to hue, a circular narcotic palette. He'd then proceed to swallow them, one by one. Sometimes he'd move from light to dark ('like retreating into a cozy cave'), other times from dark to light ('like basking in the sun'). Sometimes he'd recline on the sofa, lining the pills on the island of his belly, as if traveling up the slope, reaching a peak at his navel, and back down the other side. Lee would observe as the children watched Truman with fixed, frightened eyes.

She missed who he had once been. She could have used a dose of the Truman who'd arrive for a lunch date breathless with some scheme or another to make her very fortune—to etch her name in the heavens.

Lee had always sensed she was a special soul—an artist—ever since childhood.

Truman had spotted it straight away. He who *knew* talent saw the glimmer of it in her, and did all that he could to nurture it.

When he decided she'd be perfect to play the Kate Hepburn role in *The Philadelphia Story* and arranged a production in Chicago, who was Lee to argue? He sat in the darkened theater through each rehearsal, when everyone around them said he should have been writing his next masterpiece. '*Lee's* my next masterpiece,' she'd overheard him saying, and when he clapped enthusiastically from the shadows of the empty house, '*Yeeeeeeeeesss*, Lee! But that's marrrrrrrrvelous, darling!' she believed him. Of course when the audience came to see 'Lee Bouvier' (as she insisted she be billed) in her Saint Laurent costumes, with her lion's mane by Kenneth, they weren't coming to see her acting. They were coming to see Princess Radziwill: Jackie Kennedy's kid sister. No matter. The houses sold out, didn't they? When her cast-mates rolled their eyes (they *thought* behind her back . . .) and mocked her Miss Porter's prep school accent, she took comfort in Truman's reassurance, 'Honey, whaddaya want? They're jealous of your fame!'

When the critics cruelly declared after opening night: LEE LAYS A GOLDEN EGG and A STAR IS NOT BORN, Truman lovingly convinced her that they'd made up their minds ahead of time. 'Why Princess dear, they wrote those *weeks* ago—before you'd even started rehearsals!' When Jackie managed to be 'out of town' (for the entirety of the run), Truman pointed out, 'She simply can't *stand* you having the spotlight!'

When he'd used his notoriety to get her a TV gig, adapting the classic film *Laura* for the small screen for Lee to play the eponymous role, he'd convinced her that acting for the *camera* was her birthright. On the night that *Laura* aired he begged Carson to host a viewing party at his UN Plaza penthouse, just a few floors up from his own. Johnny's wife Joanne—so desperate to impress—planned a spread fit for a conquering army. Caviar and blinis and champagne on ice. Finest Russian vodka and a cake made in Lee's image. TVs were set in every corner of the space, three to a room, all tuned to CBS, primed for Lee's triumph. After a gushing speech by Truman, the guests raised their glasses, and settled in to watch. It took a scene or two to spot . . . Gene Tierney, Lee was not.

One by one, first in quiet singles and pairs, then in a thin trickle, guests rose to tiptoe out to balconies for cigarettes, leaving Tru, Lee, and Joanne Carson to watch the disaster in silence.

Lee knew that Truman defended her, like he always had. *Someone* had to believe in Lee. And wasn't it flattering that the genius of his generation was her champion . . . ? God love Truman. And then goddamn him! She'd trusted him so, she would have followed him to the ends of the earth. Why did he have to change? Why did he have to become what he had? A ghoul. A bore. Transformed into a grotesquerie of all she once had loved about him. The imp had turned twisted goblin, with a dark shade around him that left her feeling queasy.

SHE FIRST CAUGHT GLIMPSES OF IT during what should have been a purely rapturous summer.

It was when Lee was hot and heavy with the photographer Peter Beard. Beard had been commissioned by *Rolling Stone* magazine to travel with The Rolling Stones on their 1972 *Exile on Main St.* tour and document it all. Truman had been enlisted to write about it in a long-form piece of music journalism, tentatively titled 'It Will Soon Be Here.' The phrase he took from a painting he had seen. A stark American gothic. A group of farmers, shoveling bales of hay, oblivious as a storm cloud approaches. ('It's a perfect metaphor,' Truman had pitched Jann Wenner. Heady stuff for rock and roll, Lee thought.) Because her two 'boyfriends' were covering the gigs, the newly divorced Princess Radziwill was invited along. The trio was to travel with the Stones on board their plane, stay in their hotels. Live alongside them, in order to capture the madness.

For Lee, after the formal courts of Camelot and European royalty, it was like running away with the circus. The Stones liked her—she was pretty and thin and kept to herself. They bestowed upon her the affectionate nickname of 'Radish.'

It was the chimera of the era—to go on tour with the band. The plane was packed with champagne and cocaine. With girls who serviced the group in a private, fur-strewn compartment, while the entourage pretended to be too jaded to notice. Everyone vaguely involved was in on the action, from the roadies to electricians to bespectacled PR men.

'It's such an *obvious* orgy,' Tru would grumble to Lee, 'it's practically *puritan* in its prescriptiveness. Yawn-Mc*Yawn*. Where's the *mystery*, for Chrissakes?'

There was a private physician who hailed from San Francisco, a poor man's Timothy Leary, who served up a smörgåsbord of pills of every color and size—'from Vitamin A to Sedative Z'—passing them through the cabin on a tray on each flight, as if distributing hors d'oeuvres. At first this delighted Truman, though the relentless regularity soon diminished the pleasure. Like the sex, Dr. Feelgood's offerings felt so *inevitable*, so paint-by-numbers, Tru felt they robbed the aficionado of his artistry.

What he *did* enjoy was the Stones' cocktail of choice, the unofficial beverage of the tour—the Tequila Sunrise, which they'd recently discovered in a bar in Sausalito. A three-toned delight of tequila, OJ, and grenadine, Truman loved that it mimicked a landscape—a wildly romantic take on his standard Orange Drink.

During the nightly performances, Lee and Truman would stand backstage in their matching shades, she in a tank top and bell-bottomed jeans, or a white jumpsuit, not unlike Mick Jagger's own. Tru in flagrantly preppy attire, often pastel polo shirts paired with a wide-brimmed fedora. At first, Lee observed, Truman relished the energy of it all. After a few weeks, however, she saw his interest wane. It gradually became apparent that he hadn't written a syllable of 'It Will Soon Be Here' and appeared unlikely to do so anytime soon.

Lee followed as Truman grudgingly climbed into the limousine each night, trailing the band to whatever venue was next.

The sameness of it bored him. He began to complain about the noise levels backstage. He would loiter behind the scenes, befriending the stagehands—who he claimed were infinitely more interesting than the band. He took to smoking joints just outside the stage door, talking to the teenage groupies who waited there nightly for a glimpse of their heroes, desperate to be plucked from obscurity. Truman would inevitably sniff out the reporter in the bunch, eager to write a story for her school newspaper. He would get her a pass and give her a backstage tour. 'Unlimited access, honey.' Lee thought it ironic that he seemed more interested in their fledgling pieces than his own for *Rolling Stone*.

The one moment each evening when Truman did perk up was late in the proceedings when Mick would toast the crowd (the same shtick each night), slugging from a bottle of Jack Daniel's (which Truman would mimic with his hip flask), take out his harmonica, and the band would launch into 'Midnight Rambler.' This never failed to excite.

'It's the one thing they do that's unique. The tempo variations. The *narrative*. It's like a mini-opera. Like—dare I say—a *novella*?' Indeed, Mick was playing a character, and it was performance art at its finest. The song was meant to invoke the Boston Strangler. Each night at precisely seven minutes into the song, Jagger would remove the belt from his jumpsuit and drop to the floor, after a series of primal screams against a frenzied, blues-soaked guitar duel; at eight minutes and twenty-three seconds, he would *become* the Strangler DeSalvo, simulating the striking of his victims. The lights would turn the color of blood. When Lee looked to Truman she would find him quite altered, as if in a spell, mirroring Mick's movements. When the tempo built once more, Truman was like a man possessed, launching into a maniacal jig with an intensity that frightened her. Eyes wild, sweat pouring from his forehead, soaking his shirt. Then, as suddenly and intensely as he had engaged, it was as if a switch flipped and Truman's indifference would resume. He'd turn and walk back to an empty dressing room and sit very quiet. Pale. Sometimes nursing his hip flask, as if seeking some elusive drop of succor.

Lee often followed him out of concern. One night when he looked particularly shaken, she slipped into the room and sat down beside him.

'Truman . . . ? Are you all right?'

He met her gaze in the mirror before them. Trembling.

'I don't know . . .'

'What is it? About that song in particular . . .?'

He stared at his reflection, as if searching for something, then cut his eyes back to Lee's.

'Perry.'

'What?'

'Perry Smith. I feel him in that song, every night. It's as if he takes me over, and we become the same. The same soul . . . You see?'

'Yes, Truman. I see.'

And it was then Lee realized that Truman was *not* in fact all right.

THE PHONE IN LEE'S BROWNSTONE BLARED, startling her from reverie.

'Hello? Lee?'

'Speaking . . .'

'It's Liz—Liz Smith.'

Christ. Liz Smith. Gossip columnist, a prolific one, for the *New York Daily News*. A hard-talking, good-natured Texan broad, with a low, guttural voice and a no-bullshit air, which Lee preferred to the more pretentious breed of society columnist. Still, this was the last thing she needed—the goddamn press.

'How can I help you, Liz? I presume this isn't a social call . . .'

'No, it's not. Look, Lee, this is rather awkward . . . I guess I'll just come out and say it. It's about Truman.'

'What about him?'

'It's about this lawsuit. With Gore . . .'

Fucking hell. Not *this* again. That must be what his catalog of calls at the office had been about. Well, she for one was over it. Had been over it for *months*.

'What about it . . . ?'

'Well,' Liz tried again, 'it's just that Gore is suing, you know, Truman for an enormous amount of money—a million, I think it is—for libel, over something *you* told him . . .'

'Allegedly.'

'About Gore being thrown *bodily* from the White House . . . ?'

'Liz, we both know that's ancient history.'

'Of course, but—'

'I frankly don't see what this has to do with me.'

'Well, Truman says that *you* were his source—for the bit about Gore being bodily thrown. That seems to be the operative word here. *Bodily*. The whole case hinges on it.'

Lee sighed. She moved to a sideboard beneath her glorious *Man in a Cage*. Poured herself a Scotch. It was only eleven, but *really*. That she'd have to endure this inquisition—with all that she was grappling with . . . ? Cash-strapped. Husbandless. Soon-to-be-homeless. How dare he . . . Really, how *dare* he . . . ?

'Look, Liz. I don't recall telling Truman any such thing. Besides that, he's unwell. You know it. I know it. It's plain as day to any of us. He's sick and he needs help. I think he's—'

'He recently got out of rehab, and says you won't return his calls.'

'I've had a lot on my plate.'

'Yes, of course. Look, Lee, I know this is damn awkward, but he asked me to call you and see if you'd reconsider testifying on his behalf.'

'And implicate myself, so that bat-shit Gore can come after *me* as well? I'll do no such thing.' She found herself channeling Jackie: 'I simply can't afford it, financially.'

'Yes, I understand. But Truman loves you so, he did seem to hope that you'd stand by him . . . Just to say that the incident happened. To say: "Mr. Capote didn't make it up." One word from you and Gore doesn't have a stub-leg to stand on.'

Lee gulped her Scotch. Took a cigarette from a silver tray on the sideboard. Lit it. She'd been trying to quit of late, but fuck it. She sighed heavily.

'Well, Liz, that's something I just can't do. You might as well know, I've been subpoenaed by Gore's lawyers, which puts me in a very awkward position. Truman's going to have to find out sooner or later—I signed a deposition.'

'For *Gore* . . . ?!'

'For *myself.*' Christ! What was *wrong* with these people?

'What did you tell them?'

'That I don't recall ever discussing the events of the evening in question with the defendant, Truman Capote, and that I, in fact, wasn't present in the room to witness the alleged episode.'

'But Truman says—'

'I don't give two shits what Truman says. I *won't* risk being sued for libel over a spat that has nothing to do with me. Truman and Gore have been at each other's throats since I was in grade school. Why should I get dragged into this?'

She was livid with Truman. Absolutely *livid*. How dare he expect her to risk everything, just because he'd chosen to run his mouth? She wanted Liz off the phone.

'Oh my . . . Lee, Truman *so* adores you, this might just crush him.'

Lee let her anger rip. 'Come on, Liz. This is just too much. I'm done. I'm sick of Truman riding my coattails, little social climber. And really, what does it matter . . . ? They're just a couple of fags.'

BY THE NEXT DAY, THE WORD WAS OUT.

Lee had received multiple calls and been taken aside by several concerned parties at Vadis when she arrived at noon to meet Jackie for lunch. It appeared that all of Manhattan knew that Lee had said something to Liz Smith that was reported back to Truman. The sleeping dwarf had been kicked. Overnight he had vowed revenge, and had apparently booked a spot on *The Stanley Siegel Show* for Monday at 9 a.m.

Her face a veil of serenity, aware that all eyes in the room were upon them, Jackie leaned in close, pretending to sip her aperitif. In a low voice, 'Peaks, whatever did you *say*?'

'Oh God, Jacks. It's about this ludicrous bitch-spat between Truman and Gore. That's all.'

'But you must have said something that riled him specifically.'

'I simply asked Liz what did it matter, they were just a couple of . . .' Lee suddenly heard her own statement through Truman's ears. 'Fags.'

Shit. She watched Jackie's plastic smile waver.

'Jesus, Lee.' Jackie lit a cigarette, taking a painfully casual drag.

'What?! *Everyone* thinks it.'

'Everyone thinks it, but not everyone *says* so to dyke gossip columnists for the *Daily News*. You're no better than *he* is!'

'What does he mean, "revenge"? Typical Truman-threats! What . . . he'll put me in his goddamn opus, which we know he'll never finish? Really, I'm quaking in my boots.'

'You just better hope he hasn't something more *drastic* in mind.'

'Well, he can say what he wants. He'll only be proving my point.'

They continued their lunch, each lost in their own thoughts.

Mercifully, the waiter arrived with another round of Scotch.

LEE HAD PROMISED HERSELF THAT SHE WOULDN'T TUNE IN. That she'd simply refuse to give the little terrorist the power to frighten her. She had a busy day ahead, packing. Calls to realtors. An appointment with Sotheby's about the Bacon. A full day of keeping disaster at bay.

She'd be damned if she'd let Truman and his drama impact her life. She popped a Valium with the dregs of a Scotch, left on the counter the night before. It seemed to calm her, so she added but a splash to her morning coffee, which she otherwise drank black. Two cups in, and Lee found herself in front of the television, tuning into ABC at five minutes to nine.

She had, over the previous two days, received calls from worried allies. Rumor had it that Truman was planning a piece of performance art for Siegel. He was preparing a character he meant to debut, the self-proclaimed 'Southern Fag.' It was in this guise that he planned to take his revenge—she'd been told—and had put the word out that she'd best be running scared.

Lee found herself overcome with an eerie sense of calm as she sat staring at morning ads for dish soap and baby food and housewife-geared appliances. Surely his fealty was still intact, somewhere beneath this routine. Surely his love for her would curb his anger in the end.

When the phone went, she allowed herself the flutter of hope: Truman, calling from the studio, with a ninth-inning crisis of conscience?

She lifted the receiver and simply answered, 'Yes?'

'Are you watching?' Jackie. Of course.

'Sort of,' Lee replied, with a sip of Scotch-spiked caffeine. They lapsed into silence as a swell of orchestration announced the start of the program: Liberace piano trills. Garish neon lights flashed 'THE STANLEY SIEGEL SHOW' in the style of a Vegas casino sign.

Two orange swivel chairs sat waiting before potted palms.

Out walked Siegel in a periwinkle suit. A microphone was clipped to the tie at his neck, yet he carried a long, slender hand-mic for effect. An extraneous prop.

'Could he look more like a used car salesman if he tried?' she snorted.

Jackie said nothing.

After an initial round of banter, Siegel introduced his guest.

Out walked Truman, carefully costumed, Lee noted. It was one of his 'Nina' ensembles—the kind reserved for nice Southern boys—pale linen Brooks Brothers suit, sweater vest, and bow tie. He'd even gone so far as to add the jaunty touch of a straw boater, as if he'd just wandered out of a Tennessee Williams play. He weaved a bit, walking to shake Siegel's hand, but covered his unsteadiness with a loosey-goosey box-step, as if it was intentional.

'He's high,' Lee said to Jackie.

Truman and his host sat down in their swivel chairs, the guest looking très 'chat qui a mangé le canari.' Lee had to admit that he looked better than he had in some time. He'd lost weight. His skin was taut and his thinning hair seemed magically restored (plugs and a facelift, she'd later learn), evoking a Truman of decades before. His eyes appeared to sparkle behind his tortoise glasses and he wore the healthy glow of time spent in the sun.

Siegel greeted him warmly. Like a long-lost friend.

'Well, hello, Truman. How are you?'

'I's fiiiinne and dandy, sho'nuff,' answered his guest, playing up the hillbilly drawl.

'I'm pleased to say, you look much better than the *last* time we saw you . . .'

'Weeeeeeullll, yaaaaaaaaassssss. I's been to rehab and back and bless my soul, they done cured me!'

Lee rolled her eyes at *that* notion.

'Well, we're pleased to welcome you back. Am I correct in saying that it was *you* who called *us*, Truman? Because you had something you wanted to talk about?'

'Yaaaaaaaaaassssssa. As a matter of fact, I do! But I'll be warnin' ya, what I've gotta say, it isn't very gentlemanly . . .'

'It isn't?' Siegel, playing the innocent.

'Noooooooo way, no how. You see, it involves a veeeerrrrrrrrrry *close* friend of mine. The divine, dear Principessa *Radzilla* . . . Like Godzilla, but she ain't nearly so friendly.'

'Now, correct me if I'm wrong, Truman, but isn't Princess Radziwill Mrs. Kennedy's sister . . . ?'

'Oh God,' Jackie breathed. 'Of course *I'd* be dragged into this.'

Shut up, Jacks, Lee thought, but managed to hold her tongue.

'Yuuuuuup, Radziwilla is the baby sis of Jackie Oh-No. And both a pair of gold-diggers if I ever done seen 'em!'

'But Truman, isn't Princess Radziwill one of your dearest friends?'

'She sho'nuff *was*, Stanny boy oh Stanny boy. But you seeeee, that was several days ago, after such time the *Principessa* decided to call me a *fag* to one of this city's finest gossip columnists, one Mizzz Lizz Smith, a tall drink of water who is herself of the homosexual persuasion. What I came to discuss is this very thing, which I must say confuses me greatly.' He was really warming up, enjoying the cadence of his text. '*If* the *Principessa* held such a low opinion of *fags*, wasn't it unwise of her to *trust* one all these years?'

He smiled, coquettishly, at Siegel.

'And did she trust you, Truman?'

'Ohhhhhhhhh yaaaaaaaass suh. With *all* her dirty secrets. And that was a tragic mistake on her part, because I's not just a fag. I's a *Southern* fag. And I'm here to tell ya, we *Southern* fags is *mean*.'

'Lee . . .' Jackie breathed on the line.

Lee reached for her decanter of Scotch.

The little shit . . .

'Unfortunately for Principessa Radzilla, *this* Southern fag is just getting started.' Truman grinned at the camera, as if looking into Lee's very soul.

'Fuck,' she said aloud, spotting the killer within.

THOSE OF US NEAR TVs in the New York metropolitan area were hanging on every word from our boudoirs and living room sofas and breakfast tables. Using the event as an excuse for an early cigarette or a Bloody Mary or a clandestine fig Danish from Rigo's on Madison. In our robes or fully dressed. On the phone with one another like the Bouviers, or taking it in alone.

'So,' Siegel clarified in his schlocky therapist's tone, 'you're here because Princess Radziwill hurt you. Is that right?'

'I gots an hour, and I'm here to tell what I know. And trust me . . . I know it *all*.'

Truman cut his eyes to a woman sitting off-camera, watching: Sally Quinn of the *Washington Post*, a favor called in to his precious Kay-Kay, now in her tenth year as editor.

The moment Liz told Tru of Lee's treachery, he'd set his plan in motion. He had rung up the folks at *Siegel*, knowing they'd jump at a repeat performance. *Then* he'd called Kay to request a reporter cover the whole revenge mission.

'Kay-Kay, it'll be a comedy classic for the ages, lemme *tell* you. I want someone reputable there to cover history being made.' Against her better judgment, Kay had obliged.

On air, Siegel nodded. 'Well, Truman, I would hope, for the sake of your long friendship, that it won't prove *too* salacious.' (*Bullshit*, we longed to cry. The little twerp would simply welcome the ratings leap of another Capote meltdown.)

'Weeeeulll, Stan, the lovely, ethereal *Principessa* has gone so far, after our long, bosom friendship, to dismiss me as a fag. Fags are supposed to be bitchy, I'm afraid. So let's go . . .'

It was clear to any of us what he had in mind. He intended to bring Lee down. To do his damndest to ruin she who had so casually betrayed him, after all that he had done for her. To use every weapon he had stockpiled over decades, and she had handed him a veritable arsenal.

Sally Quinn would later report that Truman had planned his performance to the *n*th degree. A monologue to end all monologues, over which he had taken the care he usually reserved for his prose. He had calculated the rhythms of each sentence. He'd memorized his dialogue. Had rehearsed his delivery. And while he seemed woozy to the outside observer, this was merely euphoria.

'I wish poor old Stas was alive to see today's little display,' Tru had told Sally Quinn in the car on the way to the studio. 'Once, when I was doing all I did for Lee, getting her film parts and book deals and setting her up to succeed, Stas—who she always took for granted in my view—said to me that if I went to such lengths for someone that I loved, what must I do for someone that I *loathed*. Well, we're about to find out. By the time I'm done, all of New York will know what a narcissistic cunt that girl is.'

ON AIR, LIVE: 'Lorrrddeeee mercy, *where* to begin . . . ? I wanna ease into things. I wouldn't want the Princess Pee to hafta call for the ambulance *too* early on . . . She might miss the best bits!' He tilted his hat roguishly over one eye. 'Let's start with her *numerous* beaux—though I must say, *conquests* might prove more appropriate, statistically. The *unrequited* ones in particular.'

He knew her well enough to suspect she might be watching with Jackie, and went directly for the jugular.

'Well, to begin with, *Principessa* thought she'd nailed Onassis down 'fo herself, so imagine just how wounded she was when big sistah snatched him away. She wouldn't want me a-tellin' you this, but Radzilla was in an absolute *state* . . . ! Not that she cared for that wrinkled old prune, but she was *quite* besotted with those *oil* tankers. Of course, *both* Bouviers lured him away from that dear Maria Callas, who made the mistake of loving him and actually *having* talent. Of course Lee is terribly jealous of Jackie, and Jackie jealous of Lee in a way. Ms. Jacks certainly wasn't happy when Lee went after Peter Beard. *Lawdy!* He was too hot for either of those ice queens to handle—had 'em both in little puddles on the floor when he was done. He dallied with Radzilla for a time, but she raised holy hell when he refused to be faithful—she took to stalking his other young ladies. *Naturally* he traded her in for a model with less mileage—as if *that* was a surprise to either of those Bouviers, who think by speaking in baby tones we'll all forget their dates o' birth and treat 'em like they're twenty. Nags gussied up as fillies, the pair of 'em!'

He grinned genially, the most benign of narrators. There really was a kind of mad brilliance in the performance. The only one *not* enjoying it appeared to be Siegel himself, who squirmed uncomfortably in his seat. Truman swiveled happily from side to side in his own.

'I see, Truman. However—'

'Sometimes it's been downright comical,' Truman drawled, drowning him out. 'For instance, Radzilla was all tangled up in *Nureyev's* tights—and to think she failed to spot that he done pitched fo' the other team . . . Imagine her surprrrrrrrrrrriiiiiise when she went to decorate his pied-à-terre, only to stumble upon drawers full of pictures of simply mouthwatering *cocks*—'

Siegel cut in, desperate to rein in his guest. 'Yes, Truman. That's all fine. We can see that you've been terribly hurt by the Princess—'

'You bet your bottom I'm hurt, sho'nuff! "Coattails"? I *saved* that ungrateful little—'

'I hear, Truman,' Siegel interrupted again in an effort to change the subject, 'that you've just come out of Hazelden, is that true?'

'I—' Truman looked disoriented. As if Siegel had turned a blowtorch on his waxen wings and like Icarus he was falling downward, downward, back to earth.

'I was just wondering how things are going for you.'

The Southern Fag blinked. Siegel had broken the beauty of his cadence, so carefully rehearsed. He removed his glasses and rubbed his eyes, rendering him less Southern Fag and more Trumanesque by the moment. 'Well. You've *certainly* ruined the fun of that, I must say.'

Siegel, chastised. 'I'm sorry, Truman. Go right ahead.'

Truman attempted to recover his rhythm. 'And then . . . then there was Buckley—one William F.—Radzilla had the—she tried to—' He struggled in vain to find his place in the script once more. '—tried to seduce him away from his wife, by asking the aging altar boy for *spiritual* advice!' He laughed at his own punchline, a little too eagerly.

'Do you think you've managed to kick the drugs, Truman?'

'What about Radzilla? I don't exactly see *her* laying off the sauce.'

'Yes, well.' Siegel laughed, uneasily. He looked to his producer in the booth, signaling him to cut to a break. 'We'll resume our chat after a quick word from our sponsors.'

The Southern Fag simply stared at him, his rattle played out like a pair of mute maracas.

The crew cut quickly to a commercial break, at which point Truman rose, disconnected his mic, and left it on the rough orange surface of his swivel chair.

Without further word to Siegel, he moved to Sally Quinn.

'C'mon, honey. Let's blow this popsicle stand.'

CODA

IN THE LIMOUSINE, TRUMAN POURED TWO GLASSES of bubbly from the open bottle, though the ritual lacked the spirit of triumph he had anticipated when he left it.

He smiled at Sally Quinn, deflated. A maestro who had *almost* pulled off a virtuoso performance—who knew his own potential, but had fallen just short.

'It was *theater*,' Truman lamented. 'Couldn't he *see* that?'

'Apparently not.'

'I mean, it's clear the man's not the *sharpest* tool in the shed, but my *gawd*.'

'For what it's worth, I thought it was a superb performance.'

At this, the woebegone face brightened. Ever a sucker for a compliment.

'Why *thank* you, sugar. It means so much that *you* recognized what I was going for. It's why I asked Kay-Kay for you to be here to bear witness. Lee dismissed me, so I turned myself into an extreme version of *exactly* what she accused me of being. I was *supposed* to be playing some crazy, monstrous queen you'd meet in a bar.'

'It's too bad you didn't get to finish your act.'

'Oh, but I *willlllll*, sugar. That's what *you're* here for. I still got lots pent up inside me that I just gotta purge! Now, we can go for a nice luncheon out, or you can come back to *chez moi* and we'll have something in. Whaddaya fancy?'

SALLY HAD CHOSEN TO GO BACK to Truman's apartment, reasoning he'd be more candid there.

When they'd settled into his Victoriana nest of a living room with a pot of tea, the author relaxed and the showman returned. Sally set up her tape recorder and pointed it toward him. He gave her a coy smile.

'Are you *certain* you want to hear this . . . ?'

'Absolutely.'

'What bits would you like? 'Cause trust me, I's got the goods.'

'What do you want to tell?'

'Oh, there's so much, it could take days. About every man the Bouviers have ever used. About their sense of entitlement. About their obsession with one another. They're like the Kennedy boys—they keep covering the same ground, sexually, those two. Talk about share and share alike! But it isn't sharing, if it's some sort of sick competition. Why, Jackie couldn't even give *birth* without Lee gunning to get into Jack's trousers. And of all the sugar daddies for Jackie to hitch her wagon to . . . The very one that baby sis had her heart set on . . . ? Of course, the irony *there* is that *Bobby* asked Lee to break things off with Ari *years* before. Said it would look bad for the President's dear sister-in-law to run off with such a reprobate. That Jackie snapped him up herself after Jack and Bobby were gone is simply *too* ironic.'

'It all feels quite incestuous.'

'Honey, you don't know the *half* of it. It's as if those girls live, breathe, and think in the royal "We" . . . *Until* it comes to each other, then it's every gal for herself.'

'And Lee confided all of this to you? Over all these years?'

'Radzilla told me *everything*. She couldn't fart without knowing what I thought. But my gawd, how I loved that girl—I saved her, you know. Multiple times. That's why it's so treacherous, her dropping me as she did.' He smiled, sadly. 'You know, I can joke and make light of it. They are pathetic figures after all, and I can certainly spin a good yarn round 'em both. But truth is, I was there for Lee Radziwill when no one else was. I put my own career on hold to bolster hers. (Not that she had any real talent in the end, gawd help her.) She wasn't a kind person, Lee. Never particularly warm. In fact, most people who met her found her quite cold. The only person she was ever really interested in was herself. She was a phony, a climber, the ultimate star-fucker . . . but I loved her. I was the single most loyal friend she ever had.'

'Do you think you made a mistake in choosing someone so treacherous?'

'I made a mistake in trusting *her*. I thought that because I had been there in *her* moments of doubt or need that she would be there for me. Hell, if I had tossed Lee to the curb whenever she was low, she'd have been mowed down in traffic *decades* ago. I held her hand through the botched jobs, the failed pursuits, the wrong men. Then when it happened I needed the same from her, she goes and betrays me without a second thought. Trusting that little narcissist was the single worst misjudgment of my life.'

'I can see how you'd be hurt.'

He nodded—grateful that someone had heard him. 'Lee thought I was disposable. I haven't been very well the last few years. Oh, I'm strong as an ox now, but I was in and out of the hospital. I guess the *Principessa* thought I wasn't worth worrying about. Weeeeeeeuuuuuullllll. Unfortunately for Lee Radziwill, this Southern fag's alive and well in New York City—!'

But when the cameras went away and the tape recorders stopped, after the interviews were aired and the sound bites replayed, even after his revenge was recorded in newsprint in black and white for posterity . . . he found that he was left with a hole in the wall of his heart; that what he could not expunge was the pain of being discounted. Discounted by someone he had trusted with his innermost, private self, who said, in the end, that he didn't really matter.

His heart was enormous, he told himself. He felt that, even wounded, it continued to beat so powerfully he feared it was too big for his very chest.

But he knew there was a hole into which Lee Radziwill had plunged her harpoon, and that a piece of him could never be recovered.

TWENTY

1980

VARIATION No. 10

DON SEÑOR TRUMAN CAPOTE

REQUESTS THE PLEASURE OF YOUR COMPANY

AT HIS

REVENGE BALL

THE FIRST DAY OF SPRING,

NINETEEN HUNDRED AND EIGHTY

TEN O'CLOCK

ANDALUSIA, SPAIN

DRESS:

ANDALUSIAN ARISTOCRAT, CIRCA 1860

MASKS TILL MIDNIGHT

HE HAS HIS NEXT IDEA WHEN THE INVITATIONS CEASE.

Hardly anyone asks him anywhere anymore, and while he's put up a brave front, frankly it hurts his heart. He feels five years of penance are quite a long time to pass as a pariah, and he'd like to have a lovely time again.

March 21st. That's when he's calculated the first day of spring. The idea of pagan rites appeals, especially since this time he'll make absolutely certain—no stuffed shirts, just for the sake of their names. *Not* that he'll admit that's what he did last time . . . but no Sinatras running off to Jilly's just after two, or Gianni and his Italian mob making *una partenza anticipata*—a rudely early departure, that is—for a card game in the back room at Elaine's. Or Old Bastard Paley, who refused to cut a rug, even while Babe never left the floor.

This time the host wants pure debauchery. No rules. No societal norms. Boys with boys. Boys with girls. Girls with girls. Perhaps a combination thereof.

He's imagined the fervor that Stravinsky incited with his glorious *Rite of Spring*, causing a full-blown *riot* when first performed—inciting mayhem and chaos. That wonderful, terrible score of Igor's, unsettling in its dissonance—with Nijinsky's Ballets Russes hurled into a frenzy of erotic pagan dance. That's the kind of art and life that Truman has in mind. Where one sees or reads or hears, and stops and thinks *MY GOD*.

Isn't this what he himself has begun to achieve with *Answered Prayers*? To incite and enrage—is that not the point of art?

He wants ripping of clothing in the darkest of corners. Not simply sipping champagne, but indulging in everything else. China bowls of white powder that amps one's spirits high. Snorting and smoking and swallowing all. Costumes more than mere masks that guests remove too soon, unwilling to give his experiment a chance. He'll correct this with the next one. It will be the ball of the future, stripped of modes and mores. He begins to think how his new party might achieve this.

First of all, he'll hire The Rolling Stones. 'Mick loves me, honey,' he'll brag to anyone left to listen.

He has visions of a tennis court—a whole long string of 'em. Draped with rich-toned silks imported direct from Spain, with fans and muletas and a million paper roses. In his mind he's dressed as a miniature Don Juan, welcoming señoras and matadors as a chorus of flamenco dancers stomp feet against the floor to the sultry rhythms of Spanish guitars.

Perhaps he'll scrap the tennis courts and have his guests fly to Andalusia, which if they've never been, he's certain they'll adore. (How the Stones and flamenco speak to one another we really can't imagine, but Truman might argue that he's only in the *early* planning stages.)

Unfortunately for Truman, the best plan on earth can't unfold in a vacuum. He'd need his precious guests, most of whom wouldn't be caught dead anywhere *near* him. He starts to formulate a plan, to make a party so big, he's giving it for the masses. If last time was a dance for just five hundred of his 'close personal friends,' this will be a party for a thousand strangers. Just as he's plotting how he'll pull this off, as he's starting to seek out addresses, something extraordinary happens.

Someone else does it *for* him.

It's the nightclub of the *future*, just like Truman envisioned. But instead of high society, it's *new* society that counts. An egalitarian world, where the freak and the outcast possess the same worth as the debutante or the rock star, the fashion fiend or the actor or the member of minor royalty.

A society of misfits, of exhibitionists and balls-out whores— and while the upper crust has rejected him, in this brave new world he's become their patron saint.

He's delighted by its scope and vision, so much so he forgets his own event.

From the first night he wanders through its crumbling art deco doors, Truman is enchanted. The space itself had lived a life. As an opera house in the Twenties. A theatre in the Thirties. Studios for CBS in the decades extending beyond. Truman senses its former inhabitants in the ether—of the Harlem dancers of *Swing Mikado*, or Jack Benny with his laugh track. Truman's own publisher, Bennett Cerf—regular panelist on *What's My Line*, filmed within these very walls. Bennett had died a few years back and Tru misses him something awful. He comes to this space to commune with him again, and all the other folks who've come and gone before him.

The space has been rechristened 54 and is run by Steve Rubell—a midget outcast like Truman, the dark to Truman's light—and the gorgeous Ian Schrager—the brains with the master plan. In hand-selecting their guests, they create the perfect mélange. Something the boy, with his composition books and his

Blackwings, could only have hoped to achieve. Whether luring celebrities or plucking hopefuls from the throng outside each night, the bacchanal is perfectly cast. 'Mixing the salad,' Rubbell calls it.

The boy, for his part, is pleased by the invitations. It's been so long, after all, since he's received one. He's even more astonished to find himself wanted again. And not just wanted— he finds himself greeted with the semblance of something like reverence. When Truman enters, it's as if the court lines up and the freak show bows to worship their own little demigod. Whatever society rejected him before, he's certainly found a new one. One in which he is coddled and loved again.

Even if these are strangers, even if they're higher than the homemade kites he once flew with Sook in the fields in Monroeville, he finds that he's tremendously moved that someone might welcome his presence. Sometimes he's even given a kiss from one of the shirtless cocktail boys in their dolphin shorts—all of whom know his name, and vice-versa.

'Why Lance honey, what *fabulous* legs you have. And you can just see practically *everything* in those darling little shorts! . . . Gary, be a dear and pour me just one more *teensy* Orange Drink? . . . Now Jesús, you *are* a naughty boy—no! I don't need another line—and I certainly don't need to see your bits exposed!'

He loves the colors and the lights. The flashing strobes and the disco balls. An image of the Man in the Moon who appears hourly on a screen, a spoon of cocaine tilted to his nose.

In the bowels of the basement is the VIP room, where he can collapse onto sofas with celebrities of his ilk. The nastiest of spaces, reserved for the headiest guests, something Steve Rubell (in a Trumanesque gesture) thought naughty and fun. It's where he puts Truman and Andy and Liza. Mick and Bianca and Halston. Lolling on basement couches directly beneath the dance floor, the constant thump of the music, the primal heartbeat of the stomping of feet on the parquet floor above, the collective orgasm of indulgence.

In the bathrooms and in darkened corners, in the shadows of the balconies, the sex flows as freely as water from a tap, but Truman doesn't go there for that. He goes to forget where he *isn't* allowed to go.

Of course he can see that it's crude and cheap when compared to the drawing room at Kiluna, or the gardens in Manhasset, or on board the *Agneta*, sailing cobalt waters off the Amalfi Coast. Of course *those* are the things that move him . . . but this is what he can get. The society that he's left with. A glorious, grotesque sideshow, surpassing those he'd created long ago in Monroeville.

No one at 54—or *Cinquanta-Quattro*, as Truman likes to call it—gives two shits who Babe Paley is. Most have never heard of the savage Slim Keith or cowardess Gloria Guinness. They know C.Z., for she has been here with him before. Truman takes pleasure that the rest of us would likely not get past the ropes. We'd be deemed too stuffy, too prim, not *showy* enough for admittance within these rainbow-flashing walls. It has nothing to do with age, we're quick to note. Rubell lets Gloria Swanson in, well into her seventies, beauty mark darkened to a hideous rococo spot. Ditto the octogenarian known as Disco Sally, her weather-beaten face hidden beneath dark glasses, straddling young hunks of flesh, dancing to the latest hits in her muumuu tents and thigh-high boots—a novelty, but a memorable one. *Almost* as good as a bearded lady or a mermaid in a jar or half of a Siamese twin in Truman's sideshows of old.

No . . . We, his former coterie, would fail at 54 for the very qualities he'd most adored in each of us—our subtlety, our grace. Our understated elegance. Our ability to converse. (If this sounds vain or boastful, may we say in our defense we're merely repeating what he thinks.) If he's honest with himself, that's what the boy misses most, something the pounding beat of the dance floor renders a luxury of a distant social past. How he misses getting stuck in for a nice, cozy chat, which used to be his favorite part of any given evening. Truman now wears his caftan to Cinquanta-Quattro—the beige one he had shared with Babe, given to him by Yves. Sometimes he doesn't bother to dress, and shows up in silk pajamas. He always dons his panama hat and shouts to his seat-mates above the racket. He's starting to realize it might be a plot of Rubell's—an attempt to ban all dialogue. If revelers fail to hear one another, they're less likely to find the company lacking.

Of course most must be drunk or doped to the gills; without that they'd notice how empty it is. One can't dare hope for a witty riposte, and they certainly ain't discussing Proust. They have to keep going, keep racing, keep fueled, so the lights still seem magical, the dance floor still a wonderland. So no one notices how transient it is.

There's distraction in extremes. The exposed pipes, to which people are cuffed, the plastic mattresses strewn on the floor. The needles in unisex toilets. The sparkle of clothing made of cheap sequins, rather than beading of bespoke evening gowns.

What Truman relishes most is to climb into the DJ booth, where he likes to sit and observe from on high. Rubell has shown him how to play a record, and how to work the lights, and is perfectly happy for the little patron saint to ascend and play God for an hour or so. From his perch the bodies look gorgeous, writhing on the floor. From his new-found height he is hovering above them, flying far, far away. From a distance one could escape their hungry looks and panicked eyes. Their quiet desperation. They seem a shimmering mass of loveliness, rather than wasted youth teetering on the brink. Up in the safety of his nest, Truman can think of all the folks who've come and gone who would have loved to see this too.

Old Marcel is certainly one, observing the societal rituals of the *now* and making insightful observations. Toulouse-Lautrec is another, for there is something of the Moulin Rouge in Cinquanta-Quattro.

He thinks how much Cole Porter, darling, clever Cole, would have loved the rhythm, the beat-beat-beat of the tom-toms, albeit electronic ones. Would have loved the unhindered dancing of handsome boys with other handsome boys, the liberated feel. And Billie, Lady Day, gardenia in her hair, who he can picture chatting with Diana Ross, who played her in a film—perhaps they'd sing torch songs together, drowned by the less subtle throbbing pulse of Gaynor or Summer hits.

He thinks he would have liked to have shared this with Babe, and while a bit too trashy to be her scene, she'd have appreciated the spirit of transcendence and would have relished the stories he'd have spun.

Some nights Señor Capote wanders down to the dance floor, where, he must admit, he loves to cut loose. However, Truman will be the first to proclaim, he cannot *stand* disco.

'Honey, where's the tune? Where's the *musicality*? For that matter, gimme some *lyrics* please! *I will survive, I will survive*— Jesus H. Christ, we *get it* already! Cole is turning in his grave on a rotisserie spit at the dearth of *creativity*.'

The boy misses soul and rock and roll—the records he'd put on after dinner, when we'd all dance barefoot on the Chinese rug in his UN Plaza study. He misses the Twist and the Frug and the Camel Walk, but most of all, he misses the Big Bands of his youth.

Never one to let a detail get him down, Truman has a special power to block out the dull thud of the disco. He'll take his space on the strobe-lit floor, muting the monotonous pulse of 'I Feel Love.' While the near-naked bodies gyrate to this electronic beat, Truman instead hears his *own* sultry rhythms—the blaring clarinet of Benny Goodman, the frenzy of 'Sing Sing Sing.' The driving *da-DA-da-de-DA-da, da-DA-de-DA-da* of the drumbeat. The flights of fancy of Benny's clarinet, the sluttish blare of brass.

If he closes his eyes, he can imagine himself back at El Morocco, on the packed dance floor in the Forties, treading on Ann Woodward's clodhopper toes.

Sometimes his fellow dancers, in their spandex and sequins, glare at him like ole Bang-Bang, when he inadvertently bumps into them. They can look at him funny all they like, the boy doesn't give a hoot.

He's already sprouted wings and flown far above their tawdry company. Flown away to a time and place of his own—the time and place that he has lost, but recovers on the floor; soaring higher still to another time and place entirely, where their soulless era can no longer touch him.

Sometimes he swings Babe around the floor, and Jack, the trio of them cutting loose together, like they once had at his party.

C.Z. alone—the few times she accompanies him to the nightclub of the future—knows the truth, and can only hope that this might make him happy.

In his silk pajamas or his white linen suits with nothing underneath, panama hat pulled rakishly over one eye, Truman Lindy hops for hours among the disco darlings, sweat pouring down his rapturous face, dancing frenzied, tipsy jitterbugs to the Big Bands in his mind.

TWENTY-ONE

1983

Fantasia

Tchaikovsky, opus 20

H E CROSSES HIS PYGMY LEGS in a booth at the Turnpike Howard Johnson's, sitting across from Gloria—pleased as
punch.

He's sipping a Salty Dog, admiring its innocuous shade of pink,
rosy as a virgin's tit; Gloria, a blush-colored daiquiri to match.

It's been years since they've lunched. Years since they've *spoken*, in fact, she ever cautious, not wanting to offend Loel or Babe
or Bill.

And yet, under the circumstances, so much time having passed,
she has chosen—he supposes—to simply let bygones be bygones.

Of *course* they meet at their secret haunt, the one too gauche
for all the others. They'd decided to order clams exclusively, both
as a special treat and as a gesture of nostalgia, the Howard Johnson's shellfish specialties being their favorites. As they polish off
the first round of these, the boy laments the sorry state of affairs.

'Don't you find, Mamacita, that it often isn't worth *bothering* to
get outta bed these days?' He looks as if he only succeeded in half
the effort, in a blue seersucker suit like the ones his Mama once
bought him—though having forgotten to put on a shirt. 'I mean
really. Compared to the *old* days, where can one hope to *go* . . . ?'

Gloria sighs, fingering the stem of her daiquiri. 'Yes. Well.
When we were young we had such divine restaurants, did we
not?' (The best of which have shut in recent years, it pains us to
say, or been overrun by the *wrong* types and thus irrevocably
altered.) 'Wonderful nightclubs—'

'And the *parties* . . .' he interjects.

'*Beautiful* parties,' she beams at him, and they both know she means his Ball. She shakes her lovely head with regret. 'Now all they want to do is go to *discos*,' with palpable disdain.

'Well, Mamacita, you never went to Cinquanta-Quattro. That was a fine disco—mighty fine.' (Of course, its owners having been arrested for tax evasion, Truman's beloved 54 has shuttered its doors as well.) 'It had a magic of sorts . . . I did so want to take you there. *C.Z.* adored it . . .' He tries to sound convincing.

'Bah,' Gloria scoffs. 'It couldn't hold a candle to what *we* knew.'

'No, I guess you're right. They're a pretty-enough bunch, but they're all a flash in the pan. Nothin' but PR puppets. Not an ounce of glamour among 'em. They lack what *you* had.'

'And what's that?'

'Gravitas.'

She sips her drink, ingesting this.

'I mean, can any of that bunch compare to a Betty Bacall? Or a you or a Babe or a Slim? Even the vile Bouviers will have 'em talking decades hence for the lack of competition. This bunch . . . they're no flock of Swans. They're not even ugly ducks—they're *plastic* ones. Identical, factory-lined, mass-produced . . .'

'I think we must accept, Diablito, that the days of your Swans have passed.'

They sit, pondering this loss with a quiet reverence.

'Do you ever find,' he finally muses, a tinge of regret in his voice, 'that all the people you *really* like are dead . . . ?'

'Yes,' says Gloria with a sad, knowing smile.

He nods. They eat, content.

'I've missed you, Mamacita.'

'I've missed you too, Diablito.'

He, solicitous, 'Would you like another daiquiri, honey?'

'Why yes—I think I would.'

'More clams . . . ?'

'Please.'

Truman flags the waitress. 'I'll have a top-up on my Salty Dog. The señora would like another daiquiri—and we'll split another order of clams casino, *por favor*.'

The waitress stares at him with a wary expression. She begins to say something, then thinks better, scribbling the additions onto their ticket, setting it back on its dish beside the condiments, shuffling off to fetch their drinks.

'Gracious! The way Flo there looked at me, you'd think I'd turned blue and sprouted six heads!'

'Perhaps, Diablito, she failed to understand your order.'

'Well, she can kiss my grits!'

Truman twists in his seat to keep an eye on the waitress in her polyester frock. 'How dare she judge us for wanting another plate of those marvelous little— —'

He turns back, startled to find the booth opposite empty. He looks around for Gloria, but there's no trace of her. The bell on the chapel-style door jingles softly, but no one comes or goes. The waitress eventually returns with a tray laden with clams, Salty Dog . . .

'And a daiquiri for your . . . friend.'

THAT NIGHT, DINING WITH JACK at La Petite Marmite across from the UN Plaza:

'You've hardly touched your food,' Jack says as the boy cuts his meat into tiny, unappetizing cubes.

'I'll get a doggie bag. Truth be told, I'm stuffed fulla clams.'

'Oh?'

'I had lunch with Gloria today.'

'Truman.' Jack pauses. 'Gloria's dead.'

'Yes, I think I knew that . . .' Then, calmly—'When?'

'Two years ago?'

'How . . . ?' He saws at his steak.

Jack studies him, concerned. 'Do you really not remember?'

'I'm—not sure.'

'Heart attack. Loel found her lying on the floor of their bathroom in Lucerne.'

412

'Oh.'

'But some say she went like your mother . . .'

'I see.'

'That she got tired and called it a day.'

'Hmmm.'

'Seconal, they think.'

'Weeeeuulll.' The boy tries to sort this out in his mind, along with what he knows to be true. 'We had lunch today and she told me to tell you hello,' beaming Panglossian pleasure.

A beat. Jack rises.

'I'll see you back home,' he says, leaving Truman alone at the table to ponder the loss.

THE BOY ISN'T CERTAIN, but he's almost positive that Jack is holding him hostage.

He's convinced that his life is in danger. He wants to make calls, to phone for reinforcements, but there are so few left who'll answer.

'Dahling,' C.Z. tells him in her stern boss-lady tone on the line from Palm Beach, 'Jahck is not trying to kidnahp you. In fact, quite the *reverse*. Now, you go play nice or he'll be off on the first plane bahck to Verbier, fahster than your head can spin!'

'But Sissy . . . he keeps talking about me in the *past tense*. As if I'm already gone.'

'Maybe, bustah, you should spend a bit more time on your *own* prose rahther than deconstructing Jahck's.' Silence. 'Truman? Do you hear me?'

'Yes, Sis.'

He hangs up and returns to his bed. Lying flat, staring at the ceiling. Watching a spiral of dust in the air—air as heavy as the particles' weightlessness. He feels his heart racing, tripping over itself to— —

He stops. Exhales. Slooooow the pace. *Sloooooooow.*

He feels his pulse revving like a—? He can picture it, that object of transport Gianni owns . . . Not simply a speedboat but a—? Just as it's about to come to him, he abandons the effort. Has it really come to this . . . ? Lost words, tired metaphors. Hackneyed— Images he never would have— Even when he was little more than a kid with a Remington with keys that stuck, that he found in his— Was he not the writer who once insisted an entire work could be ruined by the faulty rhythm in a sentence? These days it feels he can barely write his name. Speedboats . . . Were they what he—? Or did that only pop into his head because he had Marella on the brain? There was something he saw—no, read—? that he found he wanted to tell her, something he felt sure would amuse her, but he'd promptly forgotten whatever it might—

A sharp pain. He grips his chest. He can feel his heart breaking into a thousand lethal— as if struck by a—? His grasp of language has— It's like the fluttering wings of a—

Fucking *hell*. Is it a—? The words elude him. He can see the objects in his head, but cannot for the life of him remember what they're called. Perhaps if he can manage to hold his heart inside the cavity of his chest—like Jackie held fragments of Jack's skull in place in the back of a car in a plaza called Dealey, desperate to keep that precious brain matter from seeping out. If he can just keep his own heart from exploding; prevent his brilliant brain from leaking.

He thinks there is nothing so terrifying as reaching into the clouds each day, trying to pull down the words from the sky—to graft—no, to *pin* them to the blank sheet of—

He crumples the mental paper.

Oh Lord, the terror—the sheer terror of the gamble, for that's what it was, was it not? If he could only catch the words and secure them to the page.

He no longer believes that words and phrases are generated *from* him. Rather that they exist as independent entities, and the best one can hope for is to lure one or more of them into a trap in order to use for narrative purposes. He no longer has faith that even a boy genius could hope to act as anything more than hapless hunter. Even then, they might—possessing minds of their own—choose not to cooperate.

Just as one's subjects might choose to resist.

It's been so long since the words have come, he has forgotten what they—

He stops. Scribbling through the thoughts in his mind.

Exhaling his strangled breath in three staccato puffs. He lies perfectly flat—on bed or floor or sofa—no longer bothering to arrange his chintz pillows, a ritual which once seemed to serve him. Ditto the legal pads, the Blackwings, and the weighty Smith Corona. He no longer bothers with props. By the time he collects them, the glimmer of promise he initially felt will have faded, leaving him overwhelmed with fatigue for having failed before he started.

MANHATTAN FEELS CROWDED THESE DAYS.

When he cannot pin down the words—which, let's face it, is far more often than not—he prowls the city streets, amazed to encounter so many people that he recognizes.

Strolling down Fifth Avenue one rainy afternoon, he spots a woman in a mackintosh, standing in front of the window at Tiffany's. Her gazelle legs extend from the hem, and even wrapped in the all-weather shield, her lithe, boyish frame is apparent. Her cropped hair is colored a multitude of hues—beige and caramel, streaked with champagne. Dark glasses shade her eyes, consuming her pixie countenance.

'Holly . . .' he breathes. He inches closer, careful not to spook the skittish creature, his clumsy stealth having the opposite effect. The girl suddenly turns, regarding him as a stalker sneaking up on her—perhaps a flasher in his *own* trench. She backs away, and he sees in an instant that she is not the girl he thought she was.

It's in a less salubrious setting that very week that he encounters another familiar face. It happens at Twilight, an underground saloon on the East Side in the twenties, where older men go to meet beautiful boys and where beautiful boys vie for the affections of the old. He's fled there after a fight with Jack, thinking himself one of the youngsters among the clientele, and is rather shocked upon arrival to find himself an elder. As he sits at the bar, drooped over a glass of bourbon, his cherub eyes catch the reflection of an ancient man in the mirror opposite. It takes a moment for him to recognize himself. He's pondering how this might have happened, how he's transformed from a golden baby doll to a shriveled *Testudo graeca* alone at a bar, when a young man approaches him. Dark features. Sensitive eyes. Walking with a limp.

'Evening, *amigo*.'

The tortoise peeks from its shell, recognizing the voice.

'Perry . . . ?' He squints in the dimness of the tavern.

The young man smiles, a lopsided grin he remembers.

'Sure. If that works for you.'

'My *gawd* . . . I've never been so *relieved*. I thought—I saw you—' He finds he can't bear to say the word 'hanged,' so instead he simply smiles, grateful that it's clearly no longer the case. 'I supppooooose,' he ponders aloud, 'a mistake must have been made. How *are* you?'

'Swell. You?'

'Over-the-moon, having seen you.'

'Well, isn't *that* great news.'

'Care for a drink?'

'Don't mind if I do,' the young man replies.

A couple of whiskeys in and he takes the trembling tortoise face in his hands, sharing a sloppy kiss laced with Mama-juice. How warm the youth's lips feel. They taste of licorice and nicotine and the traces of other men. How he had longed to kiss them those many years ago, visiting a cell under the watchful gaze of wardens who might have prevented him access had he been caught indulging the personal. The *book* was what had mattered, more than his desire, which flared and faded with the force of his will. But here, now, the lips are his. *Perry* . . .

He lingers, eyes shut tight. Drinking him in.

'My name's Fred, by the way.'

x

'What?' the tortoise asks, eyes still closed with the rapture of it all.

'Name's Fred. But you can call me Terry if you like.'

'*Perry*,' he corrects. The leatherback lids flutter open and he sees . . .

A youth with Latin features, teeth like cracked piano keys. A cast on his foot explaining the limp. Not the character the tortoise had mistaken him for.

'Whatever you say, *amigo* . . .' The youth goes in for another greedy kiss, but it's not the same. Truman drops a crumpled bill on the counter, hurrying out to the street.

NOT ALL OF THESE ENCOUNTERS ARE WELCOME ONES.

Sitting at the Colony, tucked into a booth in the bar, nose in a book, slurping a bowl of mulligatawny on the table before him, he feels the sensation of being watched.

An eldritch gaze . . .

In the far corner of the room, he notices a woman, observing him.

She sits alone, a bottle-blonde. Dressed in subdued tones, yet emanating a shimmer of tinsel beneath the surface. Frosted lips. Painted eyes and cheeks. The spitting image of . . .

'*Bang-Bang* . . .' he stammers, in a state of disbelief.

The woman says nothing. Eats nothing. Drinks nothing.

Simply sits and stares.

He motions the waiter over. 'Honey, how long has Mrs. Woodward been sitting there?' He nods at the blonde across the room. The waiter turns, scanning the tables.

'We have no Mrs. Woodward today, Mr. Capote. Mrs. *Vanderbilt* has been at her table since twelve.' He nods toward an ashen matron in the next booth.

'Not Mrs. *Vanderbilt*. Mrs. Woodward, beside her. Mrs. *Ann* Woodward.'

The waiter shifts uncomfortably. 'I'm sorry, Mr. Capote, but I know nothing of the lady that you mention.'

Across the room, the blonde smiles at him—mockingly?

'*Ann goddamn Woodward*, sitting right over there—plain as day!'

'Oh, yes. Well. Of course. Mr. Capote, may I bring you another Orange Drink?'

The boy nods, absently.

As soon as the waiter disappears, Ann Woodward raises her fingers, curling them into the shape of a pantomime gun. Pointing it directly at Truman, her ruby nails pull the trigger. He leaps up and all but sprints from the restaurant, not bothering to wait for his check.

A FEW NIGHTS LATER, THE BREAK-IN OCCURS.

It so happens it's Christmas Eve. The boy has taken great care to have an evergreen delivered to the twenty-second floor. He ordered a box of ornaments from Tiffany's, and bought a silver star-topper from the Bronx five and dime. He's indulged visions of carols around the tree, of endless cups of eggnog. Of presents wrapped and opened and of fireside canoodling.

He's begged Jack to come home from Verbier in order that they might spend Christmas together, something they haven't done in years. Tru has come to hate the Swiss, Jack to loathe New York, he refusing to leave the Alps at the height of ski season. Still, hearing the anxiousness in Truman's tone, Jack conceded this once.

Upon arrival, Jack clears the liquor from the cabinets, dumping bottles into trash bags, along with Truman's pills. He has yet to discover the stash of cocaine tucked between the pages of books on Truman's shelves, making passages he loves to revisit all the more pleasurable—favorite lines of Flaubert or Proust guarding other sorts of lines entirely, which he likes to snort on the sly. The boy grows so giddy with the notion of having Jack home, he pops a few Thorazine to enjoy the feeling all the more— Thorazine which he chases with a fifth of vodka, cleverly hidden in a NyQuil bottle. Jack takes one look at the lolling tongue, the rolling eyes, and marches straight to the bedroom to dress, reemerging in evening clothes. Truman begs him to stay, but Jack seems unwilling to trade Verdi's *Macbeth* for less interesting tragedy at home.

The boy retires to his study, where he pulls *À la Recherche du Temps Perdu* from the shelf, opening its clean white pages, snorting a neat line of blow directly from a madeleine. In half an hour's time, he's fallen asleep slumped on the Victorian sofa with old Marcel in his lap.

It's past twelve when he hears it. A sort of . . . ? He can't find the—

Flapping, we supply. (Might as well throw him a bone.)

Flapping! (As if he'd thought of it!)

The beating of something, rapidly, was it in the next room—? The thrumming— —of several— —A low hum. Whoever or whatever it is, there is more than one of it, of that he feels certain. He tiptoes into the hall, making his way to the living room, peering around the corner where his evergreen looms. The scene where he'd imagined carols and canoodling. *Seven swans a-swimming, six geese a-laying, five gold—* —His eyes dart to the packages tucked beneath, having bought and carefully wrapped for Jack a thin gold band from Cartier, tied with a robin's-egg bow.

The branches of the tree cast shadows that loom; ominous, rustling slightly. The window open, chintz curtains fluttering in the breeze. His blood trickles cold. While not operating at full capacity, he knows he didn't leave said window open, and it seems even less likely that Jack would, it being much more in Jack's temperament to *close* that which Truman has opened.

A rustle from behind the fir. Tinsel jostles.

Someone, *something*, is hiding behind it.

'Hello?' he calls, trying to sound less frightened than he is. 'Hello? I can *see* you—I know you're there . . .' Shadows moving behind. 'Just so you know, I'm calling the police . . .' As he flips on the light switch, a fuse blows. A *flash!* in which he thinks he spots the gleam of several sets of eyes—and the tree lights are out.

He is in darkness. Alone. Abandoned—He shrieks and makes a break for it, running for the door, groping for the cold brass knob. Turns it one way—then the other. Won't budge.

From behind, he thinks that he hears laughter, a low, dangerous hum.

He turns the knob again, throwing all of his weight against it. It flies open, propelling him into the hallway. He races—this a boy who once proclaimed that he only ran when chased—to his nearest neighbors, pounding on their door. '*Help!* Help me!' he shouts.

After a minute or two, the door opens, and Mr. Rothstein, Truman's neighbor, peers out, groggy-eyed. 'Mr. *Rothstein*, thank goodness! There's been a break-in! *Intruders!*'

He practically pushes past the poor man and his wife, who appears in her housecoat and curlers. They stare at their unexpected guest, his robe hanging open, nakedness on display. Mrs. Rothstein recovers first, leading him inside.

'Truman, you poor dear, may I get you anything?'

'Yes, sugar— I *do* hate to ask, but I'm in desperate need of a little tipple to steady my nerves. And I need to borrow your phone to call the police! *They* may still be in there!'

When the cops arrive half an hour later, Truman has depleted half a bottle of the Rothsteins' vodka, and is busy relaying his conspiracy theory of one Jack Dunphy, his *former* lover, holding him hostage—worse still, plotting to kill him.

'I just know he left tonight so they could come and do the deed.'

How did 'they' get in?

'Oh honey, through the window. *I* didn't leave it open!'

Up twenty-two flights?

'Well, *I* don't know their *techniques*, but surely they have their *ways*. They don't just burgle ground floors, you know.'

Could he describe the intruders?

'*Assassins.*'

Could he describe the assassins?

'Weeuull . . . I think *one* of them was I-talian.' Even describing them in detail, he senses that they're fiction. But in the thick of it he's convinced that he has seen them. As the cops are searching his apartment, he turns to Mrs. Rothstein.

'Mimi, that reminds me—may I use your phone one more time? I need to get hold of Liz Smith at *New York* magazine. She'll print the truth, so when Jack succeeds in bumping me off, people'll know what happened to li'l ole Caposey . . .'

When Jack arrives home from his Verdi and a late supper (having stayed out longer in the hopes that Truman might be asleep when he returned) he finds the twenty-second floor of the United Nations Plaza crawling with cops. He's taken in for questioning, a matter of routine, where it becomes quickly apparent how bogus the accusations are and how round the twist his accuser. When the police have gone, Jack packs a single suitcase and departs for his house in Sagaponack, given to him long ago by a boy he once loved.

'But Jack, what did I *do*? What did I *doooooo*?' Truman will wail in the coming weeks, no memory of the episode, assassins long forgotten.

Jack refuses to yield, his only comment on the matter: 'There's only so long you can watch something you love burn to bits before your very eyes before it starts to take you with it.'

ON CHRISTMAS MORNING, THE BOY TAKES THE ELEVATOR up to the roof.

It's a crisp, clear December dawn, snow having fallen in the night.

He walks to the edge and looks down at the street. Cars crawling like fire ants below. He thinks of Maggie Case, standing in just such a spot, before the wind filled her coat with air as she leaped to the ground, suspended like a parachute in a final moment of flight.

I've got two wings for to veil my face . . . Two wings for to fly . . . He can almost hear a Baptist chorus of angels, as sublime as any requiem. *Fly away . . .*

He looks to the building opposite, where he's surprised to see a figure, mirroring his own.

Dark features. *Like* Perry's, but not . . . Where does he know the face from?

The sun is rising behind the figure, features obscured, surrounded by a halo of— —

Truman nods across the divide, and imagines that he sees the form return the gesture. And with that he turns and walks back to the elevator, back down to his evergreen, where he opens the gold band he bought for Jack, placing it on his own finger for safe keeping.

THE BOY ISN'T SURE WHAT'S REAL ANYMORE, but he *does* know what is false.

What is false, bearing no semblance of truth whatsoever, is a vile book that his publisher informs him has been written about him, by Marie 'Tiny' Rudisill, Lillie Mae's black-sheep sister. An aunt he never knew. Spreading lies about his boyhood—calling him abnormal and his Mama a filthy whore. At least he has his defenders—another aunt whom he *did* know, Mary Ida, the boy's last simpatico relative, who claimed she used its slanderous pages as a toilet roll in her privy, a gesture that oddly moved him.

Perhaps more important, his greatest ally has emerged from the shadows of time. He always knew she had his back when push came to shove.

'Truman?' Her voice on the line, for the first time in years—he can't remember why.

'Nelle!' He almost weeps, so comforted is he to hear her. 'Have you read it?'

'I never read so many goddamn lies in one place!'

He feels a sudden wash of relief and a yearning for the past. He remembers in a flash that together they could outsmart the whole damn bunch. She's his one true friend and he hers.

WITHIN A WEEK HE'S AT THE AIRPORT to catch a plane headed home.

Just hearing the colt-girl's whinny has made him miss the South something awful. Forget that Nelle lives half the year in Brooklyn, where he hardly ever sees her. Forget that it was *her* great success—never part of his master plan—that had created the space between them. He hears the wind-voices drawing him back home, toward porch chat and creek beds and time the pace of molasses.

'I'm throwin' my knapsack on my shoulder, puttin' on my old shoes, and returnin' to my homeland where the decent folks live,' he'll tell anyone who'll listen—the sum total being his lawyer, his publisher, Sidney the doorman, and the dentist where he finds himself waiting in a lobby, flipping through the *New Yorker*, a sad fuck with a root canal.

At the Pan Am counter, he's pleased to find the sartorial state of affairs much improved since he last traveled, the counter girls having resurrected headgear—not the pillbox hats of old, but navy felt fedoras. 'Honey, we match,' he enthuses as they check him in. He's wearing his straw panama, which he's decided has something of the Southern gent about it, and thus selected it specially. 'You look just like Ingrid Bergman in *Casablanca*, about to get on that plane and fly off with Victor Lazlo, leaving poor Rick behind. Of course I knew Ingrid—*and* Bogie. Terrible shame that both of them are gone.' Blank stares. 'Why sugar, don't you know *Casablanca*?' The Misses Pan Am shake collective heads. He smiles. 'Well, I supppooooose it was before your time.' He takes care to keep up with the carry-on bag containing his precious pages, *this* time strapped to his person, all too aware of what might happen when travel distracts.

On the plane when the hostess makes her rounds, there's something about her pantsuit that makes him think of Jagger. Oddly nostalgic for a time he hadn't particularly cared for, he orders a Tequila Sunrise in homage. He finds, to his dismay, that the taste calls Lee to mind, turning acrid on his tongue with the very thought. He calls the hostess back, and trading Sunrise for old-fashioned, settles back in his seat.

It's as he's drifting off that he feels her presence beside him. He reaches for the armrest and feels her fingers stroke his arm. Manicured nails. Oxblood, buffed to perfection . . .

Babe.

'Soon, Truman ...'

'Babyling.'

'You'll be home soon, and just think how nice that will be.'

Closing his eyes he smiles, nods . . . falling asleep on her shoulder.

He wakes in two hours' time when the hostess gently shakes him, asking him to restore his seat and tray-table to their full, upright positions. He wipes groggy eyes. The seat beside him is empty, but for a plastic cup bearing the hint of a lipstick-mark, which does not surprise him in the slightest. He thinks that he can smell the faintest scent of heliotrope sweetening the stale air of the cabin, but of this he can't be certain.

He descends the stairs to the tarmac, smacked with the brick wall of humidity he's long since forgotten, soaking his shirt and linen suit before he's collected his bags and managed to find the driver that he'd ordered, standing just outside the whirl of the baggage carousels, holding a sign: 'CAPOTE' scrawled in red marker.

The driver—a gaunt man, who the boy thinks the spitting image of Skin-and-Bones from the railroad tracks in Monroeville—collects his luggage, a lone Vuitton suitcase, fraying with overuse. Could it possibly——? But the derelict had been ancient when the boy was but a child. Now that the boy is aging himself, surely poor ole Skin-and-Bones is long, *long* gone.

'The Holiday Inn, *s'il vous plaît,*' he squawks from the back of the town car, for he could find no limousine to drive him from Birmingham to Montgomery, much less Monroeville.

'Yesssir. I got instructions here.' The driver waves a paper in the rearview mirror.

Truman scans the backseat, knowing better than to expect a bottle of anything, and removes his hip flask from his pocket.

'You don't mind if I have a few sips from my trusty flask here ... ?'

The driver merely shrugs.

Truman tries again to drum up conversation. 'You know, *I'm* from Alabama—well, originally from N'awlins, but I grew up in Alabama all the same.' This too fails to elicit a response. 'I left for New York City when I was all of twelve, and I've hardly been back since. I did bring the dreadful Princess Radzilla back with me once to have a gander at hicksville, and the whole dang town thought we were *engaged*, thanks to my Daddy spreading *that* whopper.' Silence from Skin-and-Bones-as-Chauffeur.

Truman, agitated, 'Have you never heard of Lee Radziwill?'

'Nah, sir.'

'Surely you've heard of her sister, Mrs. Onassis . . .'

'Nope.'

Failing to impress, the pint-sized raconteur slumps back in his seat, watching dull, ugly landscapes fly past, beginning to remember precisely what it was he'd been so desperate to escape.

DROPPED AT THE HOLIDAY INN—a chain he's always loved for their blessed anonymity—he's checked in by midday, enjoying the familiar hum of the ice machine as he fills his bucket, shuffling back to the room where he pours a li'l-something-on-the-rocks. He removes the trio of Fabergé paperweights he'd brought from his collection, carefully chosen to make the space feel personal. Harvest golds and greens, calling to mind Babe's miniature vegetables, which never cease to warm his heart. Her impossibly minuscule carrots, sweet peas, and ears of baby corn. These he sets like a shrine on the nightstand, assured that in the evening they'll sparkle in the lamplight like bottles of Mama-juice, of which he's brought ample supplies.

He's donned swimming trunks and a terrycloth robe, plucked from a hook on the door. He's made his way down to a communal swimming pool, waded in, and started his dog-paddle laps. He's left his hat on his lounger so that he might turn backflips in the water, something that once gave him pleasure. He wants to explore all the simple things he's forgotten over the years. Perhaps he'll restore his name to 'Persons'; move back to the podunk town where authors with vision might speak their minds without causing a fuss . . .

He's so taken with the notion, he hurls his guppy frame backward in the deep end, feeling it swish around him as he turns in an endless series of loops. He can do so without getting dizzy—this he knows from boyhood. It's one of his special talents. He tries to shout for joy beneath the surface, mid-flip. He'd like to reproduce the operatic gurgles of humpback whales, which he's listened to on vinyl. His submerged shouts come out a pipsqueak peep, far from the sonar-song of the creatures of the deep with whom he feels a kinship. Still, he enjoys the sound of his own weak echo, until it blends with another . . .

Did you really think you could escape us, Truman . . . ?

Glug . . . glug . . . Fuck.

Not *that*, we know he thinks, for we can read his very mind. Not *here* . . .

You can't just go back to where you started and forget it ever happened. You'll never escape it. Never! Wherever you go you'll be locked inside—alone. Abandoned . . .

The boy shoots to the surface, choking for breath.

BACK IN HIS ROOM, RATTLED, he downs a glass of bourbon at Agnelli speed.

He gropes in his carry-on for a bottle of his pills—*any* pills— the three he extracts matching his Fabergé shrine to Babe almost exactly. Within minutes he's sprawled on the russett bedspread, floating on a liquid Orange Drink. The hotel staff have knocked repeatedly, guests having seen him retreat in a state. Concerned for his well-being, with no answer coming from within—'Mr. Capote? We just wanna make sure you're all right . . . Mr. Capote, please open the door.' He can hear them as if trapped in an echo chamber, but cannot bring himself to move, the old venom running through his veins.

'Mr. Capote, we're comin' in now.' He hears a skeleton key jimmy the lock. Hears their cautious tread, drawing close. As the manager stands over him, examining his paralyzed form, the boy feels a rush of terror that they're taking him away; stuffing him in a casket to bury him alive. Worse still, perhaps they're here to steal his precious pages, which he's carefully hidden in the room safe. The fight floods back into him as it so often does on the brink, and he attacks—his stubby little legs kicking with all their might, nearly knocking Mr. Manager in the head, grazing his ear instead. There's enough vitriol left in that midget carcass to have done serious damage, so the staff will later say they considered themselves lucky. They couldn't believe someone that shrunken had so much force in them, a dying beast, poked with a stick. Rabid. Desperate. He feels his limbs contract, then . . . nothingness.

It's terribly anticlimactic when he's rushed to the Baptist Medical Center and it turns out to be nothing more than a seizure, which he's suffered on and off for the last several years and thus has come to bore us. There was the usual siren's wails and ambulance and solicitous team of doctors. Forty-six roses from Governor Wallace, and a plant from his aunt Mary Ida. After two days' observation he's released, the *jouissance* of his visit home seized clean out of him.

BANNED FROM THE HOLIDAY INN FOR OBVIOUS REASONS, he checks into a nearby motor lodge—Doby's Hotel Court on Mobile Road, just off the Dixie Highway. He likes the bungalows with their faux porches. It seems a fated place to get back on one's feet. He pays a week in advance to stay and recuperate.

It's here that the colt-girl finds him. She of the gangly limbs and bowl-cut bob—the same traits he remembers, now stuck on a middle-aged lady. He says nothing, nor does she, sitting down in the rocking chair beside him, her down-tilts acting as counterpoints to his.

The only thing missing is the buzzing of the porch chat, but that will come. For two souls who love words, between them they hardly seem necessary.

That night over dinner—takeout fried chicken, which they eat on trays in the room that Nelle has moved into—they find they've been thinking the same thought.

'What does this remind you of?' she asks, a gleam in her eye.

Without skipping a beat—'That hotel in Garden City. *Spitting* image.'

'It's as if they picked it up in Kansas and plunked it down here.'

They smile, remembering the feeling of arriving together in that land of barren plains, Nelle having agreed to act as his Girl-Friday when he decided to travel to Holcomb to research the Clutter case. She had just delivered *Mockingbird* to Lippincott and it seemed an adventure. A grown-up version of their childhood snooping. Little did they know, in those early, innocent days, that by the end of six years they would both have succeeded beyond their wildest imaginings, though at what price was another matter.

He studies her sideways, taking in the strong jaw, the beauty that exists in her for him as it always had, if beauty might exist in plainness. Ever the midget suitor, he leans in close.

'Did I ever properly thank you, by the way?'

Same old Nelle, she refuses to indulge him. 'No, Truman. Matter of fact, you didn't.'

'But I *dedicated* it to you! *To Harper Lee with love and gratitude*—What?' off her look. '*What?*'

'*To Jack Dunphy and Harper Lee,*' she challenges in her tough Southern drawl. 'I think for the sake of all that work I deserved a bit more than unspecified "gratitude" alongside Jack, much as I love him. All Jack did was put up with *you*. Which as we know—'

'—is no small feat,' they finish together, laughing.

'Well, did *you* thank *me* for Dill in *Mockingbird* . . . ? I like to think he couldn't *exist* without me. You simply *stole* all of my mannerisms! Like a shameless soul-snatcher! My looks, my speech, my whole damn background!' He feigns upset, but she knows him too well. It's merely verbal jousting. Lance-blows he's better at throwing than receiving . . .

'Like what you did to Slim and Babe . . . ?'

He takes the jab. '*That* . . . is an entirely different matter and you know it.'

'Is it though?' When he shuts down, picking the skin from his chicken, she changes the subject. 'How is Jack?'

He shrugs.

'*Truman.* How's *Jack?*' The second time more a warning to pony up the goods.

'I think Jack hates me.'

'That can't be true.'

'Well, it is. He talks about me like I have a fatal illness.'

'Maybe you should listen to him.'

'And do what?'

'Get some help, for Chrissakes. You've done it before, you can do it again.'

'Aaactually, I'm not sure I can.'

'Truman, you look like hell on a plate. I'm worried. I'm sure Jack is too.'

'Don't laugh'—almost a whisper—'but I think that Jack is shape-shifting into Nina—I *said* don't laugh! I've seen it happen! One minute he's yelling at me, harping on about this or that—he leaves the room as Jack and walks back in as *her*. I swear to God, Nelle. He goes away and she appears. Then she'll leave the room and it's Jack who's back yelling. I promise you, he's possessed by Nina's spirit.'

'I can't think of two people more different than your Mama and Jack Dunphy. Now, you get your act together or you'll scare that poor man away.'

He doesn't bother to tell her that's what C.Z. told him, or about Christmas or the break-in or the hit men. That he's likely already sent Jack packing for good.

Softening, she places a hand on his arm. 'Truman . . . I called the hospital. They said you attacked that man because you were having a seizure.'

Silence.

'How long?'

'Hmmmmmm?'

'How *long* has this been going on?'

He starts to lie, but he knows she'll see through him—like an old country wife with the gift of prophecy. 'About two years.'

Nelle's eyes widen. 'And what have you done about it?'

'Nothin',' almost cheerful in his casualness.

'Truman . . .'

'Can I tell you a secret, Nelle?'

She nods as he lowers his voice, quivering with excitement, reminding her of a kid who used to speak the same way when he had a Big Idea to share.

He takes a breath before imparting his secret. 'You can't tell a soul, or *quelle* mess! How the folks who hate me would just *loooove* to get hold of *this* tidbit . . .'

He makes her cross her heart, that childhood gesture of utmost seriousness, then he tells her—'I *died* last summer. Not once . . . but *twice!*' He beams proudly.

'You what?' She frowns, skeptical, sure that he's gotten his facts wrong.

'I literally died—two separate times. The first time I was dead for thirty seconds. Then I was alive for four hours. Then I was dead again for thirty-*five* seconds. And let me tell you, it wasn't in *any* way unpleasant. I don't know why we're taught as kids that death is something to be scared of. I had two *different* deaths, both of them fascinating . . .'

'Where was this?'

'The hospital in Southampton. My doctor told me all about it, but he didn't have to. I remember it clear as that bottla' gin over there.'

Nelle looks to the gin, thinking (as we do) that maybe *that's* the problem.

'Well . . . ? Don't you wanna hear what happened?'

'Sure.'

'First of all, there's no sense of time. It coulda been thirty seconds or thirty minutes, or frankly thirty days. It isn't about that. The first time it happened I was on a riverboat, like the ones that used to dock in N'awlins? And I was on a stage—a rough old vaudeville stage—planks of wood, footlights, very crude. Like in *Showboat*, y'know? Anyhoo, I had my taps on, and I was in the most darling tux with tails and a tall top hat. And I was dancing like I've never danced in all my days. It was like one last glorious curtain call. You were there with your Daddy, and Ole Mrs. Busybody—'

'You mean my mother.'

'Uh-huh. And Nina and Joe and Sook and Cousin Jenny, but not just folks from here. Everyone was there, and I mean *everyone*. Those dimwit schoolmarms, and the men who saved me with their briefcases and IQ tests. Mean ole Robert Frost and that vile cunt Hemingway. Everyone I've worked with, everyone I've *known*. All the guests at my party, masks resurrected. Madge and Gladys and Ruthie, from Bobby Van's in Bridgehampton. George and Gene from the Colony. Bogie and Betty and Big John Huston. All clapping, wildly, applauding my efforts. Even *Gore* was forced to clap, and we know how much he'd *hate* that! The Barnacle Bouviers and the Kennedy boys, looking young and fine and alive. C.Z. and Winston and the Duke and Duchess of Windsor. Gloria and Loel and Gianni and Marella. My doctors and lawyers and publishers, naturally. Oh, and *la famille* Felker—Clay and Gail and clever little Maura. Cole and White— from my sideshow in Monroeville. And that horrid Chipper Daniels, who laughed at my bathing costume! My lovely, lovely Jack, beaming with pride. Maggie and Bunky and Charlie J. Fatburger, howling with deeelight. Gawd, so *many*, Nelle . . . Everyone I've ever met, cheering my last appearance on the great stage of life! Leland was watching in the wings and offered me a Broadway gig before my— —'

'Was *Slim* there, Truman?' Nelle's drawl cuts through his rhapsody. 'And *Babe* . . . ?'

He stops, pained. Nods.

'You know . . .' Nelle pulls a cigarette from her handbag and lights it, perhaps in subconscious tribute, 'I saw Babe . . . Not long before she died.'

He stares at her. *That* certainly shut him down. 'You—never told me that.'

'We weren't seeing much of each other at the time. Besides, I wasn't sure if you could handle it.'

He nods, looking very small.

'Anyway,' Nelle exhales a puff of smoke, 'it was at a dinner. Neither of us knew that the other knew the host. She wasn't going out much in those days—it was pretty near the end.'

'What happened?' his voice timorous.

'She was going into the powder room, I was coming out. We bumped smack into each other. Well, she took one look at me and burst into tears. She apologized time and again throughout the evening, hugged me as only Babe could, and told me how pleased she was to see me. But she couldn't stop crying. She felt just awful about it.'

'Why did she cry, Nelle?'

'Oh, Truman. For someone as smart as you, you can be so *awfully* thick.'

He stares at her, blinking. Waiting.

'She cried because she hadn't expected to see me . . . And she couldn't look at *me* without thinking of *you*.'

LATER THAT EVENING THEY SIT BACK OUT on the faux porch, creaking in their rocking chairs. The faintest trace of a breeze. Night descending like a veil over the purple hues of dusk.

'Would you like to hear about the second time I died?'

'Let me guess. Jesus gave you the Nobel Prize.'

'No. It was much simpler than that. I was in an airport, being checked in by those darling girls at the Aeroméxico counter—those ones in the smart pillbox hats—?'

Just like Jackie used to wear . . . by now an acknowledged refrain.

'Exactly,' unaware of the extent to which his stories have become *ours*. 'Anyhoo. They printed up my ticket and I picked up my bag and proceeded down a conveyor belt. It was in a hallway, the longest I've ever been in. And ahead of me in the distance was a figure . . . waiting.'

'God?'

'I don't *think* so, seeing as I don't believe in him.'

'Babe . . . ?'

'No.'

'Your Mama?'

'No . . . I'm pretty sure it was a man.'

'Jack?'

'That's preposterous, Nelle. I *live* with Jack. In the here and now.'

'Okay, then who . . . ?'

'I'm not sure. There was light at his back, so I couldn't make out his features. But I thought I saw the flash of a golden wing . . . an appendage wrapped in Cartier.'

'Oh, Truman. Cartier? What's goddamn Cartier gotta do with heaven?'

'I don't know . . .' he says cryptically. 'It just reminded me of someone I met once. I did something kind for him, and he did something kind for me in return.'

'And what was that?'

'I lost my words, and he gave them back to me.'

Nelle snorts. 'Well, I don't know if we should thank him for that, or issue a warrant.'

'It was thirty-five seconds, the whole shebang. Apparently if I'd been dead three more, I woulda been dead for good.'

'Well, thank your lucky stars.'

'Nelle? Do you remember, with the contest—in the children's Sunshine Page?'

'You've never let me forget it.'

'Well, do you remember the prize? The one they promised me?'

'I remember licking a hundred envelopes when you didn't get whatever it was.'

'It was a puppy. A beagle puppy.'

'What about it?'

'Don't you ever think how obscene it was that they denied me that? My whole life, all I ever wanted was a dog—then I *won* one, fair and square, and they prevented me from having it! To deny a child like that . . . Don't you think that's an act of deliberate cruelty? There's nothing that I hate more than deliberate cruelty. It's the one unforgivable sin in my view.'

Nelle looks perplexed. 'But Truman . . . you *had* a dog as a child.'

'I— —?' As if he can't believe his ears. As if Nelle holds the key to a part of his story he's long forgotten, lost in lies and narrative tales and manipulated half-truths.

'A sweet little mutt named Queenie. Sook bought her for you. Don't you remember?'

The man-boy shakes his head, trying with every ounce of his shrimpo being to separate fact from fiction.

THE NEXT MORNING HE'S CALLED TO THE LOBBY to find a telegram waiting. It's been so long since someone's thought to send him one, he feels that forgotten thrill of self-importance.

He looks closer— 'LADY SLIM KEITH' printed on the envelope as the sender.

His heart leaps in its bone-cage.

Perhaps she's chosen to forgive him! He's always held out hope . . . There isn't a day that he doesn't think of ringing her, or simply arriving on her doorstep, begging her pardon. He was sure she would forgive him with time. How did she know where he was, he wonders? Perhaps his trip home had worked some sort of voodoo, restoring her courtly favor. He rips the envelope open, anxious for what awaits . . .

SOMEONE SENT AUNT TINY'S BOOK. SO AMUSING TO
READ OF YOUR PATHETIC ANTECEDENTS AND CHILDHOOD.
    —SLIM

He stares at the paper, as if Slim herself had flicked her tongue out from the text and struck his hand as it clutched the venomed missive.

He returns to the room where Nelle is packing her belongings. She looks up to find his face ashen. 'Would you like to go to breakfast?' he asks, antsy.

'I thought we were waiting till lunch.'

'Can we reconsider—I really do feel like breakfast.'

'I suppose, but I thought we were going to—'

'Dammit, Nelle—I just need a *drink*!' he erupts. Then, hanging his head, he whispers, 'Sorry.' She watches as he pulls his snuffbox from his pocket and chokes down an undisclosed number of pills. He passes her Slim's telegram. Nelle reads it, eyes clouding with sympathy.

'Oh, Truman . . . I'm so sorry.'

'Can we please get a Bloody-Blood?'

SEATED AT A COUNTER AT THE HOTEL RESTAURANT, having slipped the waitress a ten-dollar bill to spike their tomato juice, Nelle holds Truman's trembling hand.

'Can't you just finish the damn thing? Maybe if it's out there, maybe if it's *done*, you can start something new and put all this behind you.'

'No . . . I've waited too long.' He shakes his head in his skeletal hand. The hand, Nelle notes, of an elderly man, yet Truman is still in his fifties. 'It's gotta be *perfect*, after all this. It can't just be good. It's got to be *great*. The best thing I ever wrote. The sum of all my talents.'

'But Truman, these are *bone*-crushing standards.'

'Exactly.' He leans in toward her, whispering his greatest fear. 'I'm worried . . . that it's killing me.' The terror bright in his eyes.

Nelle, touching her forehead to his, 'Why not just jump ship? You did with *Summer Crossing*—and you then wrote *Other Voices*. Frankly, you did it with *this* one and wrote *In Cold Blood*. Who's to say you won't write something else? Something *better* . . .'

'I can't give it up, Nelle. It's become a way of life. To finish it would be like taking a beautiful dog or a child out into the yard and shooting it in the head. It would never be mine again . . . and I'm not sure I could bear it.' He meets her gaze, shyly. 'I dream about it, you know? I *see* it, as real as you sitting there. The whole damn book.'

Nelle watches his eyes glaze with wonder, imagining his nocturnal visions, their splendor far removed from the harsh morning light in a cheap motel over watered-down Bloody Marys.

'It's gotta be *perfect*. It has to be worth all that I've lost.'

She shakes her head, watching obsession engulf him. 'Truman. Listen to me. Can't you just talk to them—the ones who are left—and admit that you made a mistake?'

'Ohhhhh no. Notta *chance*,' he laughs. The old moxy returns, fueled by a cocktail of vodka and defiance. The rage he feels for each of us, in tandem with the love. The fury for our having failed to understand him. 'The minute they smell the weakness, they'll come for me like sharks sniffing blood in the water. Besides, why should *I* back down? I'm in the right! They're the ones who are wrong! I have a responsibility to my art—to my talent!'

She touches his cheek, at once ancient and newborn.

'It's so beautiful, Nelle, when I see it before me . . . I can hardly believe anyone could be capable of writing such beautiful prose. I have to try . . . you know? To see it through to the end.'

'That's what worries me.'

'Don't worry, Nelle's Bells. I'll come through this—you'll see.'

THE BOY RETURNS TO AN EMPTY APARTMENT.

No Jack. No Nelle.

It's the quiet that troubles him most. He finds it unnerving.

He hasn't been sleeping of late. Two hours a night at most? His jangling nerves prevent more, even should he desire it. He's procured from his doctor a new pill to treat insomnia, which appeals for the fact it's poetically named: Halcion.

Even with the spelling gaffe, he likes to think the pale blue oval a magical passport to the shimmering days of old. Each night his greatest pleasure is the moment when he can place that sacred object on his tongue, swallowing halcyon days as he once gulped his Mama's Shalimar, hoping against all hope that by ingesting it he might find himself happily possessed. These moments are sacrosanct, his own special communion with all that he's loved and lost.

Upon his return from Montgomery, Sidney carries his luggage to his door, but more than that he has traveled the twenty-two flights for moral support, spotting that the boy seems too frightened to make the journey alone. He opens the door with Truman's keys, turns on the lights for him, and sets his suitcase in the hall. 'There you go, Mr. Truman. All set.'

'Sidney—' The boy stops him as he turns to go. 'Could you do me the hugest of favors and check each of the rooms?'

'Check them . . . for what?'

'Oh. You know. *People.* If you could do that for me and turn on a light in each, I'd be *so* grateful.'

'Sure thing, Mr. Truman,' Sidney humors him. He moves from room to room, the boy hanging back, lingering in thresholds. Kitchen to study to hallway to beds.

'All clear,' the doorman says brightly, emerging from Truman's boudoir.

'Could you possibly—I know it sounds silly, but would you mind looking in the closet? And under my bed? I've just been so damn *jumpy* since the break-in . . .'

Sidney complies, though rumors in the building have circulated that there *was* no break-in, nor were there assassins. It was just Mr. Capote, going around the bend.

'All good, sir,' Sidney reports in the end. 'And don't you worry—I'm right downstairs if you need anything.'

'Sidney, that really is terrific,' then, in his most *confidential* tone, 'And that little *favor* we discussed before I left . . . Did you manage to get around to that?'

'Of course, Mr. Truman. It's waiting in the freezer.'

Truman looks relieved. 'That's fine, Sidney. Just fine.' He walks him to the door.

'You have a good night, sir.'

'Sidney, wait—' Truman pulls up his sleeve, removing his watch, pressing it into the doorman's hand. 'For you. Bogie had one, Francis has one. I've got . . .' He forgets the rest.

'Oh no, Mr. Truman, I couldn't possibly.'

'Don't offend me, Sidney—for your trouble.'

'Beg your pardon, sir, but I consider you a friend.'

Truman brightens. 'You do?'

'Of course, sir. I appreciate the gesture, but why don't we save it for my birthday. That's what friends would do.'

'That's a terrific idea! When's your birthday, honey? I'll jot it down.'

'Fifth of July.'

'Done!' Truman beams.

'Goodnight, sir.'

'Nighty-night, Sidney.' He closes the door, walking back to his study, where he removes his battered datebook. Flips to the 5th of July, thinking with pleasure how close it is to the Fourth, which he loves, with its explosions and homemade bombs and spurts of Roman candles. Flipping another page he sees what he knew he'd find: 5 July . . . Barbara Paley.

Of course. *Babe's* birthday. Before the gloom has time to settle, he scrawls Sidney's name below hers, and makes his way to the kitchen.

He opens the freezer to find a pristine bottle of Stoli, purchased by Sidney in his absence. No one to stop him, Truman pours himself a generous Orange Drink, his 'friend' having thoughtfully left a fresh carton of OJ in the fridge as well. The boy sips with delight. He pulls his pillbox from his coat pocket, placing a lilac pill into his mouth then a green one, together blooming like a vine of inflorescence, which makes him think of Babe all the more . . . *Gawd* but he misses her in moments like these. Finally, the *pièce de résistance*: the oval tablet of Halcion, which he savors like a nun with a Eucharist wafer.

He makes his way down the hall to his own bedroom, where he changes into a pair of black silk pajamas. As he shuts the wardrobe door he sees a figure standing behind him in the glass.

He jumps with fright—the hit men—the assassins! (Who on some level he *knows* don't really exist. There are intruders in his house all right, but they're of quite another nature.)

He starts to scream, but stops, recognizing the figure behind him.

'*Joe* . . . ? Is it you?'

In the mirror, Joe Capote—whom he'd seen less and less since Nina died, hardly at all since his third wife stalked the boy genius. Could this be his comeuppance?

He rubs his eyes roughly, steeling himself to look back toward the mirror. When he does, the vision is gone. Not a trace of Steppapa Joe. He takes deep breaths, taking a vial of Dilantin from his medicine cabinet. He's been told to take these to stave off the seizures, which at this point he's keen to avoid. 'Christ, let's hope he didn't bring *Nina* with him,' Truman mutters to himself, sounding more flippant than he feels. He recovers his Orange Drink and moves to his study. He hears something . . . Soft. A thrumming of sorts?

He looks to see a moth, wings fluttering, caught inside his Tiffany lamp, drawn to the light, its whisper-weight beating against the bulb. Only a moth, he laughs at himself. Even so, he sits on the Victorian sofa, his back to the wall, so nothing might sneak up behind him.

It's then that he hears it properly. Not the moth wings, but beating all the same. *Thrumming* . . . Louder. Over it, something like Babe's laughter, rippling . . . then Gloria's. He turns to catch what he imagines might be their shadows crossing the room, or perhaps its just a trick of the light. On the windowsill, beside the chintz curtain, two perfectly white feathers. A pigeon's, he tells himself, blown in from the ledge. But when he reaches a hand out to grasp them, he's more convinced than ever of their origin, as little sense as it makes.

Two perfect, white swan feathers.

He moves back to the sofa, trembling now. A joke? A terrible joke that Jack has played to scare him onto the straight and narrow? Or could this be a plot to sneak in and steal his precious manuscript? His manuscript! He throws caution to the wind, racing to the hallway where his bag and suitcase lie, only to discover that the latter has been opened, guts rifled, every conceivable item tossed from its cavities. He stops—confused, losing the plot. He lunges for his carry-on—and *lawdy-mercy-praise-jesus* there it is.

Eight hundred pages, wrapped in brown— —

Of course he hadn't lost it! He'd learned that lesson years ago, when he first began to hear us. He returns to the study, unwrapping the paper, anxious to ensure that all is there. He holds it close, shielding the pages from phantom eyes, checking each chapter—snickering at moments that tickle his fancy. Brows furrowing critically on occasion, grasping for a Blackwing to alter wayward typos. Others he considers with a ruminative gaze, besotted with his own prose. He places the manuscript carefully on the table, and feeling thus secure, returns to the kitchen for a top-up of his Orange Drink.

He pauses . . . What's *that* he smells . . . ? Cigarette smoke? It couldn't be—he gave up years ago, after what it did to Babe. Could it be seeping through the walls? Do the Rothsteins smoke? One never knows these days. He sniffs the air with a sommelier's skill, detecting floral notes in the cigarette smolder. Perfume. Not one, but several. The scents he used to relish at cocktail parties, when women left their signature fragrances lingering in their wake, a sign of their presence as they moved from room to room. He thinks he detects the sweet fragrance of jasmine that Babe so often wore, though it equally reminds him of Marella, hers brightened with top notes of bergamot. He catches a hint of the spicy musk of Gloria, the orchid milk of Lee, which peppers the air with danger. The fresh simplicity of C.Z. and her tuberose, or Slim and her wet gardenias, mixed with Leland's bay rum, lingering on her skin.

As the boy moves through the kitchen, it seems that he can smell a bouquet, as if each of us has been present and chosen to exit the room.

From the study he hears a *bang!* A blunt crack, like a gunshot. He rushes back in, where he finds the curtains billowing. The wind having blown the window open—just like the night of the break-in. A gust sends his manuscript pages scattering across the room, several sliding under the sofa, which he scrambles on hands and knees to retrieve.

Make sure it's all there, Truman. You wouldn't want to miss a page . . .

He practically leaps from his skin. He scuttles back to his sofa. The flapping escalates in volume, surrounding him. Wings . . . Sets of wings, descending. Imperceptible.

Shining from various points around the room, a dozen eyes, liquid, lustrous black, a constellation of stars. Cygnus—the Northern Cross.

He scrambles back to his perch with the wall at his back and stares. At nothing, at everything. At that which he cannot see, but *feels*. He knows he's in the presence of *something*, but knows not what. He waits. And we wait. We have all the time in the world.

Finally, he ventures—'Hello?'

Silence.

'Is anyone there?'

Silence, but for the battering of wind against the pane.

'Nina . . . ?'

No . . .

With a mixture of fear and what can only be described as a rush of hope—'Babyling . . . ?'

And . . . (we prompt him).

'Mamacita . . . ?'

Our collective sigh ruffles the curtains. *Truman. Do you really not know us by now?*

We watch his dull little brain begin to piece it all together, which he's done before but forgotten, dismissing the revelations as the fleeting products of barbital or Thorazine or any number of others. It's not so far-fetched after all! (Mind, this might be the Halcion talking.)

'*All* of you— —?'

He can feel a wave of warmth from our collective pleasure at his having guessed.

He waits, and we wait. Listening and lurking.

'Whh–what do you want?'

Did you know, Truman, that swans—while undeniably graceful and usually benign—can fight like hell when they're under attack? When their mates are threatened, or their nests are at risk . . . ? They can go from serene to vicious in an instant.

We assume that he knows this—his head is stuffed with hundreds of useless animal facts—but being so addressed, he isn't sure how to reply.

Did you know, for instance, that their wings possess the power to break a human limb . . . ?

He shakes a feverish head.

Did you know that they're the fastest of all waterfowl and migrate in V formation? They've learned, you see, that by staying alongside the wing-tip vortices created by their neighbors, they might exploit the wake of the upwash—propelling themselves with the force of the whole. Can you guess what that means?

'No.'

It means that there's strength in numbers. And—this bit we feel you must know, it being right up your street—they can be referred to by a slew of collective nouns. A bevy. A bank. An eyrar.

442

A drift, a game, a herd. A lamentation—we like that one best. It's poetic, wouldn't you say? Of course it's referring to the dying swan's lament . . .

How his heart is racing. How he wishes we'd go away. He'd love to pop another Halcion, but fears what we'll do should he dare move a muscle.

Surely you know that swans sense their own death approaching, and sing the most beautiful of songs, right at the moment of expiration? They literally sing and then . . . finito.

His little chest puffs in silence, too wary to brag, lest he might be punished for it. Of *course* he knows this. He knows it from Shakespeare and Tennyson and Dryden and Proust. Some of his closest pals growing up. '*Like a long team of snowy swans on high / Which clap their wings and cleave the liquid sky,*' he almost whispers. He wouldn't dare test our patience with a longer recitation, but reckons a heroic couplet couldn't hurt.

So. Silence.

What about the book, Truman? What about Answered Prayers*?*

'What about it?' (Is that defensiveness we detect in his tone?)

How's it coming?

'Fine.'

Is it done?

'No.'

Is it close to being done?

'. . . Yes.'

Liar. Have you written any of it—beyond that shit in Esquire*?*

'Yes!'

You do know time is ticking . . .

We feel his pulse speed, watch him press a hand to his chest.

'Please stop! I don't want to discuss—'

Don't you just feel that clock in the sky, ticking away?

'I keep thinking I'm *almost* done—just a breath away! That all I need is one more day, one more day to get it right, to finish—the ultimate state of grace. But the *time* . . . !

Tick. Tick. Tick.

'It feels like there's an organ-grinder speeding time up, cranking it faster and faster. And I'm just the monkey, chained to his box, forced to dance at warp speed, desperate to keep up! A day becomes a week becomes a month becomes a year—'

Becomes five, ten, fifteen . . . ?

'I'm begging you—'

Have you ever stopped to consider, Truheart . . . who is writing who?

'What?'

Is it you who is telling our stories, or we who are telling yours? It all seems a puzzle, a nasty ventriloquial game.

If only you'd done us justice . . .

'But I *have*! It's *beautiful*—! It's Proust!'

Gossip! we find ourselves barking.

Pettegolezzo!—this from Marella.

'But *all* literature is gossip!' he cries in his defense. 'What in God's green earth is *Anna Karenina* but gossip? Or *Madame Bovary*, or *War and Peace* for Chrissake?'

What will you do now, Truman? we hear ourselves sneer. *Who are you—what are you—without your precious words?*

'I—' he begins, but we stop him, pecking our rage.

Nothing! Just a pissant rug rat from—

Unwanted—unnatural—

A monstrous little freak—

A genius, a failure, an addict—

A lethal goddamn cobra, taxidermied upright—

Alone, abandoned—

'Terrified.' Truman exhales. He's never been so close to *knowing* what his book needs to be. Yet never so far from reaching it.

If only he had it in him! He sees it all so clearly—all that he wants—*needs*—to pull from the heavens and render immortal. The cast of thousands, all mixing and mingling at a glorious soirée in Shangdu—that ancient Chinese city in Mongolia, the Xanadu old Coleridge had in mind when he penned *Kubla Khan*, on a peacock fan of hallucinogens himself. There the boy sees shimmering rivers, on which one might float. Wavering wheat. Lapis seas. Sleek structures of glass and steel, rising from desert floors. Big drafty farmhouses with beauty in their sparseness. He sees yachts and speedboats and streamlined planes, one shape-shifting into the next. And the people . . . Everyone he's ever met. Everything he's seen.

There above it all he balances with high-wire grace, hovering over his visions, his beautiful visions; the perfect world that he's constructed in his head, from nothing more than his very own thoughts.

It makes us want to jostle the tightrope.

It gives a sick pleasure to watch him fall and fail. An incestuous spirit of schadenfreude, given how closely we're linked. We'll concede that there is no us without Truman, but neither is there Truman without us. He's been forced to coexist with us as we honk and bark and rage. He lives with our resentment festering within him. We are the cancer eating his insides—a dilemma, when one considers it. We cannot exist without the host, yet we take solace in destroying him.

It would seem to beg the question, are we committing some sick form of mass hara-kiri? But we could frankly *give* a fuck. It's revenge that we seek. At any price.

'I just wanted to tell your *stories*,' he wails. 'Like the most sublime of novels. I *loved* who you were—total self-creations, like the great heroines of literature—Karenina or Bovary, only better. *Soooooo* much better! Because you're *real*.'

We aren't characters for your amusement, Truman. We're women. Real women. And those are our lives *you're so casually scribbling.*

'Trust me, honey—there's nothin' *casual* about it!'

Our lives—not fiction! You said the most horrible things—

'*I* didn't say them—P.B. did! You can't blame a writer for what his characters say!'

Who the hell SHOULD we blame?

'I don't know,' he's weeping now. 'I just don't know ...'

You know, there's only one thing that cannot be forgiven ...

'Yes! *Deliberate cruelty!*' he shouts, *j'accuse, j'accuse, j'accuse.*
'*You're* the monsters! What can be crueler than to reject someone flat out? Someone who loved you as much as I did?'

You left us little choice ...

'I was an artist—always an artist!'

Is any art worth this ... ? Killing us and killing you—for something you'll never finish—?

'I'm trying as hard as I know how!' he sobs. 'And I'm *tired* ... so tired.'

Maybe ... we pause, holding his attention, *it isn't meant to be finished ...*

Silence.

Because you can't do it anymore ... can you, Truman?

He shakes his weighty head in his hands.

'No,' he whispers, relieved that someone has said what he cannot. That he cannot accomplish the one shimmering thing he most wants. That we're the ones who have guessed it moves him inexplicably.

You want to be done, don't you ... ?

A mournful little nod. 'Awfully. Oh so awfully.' He no longer seems a tightrope artist hovering above, hoping to maintain his balance, but a creature below, standing at the bottom of the sea, staring up at the light above the surface. And that's when it strikes him.

So simple, so clear. Suddenly he knows, regardless of the outcome ...

Sometimes *no* words are better than the wrong ones.

It's then that he hears it ...

A great glorious symphony of voices, trumpeting the old, heralding the new. A crescendo of joy, drowning the loss and the pain. Honking, wailing, sweet Cygnus release! The swan song of swan songs, perhaps what he's been working toward all along.

He can hear Our voices, blending in concert, yet he can hear each of us as he knows us, soloists rising above the chorus. Babe's silver timbre, a familiar tune, deepening and ripening with time, with the counterpoint of uncertainty. Slim's death rattle, the rhythmic clack of the castanets, dancers whirling round his tiny room. He hears Gloria's primal cry—the tale of epic exploits. A mariachi waltz, taunting the mandolins of doomed Casanovas. The coloraturas of Marella's impassioned arias soaring higher, ever higher, then plunging back down. Colliding with harmonics of a low, bluesy wail. The exhaled puff of Lee's cigarette smoke rising and swirling with visions of gin-soaked bar-room queens and midnight ramblers, of the undulating beat of rhythm and blues. He can hear old vaudeville tunes, crackling on a gramophone. The razzmatazz of showfolk, of C.Z.'s off-key trill. Taps on uneven planks of riverboat stages—*stomp-hop-shuffle-step-flap-step, stomp-hop-shuffle-step-flap-step.* Trumpets' wails, jangling pianolas. Lullabies in dulcet tones; a mama's voice, honeyed. Singing to a boy she never asked for, who thought hers the sweetest of songs, given her smile as she cradled him close.

Over it all, the sweet cry of waterfowl, like the blare of brass and woodwinds.

The flock of Apollo, opening lovely, lengthy throats and issuing a final collective howl, traveling up the long, curving chambers, miles long, and bursting forth like a thousand rays from a single celestial sun. Flying closer, ever closer toward that brilliant orb, heralding the dawn with an eternal moan of joy.

The boy feels two muscular pinions extend through the wall and surround him, the Cartier watch ticking closer to the dawn. Without looking, he knows to whom they belong.

'Vi-chen-tee? Did you hear it?' He leans back into the crook of a golden wing, which folds protectively across his concave chest. '*That* was *Answered Prayers*. And it's beautiful.'

With that the boy loosens his grip, pages fluttering to the ground like tufts of eiderdown. His heart's still full, *so full* . . . but his mind is light as a feather.

Floating on clean white pages, so long a life raft—besieged—now a pleasure cruise through glimmering emerald grottos, cutting through the Aegean, finally drifting languidly down placid streams of blessedly empty thoughts.

T HE BOY IS FIFTY-NINE when he finally goes to China.
It's the only country he has yet to visit, the last stop on a well-traveled wish list. It's in the last stifling days of August, almost a month to the day from his birthday.

He's planning to celebrate reaching his sixtieth year in grand style, for while it *sounds* old, the boy feels unnaturally young.

He's staying with Joanne Carson, one of the few 'La Côte Basque' victims still speaking to him. Something of a Truman sycophant, she was delighted to find herself featured in his opus, even if painted as a bitter cuckquean with a flagrant case of the clap. Eager to be linked to his literary legend, she's desperate to be ensconced in the pantheon of Swans, though we'll never think of her as anything more than a second-string cygnet at best.

She devotes herself to her houseguest's needs whenever he deigns to visit, keeping her swimming pool heated at Jacuzzi temperatures so that he might sit on the first step year round, armed with a composition book, pretending to write—something he does with panache.

He ponders—as he steeps in the steaming chlorine bath—if he has the energy to dog-paddle a lap, keeping his panama hat above water. More often than not he prefers to float on a plastic raft, gazing through his insect shades into a tangle of eucalyptus branches.

Joanne has filled the rambling ranch house (a one-story monstrosity on a particularly perilous stretch of Sunset) with llama skins and wicker swings and yogi memorabilia. It's been designed to invoke a Tibetan monastery, candles a flickering constant. She used to light these on special occasions, but the boy has insisted that every day they spend together is an 'Occasion,' and has thus kept the wax trade thriving in Bel Air.

We muse that Carson must be paying hefty alimony, given that Joanne's lifestyle isn't exactly commensurate with her second-act career as a 'holistic nutritionist.'

She's gotten the boy into that shit—feeding him hemp seed and tiger's milk and wheatgrass in excess. She brags that when he stays with her, his vices seem to vanish.

'Sugar,' he'll tell the last stragglers in his weary entourage, 'California may gobble your brain cells, but the food there is so damn *healthy*. Joanne makes me fresh-squeezed juice in a special machine every morning. Carrot-and-apple-and-grapefruit, oh my!'

He balances a highball of juice on his gut as he lolls on the raft in Joanne's pool. We—and Jack—and anyone who knows him—have to wonder where he's stashed the vodka. As he sips and floats with what we suspect is his traditional Orange Drink, his thoughts turn to his former pool in Palm Springs, to the house at Thirst's End. The unrelenting midday heat makes him think of Maggie, lying in the desert sun with her steady, listless panting. He knows how hard Jack fought to save her in the end, when her hind legs were paralyzed, and regrets with all his heart suggesting otherwise in a blind moment of rage.

He thinks of Jack, who he misses terribly.

Not the harridan Jack of now, who berates him each time the boy lands himself in the hospital, who regulates his meds when they happen to occupy the same space, though that happens less and less frequently. Not the Jack who still resents him for turning their romance chaste—certainly not the prudish Jack who, when the boy attempts to undo his poor choice and make love, fails to become aroused, mechanics prevented by spite.

It is the Jack of his youth that he craves.

When he closes his eyes and inhales the eucalyptus and the fragrant scent of Joanne's climbing jasmine, the boy allows himself to travel in his mind. As the August heat seeps into his skin, he wills himself to another heat-soaked clime . . .

Not to sweltering days in Monroeville, though he travels there too sometimes, to visit Nelle and Sook and his Mama—who, in the Monroeville of his choosing, is not driving down the long dirt road, leaving him behind, but rather sitting *with* him. They sunbathe on the soft grass in the Faulk cousins' yard, watching ice cubes melt atop the griddles of their chests. They swing together on porch swings, enjoying the harmony of creaking back and forth together. When and if the boy allows the drama of a snakebite to intrude, it's the boy's Mama who kills five chickens to drain their blood for his cure. It is she who holds his hand and strokes his fringe and tells him what a fine boy he is, while he glugs from a bottle of crystal-clear Mama-juice, its fire trickling like lava down his— —

But that's not his memory of choice now.

Today, lying on the plastic float in Joanne Carson's pool, he's traveled further afield, to more exotic landscapes. He has sprouted wings and flown elsewhere, transported through the heat and botanicals to a secluded beach in Morocco.

The boy is twenty-four.

He knows this because today is Jack's birthday and in memory he's about to turn thirty-five again, rather than the seventy years of now.

They wake in each other's arms.

He has forgotten just how soft Jack's skin can be, having not run his fingers over its freckled terrain in some time. The boy, in his reverie, takes full advantage of the chance when it comes, attempting to kiss his way along the patterns that he worships, to find logic in their clusters. Jack laughs, his low, resonant laugh. *Gawd*, it's been so long since he's heard that laugh, it nearly breaks his heart with delight.

Jack loves him again—the boy can tell. He's waited for this love to return, waited through ill-fated conquests, through brawls and petty feuding. Through betrayals and defections. Through the unbearable loneliness.

The boy has needed Jack's love more than ever these last years. Needed the person he's most adored to understand the scope of his loss. To feel with him what it is to be bereft. To have done something so heinous, without *meaning* to, he's been forever barred from paradise. To be denied the chance to make amends, which is perhaps what has hurt him most.

We know he has a big heart, the boy. Perhaps that's his problem—an oversized heart, bursting with limitless love. There's so much of it stored up now, prevented from release, it's constricting his very breath.

His heart feels as big as that of a great blue whale, which he's read has the largest heart of any living creature. Their hearts alone weigh as much as a jet plane, their tongues as much as an elephant. The aorta is big enough for a grown man to crawl through. The boy feels like a *Balaenoptera musculus* trapped in a shrimpo body.

It hurts to have that much love to give and no one left to give it to.

He thought that Jack would understand, but his patience ran thin quick—his patience for such things being limited to begin with. A wedge had been driven between them, so in addition to losing *us*, he's lost Jack too in a way. He would never again be the pure, joyous sprite Jack had fallen in love with; he would always be marred by pain.

Jack hadn't fallen in love with a boy with a broken blue whale heart. The loss of Babe, of Slim, of each of us, has altered the boy's anatomy. Jack has not been certain what mammal he's now dealing with, and being thus unsure is incapable of communing with it.

But here in the travels of the boy's imaginings, Jack loves him without reservation.

THEY'D FIRST GONE TO TANGIER to meet Cecil Beaton. Jack would have happily remained ensconced in their rented house on the cliff in Taormina, with its bougainvillea and its citrus trees, laden with fragrant blood oranges.

But Truman wanted Tangier and Jack couldn't resist indulging him in those early days. Cecil was someone the boy had long admired. He'd studied him from afar—fascinated by the artist who mingled with society—'Sugar, with the *royals*, no less!'

Cecil had taken to Truman, had adopted him as a protégé of sorts. They made quite the double act—the lanky, posh Englishman and the brash midget hillbilly. But they were a friendship made in paradise. Thanks to Cecil, they found themselves (to Truman's delight and Jack's dismay) part of an expat community of artists . . . Cecil and Jane and Paul Bowles, and nasty little Gore Vidal, who loathed the boy as much as he was loathed in— —

No, the boy will not allow washed-up grudges to taint his memory. He inhales the wisteria once more, feels the faintly medicinal eucalyptus cooling his overburdened lungs. He forces himself back onto a beach, the day of Jack's thirty-fifth birthday.

He has been planning to give his darling Jack and the tiny expat town a fête they won't soon forget. He and Cecil have spent the better part of two weeks down on the beach, at the Cave of Hercules in the Cape Spartel, near the summer palace of Moroccan kings.

They've devoted their combined talents to setting the stage for a celebration of epic proportions. They've draped the inside of the cave with Moroccan tapestries. Covered the sandy floor with cement tiles shipped in a crate from Marrakech. They've procured every lantern in the remote town. It will be lit from within, turning the abandoned beach into a sultan's harem.

'Cecil baby,' the boy tells him as they arrange rugs and ottomans, hookahs and furs, 'you know, inside the harems there were often bang-up parties. Those poor little gals were slaves, but that didn't stop 'em from kicking their heels up now and again. They would swim in sea hammams—private beaches like this one, where they'd play musical instruments and sing and paint and dance, naked as jaybirds . . .'

Cecil half-listens. He's far more interested in how it looks than what it means.

'They say that Hercules slept in this cave before performing his eleventh labor—snatching golden apples from the Hesperides' Garden,' the boy continues, undeterred. 'I don't care if we have apples—or food for that matter. It's my party—'

'And Jack's,' Cecil reminds him, in clipped English vowels.

'Of course Jack's! I'm doing this for him, aren't I . . . ?' He then enthuses, 'There'll be nothin' but bottles and bottles of lovely fizz and hookahs full of hashish!'

And so it comes to pass, as the party makes its way down the brittle cliffs in the dark, led by shirtless Moroccans wielding torches, and when they discover the glowing jewel-box cave, even the most cynical of them catches their breath. Jack takes it all in, pragmatism silenced by awe.

'Jack . . . ! Jack . . . ! Look up, Jack!'

The party turns to see Truman, every bit the pasha, sitting cross-legged, being hoisted on a makeshift palanquin by four strapping Moroccans.

'Helloooooooo, Jack!' The boy can see his beloved on the beach as he makes his descent, drawing near and nearer. Jack stands in a field of lanterns, surrounded by a halo of light. His features are obscured, but the boy is certain the faint lines around those green Irish eyes are softening his countenance, as they tend to when he smiles. It's an image the boy will sear into his memory to relive again and again.

'Jack!' he calls to him and waves, as if he's brand new to him. It's how he'll always say Jack's name—as if he's something new and wondrous that he will never tire of.

And from a pool in California, the boy dips his limbs in the water as he remembers a beach in Morocco, where revelers ran naked into the ocean in the pale moonlight, as the Andaluz band played on.

JOANNE HAS SET UP A 'WRITING ROOM' for Truman in her ashram of a ranch house.

Naturally we've never seen it, but we have heard . . . and photos will later be printed by the tabloids. We're all struck by the tawdriness of it. She can call it a 'Writing Room' all she wants, but we can see what it is . . . the maid's quarters. A tiny, bare space, just off the kitchen, originally designed for the staff.

She's christened the maid's rathole Truman's, and keeps things there we can't fathom him stomaching. For someone who worships beauty as much as Tru, the contents of the space seem especially obscene: a fraying wicker peacock chair, a mass-produced sepia Madonna and Child—these for a boy who values antiques and loathes art that we've heard him dismiss as 'religious propaganda' in famed galleries. A half-deflated party balloon, dejected in its flaccid state. A four-poster canopy bed that looks like a hand-me-down from a ten-year-old girl's room. From its iron posts hang two kitsch piñatas. (We all know that since watching what happened to Dick and Perry, Truman is squeamish about hangings of any sort; he must lie awake at night, staring at those papier-mâché donkeys strung up by their necks, and shudder.)

Joanne swears that he relishes the solitude. That he comes to her to get healthy (even though she—the nutritionist—keeps his nightstand stuffed with Snickers bars and M&Ms and peanut-butter cups left as offerings). There are 'no drugs' in her monastery, she insists—though presumably she hasn't bothered to count Truman's black doctor's satchel of prescription bottles, supplying everything from Quaaludes to codeine. Dilantin, Thorazine, Valium—you name it.

'Sugar, I just love my little pills—they make one feel so cozy. I pop a few and it's like cuddling up with them for the evening.'

He 'doesn't drink' in her palace of wellness either, according to Joanne. This too we have our doubts about, Truman being better than a speakeasy barman at hiding the hooch. We're certain he'll be secretly spiking all that juice Joanne is plying him with. In fact, the health nut would be stunned to learn that the protein shakes

Truman mixes in her blender contain a healthy splash of bourbon from a discreetly concealed hip flask.

Still, on days when he feels ambitious, they drive to the beach in Malibu, where they fly homemade kites, like the ones he'd flown with Sook when he was her 'Buddy' in Monroeville. On rare days he summons the strength to dog-paddle the length of the pool a few times.

He tells Joanne that he's writing, but she has not, by her own admission, seen pages emerge. She's received the same verbal recitation of the *Answered Prayers* extracts, but we suspect he'll be bullshitting her, just as he's done with the rest of us. She claims she once saw an elusive missing chapter—the inflammatory 'Father Flanagan's All-Night Nigger Queen Kosher Cafe,' which the mighty Clay Felker never did get his hands on.

After ten years of Tru running his mouth about these famous 'chapters,' most of us suspect they don't exist—that they're but another of the boy's tall tales.

Lee thinks he wrote the whole frigging opus, all eight hundred pages, but destroyed it when the fallout occurred. C.Z., for her part, feels certain if he had something written, there's no way he would have delayed publication. At this point he has nothing left to lose. Babe and Gloria, had they been here to conjecture, would continue to hope that he's hidden his pages away, to be found at an opportune moment. (Perhaps where *they've* gone they know the answer to such questions, which we'll one day learn when we join them.)

Slim says she wouldn't doubt it if he never wrote a syllable beyond the original hatchet job. He is, as we know, appallingly lazy . . . But Marella puts her two cents in—in her cryptic post-antiquaire way, 'I promise you, there's *more*. He told me what he plans to say. He's written it, and it's lethal.'

Ever one to manipulate a tale for entertainment's sake, Truman yammers on of late about random keys and bank vaults and fabricated theft. He's taunted eager journalists with tales of lockers in stations. Of safety-deposit boxes, secured with indefinite payments. His publisher has been mailed a cryptic list of far-flung Greyhound depots; his lawyer instructed to file suits against likely culprits of theft. Planting the seeds of his own bespoke conspiracy, he's been consistently inconsistent.

TRUMAN AND JOANNE TRAVEL TO VARIOUS COUNTRIES, he having determined their itineraries beforehand.

'We're going to Barcelona tomorrow,' he might declare upon arrival.

The following morn he'd present his hostess with a tray of churros and *café con leche*. They'd spend the afternoon taking art books from the library, poring over photos of Gaudí's architecture as they lunch, nibbling plates of tapas and sipping Tempranillo. They'd listen to Spanish guitar records and critique the works of Picasso and Dalí.

They'd been to Paris, Berlin, Tokyo, Moscow . . . all without stepping on a plane.

On this particular visit, Tru reveals their destination, mimicking Johnny's *Tonight Show* catchphrase—'Heeeeeeeeeeeeere's *China*!'

'Where in China?' Joanne asks.

'Shanghai. I'm simply dying to go. Y'know it's the only place on earth I haven't been?'

They order a takeout, which they eat on the floor by the fire, studying maps and sketches of the Great Wall. They eat dim sum with chopsticks and look at photos of the Bund. Of Old Shanghai in the Thirties, in all its glorious excess. As they sip their oolong tea, Tru tells Joanne about the bruisers he'd hired in Monroeville to dig up his cousin Jenny's vegetable patch in search of Oriental treasure. He presents her with a gift of a tiny porcelain medicine jar, procured at a shop in Chinatown.

Curiously, while flipping through an atlas, Truman pauses and says—'I really am going to China, you know.'

'That's wonderful, Truman. When?'

'Oh, I dunno. Soon . . . But I'm going.'

457

What he doesn't discuss is the one-way ticket to Los Angeles he purchased the week before, at a higher rate than usual. What he hasn't told a soul—not even Jack—is that after being released from the hospital in Southampton, he'd returned to the city, and within the walls of his UN Plaza digs they started up again . . .

The voices. Our voice.

It's getting close, Truman . . . isn't it? Not only can he hear us, he's accepted our presence as something that is part of him.

It will soon be here . . . It will soon be here . . .

'Stop it!' he hisses, to no one in particular. He pops a little lilac pill—a new acquisition called Lotusate, which he finds works a treat for keeping unwelcome warnings at bay.

Truman had arrived at Joanne's the previous day hoping for the best, though he now fears his body is failing him. She assumes this means he's been drugging, despite his doctors' warnings.

'No,' he says quietly, 'I've taken nothing.'

(Not exactly true, but a cocktail of barbiturates is something he considers the 'norm.')

He looks so weak she makes him scrambled eggs on toast, as basic as it gets. Afterward, he asks her for the stack of his books she gives as Christmas gifts each year, which she always asked him to personalize.

'But it's only August,' she objects.

'I'll just feel better, knowing that they're done,' he says.

He works his way through her stockpile of *Music for Chameleons*, then continues scrawling his signature on blank scraps of paper. When Joanne looks confused, he explains—'You can save them and tape them into books in the future.'

When he finishes signing her scraps for future books, it is he who surprises her, with a cake and candles, her birthday being just before his own.

'Darling, what can I get you for your birthday? Is there anything that you want?'

'I want you to write. That's all. Please, Truman—just write.'

Yes, Truman, write, but not that shit-on-a-shingle gossip . . .

Write something worthy.

He pats her arm and wanders out into the sun, where he sits in a lounger for the better part of the afternoon. He returns, not with an excerpt from *Answered Prayers*, but a simple portrait, exquisitely penned: 'Remembering Willa Cather.'

He talks about her writing and recalls her kindness to him in his youth. They'd met by chance in the Reading Room of the New York Public Library when he was just a loud-mouthed nobody. She speaks to him now—the voice of an author with a cadence like his own.

He hands the pages to Joanne as he retreats to his room.

'There you go, Jo. Happy birthday.'

THE NEXT DAY HE RISES and begins to dress for his morning swim.

It is earlier than usual—barely five o'clock. The boy knows this because he can just see the sun rising outside his postage-stamp window.

As he reaches to pull his swimming trunks on, his strength fails him.

He sits back on the bed, exposed. He feels his blue whale heart race with a surge of something he can't control.

He cries out—'Jo-Jo?' No answer. '*Jo-Jo . . . ?!*' Then, growing desperate as he had been in fleabag motels when his Mama locked him in while she stole out with her lovers, the boy shrieks in earnest—'*JO!*'

You're just the same as you always were, Truman.

You weren't fooling any of us . . .

Just look at you . . .

Unlike his Mama, unlike *us*, Joanne comes running.

'Truman, what is it . . . ? Whatever's wrong?'

He's sitting on the bed, naked. Madras swimming trunks halfway up his legs, a deflated fabric inner tube, dangling around his calves. Frozen in the effort of pulling them to his waist.

He looks at her with fixed, frightened eyes.

'I think I'm dying,' he tells her simply.

She checks his pulse, which is racing, but she'll think what *we'd* think . . . Take it with a grain of salt; he's always been high-strung.

Joanne rises. 'I'll go get you some juice.'

The boy pulls her back—'No. Just sit with me. Sit with me so I'll have someone to *talk* to.'

She relents and sits down beside him on the bed. The boy begins to talk, if only to enjoy the familiar timbre of his own voice. She feels his pulse as he recounts all the things he loves—about Jack, and Slim and Babe, about his inconsistent Mama. His pulse flutters, the whisper-weight of a moth, trapped inside his bone-cage.

'Truman,' Joanne says, fingers pressed to his wrist, 'I think you're in a little trouble . . . I need to call an ambulance. Let's get you to the hospital right away.'

'Honey, *no*.' The boy grasps her arm with his deceptively strong grip.

'You need a doctor—'

He looks at her. Imploring. Certain.

'*Please*. No more doctors. No more hospitals. If you love me, let me go.'

Joanne's eyes meet his, welling with tears. 'What do you mean, let you go?'

'Exactly what you think I mean.'

'I can't do that, Truman. You need *help*.'

'Jo. Just let whatever's gonna happen happen,' he says, a sense of calm overtaking him. 'I wanna leave—let me.'

Joanne shakes her head. 'I can't—I'm a doctor.' (We're not sure how being a nutritionist qualifies Joanne as a *doctor* . . .) 'What will I tell them when they find out I knew you were in danger and didn't call? I could get into trouble . . .'

'Well, don't tell them, dummy.'

Joanne will report she felt a sob escape her throat. 'Truman, I can't. Please don't ask me this. I can't bear to lose you.'

As he sits in this state, childlike, drained of ambition, the rattler's venom sucked clean out of him, we're stunned to find that we feel for him too.

'Just think of me as going off to China. There's no phones or mail service there, so think of me as being away . . .' He shivers as he says it. 'I'm cold . . . so cold. Hold me . . . ?'

Joanne swaddles him in a blanket and wraps her arms around him, rocking him. She quietly sobbing. He talking, ever so softly. (We can hear him, even if she can't.)

He imagines that her arms are Jack's, holding him tight in his protective grasp. Or his Mama, cradling him close, telling him in dulcet tones what a fine boy he is.

He thinks of how he'd longed to have been there for Babe in the end. How he would have held her close and told her how very much he loved her—how she was the most beautiful creature he'd ever met. Inside and out. How he never meant to hurt her—or any of us.

He has flashes of us, the idealized snapshots he treasures for each.

Clinging to Slim on a freezing Russian train, wrapped in a dozen coats to stave off the ferocious cold, knocking back shot after shot of crystal-clear Mama-juice as it trickles like lava down their throats. Of Lee, back when she was lovely in a white bathing suit, before she could fathom betraying him, sipping frothy piña coladas from coconut shells in matching insect shades. Of C.Z. in her garden, in jodhpurs and pearls, garden mitts up to her elbows like a pair of mud-caked debutante gloves, telling him all about the first flowers to grace the new branches of spring. Of Gloria, in Acapulco, her olive skin all the more so against her crisp striped djellaba—beneath her domed palapa, where she drops international graces and sets the uncensored Latina in her free, at home in her natural habitat. Of Marella, on

461

their first Amalfi tour, sunbathing topless on the polished deck, when a Corsican swallowtail lands on her exposed breast . . .

Or, wait—was that not Babe?

Babe comes to him in a hundred images all at once, perhaps the most indelible of which is her beautiful face leaning across an intimate luncheon table, whispering, close to his own . . .

'Babe!' he cries out loud, telling her, under his breath, all that he needs to say to her; all that he never got to say in the end.

The boy talks and talks in the canopy bed—its four posters the gallows for a pair of piñatas he'll never crack open—the words that once eluded him flowing like a cool Alabama stream.

He sees it all, in filmic flashes——the snippets of memory he cherishes. What he'll remember . . . What will flicker before him when the end finally comes.

The last words of *Answered Prayers*, which he wrote before his first. The final page, which he's kept in a very special place since 1954, since the day that his Mama killed herself. It was always for her that he did what he did.

More tears are shed over answered prayers than unanswered ones . . .

The boy finds it difficult to get air into his cetacean lungs—or is it his heart?

It feels like he's drowning. He imagines himself by the river dock . . . He's fallen into the water. He can't swim, in this version of the fiction. All he can do is let the gentle current take him, gasping for air, clinging to his memories.

It's a sweltering day in Monroeville.

The kind of day when lizards sizzle on the pavement,

The kind that sears the tender pads of doggies' paws.

The boy is eight, maybe nine, in a garden thrumming with bees. He's digging up his cousin Jenny's vegetable patch himself, desperate to tunnel his way to China.

He picks round ripe tomatoes from the vine, the heirlooms he and a kind man called Jack once ate with fresh-caught redfish after a swim.

He runs through a cedar forest toward a crystal creek, where he washes the tomatoes and peels back their outer skin to reveal slushy inner guts.

In the distance a dog barks, possibly the beagle he'd won for his stories and never received. He can just hear the snippets of the Negro spiritual from the First Baptist Church in the little ole country town . . . *I've got two wings for to veil my face, I got two wings for to fly away . . .*

Fly away . . .

The boy bathes himself in the creek, to the cadence of cicadas, to the clucks of the porch chat and the trill of Nelle's mockingbirds.

To a porch swing with croaks like the bullfrogs at the swimming hole.

Then, gliding through the river water, he sees it—a snake.

The very water moccasin that bit him years before, when the farmer's wife and his Faulk Carter cousins slaughtered five fresh hens, dousing his bite with poultry blood to cure him. He watches the serpent writhing in the water, setting it a-ripple. Swimming ever closer . . .

But the boy is not afraid. Ophidian ribboning toward him, he stands stock-still, just as his Daddy once taught him—cool as a cucumber.

This is his species, after all.

Are you sure you aren't afraid, Truman . . . ?

'*Stop*,' the boy says aloud, to no one in particular.

The scene shifts—it's ten years later.

He's nineteen, but he still looks twelve. He's in a smoky jazz club in Manhattan, on West 52nd. The Famous Door.

He sits enraptured, watching Lady Day, signature gardenia in her hair, though he chooses now to remember it as a Little Gem magnolia—just like the ones Nina kept out on a crummy fire escape in her Bronx walk-up. Just like the kind Big Daddy removed from its plastic coffin and pinned in Big Mama's butterscotch mane. He watches, mesmerized, as Miss Holiday's heroin-dimmed eyes gaze into the cheap glow of a lavender follow spot. A look the boy will come to share in decades' time, squinting into the rose-hued strobe light on the floor at 54, dancing a frenzied, tipsy jitterbug to the Big Bands in his mind.

Good morning, heartache, thought we'd said goodbye last night . . .

The boy is twenty-nine. He is in Italy. He is in love . . .

He is standing on a terrace in Taormina. Stucco covered in bougainvillea, the scent of ripe blood oranges perfuming the air.

A passenger boat is arriving from the mainland. On the wharf, carrying a suitcase, is someone the boy knows well—a man's man with freckles and dark auburn hair. A man who had said goodbye, for all the reasons you'd expect, but who has come back. A man who's changed his mind. A man walking toward him, choosing him.

'*Jack!*' the boy calls out, as if he's still wondrous new to him.

Something he'll never tire of.

The boy ages in an instant to a ripe old forty-one.

He knows this because he's both waited for this day and dreaded it for six long years. It is the day that will make him as an artist, but destroy him as a man. Another man approaches, this one limping toward him, wearing a leather harness. He trembles as a cigarette is lifted to his lips and he takes a last drag. He smiles at the boy, and whispers in his ear—

'*Amigo.*'

He shakes the hand of the lawman who captured him, as if encountering a long-lost friend. Twenty minutes later he is dead, twitching at the end of a rope, eyes bulging beneath a delicate black mask that has been tied over them to conceal the barbarity of his passing.

The images are coming faster now, along with his racing pulse—

A drive through the Alps, with air so crisp it scrapes the mucus from his lungs. A thunderstorm in Central Park, breathtaking pyrotechnics.

Streamers on the Champs-Élysées, sticking to shoe heels like soggy seaweed, just before he gets the call his Mama's gone away for good. Billows of reddest smoke from her prior attempts to leave him.

The Ritz bar in Paris. Lilac in a lobby.

A bulldog pup, howling in the dunes—though he's uncertain if it's a girl called Maggie or a boy called Charlie J. Fatburger.

Hope's End . . . a garden in the desert, a brittle, thirsty landscape.

The rustle of branches in the chinaberry trees, and the laughter of a colt-girl who climbs them in record time.

Love, pure, shimmering love. Then love, the violent, toxic kind.

A bevy of swans, their feathers trailing on the placid lake like ball gowns—or their ball gowns trailing on the dance floor like feathers . . . he can't remember which.

'Beautiful Babe—' the boy breathes.

The down-creaks of sweet Sook's rocking chair as she mends long johns to his high, melodic voice, reading aloud from the Obits, 'bout all the folks who've come and gone, and all the folks who'll carry on without them.

An old lady with the soul of a child and a small child with the soul of a very old man, flying homemade kites together.

'Sook—wait! It's Buddy . . . I'm coming!'

And then there she is—Nina.

Barely more than a girl herself, her honeyed pin-curls restored. Lips redder than a tin fire engine a con man called Daddy once gave him. She hands him a cup of Mama-juice, stroking the white fringe that tops his head once more, telling him what a fine boy he is . . .

'Mama!' he says aloud.

Warm, amniotic fluid against his heart. Or is it the stuff he's expelled from his lips, the body possessing a will of its own?

She smiles at him, offering her hand; he stretches his toy limb out to grasp it.

'Mama!' he calls again. As Joanne Carson rocks him gently, the boy mistakes her for Lillie Mae. He has already sprouted wings and flown away, soaring over the Bund.

Suddenly, he finds himself back in the Alabama river, with its gentle currents, on which he floats. He sees the cottonmouth circling, but he has ceased to care. He thinks he sees the face of an angel, features obscured, surrounded by a halo of light . . .

Mr. Angelotti, have we reached the city of your kind . . . ?

'Mama . . .' he exhales, a third and final time.

And just like that, she brushing his cheek with her tender lips, his blue whale heart bursts, his Mean Reds and wasted love exploding into an invisible shower of crimson confetti.

Coda

THE NIGHT BEFORE HIS HEART BURST, he'd reached into the pockets of his Fu Manchu pajamas and procured a key from their silken folds.

He handed it wordlessly to Joanne, between the wontons and shumai and Eight Treasure Chicken (he having informed the delivery boy that eight was a lucky number in Chinese culture).

'What's this?' she had asked him.

'*Answered Prayers,*' he'd smiled.

'Where is it?'

Truman had shrugged with a cryptic grin. He'd always loved a secret.

'Oh . . . any number of places. It could be in a Greyhound depot in Houston or N'awlins . . . Or it could be in a deposit box, in a bank in Zurich or Wall Street. Once I left it in the safe behind the counter in Harry's Bar in Venice. But I thought better of that and moved it to a strongbox at the Ritz. In fact . . . I moved it around so many times, I can't quite remember where I left it in the end.'

'But how will I know how to find it, Truman?'

He'd paused, thought for a long moment, then replied, something we feel certain that he's sure of— 'Oh, I wouldn't worry about *that*. It'll be found . . . when it wants to be found.'

Grinning, he nibbled at an egg roll— beside himself.

ACKNOWLEDGEMENTS

So many people contribute to the creation of a book. Especially one that's taken a decade to research and four years to write. As Truman famously said, 'Anyone who ever gave you confidence, you owe them a lot.' I owe the following 'a lot' and *then* some...

First and foremost, my brilliant co-conspirators, honourary Swans: My agent, Karolina Sutton—champion, truth-teller, matchmaker extraordinaire—whose passion for good writing has emboldened every choice, and whose investment in the long game inspires all that will come. And Jocasta Hamilton—who was the only editor for Truman and our Swans, who understood the depth and pathos beneath their glamour from the 'third scotch and first lie,' and who has allowed me every experiment and freedom in the manner of telling their tales.

To Joan Didion for so generously allowing me to introduce my words with hers—words that have meant so much to me over the years, the details of which prove eerily apt here.

The germ of the idea for this narrative came to me in Provence in 2006. Thanks to Michael Ondaatje, Alan Lightman and Russell Celyn Jones for early inspiration.

Swan Song was born of the UEA-Guardian Masterclass and completed on the Prose Fiction MA at the University of East Anglia, and owes a debt of gratitude to both camps.

To James Scudamore, who first heard the chorus singing, without whose early mentorship this would likely not exist. To Jon Cook, whose belief in the promise of this work helped open closed-doors and allowed me to continue the journey.

At UEA, my tutors and peers helped shepherd this book through late incarnations. To Andrew Cowan, story whisperer, who asked all the right questions. Rebecca Stott for conjuring muses past. Laura Joyce for encouraging future collectives. Joe Dunthorne for calm amidst the storm. Philip Langeskov for showcasing new work. Henry Sutton for support in the home stretch. And to my cohort-in-trenches—whose investment in Truman & Co. was essential.

Swan Song would be nowhere without the recognition of literary contests and prizes for novels-in-progress. They were my passport from a world of aspiration to one of realization.

To the Bridport Prize—Kate Wilson and all involved. I am deeply proud to be the first winner of the Peggy Chapman-Andrews Award to be published. To Aki Schilz and everyone at TLC—especially the late, great Rebecca Swift.

To my whole 'family' at the Lucy Cavendish College Fiction Prize in Cambridge, particularly Nelle Andrew, Allison Pearson, and Gillian Stern. Your platform for female debut novelists is such an important one, something I'm honoured to be a part of.

To Candida Lacey at Myriad First Drafts—who championed this book from Cygnet stage—and to Elizabeth Enfield who I was lucky enough to have as a judge and gain as a friend.

To Richard Lee and the Historical Novel Society New Novel Award. Your passion for historical fiction is invaluable for anyone who does what I do.

To Caroline Ambrose and the Bath Novel Award, a force of good for writers.

To my second sets of eyes from the get-go—Sarah Newell and Megan Davis.

To the authors who have shown *Swan Song* such generosity—particularly William Boyd, Rose Tremain, Linda Grant, Damian Barr, Fiona Melrose, Emma Flint, Emma Glass, Stuart Turton, Louise Beech, Liza Klaussmann, Kate Williams, Jonathan Ames and Dolly Alderton.

To Lucy Morris, Caitlin Leydon, Claire Nozieres and Enrichetta Frezzato at Curtis Brown— as Truman would say, '*Merci mille fois!*'

To my phenomenal team at Penguin Random House/ Hutchinson—Random House was Capote's publisher throughout his career. It's been a treat to bring him home.

To my paperback 'Team Swan' at Windmill—Laurie Ip Fung Chun, Laura Brooke and Elle Gibbons—for helping *Swan Song* soar to even greater heights. To Lauren Wakefield for her beautiful, brainy cover, and to Ceara Elliot for her equally stunning paperback design—the visual conversation between the two never ceases to delight. To Sasha Cox and my marvellous sales team; to Najma Finlay and Celeste Ward-Best. And to Isabelle Everington, who has weathered my perfectionism with patience and grace through drafts galore. To you all, I raise endless Negronis.

At the risk of sentimentality, I am both in awe of and indebted to my subjects—Slim Keith, Babe Paley, C.Z. Guest, Gloria Guinness, Lee Radziwill and Marella Agnelli. I have the utmost admiration for their extraordinary stories. And to Truman, whose prose has inspired me since childhood, who is by this point both alter ego and treasured friend, who has been the greatest of joys to write—I'll miss you most of all, Scarecrow.

I've been lucky to have encountered a wealth of support for my work these last few years. Of course there were 'No's' along the way, which in retrospect have been as valuable as the 'Yes's'. Nothing fires resilience quite like *No, you can't.*

Finally, to my parents, who have never once said 'No', only 'Yes'—*Yes, you can. Yes, you will.* That has meant everything. Your unwavering support has been my greatest strength and most cherished asset.

And to my darling Dom, who has for the last four years shared our lives with a boy genius and six glorious Swans—a packed house. Writing this has been all-consuming, and you've lived every breath and step of the journey with me, for which I'm forever grateful.

Over the years, numerous sources have been invaluable to me in recreating Capote's world. I am particularly indebted to the following authors and titles:

The collected works of Truman Capote, whose cadences are felt in anything I write. Additionally— Marella Agnelli, Marella Caracciolo Chia, *The Last Swan;* Aline Countess of Romanones, *The Spy Wore Red*; Judy Bachrach, 'La Vita Agnelli' *Vanity Fair*; Sally Bedell-Smith, *Grace and Power, Reflected Glory* and *In All His Glory*; Marilyn Bender, *The Beautiful People;* Susan Braudy, *This Crazy Thing Called Love;* Iles Brody, *The Colony;* Gerald Clarke, *Capote* and *Too Brief a Treat: The Letters of Truman Capote;* Josh Condon, *The Art of Flying;* Deborah Davis, *Party of the Century;* Diana DuBois *In Her Sister's Shadow;* John Fairchild, *The Fashionable Savages;* Nick Foulkes, *Swans: Legends of the Jet Set Society*; Alan Friedman, *Agnelli and the Network of Italian Power*; David Grafton, *The Sisters*; Lawrence Grobel, *Conversations with Capote;* C.Z. Guest, *First Garden;* Gloria Guinness, *Harper's Bazaar* columns; Anthony Haden-Guest, *The Last Party;* Brooke Hayward, *Haywire;* Clint Hill, *Mrs. Kennedy and Me;* M. Thomas Inge, *Truman Capote: Conversations;* Slim Keith, Annette Tapert, *Slim: Memories of a Rich and Imperfect Life*; Shawn Levy, *Dolce Vita Confidential*; George Plimpton, *Truman Capote: In Which Various Friends, Enemies, Acquaintances and Detractors Recall His Turbulent Career*; Darwin Porter, *Jacqueline Kennedy Onassis: Life Beyond Her Wildest Dreams*; Sally Quinn, 'In Hot Blood', 'Hot Blood - and Gore' *The Washington Post;* Lee Radziwill, *Happy Times* and *Lee;* Lanfranco Rasponi, *The International Nomads;* Susanna Salk, *C.Z. Guest: American Style Icon;* William Todd Schultz, *Tiny Terror: Why Truman Capote Almost Wrote Answered Prayers*; Liz Smith, *Natural Blonde* and 'Capote Bites the Hands That Fed Him', *New York Magazine;* William Stadiem, *Jet Set*; Annette Tapert, Diana Edkins, *The Power of Style*

SWAN SONG PLAYLIST

1) 'Bachelor #1'
The Tikiyaki Orchestra, *Swingin' Sounds for the Jungle Jetset*

2) 'Please Don't Talk About Me When I'm Gone'
Dean Martin, *This Time I'm Swingin'!*

3) 'A Sleepin' Bee'
Nancy Wilson & Cannonball Adderley
Lyrics by Truman Capote, from *House of Flowers*

4) 'Green Onions'
Booker T. & the M.G.'s, *A Single Man* (Original Motion Picture Soundtrack)

5) 'Just One of Those Things'
Ella Fitzgerald, *Ella Fitzgerald Sings the Cole Porter Songbook*

6) 'Come Fly With Me'
Frank Sinatra, *Come Fly With Me*

7) 'Nel Blu Dipinto Di Blu (Volare)'
Domenico Modugno & Orchestra Eros Sciorilli, *Vintage Italian Song No. 10*

8) MARELLA SOLO
Don Giovanni, K. 527, Act II: 'In quali eccessi, O Numi! Mi tradi quell'alma ingrata'
Wolfgang Amadeus Mozart & Lorenzo da Ponte
Maria Callas, *Callas Sings Mozart, Beethoven & Weber Arias*

Don Giovanni, K. 527, Act II: 'Deh, vieni all finestra'
Mozart & da Ponte / Nicolai Ghiaurov, *Don Giovanni*

9) SLIM SOLO
Quintet No. 4 G. 448 in D-Major for Strings and Guitar ('Fandango'),
Carmina Quartett [with Nina Corti],
Boccherini: La Musica Notturna Di Madrid

10) GLORIA SOLO
'Corrido de Valente Quintero, E'
Lucha Villa, *Sus Grandes Corridos*

11) BABE SOLO
Elegy, Op. 58
Edward Elgar / BBC Philharmonic Orchestra, Andrew Davies,
Elgar: Cello Concerto

12) C.Z. SOLO
'Shaking the Blues Away'
Vivian Blaine, *Songs from the Ziegfeld Follies*

13) LEE SOLO
'Midnight Rambler'
The Rolling Stones, *Get Yer Ya-Ya's Out! The Rolling Stones in Concert*

14) BLACK & WHITE BALL MEDLEY:
'Night and Day' / 'Something's Gotta Give' / 'My Funny
Valentine' / 'The Best Things In Life Are Free' / 'Dirty Lady' /
'Down Home Rag' Lester Lanin, *Dance to the Music of Lester Lanin*

15) 'Camel Walk'
Benny Gordon & The Soul Brothers, *100 Dance Craze Hits, Vol. 4*

16) 'I Feel Love'
Donna Summer, *I Feel Love: The Collection*

17) 'Sing, Sing, Sing'
Benny Goodman & his Orchestra, *The Essential Benny Goodman*

18) *Swan Lake*, Op. 20: Act 4 Scene Finale
Pyotr Ilyich Tchaikovsky
David Lloyd-Jones & New London Orchestra, *Swan Lake* (Matthew Bourne deluxe edition)

19) 'Good Morning Heartache'
Billie Holiday, *Lady Sings the Blues*

20) 'Let's Fly Away'
Lee Wiley, *Lee Wiley Sings the Songs of George & Ira Gershwin & Cole Porter*

21) 'Caravan'
The John Buzon Trio, *Ultra-Lounge, Vol. 4: Bachelor Pad Royale*

22) 'Mood Indigo'
Duke Ellington & Louis Armstrong, *The Great Summit: The Master Takes*

23) 'On the Street Where You Live'
Dean Martin, *This Time I'm Swingin'!*

24) 'The Lady Is a Tramp'
Frank Sinatra, *Classic Sinatra: His Great Performances 1953–1960*

25) 'Misirlou'
Martin Denny, *Ultra-Lounge, Vol. 1: Mondo Exotica*

26) 'Witchcraft'
Joe Graves & the Diggers, *Ultra-Lounge, Vol. 14: Bossa Novaville*

27) 'The Boy From Ipanema'
Lena Horne, *Ultra-Lounge: Jet Set Swingers!*

28) 'Just a Gigolo / I Ain't Got Nobody'
Louis Prima & Keely Smith, *Jump, Jive an' Wail: The Essential Louis Prima*

29) 'The Ladies Who Lunch'
Elaine Stritch, *Company* (Original Broadway Cast)

30) 'Don't Get Around Much Anymore'
Duke Ellington Orchestra, *Dinner Party Jazz*

31) 'A Whiter Shade of Pale'
Procol Harum, *A Whiter Shade of Pale*

32) 'But Not For Me'
Chet Baker, *Chet Baker Sings*

33) 'Who's Sorry Now?'
Nat 'King' Cole, *Just One of Those Things*

34) 'Ottilie and the Bee' (Bonus Track)
Truman Capote, *House of Flowers* (Original Broadway Cast Recording)

A NOTE ABOUT THE AUTHOR

Kelleigh Greenberg-Jephcott was born and raised in Houston, Texas, before coming to call Los Angeles and London her adopted homes. She is a graduate of UEA's Creative Writing MA course and was the winner of the Bridport Prize Peggy Chapman-Andrews Award. *Swan Song*, her first novel, was longlisted for the Women's Prize for Fiction 2019.